COILING DRAGON

Zhu Hongzhi

8th House Publishing
Canada

Cataloging in Publication (CIP) Data

Coiling Dragon/ By Zhu Hongzhi

Chinese Version: China Renmin University Press, 2018.05

English Version: 8th House Publishing 2020.12

ISBN 978-1-7751040-7-0

Coiling Dragon By Zhu Hongzhi

Publication: 8th House Publishing

Region: Montreal, QC, Canada

Website: http://www.8thhousepublishing.com

Edition: 1st issue, May 2018 (Chinese)
1st issue, December 2020 (English)

Impression: 1st print, December 2020

Episode 1 - Ring of Coiling Dragon

Episode 2 - Growth

Episode 4 – Dragon blood Warrior

Episode 1 - Ring of Coiling Dragon

Chapter 1 - Morning in the Town

Wushan Town was an ordinary town in Fenlai Kingdom on the west of 'Monster Mountains', the first mountain range on Yulan Continent.

The sun rose up, with cool air still permeating the town. Residents had already went out to work, and children of 6 to 7 years old also got up for traditional morning exercises.

On the open land east of Wushan Town, warm sunshine came through tree branches and cast spots on the ground.

In a glance, about 100 to 200 children were divided into three groups, and in each group, they were arranged in several rows. Every child stood quietly with solemn looks. The group on the north consisted of children aged 6 to 8, and the groups in the middle and on the south consisted of children aged 9 to 12 and 13 to 16, respectively.

In front of the group of children were 3 strong middle-aged men in short waistcoat and trousers made of coarse cloth.

"To become a great warrior, you must practice hard since childhood." The heading man spoke indifferently with hands in the back and head raised up. When he cast a cold glance at the group on the north, the 6 to 7-year-old children stared at him with their lips closed.

Hilman was the heading man's name. He was the captain of the guarding team of 'Baruch family', owners of Wushan Town.

"You are all ordinary people, unlike the noble class which owns secret vital energy guidebooks. If you want to stand out and no longer face people's contempt, you must practice physically with the most ancient, simple and basic methods. Do you understand?"

Hilman cast a glance at the group of children.

"We understand!" The children shouted.

"Good." Hilman nodded satisfactorily. The children of 6 to 7 years old showed innocence in their eyes, but the juveniles showed firm determination, because they understood Hilman's meaning.

On the entire Yulan Continent, every man needed to practice since small; otherwise he would be held in contempt in future. Only power and money could represent a man's position. Even a woman would look down upon a man without power. To win the pride of their parents, the adoration of women, and the great honor in future life, they must become great warriors.

They were all ordinary civilians and could not possibly practice according to the precious and secret vital energy books, so their only method was to practice physically and develop strength. They were destined to make more effort and practice harder than the nobles.

"In the morning, the sun rises, and everything is full of vigor. It is the best moment to absorb the essence of sky and earth and tap the potential of our body. Let's follow the old rules. Split your legs to shoulder width, bend your knees, retract your hands to the waist, and make the 'containment pose'. Remember to keep focused, be peaceful and breathe naturally." Hilman said indifferently.

The containment pose was the simplest and most effective method of physical practice, as concluded by predecessors throughout the ages.

The children, all of a sudden, posed their bodies accordingly.

"Keep focused, be peaceful, and breathe naturally!" Hilman walked in the crowd of children and said indifferently.

Obviously, every juvenile in the southern group maintained their focus, quietness and natural breath, and every one of them had attained 'depth, peace and stability'. They definitely made some achievements in practicing the 'containment pose'.

But the 6 to 7-year-old children on the north were irregular in their degrees of knee bending. They were loose in their leg pose, and had neither force nor stability.

Hilman said to another two middle-aged men: "You take charge of the groups on the south and in the middle, and I'll take care of the young kids."

"Yes, captain." The two men obeyed and watched the groups in the middle and on the south. Occasionally they kicked the legs of the juveniles to see if they were stable.

Hilman walked toward the 6 to 7-year-old children, who became nervous right away."Terrible, the devil is coming." Hadley, a child with big eyes and golden hair murmured.

Hilman walked to the center of the crowd, looked at the children with indifference, and complaint in the mind: "The small children are too weak in physical ability and intelligence. We cannot demand too much from them. But physical training should start from young childhood. If they practice hard, they will have more surviving opportunities in battlefield in future."

To teach young children, the best way was to lure them instead of forcing them, which would only produce negative effects.

"Stand nicely." Hilman said with a deep voice.

The children lifted their chest and looked ahead.

With a faint smile, Hilman walked to the front side, took off his waistcoat, and showed his muscle curves to the young children, who gazed upon them with wide-open eyes. Even the juveniles in the middle and southern groups looked at Hilman's muscles with adoration.

Besides the nearly perfect muscle curves, Hilman's upper body had dozens of knife and sword marks. All children looked at those scars with amazement.

Knife and sword marks were medals of a man!

The children admired Hilman, who was a great level-6 warrior having endured the trials of life and death. He was a great person even in big cities. And in the town of Wushan, he was a hero admired by everyone.

Hilman made a tiny smile when he saw the children's aspiring looks. Arousing admiration and desire in the children was his wish. He hoped the children could practice harder and with more motivation.

"Let me add something new." Hilman smiled in the heart, and walked to a huge stone dumbbell of 300-400 jin.

Hilman grabbed the stone dumbbell with one hand and waved it easily, as if the heavy stone dumbbell was made of wood. The children watched with wide-open eyes and mouth.

"Too light, Rory, you can make a larger one after training, if you have time." Hilman threw the dumbbell over a dozen meters to the foot of a big tree. Even the earth shook a bit with a heavy 'pum' sound. Then Hilman stepped to a pile of quarry stones.

"Hoooo..."

Hilman took a deep breath, highlighting muscles all over his body. With one blow of fist, he punched on a green stone. The split of air produced a sharp whiz, and the children watched with amazement how Hilman's fist sank on the large stone.

"Smash!" The deep sound of crash between fist and stone startled all children.

That was a hard green stone.

The stone shook, showed several cracks, and broke apart, but Hilman's fist was not even slightly wounded.

"Our captain is still so fierce." Rory, one of the other two men smiled and walked toward Hilman.The other man Roger also approached. Generally, when the children were practicing the 'containment pose', the three instructors were chatting and watching if some children loafed on their practice.

Hilman shook his head with a smile: "Not now. When I was in the military, I practiced hard every day and fought fiercely on battlefield. But now I only do some light exercises every day. I'm not as passionate as before."

All children looked at Hilman with admiration.

What kind of power could crash a large stone with one fist? And what kind of power was required to wave a stone dumbbell of 300-400 jin?

Hilman turned back, looked at the children's eyes, and seemed glad with their response.

"Remember that even if you have no skill of vital energy maneuvering, you may also become a level-6 warrior through physical training! And a level-6 warrior can easily become an intermediate officer in military and acquire vital energy maneuvering method. Not to mention level-6, you can join the military if you reach level-1, the most ordinary level. And a man cannot be called a man if he cannot reach level-1." Hilman said with cold looks.

"A man should raise his chest and welcome all challenges without fear!"

After hearing this sentence, the 6 to 7-year-old children tried to contain their laughter, because it was Hilman's mantra often used to teach the children.

"Stand stably like your brothers on the south." Hilman shouted.

The children tried their best to maintain stability.After a while, they started shaking. And with pain in their legs, they held on for a while and finally fell onto the ground.

Hilman was still cold mannered, but he was satisfied with the children's effort.

After a while, some children in the middle around 10 years old fell out of fatigue.

"You can hold on as longer as you want. There is no rigid requirement, but you have to blame yourself in future if you are weaker than others." Hilman said indifferently.

"Hmm?" Rory suddenly looked at the northern group with surprise.

At this moment, many of the children in the middle group fell onto the ground, but one six-year-old in the northern group was still insisting.

"Is Lynnray practicing for the first time? He is tough!" Rory said with surprise. Roger and Hilman also noticed this boy. Hilman looked toward the direction and saw a boy with brown hair still insisting in the northern group. The boy looked ahead firmly, with lips closed, and clenched his fist till the knuckles appeared white.

Hilman's eyes showed light of pleasant surprise.

"Good kid." Hilman praised in the mind. At only 6 years old, the boy caught up with 10-year-old children in 'containment pose'. He stood out with his talent.

Lynnray, or Lynnray Baruch, was the eldest son in Baruch family, owners of Wushan Town. Baruch family was a very old family. It thrived a long time ago, but after several thousand years, only 3 members remained till today -- the patriarch Hogg Baruch and two sons. The eldest son Lynnray Baruch was only 6 years old, and the younger son was only 2 years old. The hostess of the family passed away after giving birth to the younger son. Lynnray's grandfather also lost his life in the war.

Lynnray was trembling in the legs. Despite his strong willpower, he lost control of his aching muscles and finally sat down on the ground.

"Lynnray, how do you feel?" Hilman approached him with a smile.

Lynnray grinned, revealing his small teeth: "Nothing serious, uncle Hilman." Hilman was the captain of the guarding team of Baruch family and a witness of Lynnray's growth. They were naturally close.

"Good, you are a man." Hilman touched Lynnray's head and messed up his hair.

"Hehe." Lynnray chuckled and was happy with Hilman's praise.

……

After a short rest, the children started training again. The 6 to 7-year-olds trained with much lighter degree, but the juveniles over 10 years old were experiencing heavy training.

The juveniles, including the younger children placed their head and feet on flat stones, with body in the air, supported fully with waist strength.

"The triangle formed by waist and hips," Hilman made a gesture with his hands at the abdomen, "is the pivot of body. The core of speed and strength is located at this important triangle." Hilman walked while saying to observe if the children made the proper pose.

"Straighten up! Do not loosen your waist!" Hilman shouted.

The children tried to straighten up their waist. Lynnray was practicing this pose for the first time today. His small head and feet were backed on two flat stones, but at this moment, he was already feeling hot and sore in the waist.

"Insist, insist, I'm the best." Lynnray encouraged himself from within. Lynnray was physically fit since small and had almost never gotten ill. And with strong willpower, he naturally performed excellently in practice.

"Pit-a-pat." The first child fell.

But the flat stones used to support head and feet were only 20 cm in height. The children would not wound themselves even if they fell. (The alchemists of Yulan Continent formulated the length units '1 m = 10 dm = 100 cm = 1000 mm')

"Pit-a-pat.""Pit-a-pat."...As time passed, children fell one after another.

Lynnray gritted his teeth, and his waist was paining seriously with almost no feeling: "My body is so heavy and is about to fall. Hold on, hold on for a while." At this time, only Lynnray was insisting in the group of 6 to 8-year-olds.

Hilman was pleasantly satisfied when he saw Lynnray.

"Rory." Hilman called Rory.

"Captain." Rory stood straight and waited for Hilman's command.Hilman said: "Prepare some dye tomorrow. Place one dyed branch below their waist during training. If some child loosens and touches the branch, his waist will be tainted, and we will double his exercise."

"Yes, captain." Rory replied with a hidden smile on his face, "Our captain has ideas. The children will suffer."

Didn't he?

The juveniles showed bitterness on their face. In general situation, they could relax with tiny movements, but Hilman eliminated this possibility.

Hilman continued with cold expression: "I can tell you, when a warrior practices vital energy maneuvering, vital energy is stored at the location one fist below the navel. This location is within the core triangle. Now you understand the importance of training this area. This is the core irreplaceable with any other areas."

For the children, a good instructor was of paramount importance.

Hilman was a great warrior. He knew the key points of training, and the importance of gradual progress, because children of different ages should be subject to different training. If the training was too heavy, the children's health would collapse.

"Vital force maneuvering?"

The juveniles and younger children in rest looked at Hilman with wide-open eyes upon hearing this word.

The children of ordinary families aspired for the art of vital energy, and even Lynnray, the descendant of a declining noble family also yearned to learn vital energy maneuvering.

"Pit-a-pat."Lynnray could not insist anymore, but he supported himself on the ground with arms and fell slowly.

"I feel good." Lynnray had a numb feeling at the waist when he suddenly rested. The numb feeling was felt deeply in muscles and even the bone, and Lynnray half-closed his eyes to enjoy the feeling.

"How many people fell before me?" Lynnray opened his eyes and looked around.

All the 6 to 8-year-olds and more than half of the children about 10 years old fell, but the juveniles about 14 and 15 years old were still insisting. Hilman said with his usual cold expression:

"You should remember that your body is like a vessel, a wine glass, and vital energy is like wine! How much wine a glass can contain depends on the size of the glass. Similarly, a person's final achievement in vital energy maneuvering depends on his progress in physical training. If he is too weak physically, he could not hold much vital energy even if he studies the most powerful vital energy guidebook, and he cannot become a powerful warrior." Hilman passed on much important information to the children.

Many warriors received no guidance in younger days, and only learned of the relationship between physical fitness and vital energy maneuvering later. But when they were older in age, they could make little progress in physical training.

Many predecessors experienced trials and errors. Hilman imprinted his experience, little by little, in the children's brain through his instructions. He did not wish the children to experience the same trials and errors.

……

After practicing the 'containment pose' and coordination of the waist, legs, shoulder and back, almost all children collapsed on the ground. Hilman arranged suitable degree of training for the children.

"Now we end today's morning exercise." Hilman announced.

Training in Wushan Town was regular, performed once in the morning, and once in the evening.

"Uncle Hilman, can you tell a story for us?" Some children shouted right after dismissal. After morning exercises every day, Hilman would tell the children stories of occurrences in the military or other places on the continent.

The children, growing up in the small town, were quite curious of the happenings outside the town and in the military.

Hilman smiled slightly. Storytelling was his way to motivate the children. He believed the children would achieve bigger if they proactively desired training.

"Today I'll let you know about the legendary four ultimate warriors on the continent." Hilman also showed admiration on his face.

The children listened attentively and showed light in their eyes. Lynnray had a strong heartbeat while sitting on the ground. "The legendary four ultimate warriors?" Lynnray pricked up his ears and stared at Hilman.

Hilman said with a stable voice despite his excitement: "Several thousand years ago on our continent, there were four ultimate warriors. They had power comparable with a huge dragon, and every one of them could proceed through one million soldiers and take off the enemy general's head. Their titles were Dragonblood, Purpleflame, Tigerpattern and Immortal."

"Warriors are graded into 9 levels. As a level-6 warrior, I can easily smash a large stone and break a tree, but level-9 warriors are the topmost even in our Fenlai Kingdom. Above level-9 warriors are the four ultimate warriors. They are at the peak position and belong to the legendary holy domain." Hilman continued with respect, "The legendary holy warriors can melt huge icebergs, stir up the sea, break apart mountains, destroy a city with one million population, and create a scene in which numerous stones fall from the sky. They are the highest and insurmountable."

In quietness, all children were startled.

Hilman pointed at the mountain on the northeast.

"Look at the Wushan Mountain. Is it huge?" Hilman said with a smile.

The children, still terrified by Hilman's description, now nodded. Wushan Mountain was 1,000 meters high and several thousand meters long. It was a huge entity in humans' eyes.

"But the holy warriors can destroy it in one blink." Hilman said with affirmation.

A level-6 warrior could break a large stone with one slap, but a holy warrior could destroy a mountain. The children listened with mouth and eyes widely opened. They were overwhelmed by fear, expectation and aspiration.

"Destroy a mountain?" Hilman's words were a great shock for Lynnray.

After a while, the children went back with shock, and Hilman, Rory and Roger were the last to remain.

Watching as the children left in groups of three to five, Hilman smiled.

"These children are the hope of Wushan Town." Hilman said with a smile.

Rory and Roger also looked at the children. The children of ordinary families in almost every place of the continent practiced hard since small. When they saw these children, they seemed to be watching their own childhood and teenage period.

"Captain Hilman, you are much more capable than 'old Potter' in those years. Under your direction, I believe Wushan Town will become the most powerful among a dozen towns around." Rory said with emotion.

The instructor's capability will determine the future of a place.

"By the way, captain, how do you know about the power of holy warriors -- the four ultimate warriors?" Rory suddenly asked curiously.

Hilman smiled with embarrassment: "In fact, I don't know how powerful they were. They were legendary, anyway. People have not seen them over many years."

"Why did you cheat the children, then?" Rory and Roger had nothing else to say.

Hilman smiled: "I'm not clear about the power of four ultimate warriors, but I know about...holy magician, or a magician having entered the holy domain. They can use forbidden magic to destroy hundreds of thousands of soldiers and a city. I guess holy warriors had similar capabilities."

"Besides, I informed the children to motivate them. Didn't you see their aspiring expression after hearing these stories?" Hilman laughed with content.

Rory and Roger became speechless.

……

"Ray, goodbye."

"Hadley, goodbye."

After saying goodbye to his best friend Hadley, Lynnray walked alone to his home, and after a while, he arrived at the mansion of Baruch family.

The Baruch mansion occupied a large area. Plants such as mosses and creepers were covering the wall of mansion yard, which was worn over ages. Baruch mansion was the old house of Baruch family passed down through generations. The old house, after repeated repair and renovation over 5,000 years, was still standing.

The decline of family also caused worsening of economic condition. At last, the Baruch family had to live on their savings. About 100 years ago, the contemporary patriarch of the family determined that members of the family should live in the front part, which took up only 1/3 of the area of the mansion, and the part in the back would not be repaired and maintained. They saved a lot of money in this way.

Despite the money-saving effort, Lynnray's father Hogg Baruch had to sell off some family-owned items to maintain their livelihood.

The tall gate of the mansion was open.

"Holy warrior?" Lynnray walked while thinking, "Can I become a holy warrior in future?"

"Lynnray." Hilman's voice came from behind. Hilman, Rory and Roger, the last to leave, caught up with him now.

Lynnray looked back and addressed Hilman gladly: "Uncle Hilman!"

Lynnray then took a deep breath, looked up at Hilman, and inquired nervously with expectation: "Uncle Hilman, holy warriors are so powerful. Can I possibly become a holy warrior?" In the heart, Lynnray had the same aspiration as most children.

Hilman was taken by surprise, and Rory and Roger were also stunned.

Holy warrior?

"These kids are wild in thoughts. Fenlai Kindom has tens of millions of residents, but there has never been one holy warrior over hundreds of years. To become a holy warrior..." Hilman knew what it takes to become a holy warrior.

You need to practice diligently since small. You need family cultivation, individual talent and opportunities... Becoming a holy warrior is not easy.

Hilman remembered quite well how much bitterness he endured to become a level-6 warrior, and how many times he was on the verge of death. Reaching level-6 was so difficult, not to speak of level-7, level-8 and level-9. As to the holy domain, Hilman could only think of it in dreams.

But faced with Lynnray's eager look, he said:

"Lynnray, uncle Hilman has faith that you will surely become a holy warrior." Hilman said firmly while gazing upon Lynnray. The word of encouragement brightened Lynnray's eyes and aroused desire in his heart.

The desire carried unprecedented warmth.

"Uncle Hilman, can I train in the middle group tomorrow?" Lynnray said suddenly.

Hilman, Rory and Roger looked at Lynnray in surprise.

"My father said you must make more effort if you want to be better than others." Lynnray involuntarily imitated his father's tone.

Hilman smiled right away. As he saw in today's training, Lynnray had caught up with children of 9 and 10 in physical fitness although he was only 6, so he nodded: "OK, but do not hold back then. It is not just one or two days. You have a long way to go."

Lynnray held up his head and smiled with confidence: "I can do it."

It was an ordinary morning of Wushan Town, and similar to this morning, the children practiced under the guidance of level-6 warrior Hilman every day. The only difference was that 6-year-old Lynnray was allocated to the group of 10-year-olds.

Chapter 2 - Family of the Dragon blood (I)

Half a year passed, and Lynnray endured painstaking physical practice in warm spring and hot summer, and now stepped into cool autumn. The withered leaves of tall white poplars beside the open land in the east of Wushan Town were falling in circles with every gust of wind. And the open land was covered with withered leaves.

It was getting dark.

Today, a lot of people, nearly 300 in total, gathered on the open land.

"Now we end our evening training." Hilman smiled, "And let's express our best wishes for the children of Wushan Town joining the military."

In autumn, the time after harvest was the time for joining the military. When all people admired martial spirit on the continent, every juvenile was proud for becoming a warrior. But many people also wanted to become magicians. Becoming a magician was highly difficult, and maybe only one in ten thousand had the talent required to become a magician. Common people had better give a try on something else.

Becoming a warrior was much easier. You could join the military easily if you had reached 16 years old and level-1 in training.

"Thank you, uncle Hilman."

126 young guys of 17 to 18 years of age made a bow with respect. These young guys did not join the training, because they already reached

adulthood and had their jobs. But they had been trained by Hilman since small. Hilman was their benevolent instructor.

Before joining the military, the bid farewell to Hilman.

Hilman was full of emotion when he looked at the vigorous youngsters. These kids admired military life, but after 10 years, how many of them could return?

"I hope more than half of them can survive." Hilman wished in the heart.

Hilman looked at the kids and said: "Lads, listen carefully! You are men of Wushan Town. Men of Wushan should raise their chest and welcome challenges without fear. Do you understand?"

The young guys raised their chest and stood straight. With expectation for military life contained in their looks, they shouted: "Yes, we understand!"

"Good." Hilman also stood straight and said with military-style cold manners.

"Make preparations tonight for your departure tomorrow. I'm well aware of your capabilities. All of you can easily join the military. And I, Hilman, will await your return to Wushan Town with honor." Hilman said loudly.

The 126 young guys showed brightness in their eyes.

Returning to hometown with honor was the dream of every young guy.

"Now I order you to make preparations back in your quarters. Dismiss!" Hilman commanded.

"Yes!"

The young guys responded with respect and left in the admiring look of about 200 underage children. They were about to set foot on a new journey tomorrow.

"I have two years to reach adulthood. By then, I can also join the military."

"I want to live a passionate life in military. A whole life in Wushan Town is boring no matter how long it lasts."

......

Some juveniles of about 13 and 14 years old were having a discussion. They desired a passionate lifestyle with accomplishments, girls' admiration and praises of relatives.

That was their dream!

"Lynnray, your father Mr. Hogg has very important issues to deal with today. You can't play with other children now. Go back with us." Hilman walked toward Lynnray and looked at him with satisfaction.

Lynnray was very smart. Under father Hogg's education, Lynnray became literate and capable of reading most books. Reading was a luxurious activity exclusively belonging to nobles in general. The Baruchs were a very ancient family and had lots of books.

"I know, uncle Hilman. Dad has reminded me three times today. He has never paid so much attention to an issue before. I'm not going to play here." Lynnray grinned, revealing one line of white teeth, but with one tooth missing.

Lynnray was already changing his teeth.

"OK, one front tooth was missing. You leaked air while smiling." Hilman smiled and said: "Let's go back."

In the front yard of the old Baruch mansion, the family just had dinner, and Lynnray was playing with his younger brother of two and a half years.

"Brother, hug, hug."

Little Warton looked at Lynnray with a pure, unadulterated expression. He ran toward Lynnray happily in tottering steps and held out his small, chubby hands, and Lynnray squatted and waited for him.

"Warton, come on, come on." Lynnray encouraged his younger brother.

Little Warton ran in steps which looked like he was falling, but he finally rushed into Lynnray's chest. With tender skin shining in red color, and innocent eyes looking at Lynnray in excitement, Warton addressed Lynnray gently: "Brother, brother."

Lynnray liked his younger brother very much.

They had no mother, grandfather or grandmother, and were living under the care of their father and old steward. Lynnray, who was too mature in his age, cared for his younger brother very much. He believed the elder brother should take care of the younger one.

"Warton, what did you learn today?" Lynnray smiled.

Warton frowned in a lovely expression, thought for a second and said excitedly: "Today I learned to use the cleaning cloth."

"The cleaning cloth?" Lynnray smiled involuntarily, "What did you wipe?"

Warton counted on his fingers: "I wiped the floor, the chamber pot, and at last...the bowl. The bowl used to eat meals."

Warton looked at Lynnray excitedly in expectation of his praises.

"You wiped the chamber pot and then the bowl?" Lynnray opened his eyes widely.

"Am I wrong? I cleaned these items." Warton raised his head and looked at his brother in confusion.

"Lynnray, your father needs you now. Let me take care of Warton." A benevolent old man with a wine nose walked toward him. The old man was Baruch family's steward Hilly. The family had not even one housemaid or servant beside the steward.

Lynnray had no time talking with Warton, so he handed Warton to Hilly and walked toward the living room.

"Dad, what's the matter?" Even in his young age, Lynnray could sense an unusual air.

A desk clock taller than Lynnray was placed in one corner of the living room.

Desk clock was an object of high taste, and was generally the property of wealthy or noble families. Lynnray's father was sitting in front of the fireplace, which was sending out light of flame and the cracking sound of wood.

"Hmm? Why did dad change his clothes?" Lynnray was surprised at his father's wearing. Generally, Lynnray's father wore simple clothes at home. His dress-up was ordinary at dinner, but now he changed into a high-grade piece of clothing.

Hogg had a special temperament exclusively belonging to ancient nobles. Such a temperament could not be seen in families which only had large amount of wealth. It was cultivated in ancient family tradition, and a family with 5,000 years' history could easily stood out among all.

Hogg stood up and turned back. His eyes showed light when he saw Lynnray.

"Lynnray, follow me to the ancestral temple. Uncle Hilly, you also know about our family, Please come along." Hogg smiled.

"To the ancestral temple?" Lynnray was surprised.

Generally, members of the Baruch family lived in the front part of the mansion, and the back yards had no one to maintain or clean them. In the back part, only an ancestral temple used to offer sacrifice to the ancestors was cleaned every month.

"It's not the time to offer sacrifice. Why are we heading for the ancestral temple?" Lynnray was confused in the heart.

After exiting the living room, Hogg, Lynnray and Hilly, who was holding Warton in his arms, walked toward the back yards along the stone path covered with moss through history.

It was late autumn, and the evening air was as cool as water.

Cold wind came and Lynnray shivered. But he did not make a sound because of the unusual atmosphere. They followed with Lynnray's father into the ancestral temple.

"Clik." The temple door was closed.

A row of candles were lit up. Illuminating the entire temple. At one glance, Lynnray saw the memorial tablets of ancestors placed in the front. The densely packed memorial tablets indicated the old age of Baruch family.

Hogg stood quietly in front of the memorial tablets.

Lynnray was quite nervous, and only candle burning sounds could be heard at present. The quietness was scary and suppressing.

Suddenly, Hogg turned back, stared at Lynnray and said solemnly, "Lynnray, we have many things to do today, but I have to first tell you something about Baruch family."

Lynnray could felt the strong beating of his heart -- 'thump, thump'.

"Family affair? What kind of affair of family?" Lynnray was curious but dare not speak.

Hogg said aloud with pride: "Lynnray, our Baruch family has passed down over 5,000 years. There is no family in Fenlai Kingdom comparable with us in old age." Hogg showed absolute pride in his voice.

Old age was a great merit for some nobles.

"Lynnray, do you know about the legendary four ultimate warriors on Yulan Continent?" Hogg looked back at Lynnray.

Lynnray nodded excitedly: "I know. Uncle Hilman told us that the four ultimate warriors were Dragonblood, Purpleflame, Tigerpattern and Immortal."

Hogg nodded satisfactorily: "Yes, and I'm telling you the four ultimate warriors represented four ancient families, and our Baruch family is an old family carrying the blood of noble Dragonblood warriors."

Chapter 3 - Family of the Dragonblood (II)

"Family of the Dragon blood?" Lynnray felt a buzz in his brain.

Lynnray thought his family was only an ancient family in decline. How was it connected with the four ultimate warriors?

"You don't believe it?" Hogg said proudly, "Lynnray, you can examine the memorial tablets. You are literate now. On the reverse side of every tablet was inscribed the deeds of the ancestor. The ancestors represented by the topmost three tablets were all Dragon blood warriors.

Hogg pulled Lynnray's hand: "Follow me."

They walked to the back side of tablets. Hogg held Lynnray up: "You can take a good look at those deeds inscribed on the back."

Lynnray looked ahead with wide-open eyes.

The inscription on the tablet at the top was deep and clear. The age-old handwriting with 5,000 years' history was narrating world-shaking stories one after another.

"Baruch, the first Dragon blood warrior on Yulan Continent. In the year 4560 of Yulan calendar, Baruch battled against ice dragon and black dragon under Linnan City, and became famous all over the world as their killer. In 4579 of Yulan calendar, Baruch battled against the nine-head serpent king on the northern shoreline. On the day, tsunami attacked continuously and cities fell apart. After one day and night,

Baruch finally killed the nine-heat serpent king... He founded the Baruch family as the first patriarch."

"Ryan Baruch, the second Dragonblood warrior on Yulan Continent. In the year 4690 of Yulan calendar, Ryan defeated and subdued a holy golden dragon and became its holy rider. In 4697 of Yulan calender..."

"Hazzard Baruch, the third Dragonblood warrior on Yulan Continent, born in 5360 of Yulan calendar. In his first battle with the monster lion with bloody eyes and brown mane in Sunset Mountains, he defeated and drove away the monster lion and gained fame around the world..."

......

One after another great names and deeds aroused Lynnray's emotion.

"My family is the family of Dragonblood?" Lynnray said excitedly.

Hogg, standing beside Lynnray, said with a low voice: "We had Dragonblood warriors across three generations in a row. Once one became a Dragonblood, he would have a long lifespan. The second patriarch Ryan Baruch married at 700 years old."

"What happened later?" Lynnray was confused, "Why don't we have Dragonblood warriors now?"

Hogg nodded: "The possibility of becoming a Dragonblood warrior depends on the density of Dragonblood warrior's blood in his body. And higher density indicates a greater possibility. As we pass on in generations, density of Dragonblood warrior's blood will gets lighter and lighter in members of the family. But... this is not absolute, because occasionally one member in the line may have greater density of Dragonblood warrior's blood."

"About 1,000 years after Hazzard Baruch, the fourth Dragonblood warrior appeared in our Baruch family, and after another 1,500 years, which was dozens of generations later, we had the fifth. But we had none in the following 1,000 years till now."

Hogg shook his head and sighed: "The fifth Dragonblood warrior only lived 200 years on Yulan Continent and then disappeared. And over 1,000 years, our family gradually declined."

Even the most brilliant family could decline over a period of 1,000 years.

"But there is still hope in our family. Maybe one member in a particular generation will have the density of Dragonblood warrior's blood meeting the condition for becoming a Dragonblood warrior. If so, he can become a Dragonblood warrior after decades of arduous practice, and Baruch family can restore our honor as a 'family of the Dragonblood'" Hogg said with shiny eyes, "Lynnray, you are six and a half years old. We can get a basically accurate examination of blood density in a child of six years old. Today, I will examine yours."

Lynnray was a bit surprised: "Examine my density of Dragonblood warrior's blood?" Lynnray knew his father's intention. Examination would give the result as to whether he possessed the condition for becoming a Dragonblood warrior."Lynnray, wait for a second. Let me fetch the Dragonblood needle." Hogg said excitedly and walked toward the secret chamber on the back of the temple.

"Dragonblood warrior? Will I become a Dragonblood warrior?" Lynnray was a bit nervous.

Lynnray was standing there with both expectation and fear in the heart. He feared that his blood density could not meet the requirement.

"If I fail, maybe my father will be disappointed." Lynnray thought. Since small, Lynnray had been sticking together with his father and younger brother. He did not wish to disappoint his father, but he could not determine the density of Dragonblood warrior's blood in his own body.

After a short while, Hogg walked out of the chamber with a very thin transparent needle of 20 cm in his hand.

"Dragonblood needle?" Lynnray looked at the long needle and wondered.

"OK, Lynnray, we only need to pierce the skin. There is no pain. Hold out your hand." Hogg said with a smile. Lynnray nodded and held out his right hand after a deep breath. With a nervous mood, Lynnray was shivering in his right hand.

In fact, Hogg was also feeling nervous.

"Hold on." Hogg's transparent needle pierced the skin of Lynnray's right index finger.

Lynnray felt a heart-piercing pain, and the needle turned to blood red.

In a trembling motion, Hogg placed the Dragonblood needle in front of his eyes and observed it carefully.Lynnray looked up at his father without a blink, and thought nervously: "Is my density of Dragonblood warrior's blood enough? Why is my father looking at the needle for such a long time?" Lynnray had a bad feeling.

"Alas..." With a sigh, Hogg placed the Dragonblood needle aside.

After hearing the father's sigh, Lynnray, who had been waiting nervously, now knew the Dragonblood warrior's blood in his body did not meet the requirement, so he cried all of a sudden.

"Lynnray, why are you crying? Be good. Don't cry." Hogg held Lynnray in his arms and was pained to see him crying. Anyway, Lynnray was only a six-year-old child.

"OK, I will not cry." Lynnray sobbed and held back his tears, "Dad, I'm sorry for disappointing you."

Hogg felt warm in the heart upon hearing Lynnray's words, so he held Lynnray in the arms: "Lynnray, don't be sad. I was not hopeful about it. Over 1,000 years, no one among dozens of generations became a Dragonblood warrior. It's not surprising that you cannot become one. I don't blame you."

While feeling the warmth of his father's chest, Lynnray also relaxed himself.

At this moment, Warton, who was only 2 and a half years old, was sleeping in steward Hilly's arms.

"Lynnray, there are only you, your brother and me in Baruch family. I have no big goals in this life and cannot expect to become a Dragonblood warrior." Hogg laughed at himself. How could it be so easy to become a Dragonblood warrior?

Lynnray looked up at his father.

His father seldom spoke to him like today. He was strong and strict at ordinary times.

Hogg looked at the memorial tablets and said with expectation: "In fact, my real goal was to get back the heirloom of Baruch family."

"What is our family heirloom? I haven't heard about it." Lynnray inquired curiously.

Hogg said proudly, "Our family heirloom -- saber 'Slaughter' -- was the weapon of Baruch, the first patriarch of Baruch family and first Dragonblood warrior on Yulan Continent. Alas...his descendants were disrespectful. The patriarch about 600 years ago sold the saber for his own extravagance due to family decline."

While saying the above words, Hogg trembled in anger.

"He sold the family heirloom?" Lynnray was a bit angry, too. Although he was only 6 and a half years old, he understood through extensive reading that one should not sell his family heirloom even at the most difficult times. Besides, as his father said, the patriarch sold the saber for his own extravagance.

Hogg shook his head: "Every patriarch after that generation tried to get back saber 'Slaughter', but none realized this goal over 600 years. Saber 'Slaughter' was sold for 180,000 gold coins. Even if we could offer 180,000 gold coins today, not to mention we couldn't, others would not sell it back to us."

The family of the Dragonblood sold off its heirloom.

That was a shame of the ancient family of the Dragonblood.

Every generation of family members wished to get back 'Slaughter', but they couldn't make it over 600 years.

As the current patriarch of family, Hogg also had the same wish. But the family was in very poor economic conditions. 180,000 gold coins? They could not obtain such a huge amount of wealth even if they sold off their ancestral house.

The shame of having an heirloom outside made Hogg painful sometimes. He was too ashamed to face his predecessors.

Lynnray saw his father's expression and comforted him:"Dad, rest assured that one day I'll get back our family heirloom."

"You?" Hogg laughed and touched the head of Lynnray with love.

But he was thinking: "Lynnray, do you know that I said the same words to your grandpa?" Over 600 years, so many people's efforts failed. It was not easy. Besides, the person who was capable of collecting saber 'Slaughter' was definitely not ordinary.

And that person, was surely unwilling to sell.

Even if he agreed to sell, the declining Baruch family could not afford his price.

"You don't believe me?" Lynnray raised his head and asked in confusion.

"I believe you." Hogg laughed.The father and son leaned close to each other. Only three members were left over the succession of the

Dragonblood warrior's family. When would the family restore its honor in early days? Lynnray, in his father's arms, now clenched his fist.

Chapter 4 - Growth (I)

The white poplars on the open land east of Wushan Town turned green in spring wind. A group of juveniles were training with great effort. A year and a half passed since Lynnray was tested on the density of Dragonblood warrior's blood, and now he was 8 years old. During the one and a half years, Hilman clearly found that Lynnray was training harder.

"Very good. Lynnray, hold on, hold on." Hilman said.

Lynnray was only wearing a pair of trousers, and his naked upper body was full of sweat. He was leaning on the ground, facing down, with hands supported on the ground like an old tree's root. His body was motionless, tightened up, and supported with only hands and tiptoes.

It was static tension practice, which was very simple and effective. If one could remain in this state for one hour, his body would be able to resist the attack of ordinary knifes and swords.

"Tick."

Sweat fell from his forehead along the eye corners. He had a sour feeling in his right eye, and squinted involuntarily.

"Ray is great. At only 8 years old, he has caught up with the 13 and 14-year-olds in static tension practice." The children who gave up were looking at Lynnray and conversing about him."Ray, go for it! Defeat those bigger kids of 13 and 14." The golden-hair Hadley shouted.

"Come on, Ray!" Other children also shouted.

Lynnray got along with other children very well. Although he was a noble, he treated civilian children nicely, and helped them in training at ordinary times.

"Hold on for another while." Lynnray said to himself.

But in his mind, he recalled what father told him one year ago: "Lynnray, we are a family of the Dragonblood. As a member of our family, you have both advantages and disadvantages. Even though your density of Dragonblood warrior's blood was not enough for becoming a Dragonblood warrior, your physical fitness was much better than ordinary people. Other people may not be able to reach level-6 by mere physical training, but you can reach that level easier."

"But you have disadvantages as well. As a descendant in the family of Dragonblood, you cannot practice according to secret vital energy guidebooks. Only Secret Guidebook of Dragonblood suits you because you carry the blood of Dragonblood warrior. Your body is in conflict with all other vital energy practice. One can only practice according to Secret Guidebook of Dragonblood when his density of Dragonblood warrior's blood has reached certain level. Therefore, you cannot practice vital energy maneuvering."

"And theoretically, ordinary people can become a level-6 warrior by mere physical practice. But that is in theory only. Very few people made it in reality. We are different from them, though we have only tiny amount of Dragonblood warrior's blood. We are at a higher starting point. We can reach level-6 if we only practice physically. Your great grandpa reached level-7 by mere physical practice."

The father's words were still clear in his mind.

Lynnray spoke to himself loudly in the heart: "I perform better than others because I carry the blood of Dragonblood warriors. Since I cannot practice vital energy maneuvering, I have to practice physical body with more effort. My great grandpa reached level-7 by physical training, so I...may reach level-8 or even level-9, and nothing is impossible if I try."

Level-8 warrior!

A level-9 warrior would be a top master in Fenlai Kingdom. If Lynnray became a level-8, he could greatly improve his family condition even though he could not restore the honor of his family 5,000 years ago.

"Hold on." Lynnray grit his teeth.

At this moment, Lynnray felt pain in both arms as if numerous ants were biting him. He was trembling all over and clearly in every muscle.

After a while, with a "pit-a-pat" sound, Lynnray collapsed on the ground weakly.

"So comfortable." Now lying on the ground in relaxation, Lynnray had a numb and itching feeling in all parts of the body. His muscles were slowly growing after practice. Such growth was not obvious after only one or two sessions of practice, but could be felt in the long term.

Hilman, who was standing at one side, nodded satisfactorily.Then Hilman walked to the group of 14 to 15-year-old juveniles and said coldly: "Hold on, everyone. Lynnray is only 8 years old, but you are about to reach adulthood now. Don't be defeated by a child."

After morning exercises, Lynnray said goodbye to his good friends and went back to Baruch mansion. Although Lynnray was only 8 years old, he appeared to be a juvenile of 11 or 12 years old for those who did not know him.

Children of Baruch family were indeed out of ordinary.

"Brother." Warton, who had a dignified look, rushed toward Lynnray upon seeing him.

"OK, Warton, I sweated all over. Let me first take a bath." Lynnray pinched Warton's small cheeks and said with a smile.

Warton snorted: "I know, you will attend classes with dad after bath."

As a member of noble family, Lynnray's education started from childhood. Baruch family was an ancient family with 5,000 years' history, so they were stricter than great nobles of the kingdom in education.

"OK, Warton, I'll play with you at noon." Lynnray smiled.

Warton was only a child, but Lynnray was much more sensible.

After washing himself, Lynnray put on clean clothes and entered the living room. At this moment, his father Hogg Baruch was sitting straight beside the dining table. In front of Hogg were three thick books.

"Dad!" Lynnray offered his respect.

Hogg nodded indifferently, and Lynnray stood by his side."Yesterday I told you about all the countries on Yulan Continent. Now you should repeat it to me." Hogg said indifferently.

That was Hogg's real attitude toward Lynnray.

When he held Lynnray in ancestral temple, he put on a mild face, which was rarely seen. But at ordinary times, Hogg was harsh on Lynnray and sought perfection in all aspects. He did not allow even a tiny mistake.

"Yes, dad." Lynnray said calmly.

"Yulan Continent has three dangerous places, which include the first range 'Monster Mountains', the second range 'Sunset Mountains' and the first forest 'Dark Forest'. All three dangerous places occupy vast areas. The Monster Mountains span across the continent from south to north and are more than 10,000 li in length. Numerous monsters, and even the holy monster with power to destroy the world are living in the mountains. Because of Monster Mountains, the entire continent formed a different pattern."

"On the west of Monster Mountains are 12 kingdoms and 32 principalities. The kingdoms and principalities on the west of Monster Mountains are divided into two forces -- one is the Holy Alliance headed by Fenlai Kingdom, and the other is Dark Alliance headed by Blacklion Kingdom. The Holy Alliance belongs to the 'Church of Light', whereas the Dark Alliance belongs to the 'Church of Darkness'; so they are constantly in war against each other."

"On the east of Monster Mountains are 4 empires, 6 kingdoms and many principalities. The 4 empires are the biggest and not affected by the Church of Light and Church of Darkness. In the 4 empires, imperial power is regarded as the highest power. And every one of the 4 empires is as powerful as the Holy Alliance.""The 4 empires consist of 'Yulan Empire' in the middle, 'Rhine Empire' in the southeast, 'Rio Empire' in the east, and 'O'Brien Empire' in the north." Lynnray was relieved after saying these words.

"That's all?" Hogg put on a cold face.

Lynnray was about to continue, but Hogg asked him directly: "How many kingdoms and principalities does our Holy Alliance include?"

"Our Holy Alliance consists of 6 kingdoms and ten, ten..." Lynnray frowned.

How many principalities did our Holy Alliance have? Lynnray was blurred in his memory. Was it 15, or 17? Lynnray was uncertain.

"Hum."

Hogg put on a cold face and took out a twig from one side. Lynnray held out his right hand obediently.

"Thwack!" With a twitch in the eye muscles, Hogg whipped the twig heavily on Lynnray's right hand. A blood mark suddenly appeared, and Lynnray grit his teeth without uttering a sound.

"Lynnray, we are part of the Holy Alliance, so we must understand it well." Hogg looked at his son indifferently, "There are mainly 6 forces on Yulan Continent, which include 4 empires and 2 alliances."

Lynnray nodded.

The father put it in a simple way to facilitate understanding."The Holy Alliance borders O'Brien Empire in the far north, and the Dark Alliance borders Yulan Empire in the south. Under the leadership of Church of Light, our Holy Alliance is as united as the four empires."

Lynnray agreed with his father's words.

He leafed through many books yesterday. Obviously, Holy Alliance was the 'art center' of the entire Yulan Continent, and the economy of Holy Alliance located on Yulan Continent was comparable with Yulan Empire, the first power in economy.

With Church of Light as the back-up force, Holy Alliance was indeed very powerful.

"Today, let's learn art." Hogg said coldly, "A noble must be proficient in art, and through art, a noble can cultivate his inner temperament." Hogg took out a book as thick as a fist, and opened it.

"In the year 3578 of Yulan calendar, the great stone sculptor Brooks was born in..."

While Hogg was passing on knowledge in a strict manner, Lynnray tried hard to understand and memorize it in order to meet Hogg's requirements.

Chapter 5 - Growth (II)

Time passed quickly. As the desk clock in the living room struck 11 times, it was 11 o'clock at noon.

"Is Mr. Hogg in?" a clear voice was heard. There was no gatekeeper in Baruch mansion. Obviously the guest had arrived at the front yard.

Hogg frowned and put down the thick book in his hand: "Lynnray, so much for today." After a faint smile, Hogg walked to the outside.

"Oh, Hogg, my dear friend. When I heard the chirping of cuckoos, I knew a happy event must be taking place. And at noon, I received your letter with excitement."

"Dear Philip, I'm also glad to see you. Hilman, move my stone sculpture 'Fierce Lion' here. Philip, now let's go to the living room. The stone sculpture will arrive soon."

Lynnray had a sorrowful feeling upon hearing their conversation.

"Are we selling items again?" Lynnray knew the stone sculpture 'Fierce Lion' was his father's favorite. But Baruch family, who did not collect heavy tax from Wushan Town, was now in financial difficulty.

Since Baruch family was an old family, it had many objects with a long history.

But no matter how many objects they had, they would lose a great number over many years. Now they had very few valuable objects.Lynnray looked at the desk clock in the living room: "I don't know when this desk clock will be sold also."

A middle-aged man with golden hair and noble temperament walked into the living room together with Hogg. Lynnray knew he must be 'Philip'.

"Oh, this lovely boy must be your son." Philip laughed warmly, looked at Lynnray and said: "Lynnray Baruch, right? Can I call you Lynnray?"

"My honor, sir." Lynnray put his left hand in front of his chest and made a bow.

"This boy is lovely." Philip seemed very happy.

But Hogg smiled: "Philip, don't joke with the boy, because the 'Fierce Lion' you dreamed of is arriving." Hilman entered the living room with a stone lion easily held on his both hands, and then he gently put down the lion on the ground.

The stone sculpture was nearly 1,000 jin in weight, but was carried by Hilman like a toy. Hilman was indeed powerful.

"Mr. Hilman, your power is astonishing. In my manor, I don't have such a powerful captain of guards as you, even though I own the territory of 12 towns." Philip said with a smile, but his words carried an obvious intention to recruit Hilman.

Hilman said indifferently: "Wushan Town is my hometown, sir."

"Sorry." Philip apologized.

Philip looked at Hogg and said: "Hogg, I like your stone sculpture, but I have to say its sculpting technique is not first-class and cannot be compared with those masters."

"Philip, if you don't want to buy, it's OK." Hogg was straightforward.

Philip squinted and laughed: "Haha... Hogg, don't be angry. I'm not saying I don't want to buy. I was just speaking of a fact. I can pay you 500 gold coins, is it OK?"

"500 gold coins?" Hogg frowned.

This price was much lower than Hogg's expected price of 800 gold coins.

In Yulan Continent, 1 gold coin = 10 silver coins = 1,000 copper coins. An ordinary civilian could get 20 to 30 gold coins for one year's work. And a soldier in the military could get 100 gold coins in one year.

"Price is too low." Hogg shook his head.

"As you know, Hogg, there are a large number of stone sculptures with 10,000 years' history on Yulan Continent, but a stone sculpture's real value is in its artistic quality. The artistic quality of this one... I just like it myself. 500 gold coins is my highest price. We can't make a deal if you don't agree."

Philip turned his head and looked at the desk clock with shining eyes, "Hogg, I'm willing to pay 1,000 gold coins if you can sell the desk clock."

Hogg's face turned pale.

"Oh, 2,000 gold coins is also all right. That's the highest price." Philip said in a hurry.

Hogg shook his head and said resolutely:"I don't sell the clock. I only charge 600 gold coins for the stone sculpture. You can take it if you agree."

Philip observed Hogg for a moment, and then laughed: "OK, Hogg, I can give you a favor, 600 gold coins. Steward, please bring me 600 gold coins." The steward, who was waiting out of the living room, brought 600 gold coins to Philip.

It was 6 yellow bags.

"600 gold coins, count it, Mr. Hogg." Philip smiled.

Hogg held the bags and confirmed the payment by weight and volume. It was indeed 6 bags of gold coins, with 100 in each bag. Hogg nodded with a smile: "Philip, maybe you can stay and have lunch with us."

"No, I have to go back." Philip smiled.

And Philip's old steward asked two strong soldiers to carry the stone sculpture.

After Philip and his attendants left, Hogg looked at the 6 bags of gold coins sadly. He sold his stone sculpture this time, but what about the next time? Although there were many items at home, they would still be sold off one day.

"Dad, I want to learn stone sculpting." Lynnray said suddenly.

Lynnray knew well that works of famous sculptors on Yulan Continent could be sold at more than 10,000 gold coins, and some famous works were worth hundreds of thousands of gold coins. The sculpting masters were not only rich, but had high position in society.

"If I become a sculpting master, my father will not have to sell family belongings." Lynnray thought.

"Stone sculpting?" Hogg looked at Lynnray and said in a cold voice.

"Lynnray, do you know that among hundreds of millions of people in Holy Alliance, at least several million learned stone sculpting. But the number of real sculpting masters can be counted on fingers. Besides, without a good teacher, you cannot become a sculptor by self-study."

"Ordinary people cannot enter the circle of stone sculpting. One piece of work of a sculpting master is worth tens of thousands of gold coins, or even higher, but do you know that the yearly salary of most stone craftsmen was only dozens of gold coins?"

Hogg said these words gravely.

Lynnray was startled. He raised the subject with an intention to improve family condition, but he did not expect his father to talk so much and with a serious tone.

"OK, the ancestral temple should be cleaned now. Clean it after lunch." Hogg said coldly.

"Yes, father." Lynnray replied.

Hogg looked at Lynnray and sighed in his mind: "Stone sculpting? Do you know that I learned stone sculpting for 10 years, but my works were valueless." Hogg also tried to become a master in stone sculpting in order to greatly improve his family's financial condition.

But he was caught in a helpless situation. Despite 10 years' learning, his works were still valueless. The circle of master sculptors was like a pyramid.

Famous sculpting masters were at the top of the pyramid. At the highest position, one work of theirs was worth tens of thousands or hundreds of thousands of gold coins. But numerous stone craftsmen were situated at the bottom. Their works were miserably cheap, and sold at only several silver coins to decorate the house of ordinary people.

Chapter 6 - Ring of Coiling Dragon (I)

As the sun was setting in the west, red clouds covered half of the sky area and cast red shadows on the vast land.

"Cleaning ancestral temple is a simple task."

Lynnray walked out of the ancestral temple. He expected to finish the task in one hour, but he spent only 15 minutes.

According to the calendar on Yulan Continent, one year was 12 months, one month was 30 days, one day was 24 hours, and one hour was 60 minutes. Nobles generally owned desk clocks to tell time accurately. If you were very rich or had a high social position, you could own a delicate pocket watch.

"The temple was cleaned every month. With such a frequency, it had little dirt or pollution. A random wiping could easily finish the work. The evening training will start one hour later. What should I do in the next hour?" Lynnray was a little bored, and looked around casually.

The old mansion of Baruchs had a history of 5,000 years.

The front yard was cleaned every day, but in a boarder area in the back, the houses and yards, except the ancestral temple, were covered with dust and even had cracks. Messy weeds and green mosses covered the wall corners and stone paths."Eh?" An idea came up in Lynnray's mind when he was looking at the old and wearing structures, "The back yards haven't been cleaned for more than 100 years. Are there anything old and valuable there?"

With the above thought in mind, Lynnray could almost feel his fast heartbeat.

"If I can find something valuable and give it to dad, he must be happy." Lynnray took a deep breath and walked toward the decaying house beside the temple. He made every step carefully, and with a wood stick in hand, he tore up spider webs and tried to find some special object.

After entering the old house, Lynnray sensed a decaying smell. Spiders were crawling on their webs at the wall corner.

Some spider webs were attached onto decorative objects. Under careful examination, the decorations on the wall were also very old. But these decorations had already decayed, with only forms remaining visible.

"If these decorative objects were new, they must be worth some money." Lynnray shook his head and continued his search. While removing spider webs with his wood stick, he carefully observed every object he came across.

He observed objects on the ground and wooden shelves, and examined the wall for possible hidden mechanisms.

"According to books, mechanisms are normally hidden on walls." Lynnray carefully knocked on walls and listened to the sounds of knocking.

Lynnray enjoyed the feeling of 'treasure hunt', but he might not know that his father, grandfather, and predecessors earlier in Baruch family must have certainly tried this method.Items in this old house had already been searched over and over by predecessors in Baruch family.

Lynnray was only 8 years old. Although he matured earlier than his peers because of family education, he was still far behind adults in comprehensive thinking.

"There is none in this house, I'll check the next one." Lynnray exited the first house and walked toward the second one.

There were many buildings in the back yards. The front part where Lynnray and his family were living only occupied 1/3 of the mansion's area, but the back part was much larger. It might take 1 day for Lynnray to search the back part.

"The decorations rotted away, and no valuable item can be found." Lynnray walked out of another old house.

He looked up at the sky.

"Hmm. There is about 15 minutes before evening training." Lynnray turned back and saw a very large old house at a distance. "That's it, the largest one. I'll take 10 minutes to search it before training starts."

Lynnray made the decision and ran to the old house.

The old house occupied an area much larger than even the living room of the mansion in the front yard. After entering the house, Lynnray observed carefully: "Maybe this place was where we had meals hundreds of years ago." The decoration and layout of the house showed signs of a living room.

And it was a wide and spacious living room.

"I'll search the floor at first."

Lynnray used the same method of lowering his head and opening eyes widely. He carefully searched every location, and poked every item of his interest with his wooden stick to distinguish it. He skipped useless items such as stones. Because evening training would start soon, Lynnray accelerated his search.

"Now search the wall and decorations. It's the last hope." Lynnray plumped up his mouth and looked around, "Predecessors, please leave one or two items to me, even if it may be small."

Lynnray carefully searched every location and did not even overlook the back sides of rotten decorations on the wall.

There was a wooden shelf with drawers beside the wall. Lynnray pulled out every drawer and observed carefully, but all of them were clean and empty. If there was anything in the drawers, that was only dust.

"Alas."

After checking the last drawer on the wooden shelf, Lynnray felt disappointed.

"I can't find anything valuable after searching for such a long time. Now my body is covered with sweat and dust."

Lynnray looked at his dirty body with a bit anger.

His vision scanned across the old house.

"Darn! Get back!" Lynnray threw his wooden stick at the shelf, as if he was giving vent to his anger resulting from one hour's useless work.

"Thwack!" The wooden stick hit the shelf heavily.

The wooden shelf had a long history, and with 100 years' corrosion, it had become fragile. Hitting of the stick produced a crunching sound in the wooden shelf.

Lynnray looked back and was startled upon hearing the sound: "Not good, it will collapse." While searching the old houses before this one, he accidentally broke some decorations on the ground, so he was experienced handling this issue.

He quickly dodged to one side.

The wooden shelf twice the height of Lynnray collapsed. With a "Boom", it smashed on the ground into 7 or 8 parts, and stirred up some dust in the house. In the dust, Lynnray did not notice:

With the cracking of wooden shelf, a black ring hidden for an unknown period in the shelf's inter-layer fell with the shelf onto the ground.

"Puff, puff." Lynnray spit twice and waved his sleeve to remove dust.

"Bad luck today. I got dust all over. Training will start soon. Let me take a bath and change clothes." Lynnray waved his hand and walked toward the outside.

Chapter 7 - Ring of Coiling Dragon (II)

The black ring rolled to the location of the threshold.

After walking several steps to the threshold, Lynnray suddenly stopped because he clearly felt he was stepping on something like a stone.

"When I was checking this area, there was not even one stone at the threshold, so it must be a wooden piece." Lynnray resented the collapsed wooden shelf, so he heavily trampled on the 'wooden piece'.

If it were a wooden piece, it could be smashed, but --

"Why is it so hard? What is it?" Lynnray felt it was a hard item, so he lifted his feet and examined it.

He saw a black, ring-shaped item lying on the ground. It was unattractive and covered with dust.

"Ah, is it a ring?" Lynnray looked at it with sharp eyes, picked it up happily, and wiped it with his sleeve. Then he saw the true features of the item.

The item was black in color, and it was unclear whether it was made of wood or stone.

It was a black ring made of a material similar to both wood and stone, and had a very vague and twisted carving.

"Earthworm?" Lynnray looked at the ring's carving with confusion.

At the first sight, he believed the 'twisted strip' was an earthworm.

He smiled and talked to himself: "The carving is poor in quality. Any random carver could produce a better work. Alas, there is not even a precious diamond on the ring, not to mention a more precious magic crystal."

Rings generally had a diamond or magic crystal.

But the black ring was made of a material similar to both wood and stone, and had no diamond or magic crystal. Obviously it was worthless.

Lynnray didn't know why he liked this black ring at the first sight. Maybe it was because he made so much effort in searching.

"Hmm. The ring is bigger than my fingers, so I can't wear it on my hand... I'll place a thread through it and wear it as a chest pendant." Lynnray showed light in his eyes.

As an 8-year-old boy, Lynnray's hands were much smaller than adults and could not wear the ring.

"What name should I give to the ring? Ring of earthworm? No, it sounds ugly." Lynnray thought for a while and suddenly had an idea: "Hee hee, the twisted pattern can be considered a dragon. A dragon is coiling on the ring, so it can be called Ring of Coiling Dragon." Although Lynnray believed the twisted item was more like an earthworm, he still named it 'Ring of Coiling Dragon'.

"Ring of Coiling Dragon!" Lynnray held up this black and primitive ring and laughed brilliantly.Because of difficulties in family economy, it was Lynnray's first chest pendant since childhood. Especially, the pendant was found by his own effort, so he liked it very much.

"Oops, it was the time for evening training."

Lynnray recalled his urgent business at hand. With so much dirt on this body, he was like a beggar. "Too bad." Lynnray ran out of the old house toward the bathroom.

"Splash."

Lynnray poured water onto this body. His skin was in a healthy wheat color, and pretty muscle curves had appeared. That was the result of exercises. With the flushing of water, the dust was removed quickly. He cleaned himself in the quickest way possible and put on training clothes.

"Thread, thread..." Lynnray looked for a thread to string the Ring of Coiling Dragon. When he saw a piece of broken linen clothing, he showed light in his eyes and pulled out a thin thread from the clothing.

Linen was ordinary, but tight and durable. And the thread was tight, too.

He quickly strung up the ring, and after tying a knot, he put on the ring in front of his chest.

"I'm late now, for the first time." Lynnray ran out of the house rapidly, and while running, he tucked the 'pendant of coiling dragon' under his clothes. When he felt the coolness of the pendant, he became delighted.

One late arrival was paid back with the Ring of Coiling Dragon.

Lynnray was happy with that.

Lynnray rushed out of Baruch mansion and ran to the open land on the east of Wushan Town. On the street of Wushan Town, many civilians were returning home from one day's work. They knew why Lynnray was running.

"Lynnray, don't hurry. Be careful of tripping."

"Mr. Hilman is strict. Lynnray might be punished."

……

Baruch family was friendly toward civilians, so the civilians liked Lynnray very much.

"How will uncle Hilman punish me?" Lynnray thought while running fast. He had no time talking with the adults, and after a while, he arrived at the open land east of Wushan Town.

The three groups had gathered at this time, and Hilman was addressing them. Upon hearing Lynnray's footsteps, Hilman cast a cold glance upon him.

Lynnray ran to one side of the group and stood still. He waited for Hilman's words.

"Double your training task. Return to your position." Hilman said lightly.

"Yes!" Lynnray lifted his head and chest, and responded with a loud voice.

The juveniles were whispering. The training task was doubled for Lynnray because of a few minutes' late arrival. Lynnray could not catch up with dinnertime back home today.

When Lynnray was running to his position in the group --

"Boom!" The earth was shaking with rhythm, as if a giant monster was walking on the ground.

"It's in the east." Lynnray made clear the direction.

Lynnray, Hilman, Rory and Roger looked toward the east. As the shaking sound turned clear, all juveniles knew it was a giant monster's steps.

Every shake with the steps seemed like punching on Lynnray's heart.

What was the giant monster?

Lynnray opened his eyes widely and stared in the eastern direction.

Chapter 8 - Raptor the Monster (I)

The giant monster, which was the cause of earthshaking now appeared.

Upon seeing the giant monster, Lynnray and other children were terrified. Hilman, Rory and Roger responded quickly and stood in front of the children. They watched the monster alertly.

"Level-7 monster 'Raptor'!" Hilman turned pale. And both Rory and Roger felt weakness in the legs out of fear.

"It's huge. Is it the monster in legends?" Lynnray was shocked.

The largest animal Lynnray saw since childhood might be a war horse passing through the town. The war horse was one meter and eighty centimeters high, but compared with the giant monster in front of him now, it was only a baby in front of a giant. Their difference in height was quite obvious.

The giant figure was as tall as a two-story building and was 20 to 30 meters long.

It was a raptor!

The raptor had huge, hard and red scales all over its body. Every red scale was shining with luster of metal and was scary upon sight. The four long legs of raptor covered with scales were extremely strong and as thick as two persons' arm length. The raptor was fire red in color, with only its claws in color cold, deep black.

The raptor's tail, covered by fire red scales and as long as half the length of its body, was sweeping on the floor like a whip. Every sweep would produce a deep ditch on the floor.

"Hum...."

With a low snort, the raptor sent out two streams of white smoke with the smell of sulphur. The two eyeballs as crystal-clear as diamonds showed redness in an uncanny way. The huge head of the raptor turned toward the group of juveniles including Lynnray. The cold red light shining in its eyes seized all juveniles with fear.

"Puff, puff." The raptor chewed twice and showed his saw-like teeth in two rows inside and outside. Every tooth was frightfully pale and cooled down people's heart. Nobody could doubt the sharpness of these teeth.

Lynnray's heart almost stopped beating. At this moment, the entire world seemed to have become silent.

"Too horrible, can someone withstand this giant monster?" Lynnray was petrified.

With only the sight of this huge monster, Lynnray knew he had no power to fight back. He believed that with one seep of the whip-like tail, the houses made of hard stones in Wushan Town would turn into debris.

"Is here Wushan Town?" An indifferent voice came from the top of the raptor.

The petrified juveniles looked at the large back of the raptor and saw a mysterious man in purple gown sitting cross-legged. The raptor was large in size, and so was its back. It was enough for a man to lie down or even roll over.

"Respected magician, here is Wushan Town. How can I help you?" It was Hilman's voice.

Upon hearing Hilman's voice, all people seemed to have found their backbone, and recovered from their shock and terror. But all of them, including Rory and Roger still dare not make a sound. They only looked at the giant raptor and mystery magician in purple gown behind Hilman in terror.

"Wushan Town. So I went the right way." The mystery magician said in a low voice.

Then the mystery magician stopped talking. The giant raptor glanced at Lynnray's group of people with its cold, large and red eyes, sent out two streams of smoke with its nose, and then marched forward again. While seeing the raptor walking into the town, Hilman turned pale in his looks.

"Stay here, everyone." Hilman followed the raptor.

"Uncle Rory, what is that? A monster?" Lynnray inquired.

Rory cleared his throat and was still terrified. But he nodded and said: "Yes, it's a monster. But it's a very fierce monster, level-7, a raptor."

"Raptor?"

The name was impressed in Lynnray's heart.

The raptor's giant figure, rigid scales, sharp claws and powerful tail were all scary. Lynnray believed... that a raptor could wipe out the entire Wushan Town.

"The raptor had great defense with its scales and tremendous power of attack, and it was good at fire magic which was very aggressive."

Rory was introducing to Lynnray in terror, "The raptor could slaughter a team of 1,000 persons. Only the joint force of level-6, level-7 and magicians could penetrate its scale and harm it."

Lynnray was shocked in the heart.

Even a 1,000-person team could be slaughtered?

"But the most horrible was not the raptor, but the mystery person in purple gown." Rory took two deep breaths and tried to pacify himself.

Roger also nodded: "To subdue the raptor, you must change it into a faithful servant. It means... The mystery person in purple gown was much more powerful than the 'raptor'. It must be a magician, judging from his wearing."

"A magician of at least level-7, or maybe level-8." Roger also clenched his fist, "I can't imagine such a powerful person came to our place."

Lynnray could also experience the fear in the heart of Rory and Roger.

A level-7 raptor and a mystery magician with greater power were indeed terrifying.

"The magician is more powerful than the raptor?" Lynnray still couldn't believe it.

The raptor had a huge body, hard scales, sharp claws and a strong tail... but the magician was so small in body figure.

"Howl..."

A roaring sound came from the center of Wushan Town.

"Oops." Rory and Roger were shocked. Lynnray and other children were worried. Was the raptor roaring because of Wushan Town or uncle Hilman? Nobody knew at the moment.

"Stay here, everyone." Despite fear in the heart, Rory and Roger still ran to the center of town.

Lynnray bit on his teeth:"Uncle Hilman!" Lynnray was worried about uncle Hilman and all others in town, so he followed. With attention fully attracted to the raptor, Roy and Roger gave no heed to Lynnray who followed them.

After a while, Rory and Roger ran to the center of town. Hilman was watching them from a distance.

"Why did you come?" Hilman rebuked them.

But when he saw Lynnray who was running behind Rory and Roger, he frowned and said: "Lynnray, it's dangerous here, go back now." Rory and Roger did not notice Lynnray's arrival till now.

"Lynnray, why do you..." They did not know what to say.

"Uncle Hilman, ,I will not go back." Lynnray was unwilling to go back.

Hilman shook his head. He knew Lynnray had a strong character and often insisted on what he believed to be right, so he said: "OK, stay where I am, and do not get away. I can protect you."

"Thank you, uncle Hilman, I will not run away." Lynnray was excited.

At this time, Hilman and others were looking at the place of conflict at a 100-meter distance. They saw a group of young people in front of the raptor, consisting of 4 men and 3 women.

Chapter 9 - Raptor the Monster (II)

"Captain, what's happening there?" Rory inquired in a low voice.

Hilman smiled: "The mystery magician had some conflict with the mercenaries. We only need to look, and do not interfere." As a level-6 warrior, Hilman dare not interfere, either.

The raptor alone was powerful than him, not to mention the mystery magician.

The mercenary team of seven was not weak. 5 of them were warriors and 2 were magicians. A strong man of red, messy hair, who was heading the team, was sitting on a black bull. The bull's sharp horns were shining in metal color.

And the red eyes revealed the bull's identity -- level-5 monster 'bloody bull'.

With a snort, the bull also sent out two streams of white smoke from its nose.

The mercenaries had 7 persons, including 4 men and 3 women. Magicians were women, and one woman was an archer. Besides the bloody bull, there was another monster -- a giant griffin hovering above the ground.

Griffin is a level-4 monster.

The griffin had a lion-like head and giant wings. With two monsters and two magicians, the mercenary team was out of ordinary.

"Young guys, you'd better hand over the Depro Diamond." The mystery magician said with a cold voice from the back of the raptor.

"Respected magician, we don't want to become your enemies, but we made much effort to obtain this Depro Diamond.It's worth 100,000 gold coins, but you are trying to exchange for it with only 700 gold coins. It's impossible." The strong man in messy red hair said gravely.

Now Lynnray, who was staying beside Hilman, knew what was going on.

The mystery magician tried to purchase the Depro Diamond worth 100,000 gold coins with only 700 gold coins.

"Depro Diamond is so valuable." Lynnray was surprised, "Maybe the diamond means something; otherwise it would not attract the mystery magician into a forceful purchase regardless of his identity."

No wonder the mercenaries did not agree to sell.

"humph." The mystery magician grunted.

"I only have 700 gold coins, and I'm paying. If you don't make concession, you will lose your life, and for no gold coin." The mystery magician said coldly.

"Howl.."

The raptor, which was higher than general buildings in town, made a low roaring, shaking the houses beside the street.

"Captain, we risked our lives to obtain the Depro Diamond. How can we give it to this flinching guy?" A woman in black gown said indifferently.

As senior mercenaries, the 7 persons experienced a lot of battles and would not easily compromise.

The red-hair captain said in a deep voice: "Respected magician, I belong to the Kelley family of Fenlai Kingdom..."

The captain tried to gain an upper hand with his background.

But powerful magicians generally had peculiarities and gave no respect to members of nobility.

"You are starting a battle." The mystery magician grunted.

"Be careful." The 7 mercenaries were in positions of alert. The 4 male warriors were in front, and the woman archer took out a compound bow. Another two female magicians were preparing magic.

"Howl..."

As the giant raptor opened its mouth, a thick flame came out toward the mercenaries.

Under high temperature of the flame, the stone pavement of central street expanded, rolled up and even broke. Many stone plates cracked, and the entire ground turned black.

"Be careful."

The heading red-hair man said quietly, and summoned up a red-color vital energy shield around his body. Another three warriors also activated their shield.The huge sword in the hand of the red-hair man slashed on a stone wall beside the street. With a large "pum" sound, the wall collapsed. Hundreds of stones fell onto ground, raising up loads of dust.

And the raptor's flame also wrapped up the four warriors, producing a hissing sound on their vital energy shields.

"Huh!"

The red-hair man swung his right foot onto a stone half a meter in diameter.

Other 3 male warriors used the same practice. They kicked a large stone each. And the stones were as if thrown from a catapult; they split the air, and with sharp whizzing sounds, they were about to strike the mystery magician sitting on the raptor.

"Fu!""Fu""Fu"......

One and another large stones were kicked up against the mystery magician. And in a short while, half of the fallen stones of the house in construction were used up.

Lynnray was watching the fight excitedly, with fist clenched.

"They are doing great. They kicked up stones that large." As he saw the four 'human-figure catapults', he admired the warriors very much. However, the raptor was even more horrible.

The tail of raptor swung in the air as fast as lightning.

"Pa""Pa""Pa""Pa"......The stones were smashed by raptor's tail and had no chance of hurting the magician.

"Fu..." The raptor's tail gave no heed to the surroundings. Under sweeping of a large range, one and another stone houses were destroyed, as if they were made of mud. As the stone houses collapsed, numerous stones fell and dust permeated the area.

"Howl..." The raptor was still roaring and spitting huge flames in dust.

Since the beginning, the two female magicians were chanting ancient magic mantras. The pronunciation of magic mantras was totally different from the common language on Yulan Continent and was much more complex. After a short while, they finished chanting.

"Ice armor!"

As the female magicians shouted, two white beams were sent out from each one of them, covering the four men with a layer of crystal-clear and transparent armor.

The heading red-hair man was glad with the two layers of protection -- one the ice armor and the other vital energy shield -- and was more assured in the heart.

"Attack!" The red-hair man commanded.

The four warriors kicked up a large stone each. Four large stones were striking the magician sitting on the raptor. Then the four warriors made a leap of a dozen meters and rushed toward the raptor.

Chapter 10 - Dance of Fire Serpent (I)

"Howl..." Flame from the mouth of the raptor burned an area of dozens of meters in an ocean of fire.

"Sssss..."

The raptor's fire was burning at the surface of the warriors. With the protection of ice armor and vital energy shield, the warriors could absolute withstand the heat.

The female archer reached to the back of the griffin and was shooting with arrows.

The bloody bull was protecting the two female magicians like city walls.

"Fu""Fu""Fu"!

With cold looks and stable hands, the female archer shoot three arrows at the mystery magician on the back of the raptor.

"Fuu!" The raptor's tail whipped even faster than the arrows and smashed them on the ground. Then it turned in the opposite direction toward the four male warriors. Upon hearing the whizzing sound of the tail, the four warriors turned pale in their looks. They dodged quickly like monkeys.

But the tail was not whipping in straight lines, but in a bizarre floating manner.

"Pum!"

One warrior among the four failed to dodge the tail, which cut at his waist. His ice armor and vital energy shield was penetrated in a blink. And with one curve, the tail wrapped up his body.

"Luke!" The red-hair man shouted anxiously.

"No!" Luke was also shouted in terror.

With one shake of tail, the raptor sent Luke into its mouth. Luke was bit apart in a crunching sound. And his final voice was only a painful howling.

In the middle of the raptor's saw-like teeth, Luke was dismembered, and one bloody leg fell from the corner of the monster's mouth. A section of scary white bone stuck out at the knee area.

"Don't look at it." Hilman stood in front of Lynnray to block his vision.

The scene was indeed bloody, and even terrifying for an adult if he saw it the first time. Besides, Lynnray was only an 8-year-old kid.

But he saw it.

"Hoo, hoo!" Lynnray felt as if his heart was pressed by a large stone. He couldn't breathe naturally. While gasping, he recalled over and over how the young man Luke was bit into pieces.

The split belly, separated intestines, crushed head and fallen thigh!

All these blocked Lynnray's breath and dizzied his head.Lynnray first saw a battle of such cruelty and a man bit into pieces by a huge raptor. Especially, the fallen thigh was deeply impressed in his heart.

Hilman, Rory and Roger looked at each other with worries about Lynnray.

Could Lynnray bear the bloody scene? Would it cause psychological wound in a child's heart? If a child was terrified by war, his progress would be obstructed.

"It's nothing but killing!" Lynnray said to himself, "When I join the military in future, I have to kill, too. I should tolerate this."

Lynnray was indeed smart. After extensive reading, he knew the path he was about to walk.

When a man grew up on Yulan Continent, he would naturally face life and death. Only as a child, Lynnray had not faced moments of death before. As he kept talking to himself, he reduced his fear gradually.

On the contrary, Lynnray felt the surge of blood in his body.

"The battle is indeed exciting." Without knowing the reason, Lynnray felt excited to see the bloody war and desired to fight and kill.

"Is it because of the Dragonblood warrior's blood in me?" Lynnray did not know.

He suddenly found that he was expecting such bloody battles. He made a step to the side, getting around Hilman, and looked at the battle 100 meters ahead.

"Lynnray, don't look at it." Hilman was startled when Lynnray tried to watch again.

"I'm not scared, uncle Hilman." Lynnray looked up at Hilman.

Hilman was amazed to see the excitement in Lynnray's eyes, and did not contain him further. Lynnray continued to watch the battle 100 meters ahead, which was at the most intense point.

Another three warriors made a leap toward the mystery magician on the raptor's back.

"Howl." The raptor roared, turned its head and tried to bite on a warrior. Meanwhile, its claws waved toward another, and its tail swung toward the last one with a flashing speed.

The warriors had to change their direction of advancement.

The mystery magician on the raptor's back remained still, with only lips moving. He was allowing the raptor to fight by itself.

"Dance of fire serpent!"

It was the mystery magician's cold voice. Seven fire serpents dozens of meters long were roaring and flying to all directions. Every fire serpent looked like real. They had distinctive scales and terrifying huge sizes. All people were dumbfounded at the scene.

Level-8 fire magic -- dance of fire serpent!

In fact, the mystery magician had been chanting his magic mantra in soft voice and preparing the horrible level-8 magic 'dance of fire serpent'. In the dance of serpent, seven huge serpents with terrifying power of attack were sent off. Even a raptor with powerful defense would die or be wounded heavily under the serpents' besiege.

The mercenaries might bc able to resist for a while in front of a level-7 magician, but they were in no way possible to withstand the combination of a level-8 and a raptor.

The finally knew the mystery magician was at level-8.

"It's dance of fire serpent. Flee!" The red-hair man looked pale and screamed.

And the remaining 6 mercenaries were in terror.

"It's too late. You have to accept your fate." The mystery magician's cold and mad voice touched the heart of the six mercenaries like a cold knife.

Chapter 11 - Dance of Fire Serpent (II)

The seven fire serpents flew fast and lit up all houses it passed above, creating a disastrous scene of high flames. The civilians of Wushan Town, who was watching their homes destroyed from a distance, sunk into deep sorrow.

In front of the seven fire serpents, the stone houses were destroyed like toys, with flames dancing all around.

"Let's go." The female archer gave up the fight and ordered her griffin to fly up.

In fire magic, the seven fire serpents had a range of motion. As long as the archer flew out of the range, she would be safe.

"Ssssss..." Two fire serpents twisted each other and wrapped up both female magicians and the bloody bull. A hissing sound of burning flesh came, and Lynnray almost smelt the scorched flavor of hair and skin.

"Brother Kelley, help!" The shrilling scream of female magician came from the circle of fire serpents.

"Moo, moo..." The bloody bull showed redness in its eyes, and its muscles were twisting. It grunted and tried to escape the constraint of fire serpents, but every fire serpent had strong power of bondage.

"Louisa!" The red-hair man yelled in pain.

The two pretty female magicians and the bloody bull turned into ashes in a short while, but the red-hair man had no time to mourn their death.

He and another two male warriors were about to face one fire serpent each. And they were like babies who had no power to resist.

Even though they could smash a stone with one punch, what could they do when their body was wrapped up by a fire serpent?

"Ah..." With bodies wrapped up by fire serpents, the three warriors screamed.

Their vital energy shields at the surface were broken. And in a hissing sound, their facial muscles were twisted, eyeballs stuck out, and all their hair, skin, muscles and bones were burned off. Nothing could withstand the horrifying temperature of the fire serpents.

The three powerful warriors were burned into ashes in a short while.

"Hu Hu..."

The female archer was short of breath. She finally escaped from the range of fire serpents.

"Luke, Louisa and Kelly... I will revenge for your death, for sure." The female archer wept in misery, and rode her griffin higher up to the sky.

"Boom!"

A thick lightning came from the sky on the unprepared female archer. She was directly turned into ashes, and the griffin was burned black, twitched, and fell from the sky heavily onto a stone house. It broke the roof and fell inside.

"Escape? Hum..." The mystery magician grunted.

Hilman, who saw everything from a 100-meter distance cleared his throat, and thought to himself in horror: "Amazingly, he is a level-8, and dual-series magician."

......

"That is called dance of fire serpent?" Lynnray stood still in horror..

The scene of seven flying serpents and burning flames was shocking to Lynnray unlike anything before. Every fire serpent was similar to the raptor in size, and seven of them flying together was indeed a disaster. Houses were burned and fire swallowed everything.

In such a short time, the powerful 4 warriors, 2 magicians, 1 archer and 2 monsters were dead. Only the griffin's life and death was hard to tell.

The seven huge fire serpents had disappeared, but Lynnray could still feel the hot air around the site of battle, which had become ruins. The ruins and hot air seemed to be narrating the process of the battle.

"That's terrible."

Lynnray was short of breath, and in his mind, he kept recalling the disastrous scene of 7 flying fire serpents.

Even the horrible raptor was not as scary as the fire serpents.

Lynnray glanced at the mystery magician on the raptor's back. The mystery magician's body was much smaller compared with the raptor.

"He sent out the 'dance of fire serpent' just now?" Lynnray felt hard to believe. How could a person even weaker than uncle Hilman send out such a disastrous attack?

A slight feeling of fear arosc in Lynnray's heart for the mystery magician in purple gown.

"Is this a magician?" For the first time, Lynnray had direct perception of a magician's power.

And also...

He expected to become one.

"If I can launch such an attack one day." Lynnray felt surge of blood in great excitement when he thought of the possibility in future.

At that moment...

Lynnray found his own path.

Pursuit for the peak of power.

"Dad." Lynnray suddenly saw his father Hogg. The entire Wushan Town was in accidental disaster, and as the town's owner, Hogg was unable to help.

"Do not speak." Hogg glanced at Lynnray and prevented him from speaking.

Then Hogg looked at the magician and thought: "He is a level-8 magician, and dual-series. Few could compare with him in power in the entire Fenlai Kingdom. I can't imagine such a person came into our Wushan Town."

Hogg just wished that the magician leave and peace be restored in the town.

The mystery magician jumped off the raptor easily, although the raptor was 2-stories high.

He walked to the site of the red-hair man's death. With one wave of hand, ashes were blown aside, and a purple diamond with dazzling and dreamlike light appeared. He picked up the Depro Diamond.

"Haha, I searched 10 years for Depro Diamond, and found it while passing this town in a short cut. Haha... Heymans, now I have the Depro Diamond embedded in my wand. How can you fight with me, haha..." The mystery magician laughed madly.

The noble man Hogg and civilians stayed quiet in the distance. They dare not make a sound in case irritate this mystery magician.

"Who is the owner of Wushan Town?" said the mystery magician suddenly.

"Dad." Lynnray was frightened.

Hogg came forward and said respectfully: "Great magician, Wushan Town is my territory."

"Oh." With face still covered by his purple gown, the mystery magician said lightly, "You suffered great loss this time. I killed the mercenaries who have a lot of gold coins. The gold coins were meted in 'dance of fire serpents', but still can be exchanged for money. That is my compensation."

Hogg was relaxed upon hearing the words of the magician, who would probably stop killing.

"I, Hogg, thank you for your grace on behalf of the town." Hogg offered his salute.

The magician nodded gently and walked toward the raptor. The raptor got down and stretched its front legs, and the magician stepped on the front legs, went two steps, and leaped onto the back of the raptor.

"Hum..." The raptor made a snort and sent out two streams of white smoke with sulphur smell.

Then with heavy steps, the raptor departed. When the raptor and mystery magician went farther and father and vanished at the end of streets, Wushan Town's residents were finally relieved.

Chapter 12 - A Strong Man's Heart (I)

Hogg was relieved to see the level-7 monster the raptor and mystery magician left.

"Uncle Hilly." Hogg turned his head to steward Hilly, "Arrange some people to find gold in the ashes. The team of mercenaries was uncommon. They must have some wealth to compensate for our town's loss."

Hogg looked around at the house ruins.

"Yes, sir." Hilly nodded.

"Hilman." Hogg looked to one side at Hilman and smiled: "How do you feel?"

Hilman also nodded and said: "I was scared. When I saw the level-7 monster 'raptor' and the mystery magician, I knew our Wushan Town had no power to defend against them. A noble magician at level-8 will not be criticized even for destroying our town on a whim, not to speak of punishment."

Magicians were high in social position.

An ordinary magician was as respected as a noble.

And a level-8 magician need not kneel before a king and could converse with him while standing. The noble position of a level-8 magician was obvious.

"Yes, so we should celebrate because no resident of Wushan Town died." Hogg smiled.

"Yes, it's worth celebration." Hilman nodded with a smile.

"Hilman, please lead others to assist uncle Hilly in accommodation of civilians who lost their houses." Hogg gave his instruction.

"Yes, Mr. Hogg." Hilman replied.

Hogg looked behind and asked Hilman in confusion: "Eh? Where is Lynnray? He was beside me."

"I don't know. I didn't notice him." Hilman shook his head.

"Sir, Lynnray has gone home." Hilly said, "But he was a bit distracted while walking. I don't know what he was thinking about."

Hogg nodded, as if deep in thought.

The mansion of Baruch family. The only thing the mansion had a great number of was houses. At the most prosperous time of the family, hundreds of people were living in the mansion. But much fewer people were still living there. Even Lynnray, an eight-year-old was occupying one house.

Lynnray's bedroom.

Lynnray was sitting cross-legged on bed and absorbed in thoughts.

The horrible scene of 'dance of fire serpent' kept occurring to him. As seven fire serpents as thick as a water vat and as long as dozens of meters rose, fire consumed the sky and everything on the ground. The powerful warriors and magicians of the mercenary team turned into ashes in a short while.

"Magicians are so powerful."

Lynnray was a bit excited, "Although I have the blood of Dragonblood warriors, it was low in density, and the blood of Dragonblood warriors contradicts with other methods of vital energy maneuvering... It restricted me on my path of growth as a warrior. I don't know if I can become a magician."

Lynnray suddenly wished to become a magician.

"The raptor was horrible, but if I own a raptor..."

Lynnray recalled the scene of the raptor.

The flash-like tail could smash large stones and houses in one whip. And the giant body was like a huge chariot in the military. Once it advanced fast, its body and protective scales could exhibit destructive force.

"I don't know how to own a monster." Lynnray also desired to own a monster.

For no apparent reason, Lynnray couldn't fall asleep. He tossed and turned in bed, and thought of the giant raptor and the scene of 'dance of fire serpent' again and again.

"Lynnray, what's wrong?" A familiar voice came.

Lynnray sat up and saw his father Hogg, who was looking at him with a praising smile.

"Dad." Lynnray called out, but he was also confused: "Dad is smiling at me? And with such an expression?"

Hogg was harsh on Lynnray and seldom smiled at him. His expression now was surprising.

"Good, good." Hogg praised Lynnray, "You deserve to be a man in the family of the Dragonblood and possess the best qualities of a warrior. If the descendants of Dragonblood warriors fear death and bloody fight, it would become a great joke."

Now Lynnray understood that his father was referring to his indifferent reaction upon seeing the raptor tearing up Luke in a bloody scene.

Lynnray was a bit surprised: "Dad, you saw it?"

"The raptor created a great havoc. I certainly knew it. I came out when the monster just arrived at Wushan Town, but I was in the opposite direction. I saw you were together with Hilman." Hogg nodded.

Lynnray giggled.

Lynnray was frightened in the beginning, but soon he became excited and felt the impulse of bloody fighting. He didn't know whether it was because he carried the blood of Dragonblood warriors.

Hogg smiled: "Were you in such a great shock that you forgot about dinner?"

"The dinner?" Lynnray suddenly thought of the dinner."Grooh..." Lynnray's stomach grumbled. Now he recalled that he was about to attend the evening training when the 'raptor' and mystery magician came.

At ordinary times, he would have dinner after returning home.

But now his mind was occupied by the shocking 'dance of fire serpent' and the 'raptor'.

"Dad, I'd like to ask, will it be possible for descendants of Dragonblood warriors to become magicians?" Lynnray asked, with his hand grasping the bed sheet, and eyes staring at his father.

Hogg was a bit surprised, but he knew right away that his son desired to be a magician.

"It is possible." Hogg nodded.

Lynnray showed pleasure in his eyes.

Hogg waved his hand to calm down Lynnray and said: "Lynnray, our family had magicians before, but it had only two. You should know what role talent is playing in a magician's path. Generally, only one in 10,000 has the chance to become a magician. There is only tiny hope. Don't expect much."

But Lynnray shook his head.

"Dad, I'll try even if I have only tiny hope." Lynnray was serious.

Hogg looked at the serious expression of his 8-year-old son. A child's serious expression was interesting, but Hogg didn't find it funny.

He thought for a moment and said: "Lynnray, military recruitment takes place in late autumn. There will be a test in the capital 'Fenlai City' for recruiting magic students. You can try in late autumn this year if you want to go."

"Late autumn? Only half a year from now?" Lynnray showed excitement in his eyes.

Chapter 13 – A Strong Man's Heart (II)

The three of Baruch family and steward Hilly had dinner together. Little Warton happily made noise at table, and the living room was filled with laughter. After dinner, Hilly put Warton to sleep, and Lynnray was having a conversation with his father Hogg.

"By the way, dad, which one between magician and warrior is more powerful?"

Hogg looked at Lynnray with a smile and shook his head: "Magician and warrior have their respective advantages each. A magician is slightly better than a warrior in power if they are on the same level. And most importantly... a magician has very high social status and is higher than a warrior. For example, the level-8 dual-series magician just now might be even higher than a level-9 warrior in status."

"So the magician's power is slightly greater, but why do their statuses differ so much?" Lynnray was confused.

Hogg smiled: "You need to first understand the grading of magicians. Magicians are graded into 9 levels. Level-1 and 2 are the beginning stage. Level-3 and 4 are intermediate. Level-5 and 6 are advanced. Level-7, 8 and 9 are extremely powerful. And above level-9 is the holy magician."

"Magicians have a high social status because of their destructive power." Hogg raised a glass of fruit juice and took a sip.

"Destructive power?" Lynnray looked at his father.

Hogg put down his glass and nodded: "A warrior, even a Dragonblood warrior can kill nearly 100 enemy soldiers with one wielding of sword, but in front of a huge army of millions, they can kill the commander at most. If the commander dies, the enemy can appoint another one. Then how about a holy magician? With forbidden magic, he can destroy a city and hundreds of thousands of enemy soldiers. If hundreds of thousands of soldiers have died, what will be the use of a living commander? Therefore, for a country, a holy magician would be more horrible than a military."

Lynnray understood it right away.

"Not to speak of the holy magician, even a level-8 or level-9 can exhibit astonishing power in a battle. So magicians have very high social status." Hogg said with a slight smile.

Lynnray nodded gently.

On the war-themed Yulan Continent, magicians naturally had high social positions.

"Oh, by the way, dad, I read in the books that magicians are physically weaker than warriors. But the magician I saw jumped off the raptor easily. Is he weak or not?" Lynnray questioned further.

"I'll tell you later. Lynnray, you should know that ordinary people on Yulan Continent can live up to 120 and 130 years. Powerful magicians and warriors can live longer, generally 200 to 300 years, and even 300 to 400 years. The longest lifespan of humans is 500 years. And you can have a very long and nearly indefinite lifespan only when you attain the holy domain."

Lynnray nodded.

He read it in books before.

"But, do you know why they live a long life?" Hogg asked.

Lynnray was baffled.

He took it for granted that powerful magicians and warriors live for, maybe 300 to 400 years, and did not think of the reasons behind.

Hogg saw Lynnray's expression and laughed: "In the wide area between sky and earth, there are elements carrying the properties of fire, water, wind, earth, thunder, light and darkness. Magicians and warriors practice by absorbing elements between sky and earth. Therefore, magics and vital energy techniques are different from each other in property. If you have observed carefully, you can find the vital energy of the red-hair man heading the four mercenaries was fire in property, and the other three had vital energy with the properties of wind, water, etc. Both vital energy techniques and magics are classified according to properties."

Lynnray now knew for the first time that magicians and warriors practiced themselves by absorbing elements between sky and earth.

"Powerful magicians have a long lifespan because when they absorb elements between sky and earth and refine them into magic power, the elements flow in their body and are absorbed by organs, muscles and bones. Consequently their constitution will turn better and better. Similarly, when warriors practice vital energy maneuvering, they absorb elements between sky and earth, and refine them into vital energy in their body. Circulation of elements in their body can also improve their constitution. Warriors at higher level have a better constitution and naturally, a longer lifespan." Hogg made everything clear to his son.

Now Lynnray fully understood the point.

According to his father, a magician's body was improved by using elements of sky and earth, and naturally they had better physiques.

"Dad, but why do they say magicians are weak?" Lynnray was perplexed.

Hogg shook his head: "Think carefully. When they say a magician is weak, he isn't really weak, but when he is faced with a warrior on the equal level, he is relatively weaker and his body is his weak point. For example, a level-8 magician is as strong as a level-2 or level-3 warrior if he hasn't practiced physically, but his body will become a disadvantage if faced with a level-8 warrior."

Lynnray patted on his head and smiled in embarrassment.

It was such a simple issue.

"A magician cannot fight at close quarters, but he has a way. He may use magic shield such as the 'earth shield', 'ice shield', 'wind shield', 'light shield', etc. With magic, he first defends and then attacks."

"And a powerful magician has another method, which is to subdue a monster."

Lynnray's eyes brightened up.

He also wanted to subdue a monster, such as a powerful raptor.

"A powerful monster can protect the magician and keep the enemy at a distance. In this way, the magician can toss out magic and kill the enemy." Hogg smiled.

Lynnray asked eagerly: "Dad, how to subdue a monster?"

Upon seeing Lynnray's expression, Hogg smiled and said: "You need to meet two conditions to subdue a monster. One is to make the monster willingly submissive to you, and the other is to lay out a soul contract magic circle to transform the monster into your servant."

"The first condition is difficult to meet. You have to defeat the monster straight to create willing submission. For example, to subdue a raptor, you have to defeat it first." Lynnray could understand the difficulty in those words.

He wanted to subdue a raptor, but did he have the power to defeat a raptor?

"And the second condition, lay-out of soul contract magic circle is also a tough task. You need to reach level-7 in order to make it." Hogg said solemnly.

Lynnray was a bit surprised, "Dad, so in your words, only a magician on level-7 or higher can subdue a monster?"

"Not really. If you have enough money, you can buy the 'soul contract' scroll. Tear it into pieces and a 'soul contract magic circle' will be formed. But the 'soul contract' scroll is very expensive." Hogg laughed at himself.

"How much is it?" Lynnray questioned further.

"I heard last time it is 10,000 gold coins one scroll, and a seller is difficult to find." Upon hearing these words, Lynnray could only smile bitterly in his heart.

The most difficult part of subduing a monster was to defeat it.

Of course, you could choose to subdue a weak monster, but what was the use of it? Did you have the power to defeat a strong one? And how could you create willing submission if you used tricks?

Creating willing submission was not an easy task.

And the second condition, lay-out of soul contract magic circle limited the conquerors of monsters to magicians and wealthy people. Even a person of noble class could not enjoy the luxury of spending 10,000 gold coins for a magic scroll, if he was not wealthy enough.

Lynnray closed his lips and frowned.

"Considering our family's financial condition, I have to become a level-7 magician if I want to subdue a monster." Lynnray thought to himself, and he knew this path was difficult.

And the first qualification was talent.

It was a hope of one in 10,000. If he had no talent, he could not possibly become a magician.

Chapter 14 - Battle in the Sky (I)

Morning of the next day.

As usual, a large group of children gathered on the open land east of Wushan Town. Hilman and two other instructors had not arrived. The children were in heated chit-chats on the shocking battle yesterday.

"The monster yesterday was fierce. When uncle Hilman and others went to the center of town, I followed them and watched from a distance. When the monster's claws hit the ground, the stone pavement was smashed. And the houses collapsed like made of mud." Hadley was the most eloquent in the children. He talked a lot with body gesture, as if he saw everything clearly.

And most of the children were listening with wide-open eyes.

"Hadley, you were on the open land with us, weren't you? How did you see?" A brown-hair juvenile of 13 or 14 grunted.

The older juveniles were not so easily fooled as the 7 or 8-year-olds.

Hadley stared at the juveniles and said: "Fra, you don't believe me? I never cheat people."

The brown-hair juvenile named Fra continued with scorn: "Everybody knows you as a big mouth. You seldom tell the truth. Hi, everybody, when did Hadley ever tell the truth?" Fra turned to the youngsters beside him.

The youngsters of 12 to 15 years old laughed: "Yes, Hadley the imp often tells lies." The older juveniles were obviously on Fra's side.

Hadley became anxious: "You don't believe me? OK." He looked around and found Lynnray, so he shouted, with light in his eyes: "Apart from uncle Hilman and other two instructors, Lynnray also went there. He saw it with his own eyes. Ask him to speak, and you'll know if I told a lie."

"Young master Lynnray?" The juveniles looked at Lynnray.

Lynnray had a high position among the children and juveniles. On one hand he was the eldest son of Baruch family, and on the other hand, he caught up with the 13 and 14-year-olds in physical training, as only an 8-year-old child. On Yulan Continent, a place of martial admiration, Lynnray's excellence won a lot of praises among the children of Wushan Town.

"Young master Lynnray saw it yesterday. We surely believe his words." The children nodded.

At the age of 13 or 14, the juveniles started to know something. They knew Lynnray as a noble, and different from themselves. Generally they addressed him as 'young master Lynnray', but the 7 to 8-year-olds such as Hadley just called him 'Lynnray' directly.

"Lynnray, did I tell a lie? You saw the scene." Hadley ran to Lynnray, held his hand and winked at him.

Lynnray was unwillingly involved in the dispute.

"The monster was named 'raptor'. It was a powerful level-7 monster. With hard scales all over the body, it was resistant to knife and sword. The raptor's whip-like tail and sharp claws could easily destroy stones and stone plates as if they were made of paper. And it spit fire which burned apart stone pavement.."

Lynnray described the scene as it was.

And the children were listening attentively.

"Needless to say, when you saw the raptor, you knew how fierce it was." Lynnray smiled.

The juveniles nodded.

When they saw the raptor for the first time yesterday, they were indeed frightened. The monster's giant body was like a small hill, and its fire-red large scales had a hardness visible at the first sight.

"You see, the raptor was fierce." Hadley shouted.

The juvenile named Fra stared at him and was about to speak in a loud voice.

"Uncle Hilman came." Lynnray called out when he saw Hilman, Rory and Roger arriving. All the children and juveniles quieted down and stood orderly in three groups.

Now the open land was in silence. Only the footsteps of the three instructors could be heard.The instructors walked to the front side and faced the group of children. Hilman said with a smile: "You all know what happened yesterday, right?"

"Yes, we know." The children noticed Hilman's casual attitude, so they responded in a disorderly way.

"Good." Hilman straightened up his face, "The giant monster was a raptor, and on its back was a mystery magician. They were very powerful, but you should know:"

Hilman cast a cold glance upon the children: "The mystery magician reached his current level by gradual practice. It took him many years' effort to subdue the raptor. If you want to subdue a powerful monster and become as powerful as the mystery magician, you should keep going and make continuous effort!"

"Everyone has the chance to become a strong fighter. What it takes is...effort!"

Hilman said with a resolute voice and put on a cold expression.

The children quieted down immediately. Some older children had their own purpose in the mind, so they looked differently in their eyes.

"OK, let's start our morning exercise. Old rules... Face the sun and make the 'containment pose'." Hilman was straight to the point, and the children of three groups started their training in 'containment pose'.

......

Hilman set out different training tasks for different groups, and the children had to complete the training tasks with effort under the supervision of the three instructors. Training was performed in a different atmosphere today. No child was complaining about tiredness. All of them were making great effort and tolerating difficulties.

"...Fifty, fifty-one..." Lynnray was counting in the mind. He was lying with face down, and supported on his five fingers of one hand and tiptoes of feet. With a tightened body, he was practicing support with one hand.

Support with one hand was a simple and effective way to practice the strength of fingers and arms.

To become a great warrior, one generally needs to practice according to secret vital energy books. And his achievement in vital energy practice depends on his physical fitness. A stronger body can accommodate more vital energy.

"Due to my blood of Dragonblood warriors, I cannot practice vital energy maneuvering, so I can only surpass others in physical practice." Lynnray showed firmness in his looks. With fingers grasping the ground like tree roots, he practiced once, twice, and more. He was greatly admired by the juveniles who drained completely in practice.

"Ninety-eight, ninety-nine..."

Lynnray kept going.

......

"Now we wrap up today's morning exercise." Hilman said loudly while looking at the children in three groups.

Then he took a deep breath and thought: "What story should I tell today?" At the end of morning exercise every day, Hilman would always narrate stories for the children. It had become his usual practice.

"Uncle Hilman, please..."

The child was about to speak, but stopped suddenly.

Hilman, who was preparing his stories in the heart, heard the child's incomplete sentence. He was a bit confused and looked up. Now all children looked at the sky in the east with a dumbfounded expression. And Rory and Roger also looked in the direction in shock.

"Hmm?" Hilman turned about and looked to the sky in the east.

A huge black dragon 100 meters long was hovering in the eastern sky at a height 200 to 300 meters above ground. The dragon had eyes as large as carriage wheels, a body with black scales shining in cold glimmer, and a pair of huge wings with a total length of 100 meters, which was flapping heavily.

It was the monster 'black dragon'.

Chapter 15 - Battle in the Sky (II)

Black dragon was one of the most powerful among monsters. The black dragon family consisted mostly of level-9 monsters, and the powerful ones might be holy monsters. The raptor yesterday was by no means comparable with a level-9 or a holy monster.

The children and three instructors were observing the black dragon at hundreds of meters' distance on the open land. Such a close range produced a shocking visual effect.

And the most shocking was:

On the head of the black dragon was standing a man in gray gown. Strong wind lifted the man's gown, but he was standing straight and as stable as a rock. He was staring at a middle-aged man in green clothes, who was standing in the air and carrying a long sword on the back.

The two men were standing in confrontation with each other.

Standing in the air!

Besides a wind magician proficient in level-7 flying magic, only a holy fighter could stand in the air. And the middle-aged man in green, who was carrying a long sword had proved his identity.

He was a warrior on the holy level.

"A gray-gown man who subdued the black dragon, and a holy fighter who can fly." 8-year-old Lynnray was shocked at the scene although he watched a grcat battle yesterday. Hilman, as a level-6 warrior, was also petrified.

......

"Holy fighters. They are holy fighters." Hilman murmured, and his body was shivering.

As a warrior who experienced many occasions of life and death, Hilman was the first to come to his senses. But he still felt like dreaming: "Yesterday, a level-8 dual-series magician came, but today, we have two holy fighters and one black dragon. I was never so shocked before."

Hilman felt a little dizzy in the head.

A black dragon was at the top position among monsters, and was at least level-9. The one who could subdue a black dragon was most probably a holy fighter. Besides, only a holy fighter could stand in confrontation with a holy fighter.

It means the gray-gown man was a holy fighter.

Hilman and the crowd were hundreds of meters away from the black dragon. Even with the best hearing, they could not hear the the conversation between the holy fighters standing in confrontation.

They did not know what words were exchanged between the holy fighters, but suddenly:

"Howl..."The giant black dragon roared and flapped its large wings. A horrible force was sent out in all directions, and all the people present, including Hilman felt breathless and weak in the legs.

"That is the power of a dragon?" Lynnray felt breathless, as if his heart was pressed by a large stone, but he was still excited, with blooding surging all over his body.

The black dragon was indeed powerful.

"Rudy, don't go overboard!" The middle-aged man in green shouted. His shout echoed between sky and earth like thunder. His words were heard by all in Wushan Town, including Hilman.

Upon hearing the shout, the dragon withdrew its power, and people's breath returned to normal.

Hilman was in a daze, and murmured: "Rudy? Rudy?"

He suddenly knew what was happening, so he turned back to the children and shouted in a loud voice: "Everyone, go home now! Go home and hide! Quick!" Hilman's shout and twisted expression surprised the children.

Hilman was well aware of the ongoing incident.

Obviously, the holy fighters had a conflict, and seemed to be starting a fight soon.

If the children remained on the open land without the protection of buildings, the energy of holy fighters might kill them even with a little touch. It was said holy fighters had the power to 'destroy sky and earth'. It was a little exaggerated, but they could certainly destroy a city and high mountains.

"Go now! Move! Quick!" Hilman shouted while pushing some children.

Now the children came to their senses. Although they did not know why they should go back, and wanted to watch the fight, they still followed Hilman's order to go home.

"Rory and Roger, send back the younger children of 6 and 7 years old. Quick! The fight between holy fighters may influence this area and cause unthinkable consequences."

Hilman's anxiety was obvious on his face.

"Yes, captain." Now Rory and Roger knew the mind of their captain.

They started carrying some younger children who were running slowly. Two with arms and two on the back. Hilman also joined them and carried children one after another.

"Lynnray, go home quick." When Hilman was running with children in his arms, he shouted to Lynnray.

"Yes, uncle Hilman." Lynnray said with a loud voice.

Although Lynnray was 8 years old, he ran as fast as a 14-year-old juvenile. And while running, he occasionally looked at the sky in the east. His attention was drawn to the giant black dragon and two holy fighters.

"Captain, Mr. Hogg needs us." About 11 warriors ran from the direction of Baruch mansion and shouted to Hilman.

"Quick. Send the children back." Hilman commanded."Yes, captain." The warriors responded, and started carrying the younger children who were running slowly. "Go home and hide! Protect yourself!" Hilman shouted.

Hilman had high authority in Wushan Town, and his words were the direction for all those who were frightened by the black dragon. People in Wushan Town hurried up, and all children and workers returned home and took shelter in their stone houses.

Lynnray rushed to his own home.

"Quick, hide in the basement of the warehouse." Hogg, who was standing in the courtyard, shouted to Lynnray. The basement of warehouse in Baruch mansion was strong enough to protect people's lives.

"Yes, dad." Lynnray nodded and ran to the warehouse.

Lynnray ran quickly, but his mind was still lingering on the man in gray and standing on the black dragon and the man in green, so he looked up at the sky in the east. The town's buildings were low in height, so the sky area covering hundreds of meters could be easily seen.

The black dragon was still roaring in a deep voice.

"Tillon, you can't blame me for my actions since you are so stubborn." A cold voice echoed in the sky, and the black dragon was infuriated. While roaring, it spit black fire steams.

"Rudy, I'll see how fierce you are as a holy magician!" The man in green yelled.

Chapter 16 - Disaster (I)

Obviously, the middle-aged man in green who carried a long sword was named 'Tillon', and the man in gray gown was named 'Rudy'.

The black fire coming from the dragon's mouth consumed the green-clothed man's body, which shone in green light suddenly. His body was protected by the green light from the harm of black fire. Meanwhile, wielding of sword was heard.

The sword swish was even louder than the roaring of dragon.

As the green-clothed man wielded his sword, a streak of light as long as dozens of meters crossed the sky and cut toward the gray-gown man. The gray-gown man stared at the huge light streak, remained motionless, and kept chanting magic mantras.

"Is this a light streak of sword? It is huge." Lynnray ran to the warehouse while looking at it, "How will the gray-gown man withstand it? Will he rely upon the black dragon?"

"Pum!"

Without making a defense, the black dragon allowed the light streak to cut at the gray-gown man's body. The man's gown cracked into pieces, but his shiny armor inside was revealed. The armor was emitting dazzling light as bright as diamonds.

The light streak cut at the armor, without hurting the gray-gown man even a bit.

"How's it possible?" Lynnray was petrified.

Since he was watching the sky while running, he tripped on a stone. When he fell, he was still looking at the sky in the east. "What is that armor? Great defense."

"Lynnray, quick! Don't be distracted." Hogg shouted, because Lynnray was still watching.

"Yes, dad." Lynnray was reminded of his situation, so he stood up and ran directly to the warehouse.

"Rumbling..." A horrible sound was heard in the sky, followed by screams of people in Wushan Town. Lynnray involuntarily looked at the sky again, but this time he was frightened.

In the east, a dense array of stones floated in the air, and each one of them was as large as a house.

"Fu!""Fu!""Fu!"...

All the stones crossed the sky while shining earth-yellow light, and smashed toward the green-clothed man like meteors. Every stone was about 100,000 jin in weight. Such huge stones were many times larger than the stones used by catapults in wars.

Even the city wall could not withstand such heavy strikes.

One huge stone could produce a terrifying effect, but there was a dense array of them. One and another huge stones smashed toward the green-clothed man in a shocking scene.

"Pum!"

When the first huge stone struck the green-clothed man, the man's green light turned brighter, and soon he became a dazzling 'green sun'.

Densely arranged stones were thrown upon the green-clothed man like tidal waves.

At one blink, the green-clothed man was surrounded by large numbers of stones, but his green light was still overflowing from the gaps of stones.

"Pum!"

With heavy sounds, the huge stones cracked into pieces by the horrible green vital energy. Every huge stone as large as a house broke into fragments shooting in all directions.

The stone pieces came from a height of hundreds of meters, and with the explosive power of vital energy, they were catapulted with great force and over a long distance.

"Terrible!" Hogg turned pale. And Hilman, who was still on the streets of Wushan Town, knew immediately:

It was a disaster of Wushan Town.

Numerous stone pieces, varying from the size of 2 meters and a human's head shot in all directions from a height of hundreds of meters. Every huge stone broke into dozens of or more than a hundred stone pieces, and nearly 1/5 of them came toward the area of Wushan Town.

"Dad!" Lynnray shouted to Hogg when he saw large numbers of stones falling from the sky.

"Get in quick!" Hogg shouted anxiously.

Lynnray was still dozens of meters from the warehouse. When he heard his father's anxious voice, he let go of all thoughts and ran fast toward the warehouse. With loud sounds of crash, numerous stones fell onto structures on the ground.

It was a doomsday scene with earthquakes.

"Fu!" A huge stone of several hundred jin touched Lynnray's body and smashed near his feet. It created a large and deep pit on the ground. Lynnray sweated for his good luck.

"Boom!""Boom!""Boom!""Boom!"...

The sounds of stone crash into roofs, stone plates and grounds as well as people's miserable screams were heard simultaneously. It was indeed a doomsday's scene.

"Fu!" Several large stones fell to ground in front of Lynnray, and he dodged quickly.

If he kept dodging, how could he hide in the warehouse?

"Young master Lynnray, quick!" A person rushed out of the warehouse. He was old Hilly. With a fire-red vital energy shield on his body, Hilly ran toward Lynnray.

"Brother, quick, quick!"

At the door of the warehouse, the 4-year-old Warton cried loudly to Lynnray.

"Warton, get in, quick!" Lynnray shouted.

"Fu!" A rare stone with a 2-meter size smashed rapidly toward the warehouse. Lynnray had the calculation that if the huge stone fell on the roof, Warton would be injured or even killed!

"Get in quick, Warton." Lynnray shouted anxiously as if his eye corners were ripped apart, and he himself was running fast toward the warehouse.

Disregarding the falling stones, Lynnray ran directly to Warton without dodging.

Hilly was facing Lynnray, so he did not see the huge stone smashing onto the warehouse, but Lynnray saw it. Once it fell, how could Warton's tender body resist the terror?

"Lynnray." Hilly was surprised at Lynnray's reaction.

Another two or three stones fell near Lynnray. While staring at Warton like a leopard, Lynnray made it to the warehouse quickly. Hilly turned pale when he saw behind him the huge stone 2 meters large.

"Get down!" Lynnray shouted with a twisted expression.

Little Warton never saw his brother's horrible expression, so he got down out of fear. With tears in the eyes, he stared at Lynnray and murmured: "Brother..." Lynnray threw himself upon little Warton.

At the same moment...

"Boom!"

With a huge crashing sound, the terrifying huge stone smashed onto the roof of the warehouse, which broke apart despite its strong stone plate. And the wall collapsed under strong shaking.

"Young master..." With red eyes, steward Hilly had a sudden outbreak of vital energy and threw himself to the spot. He created a vital energy shield around his body, and struck on the stone pieces of the wall with his hands. The stone pieces and steward Hilly almost fell onto Lynnray at the same time.

"Boom..."

After a short while, Warton, Lynnray and steward Hilly were buried under the collapsed wall.

In the courtyard, Hogg was holding a sword and striking away a flying stone, but when he turned his head and saw how Lynnray threw himself on Warton and steward Hilly followed to protect them, he was petrified.

The warehouse collapsed, and stones rushed down.

"Lynnray..." Hogg called him with red eyes.

At this moment, Hogg could not see clearly whether Hilly or the stone pieces fell first on Lynnray.

Chapter 17 - Disaster (II)

"Boom!""Boom!""Boom!"...

Shortly after intermittent crashing sounds, no stone piece could be seen in the sky of Wushan Town. All the huge stones were smashed by the green-clothed middle-aged man, but now the residents of Wushan Town had no time watching the fight in the sky.

"Mr. Hogg, our town is in a bad situation. Just now... Mr. Hogg? What's wrong?" Hilman was about to make a report when he noticed Hogg's petrified expression.

Hogg shivered and returned to his senses: "Lynnray." He rushed to the warehouse in a scary fast speed. Hilman also figured out something and followed.

"Pum!" Before Hogg reached the site, the stone pile pressing on Hilly, Lynnray and Warton was broken apart from within.

Steward Hilly straightened up his body.

"Uncle Hilly, how's the situation?" With trembling voice, Hogg looked at the other two, and first noticed the bloodstain on Lynnray's head. The bloodstain was so obvious that Hogg felt dizzy and shook a bit.

Lynnray was still supporting himself on the ground with his hands so that he would not press on Warton.

"Dad." A tender voice came from below.

Warton crawled out from below Lynnray. Because of his tiny body and protection of Lynnray, Warton was not even slightly injured.

"Brother, what's the matter?" Warton pushed Lynnray's body.

"Lynnray, Lynnray." Hogg called Lynnray with a trembling voice.

At the side, steward Hilly said: "I was a bit slow. I struck off one stone piece, but it still hit Lynnray's head. Fortunately the crash was not heavy."

"I'm OK." Lynnray said with a husky voice and squeezed out a smile.

When Hogg saw his son's smile, he burst into tears.

Lynnray lifted his body and sat up. He had bloodstains on his clothes, face and neck. He bled quite a lot when the stone hit his head. And he was still feeling dizzy. He looked at his father and said weakly: "Dad, you are weeping."

"Nothing serious." Hogg smiled excitedly.

"Warton, why were you at the warehouse door?" Lynnray patted on his brother's head and said with discontent.

Warton knew his mistake and lowered his head: "Sorry, brother."

At the side, Hilly said: "It was my fault, actually. The disaster came suddenly, so I brought Warton to the warehouse. When I saw young master Lynnray was in danger, I came to the rescue. But I didn't expect a huge stone fell onto the warehouse in such a short time."

"Boom!"

An intense shaking took place again.

All people looked at the sky on the east and saw a giant floating in the air. The giant was 10 meters high and had twisted muscles, cold face and earth-yellow skin. The sound of combat was like thunder when the giant fought with the green-clothed man.

The horrible force of the yellow giant was shown in the sound of combat. Every strike had far exceeded the booming of huge stones of 100,000 jin.

Lynnray watched the scene with admiration: "This yellow giant must have been summoned by the gray-gown man in magic." Lynnray figured out that the gray-gown man was a powerful holy magician.

"Lynnray, how do you feel?" Hogg asked with worries.

Lynnray squeezed out a smile: "Not serious. My head is wounded and bleeding."

"You bled too much. A person may die from bleeding, you know?" Hilly took out a piece of white gauze from the warehouse and bound up Lynnray's wound on the head.

Hogg glanced deeply at Lynnray and asked: "Uncle Hilly, how is him?"

Hilly smiled: "He's OK. He didn't pass out because of his physical fitness. Just eat some meat to enrich the blood and he'll recover."

Hogg was relieved to hear Hilly's words.

Just now, when Lynnray rushed in to protect Warton, Hogg was frightened. He was afraid his son might die in this way.

After a deep breath, Hogg looked at Hilman: "By the way, Hilman, you were reporting about Wushan Town. How's the casualties?"

"I didn't make a thorough calculation." Hilman said gravely, "But according to what I saw, some people died, some were injured or disabled. We were all unprepared. Even if I shouted to them, many people still had no time to escape into the basement."

"It came fast." Hogg raised his head and looked at the sky in the east.

A holy fighter was much more powerful than residents of Wushan Town, and could destroy the town in moments. The bombarding with huge stones and smashing of them by the green-clothed man was only the beginning stage of a battle.

But even in the beginning stage, the stone pieces resulting from the fight caused a disaster in Wushan Town.

"The legendary level-10 earth magic, and also a forbidden magic -- 'earth guarding' with earth element was indeed powerful. It could be considered the strongest single-person attack launched by a holy earth magician." Hogg looked at the yellow giant and said indifferently.

Hogg was the patriarch of a Dragonblood warrior's family. Although declining, the family kept records of powerful magic attacks over 5,000 years. So Hogg could distinguish them at the first sight.

"Level-10 magic..." Lynnray gasped.

Lynnray also hoped he could stand on a black dragon and use level-10 magic someday. He thought of the magic school recruitment. "There will be a test in the capital for recruiting magic students. Half a year from now..." Lynnray was expecting the magic recruitment test in half a year.

"Hilman, after a while, check out with me the situation of residents." Hogg said and then looked at Hilly, "Uncle Hilly, when the holy fighters leave, bring Lynnray to take a bath, change some clothes and take rest."

"Yes, sir." Hilly nodded.

Hogg turned his face to Lynnray, who was attentively watching the fight between the holy fighters, and said with a smile, "This kid still wants to watch the fight despite injuries. Luckily, the holy magician used 'guard of land'. It means the battle will end soon."

Lynnray was focused at the intense battle in the sky, and did not notice his chest pendant which was stained with blood in his clothes. Amazingly, the ring's wood-stone material absorbed blood slowly like sponge. And the surface of the ring was shining with dim shadows.

But covered by clothes, the dim shadows were unnoticed.

Chapter 18 - Spirit of Coiling Dragon (I)

In the eastern sky, the gray-gown man was standing on the head of the curling and hovering black dragon, and with a self-confident smile on his face, he was watching the fight between the green-clothed middle-aged man and the yellow giant.

"Su!"

In an air-split whiz, the green-clothed man's long sword pierced the head of the yellow giant. With a loud sound, the giant's head cracked, but he seemed to be unaware, and his stone-like fist smashed on the middle-aged man's body.

"Pu!" The middle-aged man spit blood and turned pale.

The cracked head of the yellow giant pieced up together with no harm at all.

"Tillon, you'd better hand it out. The earth guard I summoned cannot be defeated." The gray-gown man said indifferently.

The green-clothed man looked at him coldly and said with a harsh voice: "Rudy, if I can't keep it, you can't get it, either." Suddenly, green light in the hands of the middle-aged man turned much brighter, and the gray-gown man, who was standing with a straight face, now shouted in panic: "Stop!!"

"Boom!"With a loud sound, the green light in the middle-aged man's hands became as bright as the sun, and disappeared in one moment.

"Tillon, you..." The gray-gown man pointed at the green-clothed man without uttering a word.

With a pale face, the green-clothed man stared at the gray-gown man who was also in disappointment: "Now neither of us can have it. Rudy, I'm wounded, but you still can't easily kill me." With a cold laughter, the green-clothed man turned into a ray of green light and flew away in the northeast direction.

The gray-gown man watched his opponent vanishing, frowned, but did not chase him.

And the earth-yellow giant beside him also disappeared.

"Holy sword master 'Tillon'? I can't kill him now." The gray-gown man murmured, and his black dragon, which seemed to know his thoughts, fluttered its wings and soared to the southeast.

The two holy fighters vanished at horizon with the blink of an eye.

But Wushan Town was in a scene of decadence. Hundreds of houses houses collapsed, and the residents' moans, curses, shouts and weeps filled the air. In a short while, a peaceful morning turned into the day of disaster.

Hogg was alone in the living room of Baruch family.

He was sitting beside a long table with knitted brows. As the controller of Wushan Town, he had to serve the benefits of residents. With the sound of footsteps, steward Hilly came in: "Master."

"How's Lynnray?" Hogg inquired.

Hilly smiled:"Don't worry. I cleaned his wound and bound it. He had a meal, changed clothes and slept. He will feel much better after waking up."

Hogg nodded with relief, but he was still frowning.

"Are you worried about the residents of town?" inquired Hilly.

Hogg nodded and smiled bitterly: "Uncle Hilly, ordinary residents are not like us. Men are generally level-1 or level-2 warriors, but women were not. The stones kept falling, they were helpless."

Hilly nodded with agreement.

Very few people practiced vital energy maneuvering in Wushan Town. When thousands of stones fell, they had to hide in the basement or defend with a shield. If a stone hit them, they would be...

"Now we can only wait for Hilman's numbers." Hogg said anxiously.

After a long while, rapid footsteps came from outside.

Hogg brightened his eyes and looked in the direction. He saw Hilman running into the living room.

"Hilman, how's the casualties in town?" inquired Hogg eagerly.

Hilman made a sigh with lamentation: "I did a calculation just now. There are about 300 deaths and 1,000 injuries." Among the 5,000 residents, nearly 1/5 of them got injured despite protection of stone houses. The casualties were indeed serious.

"So serious?" Hogg murmured eagerly.

The most important supply for a country is grains. And a town also needs grains. They had a reduction in labor force, but so many disabled people still needed support. The town might suffer hardship in economy.

"Alas!" Hogg made a deep sigh.

He wanted to reduce taxation, but how could he help when the taxation was already too low to sustain his own family? And in some other towns, peasants were living a very hard life due to high taxation.

"Mr. Hogg, our residents are grateful for your kind treatment. They know what you did for them. So take it easy." Hilman persuaded Hogg.

Hilman was born in Wushan Town.

As a retired level-6 warrior, he could have worked as a captain guard in any noble's family in the capital, but he chose the declining Baruch family because of his gratitude for Baruchs' generous treatment of Wushan Town.

"Hilman, please take a walk in the town with other guards. Uncle Hilly, you can take a rest now."

"Yes, sir." Hilman replied.

Steward Hilly also offered his respect, then he left the living room with Hilman. Hogg was left alone in the living room.

……

In Lynnray's bedroom.

Lynnray was wounded in the head. Hilly had told everybody not to disturb him so that he could take a good rest. When the outside was in a chaos, Lynnray was enjoying his sweet dreams quietly in his bedroom.

"Ding..."

A slight beep was heard, and rays of light appeared at Lynnray's chest. The Ring of Coiling Dragon, which was in the shadow of light, slowly flew out from Lynnray's nightgown and floated at a position 10 centimeters from his chest.

When the beep got louder, the ring's glow also turned brighter.

Luckily, nobody was entering Lynnray's room to see the shocking scene, and Lynnray was in his comfortable sleep without noticing the floating ring.

"Su!" The glow of ring shrank suddenly and turned into a dim beam. The beam came out of the ring and appeared as a human beside the bed.

It was an old man with moon-white robe, white hair and beard, and a benevolent look.

At this moment, the Ring of Coiling Dragon fell onto Lynnray's chest. Lynnray slowed opened his eyes and was shocked to see the old man standing beside him. "Who are you?"

"Lad, my name is Delinkovot, holy magic master of Pron Empire!" The old man said with a smile.

Lynnray stared at him with wide-open eyes: "You, you are a holy magic master?"

The amiable old man nodded with confidence.

"No, sir, you just said Pron Empire? It perished 5,000 years ago!" Lynnray knew from continent history that Pron Empire had perished before his family existed. And Pron Empire was not one of the four great empires today.

Chapter 19 – Spirit of Coiling Dragon (II)

Pron Empire was founded as long as 8,000 years ago and lasted nearly 3,000 years before its destruction. The territory of Pron Empire included the land of Holy Alliance and Dark Alliance today.

It could be said that the 12 kingdoms and 32 principalities west of Monster Mountains used to be the territory of Pron Empire. One could imagine how large the empire was!

But Pron Empire perished a long time ago!

"5,000 years ago?" The old man paused for a moment, and sighed: "I couldn't feel the passing of time accurately in the Ring of the Land, but when I came out from it, my country had been non-existent for 5,000 years."

"Sir, what are you saying? I'm confused."

Lynnray was puzzled by the old man who appeared suddenly and said he was a holy magic master of a country which perished 5,000 years ago. Was there anything more funny than this?

Lynnray doubted if he was dreaming.

"Lad." The old man looked at Lynnray and said with a smile: "The ring on your chest is the Ring of the Land, a magic object I used before."

"Wait, wait."Lynnray lifted his head and said: "What is Ring of the Land? My ring was passed down from predecessors of my family. It is called the Ring of Coiling Dragon!"

"Ring of Coiling Dragon? Is it the original name?" The old man was surprised.

Lynnray was a bit surprised, too.

"What does original name mean?" Lynnray looked at the old man in doubt.

The old man laughed: "Oh, Ring of Coiling Dragon may be the name you or your predecessor gave it. When I discovered this ring, I could not find its name in any document, so I named it 'Ring of the Land'. I don't know its original name, either."

"You you named it by yourself, too. The ring is mine, and I named it 'Ring of Coiling Dragon'." Lynnray said stubbornly.

"OK, so let's call it Ring of Coiling Dragon." The old man did not argue with Lynnray.

"Why did you come out of the Ring of Coiling Dragon?" Lynnray furthered inquired.

The old man said with a smile: "In 4280 of Yulan calender, I..."

Lynnray was surprised upon hearing the date:"The year 4280? Now it's 9990."

"In 4280 of Yulan calendar, I came across my opponent Hamlin, another holy magic master. We battled with each other. But I didn't expect another holy fighter sneak attacked me... I lost the battle, but I didn't want my soul to be captured and tortured by Hamlin, so I sealed it inside the ring." The old man narrated his old story.

"The Ring of Coiling Dragon is miraculous. It seems not responsive, but it is a magic object. After I sealed my soul in it, Hamlin searched for a long time and could not discover me. I lived on by thanks to the ring." The old man smiled.

Lynnray nodded.

The Ring of Coiling Dragon looked quite mundane. As a successor of an old family, Lynnray knew the general features of treasures. They generally had a feel of elements. But the ring was like rotten wood.

"Sir, as you said, you were sneak attacked by a holy magic master and a holy fighter, and sealed your soul in the ring. And this ring is a treasure comparable with magic objects?" Lynnray said in conclusion.

"Yes." The old man nodded with a smile.

"Then how did you come out from the ring?" asked Lynnray.

The old man smiled: "After I sealed my soul in the ring, I lived on as part of it. Unless and until somebody became the owner of this ring, I could never come out."

"Become a owner of the ring?"

"Yes, it means your blood touches the ring." The old man smiled.

Lynnray knitted his brows and murmured: "Blood touches the ring?" Then he suddenly remembered when his head was wounded by a stone, the blood flowed onto his clothes, neck and maybe, the Ring of Coiling Dragon.

"Oh, so I'm the owner of Ring of Coiling Dragon." Lynnray nodded.

"Yes, since you became its owner, I came out and started to feel the atmosphere of Yulan Continent again." The old man asked with a smile: "By the way, lad, I told you my name. But what's your name?"

Lynnray smiled brilliantly: "I'm Lynnray, Lynnray Baruch."

"Nice name." The old man smiled.

"Sir, are you bound to the ring forever and cannot get free?" Lynnray pitied him.

The old man nodded: "As you may know, our soul goes to the lower region after death. Because I am a holy magic master, my spirit is everything, so I could resist the call of lower region for a short while, and sealed myself in the ring. Now I have only one method to leave the ring -- use up all of my spiritual force."

"Use up all spiritual force?" Lynnray didn't understand.

"Spiritual force is human's saying, but spirits call it 'soul power'. When the spiritual force is used up, the soul will vanish. In other words, when my soul vanishes, I will not be bound to this ring anymore."

The old man continued: "Although I'm still bound to the ring and restricted in a range of 3 meters, I feel good about it."

Lynnray was a bit touched. And suddenly, he really sympathized with the old man.

"Hehe, Lynnray, I'm already satisfied. You don't know... If I had been caught by Hamlin, I would have preferred death." The old man lamented.

"Sir, your name is Delinkovot, can I call you Grandpa Delin?"

Delinkovot was a great holy magic master in Pron Empire period. He had a high position and was ranked among the top 5 on Yulan Continent. His disappearance was because of the sneak attack of holy magic master Hamlin and another holy fighter.

However...

Delinkovot had no children or grandchildren. When Lynnray called him Grandpa Delin, his lonely heart warmed up.

"Good, good." Delin said happily.

Lynnray suddenly asked with expectation: "Grandpa Delin, you just said you are a holy magic master, can you teach me magic?" Faced with a holy magic master of 5,000 years ago, Lynnray could almost feel the thumping of heart.

He thought of the giant body of the raptor, the horrible scene of 'dance of fire serpent', the numerous huge stones falling from the sky, and the proud figure standing on the black dragon.

He desired that one day he could also stand on the head of the dragon and soar in the sky.

With a slight raise of white beard, Delin showed light in his eyes and said: "Certainly, your grandpa Delin is the greatest holy magic master. And among magics of all series, the earth magic is the most powerful." Old Delin was excited and energized to talk about magic.

Chapter 20 - Earth Magic (I)

Lynnray's feeling of excitement was like a volcano eruption.

"Grandpa Delin, you really can teach me magic?" Lynnray looked at old Delin with expectation.

Delin raised his white beard and said: "I'm a holy magic master, so I can teach you even if you are not talented. But the lack of talent will lead to low achievement."

Delin's words would certainly surprise other magicians if they were present.

As known to all, talent was most important for becoming a magician. One could never become a magician without good talent. But Delin said he could change a low-talent student into a magician. Such words would be considered a boast in general, but they came from the mouth of a holy magic master of 5,000 years ago.

"Low talent will lead to low achievement..." Lynnray was absorbed in thought.

He wanted to become a magician in order to restore the honor of his Baruch family, or at least, fulfill the wish of patriarchs over hundreds of years -- bring back the family's heirloom.

But power was important to realize his purpose."Don't worry, Lynnray. I haven't tested your magic talent, so we can't say it's high or low. Maybe you have good talent." Delin touched his white beard and said with a smile.

Delin's composure produced a pacifying effect on Lynnray.

"How do we test magic talent, grandpa Delin?" Lynnray asked with expectation.

"It's simple." When Delin said those words, suddenly --

Footsteps came from outside, and Lynnray said hurriedly and in a low voice: "Grandpa Delin, you have to hide. Someone is coming." If the holy magic master of Pron Empire 5,000 years ago was discovered, terrible things might happen.

But Delin smiled and did not move.

"Grandpa Delin..." Lynnray was a little worried.

"Clik." The bedroom door opened. Steward Hilly looked inside and saw Lynnray awake, so he said with a smile: "Lynnray, you woke up so early. Are you feeling better?"

Lynnray squeezed out a smile and nodded: "Thank you for your concern. I'm much better."

But he was quite anxious in the heart now. When he looked in the direction of Delin, he saw the old man still standing there with a smile: "Oh, what's wrong with grandpa Delin? It will be hard to explain if he is discovered."

"Young master, it's time for lunch. Since you are awake, you can have lunch with us." Hilly smiled.

"OK, I know." Lynnray looked again in the direction of Delin and was puzzled: "It seems that Hilly cannot see grandpa Delin. Why?"

Hilly noticed that Lynnray was looking at the area beside his bed, so he inquired: "Young master, what are you looking at? Did something fall on the ground? Maybe I can help."

"No, nothing." Lynnray rose from bed in a blink and said: "Grandpa Hilly, let's have lunch."

Steward Hilly felt a bit strange about Lynnray's reactions, but he didn't think much, so he nodded. Lynnray put on his clothes and shoes, and still looked at Delin with worries. Delin smiled toward Lynnray, moved a bit and disappeared from physical vision.

"He entered the ring." Lynnray now clearly felt a spirit's existence in the ring.

After formally becoming the owner of the ring by his blood, his feeling about the ring was taken to a new level.

"Lynnray, you don't need to say with voice, just converse with me in the heart. You are the owner of the ring, and I'm a spirit dwelling in it, so we can communicate with heart." To Lynnray's astonishment, he heard Delin's voice in the mind.

"Grandpa Delin?" Lynnray tried to communicate with his heart.

"I heard it." Delin's voice appeared in Lynnray's mind.Lynnray was so glad to communicate with Delin that he tripped on the threshold. Hilly turned back and said: "Young master, be careful during walking."

"Yes, I know." Lynnray replied with a smile.

While chatting with Delin in the mind, Lynnray entered the living room and sat down. The lunch was fancy with a delicious roast lamb. Hogg said with a smile upon seeing Lynnray: "Lynnray, take a seat." Then he tore off a lamb leg for his son.

"Thank you, dad."

Lynnray was a bit surprised. His family ate mundane meals generally because of their difficult financial condition, but they put a roast lamb on the table today. He did not know...when stones fell into Wushan Town, livestock was also killed besides humans. Therefore, even some civilians ate in luxury today, which was rare.

"Grandpa Delin, why didn't Hilly see you just now?" Lynnray asked Delin in his heart.

"Lynnray, only you can see me. I'm existing as a spirit which cannot be seen with physical eyes. You can see me because you are the owner of the ring." Delin answered carefully.

Lynnray understood his meaning. As Delin said, he was dead already, and was now existing in spirit form.

"Grandpa Delin, can you appear in front of me at any time?" Lynnray said gladly.

After saying those words, Lynnray saw Delin appearing as an old man with white robe, white beard and white hair beside him. At this moment, Hogg, Hilly and Warton were eating lunch and chatting, unaware of Delin's appearance.

"Wow..."

Lynnray was surprised that people on table did not see grandpa Delin.

"It's also not true that no one can feel my existence. People on my soul level can perceive me. Of course... if I hide in the Ring of Coiling Dragon, nobody can find me." Delin's voice sounded in Lynnray's mind.

"On the same soul level with you?" Lynnray talked with Delin while eating.

"Holy fighters are on my soul level. They can vaguely perceive my existence only when I appear outside of the ring. If I'm inside the ring, they cannot find me." Delin said with a smile.

Lynnray nodded in the heart, and gobbled the lamb leg while grabbing it with one hand.

"Lynnray, eat slowly." Hogg said with a smile.

Lynnray smiled toward his father, but was still eating fast. He soon ate up the lamb leg, made a burp, wiped his mouth and hand with a napkin, stood up and said: "Dad and Hilly, I finished, but I'm still dizzy. Let's me go back and sleep again. Warton, goodbye." Lynnray was the first to finish the meal.

"Still dizzy? Then go back and rest." said Hogg.

The incident this morning was a great shock for Hogg. He nearly believed Lynnray was dead. After this incident, Hogg became much more amiable toward Lynnray."Bye, brother." The lovely little Warton waved at Lynnray with his oily hand.

Chapter 21 - Earth Magic (II)

Lynnray ran to his room and locked the door from inside.

He quickly took off his shoes, jumped onto bed and sat down: "Grandpa Delin, can you come out and test my magic talent?" Lynnray said eagerly. He had been thinking about this issue while having lunch.

A dim light ray came out from the ring and turned into Delin beside the bed.

Delin said with a smile: "Don't worry. The first to tell you is...Without special test tools, I can only test your talent in 'earth magic'. Tools are required to test in other series."

"You can only test my talent in magic of earth series?" Lynnray was a bit disappointed.

He had heard that special tools were required to test magic talent, but he thought Delin might have some special methods as a holy magic master.

"What's wrong with earth magic? I can tell you earth magic is the strongest among all series including earth, fire, water, wind, thunder, light and darkness." Delin was obviously proud of earth magic. Anyway, he was a master in the earth series.

Lynnray found it hard to believe.

Different series of magic should be equal in potency, but why was earth magic the strongest?

"Grandpa Delin, I heard fire magic is the strongest in attack, and dark magic is the most bizarre. Why is earth magic the strongest?" Lynnray frowned.

Delin, who always had an amiable attitude, was now a little angry and discontent: "Lynnray, I can tell you, different magics are different in their power of attack."

"For example, the forbidden magic in fire series 'all-round devour' can burn out a large city. 'Absolute zero', the forbidden magic in water series can freeze hundreds of thousands of people to death. And in the thunder series, the forbidden magic 'thunder destruction' can produce thousands of lightning rays, leaving none to survive. And in the wind series, we have 'storm of destruction', summoning storm as sharp as knives. The result..."

Delin made a deep sigh.

Lynnray was listening with great shock.

He used to believe fire magic was the strongest in attack, but now he knew it was a silly thought. Magics in all series could produce massive destruction on the forbidden level.

"How about earth magic?" Lynnray didn't forget to mention the earth magic.

Delin said with self-confidence: "The earth magic is as powerful as other magics. When forbidden magic 'meteorite shower' is used, numerous meteorites will fall from the sky and ruin the city in moments. And there is 'world crack' which causes the earth to roll over like sea waves.

Houses will collapse, land will crack, and magma will erupt to kill millions."

Lynnray held his breath in shock.

"There is a forbidden defense magic in the earth series -- 'pulse defense'. When it is used, the sky, earth and space in all directions will be protected from harm of even 'thunder destruction'."

Delin described magic power in a vivid way, and then smiled: "Of course, I meant magic attack in large areas, not in single person."

Lynnray nodded.

He knew Delin was referring to destructive large-area magics.

"Grandpa Delin, it seems the earth series has relatively more forbidden magics. Why?" asked Lynnray.

Delin explained with a confident smile: "In fact, magics in all series only differ slightly. But they work in different ways in different environments. For example, in water areas such as the sea, the water magic is the strongest. And in some windy places, wind magic is the strongest."

Now Lynnray understood the point.

"Magicians on the continent fight on the land, right? And on the land, earth magicians are at an advantageous position." Delin said with a smile: "The vast land is earth magicians' greatest support."

Lynnray got the point.

Magicians in all series had places to use magic to their best capabilities.

Magicians on Yulan Continent fought on the land, most of the times. So earth magicians were at the best position.

"The earth element can best improve our body, and mother earth is the most benevolent to us." Delin said with respect, "When we sit on the land as earth magicians, we can feel how broad it is, how it pulses, and how much care it has for us."

"As to attack, we have single-person 'guard of land' and destructive 'world crack' and 'meteorite shower'. As to defense, we have 'pulse defense' and single-person 'holy armor of land guard'. We have the strongest single-person defense as earth magicians."

Delin explained with self-confidence.

"Single-person defense? We have the strongest single-person defense?" Lynnray looked at Delin in confusion.

Delin smiled and said: "Initially, an earth magician can use earth shield or earth wall to defend himself, but once he reaches level-5, he can use 'holy armor of land guard', which can become stronger as the magician progresses."

"At level-5 and level-6, the holy armor is made of rock; at level-7, it is made of jade; at level-8, it will be crystal jade; at level-9, it will evolve to platinum. And if you become a holy magician, your holy armor will be made of 'diamond', which provides the strongest protection." Delin smiled after saying these words.

Lynnray gasped in admiration in his heart.

Earth magic was indeed a strong one in all series. The 'holy armor of land guard' was made of diamond at the holy domain. Diamond was quite tough, and the 'diamond' of 'holy armor' was not ordinary, but a magic material.

"Ah, by the way..."

Lynnray suddenly recalled the holy fighters battling in the sky of Wushan Town. The green-clothed man slashed the gray-gown man with a sword ray. The gray-gown man's gown was torn apart, revealing an armor as shiny as diamond.

The holy magician named Rudy resisted Tillon's attack with the diamond armor.

"That is 'holy armor of land guard' made of diamond?" Lynnray was amazed.

It was strong enough to defend against the sword ray of a holy warrior.

"So I said earth series is the strongest in all." Delin said contently, raising his white beard a bit.

Humans live and fight on the land, after all. Therefore, earth magicians took the most advantages.

Chapter 22 - Rotation of Seasons (I)

In fact, magic in all series had their own special effects. As an earth magician, Delin certainly advocated his own series. And Lynnray, at only 8 years old, was greatly attracted by his vivid description.

"Grandpa Delin, please test me on my talent of becoming an earth magician." Lynnray said eagerly.

Delin smiled: "OK, let me test you now."

"A magician's talent is measured in two aspects, so I'll carry out my test in two stages." Delin was a bit high-spirited. After staying alone in Ring of Coiling Dragon for 5,000 years, he now had a lovely kid to instruct.

"Magic talent is measured in the student's affinity with elements and his spiritual force." Delin started his preliminary magic education.

"What are the use of the two aspects?" inquired Lynnray.

Delin said slowly: "I'd like to ask you first what a magician will use to toss out a magic?"

"Magic mantras." Lynnray answered right away.

Lynnray had seen how the mystery magician on the raptor's back use magic.

"Wrong."

"I saw they chanting magic mantras when they used magic." Lynnray refuted.

Delin touched his white beard and said contently: "A magician depends on his magic force and spiritual force to use magic. If his spiritual force is strong enough, he can use magic instantly without chanting a mantra. The mantras only play an auxiliary role."

"Use magic instantly?" Lynnray looked at Delin in confusion. He felt a broad magic world was expanding in front of him, but it was only dimly seen under a veil, and Delin was gradually pulling off the veil and revealing the world to him.

Delin nodded with a smile: "Yes, you need sufficient magic force first, and then control the magic force with spiritual force to absorb more elements of sky and earth and produce a magic."

"Elements of sky and earth?" Lynnray was surprised, "Grandpa Delin, we need to absorb external elements to use magic?"

"Haha, certainly. Do you think a powerful magic only depends on your magic force? No. In a forbidden magic, magic force of the holy magician only takes up one percent, and the remaining 90 percent is the energy of elements."

"In other words... magic force within the body is refined elements of sky and earth. Magic force is like the general, and elements are like soldiers. A magician direct his magic force outside of his body to control elements of sky and earth and produce astonishing magic, do you understand?" Delin looked at Lynnray with a smile.

Lynnray knitted his brows."Oh... I understand." Lynnray nodded, "The magic force is like uncle Hilman, and elements of sky and earth are like children. Hilman guides us in training, and maybe, in battles."

Delin nodded with a smile: "Yes, so the magic force is very important for a magician. If the magic force is not sufficient, he cannot use magic."

Lynnray nodded.

"And spiritual force is even more important than magic force." Delin smiled: "Now you know spiritual force is the 'soul power', which is a capability of control."

"With a strong magic force, we absorb elements of sky and earth. If we don't have enough spiritual force to direct so much energy, what will be the result?" Delin touched his white beard and enlightened Lynnray.

Lynnray frowned and thought by himself.

"Grandpa Delin." Lynnray said with knitted brows, "I read about art of war in some books. They say we can defeat the enemy by capturing its leader. If we kill the head of bandits, the members will disperse and escape. Spiritual force is like how the head of bandits controls the bandits. If magic force and elements are not put under control, their energy will enter a chaotic state."

Delin smiled upon hearing Lynnray's words.

"Haha, you are smart, Lynnray." Delin burst into laughter.

"Yes, magic force, elements of sky and earth and the control by spiritual force will come together and produce magic. Powerful magic would require a stronger spiritual force. So it needs the assistance of magic mantras." Delin said with a smile.Now Lynnray was clear about the basic principle of the broad field of magic.

Delin continued: "Certainly, that is only the basic principle, and the real magic world is more complicated than you imagine. The most important part is how to create a magic from magic force and elements of sky and earth."

"You may have magic force but do not know how to toss out a magic." Delin lamented: "Magic is a complex field, and magic study is very difficult and dangerous. Countries are competing with each other, and numerous magicians are researching new magics."

"In fact, they are researching how to create different magics by different arrangements of magic force and elements. But magic experiment is dangerous, especially the destructive ones. Sometimes it will cause disasters to the magicians themselves.."

With a faint smile, Delin continued: "You can only learn level-1 to level-6 in magic schools. Levels above seven and in the holy domain are confidential. You may learn some of them if you join the system of a country."

Due to extensive reading, Lynnray could easily understand Delin's point.

"If no one teaches you, you are not able to use magic regardless of your magic force or spiritual force." Delin said with a faint smile, "The secret of magic is about how to control magic force and elements to produce magic."

"After many years' exploration, a nearly perfect system of magic was developed." Delin touched his white beard and laughed, "Don't worry, Lynnray, you will not stay low in front of some big personalities, because I can teach you level-7 to level-9, and even magic in the holy domain."

Lynnray took a deep breath.

He felt he stepped onto a new path.

Under the guidance of grandpa Delin, he need not become a warrior, and he could choose the path of magicians, which had much mystery and power.

"Now let's check your affinity with elements. Sit cross-legged, close your eyes and meditate." Delin said lightly.

"Meditation?" Lynnray's heart was beating rapidly.

"How is my talent?" He thought to himself.

"Don't worry, you just need to feel and tell me whatever you have felt." Delin smiled to encourage Lynnray. And Lynnray closed his eyes and tried to calm down.

"Don't worry, just do as I said." Delin said lightly.

......

Meditation is the foundation of magic and is required in absorption of elements, refinement of elements into magic force, and improvement of spiritual force. At the first time, meditation was difficult and a little dangerous, but with the guidance of magic master Delin, Lynnray did it in an easy way.

After half an hour's induction, Lynnray entered a meditative state.

Delin looked at Lynnray with a smile, and waved his hand.

Suddenly, large amount of earth elements gathered around Lynnray. Generally, earth elements were evenly distributed in space, but by the strong spiritual force of Delin, earth elements were thickened nearly 100 times around Lynnray.

"If he can't feel earth elements in such a condition, he has no hope of becoming a magician." Delin said to himself.

Even an ordinary people could feel earth elements thickened 100 times.

Lynnray was in a happy mood in meditation. He never noticed the miracle around him before -- numerous earth-yellow light dots floating around.

Chapter 23 - Rotation of Seasons (II)

"Lynnray, can you feel it?" Delin's sound appeared in Lynnray's mind.

"I can feel it. So many earth-yellow light dots packed tightly together. Thousands of them. There are more than 100 over the back of my hand. So many." Lynnray was glad to see those light dots.

Delin was glad to hear Lynnray's words.

"OK, do as I say, slowly and quietly, without thinking of anything..." In a manner similar to hypnosis, Delin took Lynnray out of the meditative state. Meanwhile, Delin stopped controlling those earth elements, which returned to normal density quickly.

After meditation, Lynnray was greatly refreshed and felt differently from before. And even in sober state, he could feel the fluctuation of earth elements around, although it was not as clear as in meditative state.

"Grandpa Delin, even now I can still feel, although dimly, the fluctuation of light dots." Lynnray said excitedly.

He was thrilled to step into the world of magic.

"What are you saying? You can feel it now?" Delin was very surprised, because the density of elements had returned to normal, and Lynnray was not in a meditative state. In such a case, Lynnray's affinity with elements was...

"Grandpa Delin, why don't you speak? How's my affinity with elements?" Lynnray asked with worries.

He did not know how his performance was rated.

"Good, very good. You have high affinity with elements." Delin said with a smile, "As far as I know, maybe we can't even find one in a thousand to compare with you, really."

Lynnray felt the thumping of heart, and became wordless with excitement.

"Of course, affinity with elements is one hand, but the spiritual force is the most important. Magic force can improve with time, but spiritual force is the real limitation for a magician." Delin said seriously.

Lynnray took a deep breath and nodded.

"Now we test the second item -- your level of spiritual force." Delin looked at Lynnray with a serious expression.

Lynnray knew the importance of spiritual force.

"What should I do now?" Prepared for the test, Lynnray looked at Delin.

"Nothin." Delin laughed.

"Uh..." Lynnray was surprised.

"I'm a soul dwelling in the Ring of Coiling Dragon, of which you are the owner, so I can feel how much spiritual force you have. There is no need to test. I can tell you directly." Delin looked at Lynnray with a smile.

"How's my spiritual force?" Lynnray held his breath.

His spiritual force will determine his path of life.

"Your spiritual force is 10 times of your peers at the same age." Delin smiled.

Lynnray was glad to hear about the figure.

It was not a small difference.

But Delin continued: "Generally we have only one magician among 10,000 people, because we have high requirement on spiritual force. The bottom line is 5 times of peers at the same age. 10 times of peers is at the medium level in the circle of magicians."

Lynnray's heart suddenly cooled down.

"If you are taught by an ordinary magician, you can reach level-5 or level-6 at most. But I can help you attain a higher level." Delin raised his brows with confidence.

Lynnray was suddenly reminded that Delin was a holy magic master.

"As long as you are wiling to put in effort, I'm confident that you can reach level-8. But it depends on your power of understanding and opportunities if you want to attain level-9 or holy domain." Then Delin said in a harsh way, "You can blame no one for not even reaching level-6, if you don't make effort."

A teacher is one side of the coin, but the other side is oneself.

"Grandpa Delin, I will not disappoint you, and I will not disappoint my father and Baruch family." Lynnray recalled the memorial tablets in ancestral temple as well as the heroic stories inscribed on their back.

The restoration of the honor of Baruch family.

Lynnray felt the surge of emotions to move on.

"Good, I will formally teach you from tomorrow." Delin looked at Lynnray with expectation, and he regained the self-confidence as a holy magic master.

……

Since the next day, Lynnray started his life of rigorous practice.

Since Lynnray couldn't tell his father about Delin, he continued his warrior training in the morning and evening, and studied politics, religion, etiquette, art of war, geography and art with his father before noon.

Only the afternoon was his free time. He would go to Wushan Mountain northeast of the town and practice secretly in a quiet place. Under the guidance of Delin, he learned the knowledge of magic and practiced meditation to refine his magic force.

And he spent a lot of time doing meditation after dinner every day.

Lynnray only slept 6 hours ever day, and in the remaining time, he was busy in warrior training, knowledge study, magic training and meditation. Six hours could not be enough for him because he would use a lot of energy in meditation to cultivate spiritual force. He was more fatigued than a normal person. Therefore, he slept very deeply in his only 6 hours.

He lived in full these days.With the passing of time, Lynnray made significant progress, which could even be called transformation.

During his diligent practice, he experienced the pleasure of first successful absorption of elements and refinement into magic force, the first near-fainting incident due to over consumption of spiritual force in meditation, and the first use of earth magic in which he conjured up a 'ground thorn' of 20 centimeters from ground.

......

He made effort over and over.

Lynnray's perseverance and rapid progress astonished Delin, the holy magic master of Pron Empire 5,000 years ago.

Due to continuous warrior training, Lynnray's body was gradually strengthened, and the benefit of absorption of earth elements and frequent meditation appeared in his temperament. He looked calmer and stabler, which was a pleasant surprise for his father Hogg and Hilman.

With the rotation of seasons, it was autumn now, only one month from the recruitment test of magic school.

In the ancestral temple, back yard of Baruch mansion.

"Cleaning finished. It's time to practice magic. I used 'earthshaking' yesterday. It's so good." Lynnray exited the temple and closed its door in a good mood.

On the moss-covered stone pavement, Lynnray walked lightly without any sound.It was a capability of all earth magicians. They could walk quietly because earth was the source of their power.

"Eh?" Lynnray frowned.

He pricked up his ears and looked toward an old house: "Sound?" He walked to the direction quietly. His steps were very light with little sound normally, and now he purposely made light steps without producing even a slight sound.

He gradually drew near.

When he looked inside at the gate of yard, he opened widely his eyes out of amazement. "What's that?"

A black mouse of 20 centimeters was biting on a broken stone. With one flashing movement, the mouse moved swiftly to a green stone a dozen meters away and bit it several times. The mouse had soft skin, flexible eyes and a furry tail and was lovely.

And it even stood straight on two hind legs and jumped for fun.

"A lovely mouse with amazing speed." Lynnray was a bit shocked, hiding at the yard gate.

Mice were generally not that big, and appeared loathsome in the most cases, but this mouse was lovely with bright eyes seemingly able to talk. Most importantly... it was fast.

"Even uncle Hilman at level-6 cannot catch up with it. Why is it so fast?" Lynnray was amazed at the lovely creature which jumped a dozen meters in one instant.Delin flew out of the Ring of Coiling Dragon, stood beside Lynnray and observed this black mouse in amazement: "It's a monster -- 'shadow mouse'. Judging from size, it should be a juvenile."

"Shadow mouse, a monster? And a juvenile?" Lynnray looked at Delin in surprise.

Besides the bloody bull, griffin, raptor and black dragon, Lynnray now saw another monster. How can such a lovely mouse be a monster capable of using magic?

Episode 2 - Growth

Chapter 1 - Shadow Mouse the Monster

"Shadow mouse? Grandpa Delin, what's special about this shadow mouse? And what level is it at?" Lynnray communicated with Delin with heart, and looked at him with expectation.

Delin gave a faint smile, made a cough and said slowly: "I cannot tell what level shadow mouse is at, because they are a species. Murine monsters consisted of two types -- the stone-biting mouse and shadow mouse. Both of them are omnivorous. They eat stones, bones and even meat."

Lynnray nodded, because he saw the shadow mouse eating stone just now.

"Monsters are graded into 9 levels. Level-1 is the weakest, but above level-9 there is holy level." Delin looked at Lynnray with a smile, "The weakest stone-biting mouse is gray in color. Level-1 to level-3 are all gray, only varying slightly in color. Stone-biting mouse at level-4 is silver, and at level-7, they are golden. A golden-color stone-biting mouse is at level-7 at least, and may be level-8."

"Lynnray, stone-biting mouse is a horrible species because of their great number and sharp teeth. Their teeth are sharper than those of shadow mouse. If they come in countless numbers, even hundreds of thousands of soldiers cannot resist them." Delin said with a sigh.

He recalled a disaster in his years.

Stone-biting mouse was not as fast as shadow mouse, but it was as hard as steel. Harder skin and sharper teeth came along with a higher level. Although they were small, they were quite scary if they came in large numbers.

"Military weapons cannot kill stone-biting mice, but stone-biting mice can bite away the warriors easily." Delin gave another sigh.

Lynnray shivered a bit when he thought of the scene in which numerous stone-biting mice came all over the mountains, devoured the military, and bit away many and many warriors.

It was horrible.

"Stone-biting mouse has good defense and sharp teeth and is great in numbers. Shadow mouse also has a large quantity, but far less than stone-biting mouse." Delin seemed to know everything, as if he was a living encyclopedia.

"Then how about the power of shadow mouse?" Lynnray asked eagerly.

There was a black shadow mouse at the distance, so Lynnray wanted to know about its power.

"The lowest level of stone-biting mouse is level-1, but shadow mouse starts from level-3 when its hair is black. It turns cyan at level-5, and purple at level-7 or level-8." Delin made it very clear.

Lynnry nodded to himself.

Shadow mouse is not weaker than stone-biting mouse in power.

"Grandpa Delin, as you said, a shadow mouse at level-3 and 4 should be black in hair, and turn cyan at level-5. So this small one is level-3 or 4, right?" Lynnray inquired, looking at Delin.

"This black mouse is out of the ordinary."

Delin said with knitted brows, "Stone-biting mouse is well known for its strong defense and sharp teeth, but shadow mouse is well known for its high speed and sharp teeth. Speed is a good criterion for judging a shadow mouse's power."

"It moved so fast at a dozen meters in one blink. That's normal since it is a shadow mouse." Lynnray still remembered the swift movement of the mouse.

Delin nodded: "A shadow mouse is fast, naturally, but one at juvenile stage has reached the speed of an adult. That's not normal." Delin smiled.

"Out of the ordinary?" Lynnray looked at Delin.

Delin continued: "Yes, it has reached the speed of an adult at level-4, even at the juvenile stage. When it matures, it may reach level-7 the purple. I doubt its a child of a purple shadow mouse."

"A child of a purple?" Lynnray was perplexed, "But it has black hair."

Delin laughed: "The baby mice of purple or cyan are all black. With increase of power, their color will change. Hair color is a symbol of power."

Lynnray now understood: "I see."

"Grandpa Delin, as you said, the speed of this one is amazing. I think it is slightly faster than uncle Hilman, but it is only comparable with an adult mouse at level-4. An adult mouse at level-4 can be as fast as a level-6 warrior..." Lynnray sighed in amazement.

Delin smiled: "That's natural for a shadow mouse."

At the same level, a shadow mouse can leave far behind a human warrior, if they run together.

"Shadow mouse is a rare monster, and a purple one starting from level-7 is the target of treasure hunt for many magicians. But a purple mouse moves too fast. Adults are precious, but hard to subdue. A juvenile, which can become a purple one is easy to subdue, but you can hardly come across one of them." Delin looked at Lynnray with a smile.

Lynnray could understand Delin's point.

A purple mouse was at least level-7; in other words, a purple mouse was on the same level as a 'raptor'.

"Lynnray, a purple shadow mouse is the king in the shadow mouse species, and it can give order to large amount of shadow mice. Shadow mice are not as many as stone-biting mice, but they still have great numbers. The juvenile of a purple shadow mouse is protected by many shadow mice in the younger stage."

Delin glanced at the black shadow mouse, which was biting and eating a stone in the distance.

"It is strong at the juvenile stage, and is most probably the child of a purple shadow mouse. I don't know why it appeared in your mansion and has no protection by any other adult mouse." Delin said with emotion.

Lynnray agreed with Delin.

"Lynnray." Delin looked at him in a strange way, and said with a tempting voice, "We don't care why this shadow mouse is here, but do you want to subdue this one? It grows fast and will mature within 10 years. By then, you will own a monster at level-7 or 8."

Lynnray was certainly fascinated by the idea.

Level-7 and level-8 monsters were hard to subdue, but one could do it when they were young.

It was also important to distinguish them based on speed of growth. For example, some dragon species took a thousand years to reach adulthood, and a human could not wait that longer. But shadow mice grew much faster, though it was very difficult to come across a young one.

Powerful monsters would protect their children nicely. It was unknown why the young shadow mouse appeared in the Baruch mansion, but it was in front of Lynnray. That was the fact.

"Lynnray, if you own a purple shadow mouse, you own an army of them." Delin looked at Lynnray with a smile, "And this is a purple shadow mouse, which was more precious than other level-7 and level-8 monsters."

Delin pushed forward his temptation.

And Lynnray, at only 8 and a half in age, could not resist.

"How do I subdue this one." Lynnray looked at Delin in excitement.

Delin said gladly: "I can be rest assured if you subdue this shadow mouse." Delin was well aware that as a spirit, he had no magic force. And a magic master with no magic force could not attack anyone.

So he could not protect Lynnray.

During half a year's instruction, he regarded this simple and persevering child as his own grandson, so he wanted him to stand on his own.

"Be calm, Lynnray." Delin said seriously, "Even the child of a purple shadow mouse is as fast as an adult mouse at level-4, and cannot be overtaken by your uncle Hilman. You have no power to subdue it by force, and you cannot lay out a 'soul contract' magic circle."

Delin's words took Lynnray by surprise.

He cooled down and smiled bitterly: "Now I recalled the process. We have to make the monster willingly submissive, and lay out a soul contract magic circle, of which only a level-7 magician is capable."

Lynnray was a bit disappointed.

Since he was weak, he could not subdue a rare juvenile purple mouse despite his good luck.

Chapter 2 - Method for Dummies (I)

"Don't be discouraged. I just said you couldn't subdue it by force, but you could still subdue it." Delin smiled confidently: "If it were an adult mouse, I had no means to subdue it, but it is only a child. As a holy magic master, I have ways to deal with the child of a purple mouse, and you don't need to lay out a soul contract magic circle."

Lynnray regained his hope and looked at Delin with expectation.

"Grandpa Delin, tell me quick, what is your method?" Lynnray communicated with Delin excitedly in the heart.

Delin smiled confidently: "Very simple. The soul contract of magic circle is a master-servant contract in which the magician owns the monster. We cannot lay out such a contract, but we can enter into an equal contract with the shadow mouse."

"Equal contract?" Lynnray was perplexed, "What is it? I haven't heard of it before."

"It's natural you haven't heard of it. Even in my age 5,000 to 6,000 years ago, very few people knew about equal contract." Delin said with a smile, "In an equal contract, you and the monster are on an equal position. It seems less than a master-servant contract, but you can have intimate contact with the monster. When the monster helps you willingly, you and it can cooperate better."

Lynnray suddenly got the point.

"Oh, so an equal contract has a lot of advantages, but why are people not using it?" Lynnray raised his question.

Delin said with laughter: "Because an equal contract is not laid out by humans, but prepared by the monster itself."

"Prepared by the monster?" Lynnray was a bit surprised.

A soul contract magic circle was not required, because the monster could prepare a contract by itself. Delin continued: "Every monster is capable of preparing an equal contract since birth, but they can prepare an equal contract only once in a lifetime. It is unlike the master-servant contract which can be canceled, and in this case, the monster can enter into a master-servant contract with another human."

Lynnray nodded.

"But it is difficult to make a monster prepare an equal contract." Delin said seriously, "You have to make it feel you are its relative, and it doesn't want to leave you. In this way, it can enter into an equal contract with you willingly."

Lynnray nodded lightly.

"An adult monster has higher intelligence, and it is almost impossible to touch its heart and make it feel you are its relative." Delin gave a sigh and continued: "But a juvenile is different. It is easy to coax, just as human babies. Give it some tasty food, and it will like you, not to mention its intelligence, which is lower than human babies. Feed it frequently, make it like you, and play with it. After a short time it will like you. Especially, lonely juveniles separate from their peers are easier to subdue."

Lynnray now understood the method clearly upon hearing Delin's words.

"It's like coaxing babies." Lynnray smiled.

He was good at it because he had been playing with his younger brother much earlier.

"Don't be overly self-confident. There are many precautions in coaxing a monster baby. If you are careless, you may be bitten." Delin reminded Lynnray.

"Will it bite me?"

Lynnray looked at the black shadow mouse far ahead and shivered at its sound of biting a stone -- 'crunch, crunch' -- as easy as eating bread. Lynnray had no doubt about the sharpness of its teeth.

"Then what should I do?" Lynnray was uncertain about his ability.

"Don't worry. Do as I say and it will not be a problem. My method is for the dummies, but it requires patience. Do not hurry." Then Delin explained his 'method for the dummies', "Lynnray, shadow mouse is an omnivorous monster. It eats stones, bones and meat, but it likes meat most, especially roasted meat. This is the experience of predecessors."

"Kill a small-sized animal in Wushan Mountain first, roast it and place it on the ground at a distance. Remember, do not get close to the shadow mouse. Feed it and wait until it gets close to you." Delin smiled, "If you get close to it, it may be frightened and attack you. But you will be safe if it gets close to you first."

"Stupid method, but it's the safest." Delin smiled.

Lynnray got his meaning.

The method was simple and straightforward.

"Will the shadow mouse run away?" Lynnray was worried if he brought the roast meat but the shadow mouse ran away.

"It depends on your luck. But I think it will not run away in a short time." Delin said.

"OK, I will kill an animal first." Lynnray nodded and ran out. His footsteps touched the ground solidly, but with no sound. That was typical of earth magicians.

After exiting the old house cluster in the back, Lynnray returned to normal footsteps with sounds.

"Young master, are you going to Wushan Mountain?" Hilly, who was sweeping the floor saw Lynnray running, so he asked with a smile.

"Um." Lynnray replied and ran out quickly.

For half a year, Lynnray had been practicing magic in Wushan Mountain every afternoon. Others didn't know he was practicing magic, and figured he was only playing.

In the autumn, most trees on Wushan Mountain withered, but there were still many evergreen trees and also maple trees as red as fire.A swift figure passed quickly in the woods with quiet footsteps. After half a year's absorption of earth elements, Lynnray cultivated magic force in earth series and improved his physical fitness.

Now Lynnray was as strong as juveniles at 15 or 16 years old in Wushan Town, and had the power of level-1 warriors.

On Wushan Mountain, there were many squirrels and rabbits, but few fierce beasts. That was why parents allowed their children to play in the mountains. Wushan Mountain was only an ordinary mountain with few large beasts, not to mention monsters.

Lynnray stopped running upon seeing a light-yellow rabbit eating grass.

Even an alert rabbit could not notice Lynnray's approach.

"Rabbits move fast and react quickly. Let me use magic." Lynnray started chanting magic mantras.

He felt the movement of magic force in the center of his chest. Vital force of warriors was stored 10 centimeters below the navel, while magic force of magicians was stored in the center of chest, or precisely, the center of breast line. And spiritual force (soul power) was stored in the brain.

It made no difference chanting quietly, softly or loudly, but his spiritual force had to attain certain state along with the magic mantra.

In a few seconds, Lynnray, who was murmuring his mantra, now stared at the rabbit in a cold look.

Level-1 earth magic -- 'ground thorn'!

"Pu!"

A sharp thorn protruded from below the rabbit and penetrated its stomach. Blood came out and stained its soft fur at the belly. The rabbit struggled intensely under the sudden attack, but the more it struggled, the quicker it was drained of blood.

Chapter 3 - Method for Dummies (II)

Lynnray rushed to the spot and seized the rabbit's throat with one hand. With one 'snap', the painfully struggling rabbit twitched a moment and died. Since he watched the two battles half a year before, he felt a bloodthirsty feeling arose in his heart due to his blood of Dragonblood warriors.

"Now I'm a level-1 warrior and level-1 magician. I think magic is stronger than martial art in attack power." Lynnray smiled and sighed while holding the rabbit.

Magicians had nine levels. Reaching level-1 was relatively easier, but with increase of level, it took more time to move further up. And many powerful level-7 and level-8 magicians might spend a hundred years without crossing one level.

Those talented might take half a year to reach level-1. Even if an untalented person, as long as he met the conditions for becoming a magician, he could reach level-1 in three years.

Lynnray grabbed the rabbit and ran downhill.

"Lynnray, why don't you roast it? The shadow mouse like meat, but roast meat the most." Delin's voice occurred in Lynnray's mind.

"Grandpa Delin, you may not have coaxed a child before." Lynnray joked while running. Delin paused for a moment. He didn't have a grandson, and as a holy magic master, he would not coax a child.

"True, I have not." Delin admitted.

Lynnray said with self-confidence: "I coax little Warton often. I can tell you, we can't give very good things to a child, otherwise he will want better. Now the shadow mouse is biting a stone, it must be glad if I can give it raw meat. Let it eat raw meat 7 to 8 days, and then i can provide roast meat."

Delin got his point.

As a old man, Delin certainly understood the tactic. If you are a leader, you have to give your men some benefit first, and better rewards later on. If you give them too much, you cannot satisfy their desire.

"I know the reason in my books. It's about keeping monkeys. It's better to make them earn what they deserve." Lynnray giggled.

Delin suddenly felt Lynnray was smarter than some juveniles, though he was only 8 years old.

"It seems Baruch family's education did have an effect." Delin praised in his heart. Education paved the way of wisdom, but most civilians had no chance of accepting education. Even some good magic schools and warrior schools had enrollment conditions and tuition hard to accept for common civilians.

......

The residents of town did not feel strange at Lynnray going home grasping a rabbit. In fact, since Lynnray knew how to use 'ground thorn', he often brought some rabbits home.

"Young master Lynnray is great. He is grabbing a rabbit again." The residents chatted with smiles.

And Lynnray was also smiling politely on the street.

"I don't know if the shadow mouse will eat food given by humans."

With a deep breath, Lynnray went into the old house cluster in the back of the mansion, and drew near to the shadow mouse without making a sound. After a short while, he was on the spot he had been before he left.

"Where is the shadow mouse?" Lynnray looked in the yard but only saw some gravel and rotten leaves.

There were traces of bitten stones, but no sight of the shadow mouse. Feeling disappointed, Lynnray asked: "Grandpa Delin, the shadow mouse is gone. It was only one hour, did it get away?"

A beam of light flew out from the Ring of Coiling Dragon and turned into Delin, who was wearing a moon-white robe.

Delin also frowned: "It's just one hour. Has it left?"

Suddenly, a weak crunching sound was heard again. Lynnray was gladdened and walked to a decaying old house. At the threshold, he clearly saw the black shadow mouse biting a stone. It was like a sculptor carving the stone into various strange shapes.

Lynnray was standing at the shreshold.

"Pum!" He purposely made a sound by kicking on the threshold.

"Su!"

The shadow mouse instantly dodged to a dozen meters away. With rolling eyes staring in the threshold's direction, it saw Lynnray and stared at him in alert.

"Come, here's some food."

Lynnray smiled at the shadow mouse and threw the rabbit to the threshold. The shadow mouse might not understand human language, but Lynnray knew... some intelligent monsters should understand the meaning of a smile.

After all, monsters were not beasts. Their intelligence was only a little lower than humans, and some powerful monsters were quite cunning.

"Don't hurry, don't hurry." Lynnray said to himself and left unwillingly.

After Lynnray left, the shadow mouse saw the rabbit, and unable to resist the delicacy, it swooshed to the spot and looked far ahead. Lynnray was far at this time. The monster stood straight and jumped out of excitement.

"Chi..." The shadow mouse was making a happy sound.

Then it started biting the rabbit quickly with its sharp teeth. Despite its small size, it ate up the rabbit which was larger than itself, including the bones, and only left the fur out.

"Coo..." The little shadow mouse moved its throat, and patted on its belly excitedly in a humanized way.

Obviously, bloody meat was more delicious than stones.

After finishing the meal, the shadow mouse looked in the direction Lynnray left. The young monster definitely had a good impression of the boy. As only a child monster not long after birth, it was expecting that maybe the boy would give it another rabbit sometime.

Before dinner on the same day.

"I don't know if the shadow mouse will eat it." Lynnray was now walking in the house cluster to the yard where he threw the rabbit this afternoon.

"Don't worry, Lynnray. It's just a child monster. It likes food." Delin's smiling voice came into Lynnray's mind.

Lynnray nodded slightly, and walked to the threshold soon. He was glad to see the blood-stained rabbit fur and the absence of meat and bones.

"So good." Lynnray clenched his fist.

He made the first step, and then he just needed to continue.

On the morning of the next day, Lynnray killed a rabbit and a prairie chicken. He left the rabbit to grandpa Hilly for roasting at night, and placed the prairie chicken at the old location -- the threshold of the old house.

"The shadow mouse is looking at me." Lynnray saw the shadow mouse gazing upon himself.

"Lynnray, it seems things are going smoothly. It isn't running away, which means it's not hostile toward you." Delin was also glad for

Lynnray's success. It was his good luck to come across the child of a powerful monster.

"I don't know what the little mouse's parents are up to." Delin was also perplexed.

Lynnray threw the prairie chicken at the threshold, spoke something to the shadow mouse, smiled and went away. But this time he kept looking back. The shadow mouse went out and looked around. Not quite afraid of Lynnray at a distance, it started eating the prairie chicken.

……

On day 3, 4 and 5...

Time went on, and Lynnray practiced meditation and fed the shadow mouse with game every day. No one in Wushan Town, including Hogg and Hilman, did not know Lynnray was practicing magic. And they did not know he was taking care of a juvenile monster which was at level-4 in power.

Only Delin knew everything as he watched Lynnray grew up.

"This small Wushan Town cannot bind Lynnray." When Delin looked at Lynnray who was doing meditation to accumulate magic force, expectation emerged on his face, "One day, he will bring an adult purple shadow mouse and get on the broad stage of Yulan Continent."

Chapter 4 - Ernst Academy

With the passing of time, the little shadow mouse which had not felt much care let down its guard against Lynnray. On the eighth day, shortly after Lynnray put down the rabbit, the little shadow mouse rushed out and started eating, and it squeaked toward Lynnray.

On the tenth day!

"Hmm, it's the time to let it taste some roast meat." Lynnray wrapped up a roast prairie chicken with a small cloth bag, and pleasantly walked toward the old house cluster.

Delin was walking abreast of Lynnray, only nobody could see him. He smiled with raised white beard: "Nine days passed, and the shadow mouse now has no guard against you. You are bringing more delicious roast meat today. It will certainly get excited and more intimate with you."

Lynnray laughed upon hearing these words.

"Chi, Chi..." When he arrived at the threshold, the little shadow mouse swooshed to him, stood straight and kept squeaking toward him.

"It ran to me when I haven't taken food out. It is not afraid of me now." Lynnray was pleasantly surprised.

With a smile, Delin looked at the little shadow mouse, which could not feel his existence. Delin said: "Now the shadow mouse is intimate with you."

"Chi..." The shadow mouse stared at Lynnray with lovely eyes and squeaked eagerly, as if it was urging Lynnray to take out food.

"Don't hurry." Lynnray took out the roast prairie chicken from his cloth bag.

Upon smelling the flavor of roast chicken, the shadow mouse showed light in its lovely eyes and looked at Lynnray with expectation. Lynnray laughed out because when he brought delicious food to Warton, Warton also called: "I want it, brother" and looked at him in the same way.

Now the little shadow mouse had the same behavior as a child.

"Hehe, here you are." Lynnray threw the roast chicken to the shadow mouse.

The little shadow mouse squeaked happily, and after biting the roast chicken once, it quickened up enjoying the meal. After a short while, the roast chicken of the same size as the shadow mouse was eaten up.

"I don't know why you can swallow such a big one with your small belly." Lynnray laughed at the side.

The little shadow mouse seemed to be very happy with the meal. It stood straight, squeaked toward Lynnray and held his lower leg with two front legs. Lynnray was glad with such intimate behavior, which took place for the first time.

"Lynnray, try to comb its hair with hand. Monsters generally like their close human partner grooming them." Delin advised.

Lynnray tried to place his hand gently on the head of the shadow mouse, and the shadow mouse was not avoiding the touch; instead, it enjoyed the touch with closed eyes. Now with ease of heart, Lynnray combed the hair of the shadow mouse, which started snoring in comfort.

"This little animal is cute." Lynnray is now fonder of the little shadow mouse.

"Grandpa Delin, monsters are indeed strange. The raptor had a large size and rigid scales as a level-7, and this little shadow mouse will grow into a level-7, too. But why do they differ so much even at the same level?"

Lynnray stroked the shadow mouse and thought in amazement.

"We can't judge them based on appearances. Maybe an ordinary old man on the road can step on a dragon and destroy a mountain with one wave of hand." Delin said with a smile.

Lynnray understood the point.

But involuntarily, he would still judge by appearance.

The raptor's power was obviously shown in its large size and shiny scales.

"I don't know when this little mouse can enter into an equal contract with me." Lynnray murmured. Since the equal contract is laid out by the monster, Lynnray had no other means except waiting.

Delin smiled: "Things are going smoothly. Be patient."

"OK, I know." Lynnray also smiled.

……

Twenty days passed during which Lynnray fed the little shadow mouse every day. He became quite intimate with the shadow mouse, but there was still no sign of laying out an equal contract on the side of the shadow mouse.

Night covered the land and the entire Wushan Town was in tranquility.

Candlelight lit up the living room of Baruch mansion, and the three of Lynnray's family and steward Hilly were eating dinner together at the long table.

"Lynnray, I hear you often bring some roast rabbit to the old house cluster in the back." Hogg put down his knife and fork half way in the meal and said to Lynnray.

Lynnray shivered a bit in the heart.

"It seems I have to confess." Lynnray thought, and nodded to Hogg: "Dad, I found a lovely animal in the back yard, so I often bring some food to it."

"A lovely animal?" Little Warton brightened up his eyes.

"Oh."

Hogg nodded, "Few people go to the back yard. It's not surprising there are some animals. By the way, the magic recruitment test in capital Fenlai City will start in a week. You said you want to join."

"Ah, magic recruitment test?" Lynnray was suddenly reminded of the test.

An airflow only visible for Lynnray flew out from the Ring of Coiling Dragon and turned into the old man Delin with white hair and beard. Delin said to Lynnray with a smile: "Lynnray, magic recruitment test? You can go or not. My instruction will be better than those of magic teachers in school."

Lynnray agreed with Delin.

Delin was a holy magic master, and an ordinary magic school could not have a holy magic master as a teacher.

"What's up? You don't want to go?" Hogg withdrew his smile and put on a cold face with knitted brows.

Hogg remembered Lynnray wished to become a magician eagerly when he saw the battle between the level-8 dual-series magician and the mercenaries, but why was he hesitating now? And Hogg wished his son to become a magician, too.

"Dad, I..."

"No, Lynnray, please say yes." Delin frowned and explained himself.

Lynnray suddenly stopped talking, and inquired in the heart with confusion: "Grandpa Delin, aren't you teaching me? Do I still need to go to magic school with your guidance? Isn't it a waste of money?"

"No." Delin said seriously, "I have not been in contact with Yulan Continent for over 5,000 years. You know, many and many magicians were researching new magic during this period, and you don't know how many new types of magic emerged."

Lynnray suddenly got Delin's point.

"And you should also know that Wushan Town is not your stage of activity. You need a wider stage in the outside." Delin continued seriously.

"A wider stage..."

Lynnray was touched in the heart.

He involuntarily recalled the giant monster 'raptor', the horrible scene of 'dance of fire serpent', and how the holy magician Rudy easily controlled densely arranged large stones to fall from the sky.

"In future."

Lynnray felt the rapid beat of his heart. If he could stand on a huge dragon and be capable of massive destruction, he would feel so great at the peak of humanity. With such thought in mind, Lynnray felt the surge of blood in his body.

"Lynnray, what are you thinking about?" Hogg was a bit discontent, because Lynnray was distracted.

"Ah, no." Lynnray looked at Hogg and nodded, "Dad, I really want to become a magician. Please send me to capital Fenlai City to attend the magic recruitment test."

After hearing Lynnray's words, Hogg smiled brilliantly.

"Magician? Does it mean the one who can spit fire?" Little Warton clapped his hand happily.

"Warton, that's a variety show. Don't mistake it as magic." Hogg said seriously.

"Oh." Warton plumped up his mouth and did not speak.

Lynnray smiled and said to Hogg: "There should be many magic schools. Which ones are better? By the way, are magic schools combined with warrior schools?"

Hogg laughed: "The four empires and two alliances had their top schools each. You should know O'Brien Empire is the strongest in military strength."

Lynnray nodded. He knew it as common knowledge.

"And the top school O'Brien Academy of O'Brien Empire is the No.1 warrior school on Yulan Continent. As to magician school..." Hogg smiled, "The No.1 magic school of Yulan Continent is in our Holy Alliance, and named after the legendary pope Ernst of Church of Light -- 'Ernst Academy'."

Chapter 5 - Shadow Mouse 'Beibei' (I)

"Ernst Academy is the No.1 magic school of the continent. Magicians graduating from the school are at least level-6 and many are level-7. As long as we have a level-7 magician, we can get our family heirloom back."

Hogg said while looking at Lynnray in expectation.

And Lynnray could feel his father's expectation.

"We need to erase the shame of having an heirloom taken by others, as a family of the Dragonblood." Lynnray could feel the heavy burden on his shoulder.

As descendants of an ancient and great Dragonblood family, both Hogg and his predecessors over hundreds of years were proud for their identity, but they were also very ashamed for their loss of family heirloom to the outside.

Regretfully, a family which could collect saber 'Slaughter' must not be an ordinary one; whereas Baruch family today was too weak.

"Ernst? The legendary pope of Church of Light?" Delin was surprised.

"Why? Grandpa Delin?" Lynnray asked in confusion, "Hundreds of millions of residents in 6 kingdoms and 15 principalities of the Holy Alliance know about the legendary pope Ernst of Church of Light." Lynnray also knew the story of pope Ernst. Ernst improved the position of Church of Light and founded the Holy Alliance.

"I didn't imagine Ernst made such a great achievement and became a legendary pope of Church of Light." Ernst sighed with emotion.

"Grandpa Delin, do you know Pope Ernst?" Lynnray was a bit surprised.

But with a second thought, he believed it was natural. In the age of a unified Pron Empire, the Church of Light, Church of Darkness, Temple of the Land, and many other churches and temples were under the control of Pron Empire.

"Of course, Ernst was a genius. He attained the holy domain at about 50, but in my times, he was only a rising star in the new generation." Delin said lightly.

When Delin was physically alive, Ernst was in a stage of growth, and when Ernst attained the holy domain, Delin was already on the top of Yulan Continent, and the topmost even among holy fighters.

Delin had a very high position in Pron Empire far above Ernst.

Ernst would offer his salute in front of Delin.

"I didn't expect Ernst made such a great achievement after my passing." Delin smiled lightly.

Lynnray was full of admiration for Delin at this moment. As a top holy fighter in the times of Pron Empire, a top personality on Yulan Continent, Delin was now teaching Lynnray carefully. It was indeed Lynnray's good luck.

The Baruch family was in a good mood at dinner.

"Lynnray, you will go with Hilman to the capital Fenlai City in a week to take part in the magic recruitment test." Hogg smiled to Lynnray.

"Yes, dad." Lynnray nodded.

"Young master, I believe you will enter the best magic school." Steward Hilly smiled.

"The best, oh, the best." Little Warton clapped his oily hands with a smile.

Hogg smiled lightly and said: "It's not easy to become a magician. Maybe only one in 10,000 has such potential. And Ernst Academy has high requirements for enrollment, and students in this academy are all very talented. I will be satisfied if you can become a magician, whichever school you enter."

"Dad, I will not make you disappointed." Lynnray said confidently.

Because he was already at level-1 in magic.

......

One week passed quickly.

Lynnray lay on the grassland in the back yard. The little shadow mouse was jumping around him and squeaking, but Lynnray did not gave it attention.

The little shadow mouse rolled its eyes, stood straight and placed its front legs on Lynnray.

"Chi." The shadow mouse made a discontent squeak.

Lynnray touched its head: "I can't play with you. I will depart for the capital tomorrow, and go to the magic school at recruitment. Maybe I don't have much chance to stay with you."

He couldn't bring the little shadow mouse to magic school.

There was no mediocre student in the magic school. Many students were powerful magicians who might subdue the shadow mouse if it was discovered. There were level-7 and level-8 magicians who could take the shadow mouse easily.

Anyway, he was not in a contract with the shadow mouse to prevent conquering by others.

"Wu..." The shadow mouse grunted upon hearing Lynnray's words.

"You can't understand what I say." Lynnray shook his head.

"It will take a few years studying in magic school. Will we meet again after a few years?" Lynnray touched the shadow mouse's smooth hair in cherishing mood. During the one month's play, Lynnray developed some affection for the shadow mouse.

Under the touch of Lynnray, the shadow mouse squinted and grunted.

In the front yard of Baruch mansion, after lunch of the next day.

Hogg stood straight like a pillar and looked at Lynnray in the eyes: "Lynnray, Wushan Town is close to the capital at only a 90 li distance. You should arrive there before dark. Remember, do not cause trouble in the capital, because many noble persons are living there."

"Yes, dad." Lynnray said respectfully.

"Hilman, you'll take care of Lynnray." Hogg looked at Hilman, who was standing on one side.

Hilman smiled and said: "You are rest assured, Mr. Hogg."

"OK, you can set off now." Hogg laughed.

"Bye, dad." Lynnray said with respect, and then smiled to Warton: "Warton, I'll go now."

Little Warton looked at Lynnray with blinking eyes and said with affection: "Bye, brother."

Lynnray looked in the direction of back yard and thought to himself: "Nobody is feeding the shadow mouse these two days." Hilman said to Lynnray, "Don't be absent-minded. Let's go."

"Yes, uncle Hilman."

Lynnray followed Hilman and left the mansion of Baruch family.

"Chi..." On the roof of the living room, the shadow mouse was looking at Lynnray and Hilman as they left. The little monster was full of confusion, because normally Lynnray went out to catch rabbits, but today he got away with his bag and another person.

The shadow mouse liked Lynnray very much.

No relations appeared in this mouth, so the shadow mouse regarded Lynnray as its relative.

"Su!"

The little shadow mouse disappeared from the roof and swiftly moved to anther, staring at Lynnray and Hilman. In this way, it followed Lynnray out of Wushan Town.

Chapter 6 - Shadow Mouse 'Beibei' (II)

The shadow mouse had seen Lynnray heading to Wushan Mountain to catch rabbits. But this time, Lynnray was heading in another direction. So the shadow mouse became anxious.

"Chi, Chi..."

The shadow mouse rushed to Lynnray.

Lynnray was about to take a step when his foot was held. He lowered his head and saw the little shadow mouse, which stood straight, held Lynnray's foot with its front legs, and looked at Lynnray with pitiful eyes, as if it was about to weep.

"Eh, little shadow mouse, why are you coming?" Lynnray was a bit surprised.

Hilman turned his head and saw the shadow mouse in surprise: "A monster, a stone-biting mouse?" Hilman was not quite clear about the categories of monsters, but once an army was consumed by stone-biting mice, so soldiers were generally frightened by monsters in the shape of a mouse.

"Lynnray, be careful." Hilman kicked at the shadow mouse. His foot reached the shadow mouse in the blink of an eye.

But the shadow mouse was even faster. It swooshed to Lynnray's shoulder rapidly.

"Uncle Hilman, don't do that." Lynnray saw Hilman's move.

Hilman was a bit surprised.

"Uncle Hilman, this is the animal I'm feeding in the back yard." Lynnray said, "Little shadow mouse, that's it, right?"

The shadow mouse seemed to understand Lynnray's words and nodded with its small head.

Hilman looked at Lynnray in surprise: "Lynnray, you are keeping a monster?"

"Uncle Hilman, wait a moment, let me ask the shadow mouse to go back." Lynnray held the shadow mouse with his hands and said to it: "Little shadow mouse, I'll go on a trip with uncle Hilman to the capital. You can't go to the capital, do you know?"

The little shadow mouse looked at Lynnray in a pitiful way, as if weeping.

Lynnray placed the shadow mouse on the ground and waved his hand: "Go back." Then he pointed at his own road, "I'm going this way to the capital."

Lynnray went on while waving his hand.

"Chi, Chi..." The shadow mouse stood at the spot and looked at Lynnray.

"Uncle Hilman, let's go. The little shadow mouse is smart enough to understand my words." Lynnray said to Hilman. The latter looked at the exchange in surprise, but he smiled and went on with Lynnray.

The shadow mouse stood still and looked at Lynnray and Hilman as they walked away.

"Chi, Chi..."

The shadow mouse squeaked suddenly, and swooshed 20 to 30 meters in a black flash. It had scary speed and elusive movement. Lynnray and Hilman were walking and chatting when Hilman suddenly felt something rushing to them, so he turned back.

"Su..."

Faster than Hilman's defense, the shadow rushed to Lynnray's foot and bit on his lower leg.

"Ah!" With a sharp pain, Lynnray made a jump.

He saw the shadow mouse looking at him with watery eyes. He touched his lower leg and found blood oozing out. Despite his discontent, he felt hard to get angry when he saw the shadow mouse's look.

"Lynnray, are you OK?" Hilman said at one side.

"Nothing." Lynnray smiled.

Suddenly, a dense, black ray of light enveloped the shadow mouse, and drops of blood came out from the shadow mouse's mouth corner. The blood drops contained blood of the shadow mouth and his own. Strangely, two black triangles in opposite directions rose from the blood drops, and rays of black light merged with the triangles, forming a weird magic circle which was sending out a dense air of darkness.

Both Hilman and Lynnray looked at the scene in shock.

"Is this..." Lynnray guessed out something.

Delin flew out from the Ring of Coiling Dragon at this moment. He said gladly with raised white beard, "Lynnray, this little creature is laying out an equal contract."

"An equal contract?" Lynnray was a bit surprised though it was in his uncertain guessing.

The strange black circle of magic split into two -- one flew into Lynnray and the other into the shadow mouse. Hilman was a bit frightened at the moment.

"Lynnray, are you OK?" Hilman was a bit worried.

"Nothing. I'm fine." Lynnray could feel a weak soul connection with the shadow mouse.

On the quiet road of Wushan Town, Lynnray and the shadow mouse looked at each other and communicated for the first time.

"Little shadow mouse, what's your name?" Lynnray asked in the heart.

The black shadow mouse was a bit excited: "Bei, bei..."

Lynnray looked at it in confusion.

"What is it saying?" Lynnray did not understand.

Delin, with white beard and hair, now appeared beside him and said mentally: "Lynnray, this little shadow mouse is still a juvenile. It can't utter syllables accurately. It may only communicate simple ideas in mental communication." With a soul connection, Lynnray could also feel the shadow mouse's excitement, but it couldn't even utter a syllable.

"Hmm. You said Bei and what, so let me call you 'Beibei', all right?" Lynnray looked at the shadow mouse with a smile.

The shadow mouse made a pondering appearance, and then nodded happily.

"Beibei." Lynnray grinned.

"Chi Chi..." The shadow mouse jumped and responded.

"Beibei!"

"Chi Chi..."

"Beibei!"

"Chi Chi..."

......

So an eight-year-old child was talking with a little shadow mouse.

"Lynnray, what's the matter?" Hilman came to his senses and stared at Lynnray in surprise, "What was the black magic circle? What happened? Are you alright?"

Hilman heard about curse magic, one of black magics.

Was Lynnray under a curse?

With only vague impression about magic, Hilman was a bit worried.

"Haha, nothing serious. Beibei became my monster." Lynnray said gladly, "Come, Beibei, get to my shoulder." The shadow mouse squeaked happily and jumped onto Lynnray's shoulder.

"You subdued it?" Hilman was surprised.

As a person with rich experience, Hilman knew how difficult it was to subdue a monster, but Lynnray made it.

Hilman was also perplexed: "You don't have a soul contract scroll, how did you make it?"

"Fine, uncle Hilman." Lynnray giggled and said, "Let's hurry up on our journey. We still have a long way to go." Lynnray pulled Hilman's hand and continued on their journey to the capital.

The shadow mouse Beibei was happily squeaking on Lynnray's shoulder.

In this way, Lynnray, Hilman and the shadow mouse gradually vanished on the road.

Chapter 7 - Fenlai City

On the west of Monster Mountains of Yulan Continent were the Holy Alliance and Dark Alliance, and the Holy Alliance was headed by Fenlai Kingdom.

Fenlai City was the capital of Fenlai Kingdom.

It was also the holy capital of Holy Alliance, because the headquarter of Church of Light was in the western part of the city.

Fenlai City consisted of the eastern and western parts managed by Fenlai Kingdom and Church of Light, respectively. Because Fenlai City was both a royal capital and holy capital, its prosperity was unparalleled on Yulan Continent.

With a vast area, Fenlai City had millions of residents and was a super large city ranked among top five on Yulan Continent.

At sunset, Lynnray and Hilman entered Fenlai City.

"Wow."

While walking on the main street of eastern city 'Champs Avenue', Lynnray was dazzled in the eyes, and under his request, little shadow mouse Beibei hid in his clothes and only looked secretly from inside. "Chi, Chi, Chi", the little shadow mouse was shouting excitedly.

Fortunately the avenue was bustling and noisy, and no one noticed Beibei's squeaking.

"Quiet." Lynnray patted on the little shadow mouse, which stopped making noise, but it was still expressing its excitement in mental communication.

The entire Champs Avenue was paved with neat blue stone plates and could accommodate parallel passing of several carriages. On both sides of the street were hotels, clothes shops, weapon shops and bars. And there were tall and straight pine trees lined up on both sides of the avenue. Noble women and young ladies were wearing fashionable clothes, laughing and walking on the street.

When they saw Lynnray's manners, they sneered at him in a low voice and pointed at him occasionally. Lynnray was obvious as a villager, and the noble residents in capital felt some superiority over him.

"Hum, they have no courtesy." Lynnray frowned and was unhappy with the noble women's chatting about him.

With a good family education, Lynnray kept his discomfort in the heart and appeared peaceful.

"Lynnray, how's Fenlai City? It's the largest city in our Holy Alliance." Hilman was walking with Lynnray on one side of street. When he saw some warriors or a couple of magicians passing by, he sighed, "Powerful warriors and magicians are common in Fenlai City."

Lynnray smiled and nodded: "As recorded in the books, Fenlai City is the political, economic and art center of the Holy Alliance."

"It is the heaven of the wealthy and noble." Hilman nodded with a sigh.

Occasionally some luxury carriages passed on the bustling avenue. Hilman took a walk with Lynnray on the main avenue of Fenlai City -- Champs Avenue -- and found an ordinary hostel to stay.

They had dinner at a small restaurant beside the hostel.

In the hostel at night.

Lynnray and Hilman were staying in a two-bed room. Upon entering the room, the shadow mouse Beibei jumped out from Lynnray's clothes at the chest, and went around Lynnray while squeaking.

"I know you are hungry. Please eat." Lynnray threw the roast duck he brought from the restaurant on the ground, and Beibei started its feast.

"Lynnray, rest early. You will have the magic test tomorrow morning." Hilman reminded him.

"I know, uncle Hilman." But Lynnray withdrew the curtain at the window.

The hostel had three stories, and Lynnray and Hilman were staying at story-two. Three-story buildings were nowhere in Wushan Town, but very common in the capital Fenlai City. And there were also 7-story and 8-story buildings.

Lynnray looked at the outside through the window. People were still on the street at this time.

"Oops, I haven't seen a large city for a long time." A ray of dim light came out from Ring of Coiling Dragon and turned into an old man with white beard and hair. Delin and Lynnray were observing the street outside shoulder to shoulder.

"Grandpa Delin." Lynnray addressed him.

"How do you feel about arriving at a large city?" Delin asked with a smile.

"Nothing." Lynnray replied with curled mouth.

Delin gave a sigh: "You don't know about large cities. There are various luxury venues such as auctions in which some rich people will spend hundreds of thousands of or one million gold coins to purchase an object."

"One million gold coins?" Lynnray's throat dried up.

That was a huge amount of money. His family couldn't even bring out one hundred thousand gold coins.

"There are many rich people. They fight for money, power and beauties. People die every day. Sometimes you can see corpses in the sewer, and maybe they are nobles."

Delin smiled lightly, "But you need power to stand out in the world."

"Don't rely upon others' compassion. You have to depend on yourself." Delin looked at Lynnray.

The Dragonblood warrior's blood in Lynnray made him chivalrous and bloodthirsty. "If anyone threatens me or my relative, I will kill him." Lynnray said firmly. After reading about the rise and decline of families, Lynnray concluded that the mercy to enemy was cruelty to himself.

If you let the enemy go, he might kill your relatives.

"But I'm still weak." Lynnray recalled the look of contempt of the noble women when he just entered the city. In the eyes of upper class people, he was only a poor villager.

After a faint smile, he sat on bed cross-legged and started practicing meditation.

Spiritual force was trained and cultivated by using it in meditation to the bottom level, and then restoring it in sleep.

In the center Dantian at the chest.

Vague fog of earth-yellow color was floating. The fog represented earth magic force refined from earth elements. According to Delin, magic force of level-1 to level-6 magicians took the form of fog. With the magician's progress in levels, it will have better quality of magic force, and greater density of fog.

At level-7, magic force would condense into liquid.

A threshold had to be crossed from level-6 to level-7.

"Lynnray is so hardworking. He is practicing spiritual force at night." Hilman praised Lynnray in the heart when he saw Lynnray doing meditation. Spiritual force was very important for both magicians and warriors.

On Greenleaf Road of eastern city, the morning of the next day. Greenleaf Road was one of the several trunk roads in Fenlai City, with many luxury mansions and government buildings lined up on both sides. The highest building was the Church of Light.

The Holy Alliance included 6 kingdoms and 15 principalities and was controlled by Church of Light.

The Pope of Light had the highest position and the right to dismiss the king of any kingdom. Therefore, in the eastern part of Fenlai City, the highest building was the Church of Light.

In the morning, many people, mostly nobles in luxury clothing gathered at the gate of the Church of Light. Carriages filled the square in front of the church, and the nobles were greeting each other.

Lynnray and Hilman also arrived there.

"Uncle Hilman, many people are here today, and many nobles are bringing their children." Lynnray smiled to Hilman. The shadow mouse Beibei was hiding in Lynnray's clothes and looking to the outside secretly.

Hilman nodded with a smile: "Noble? Any magician graduating from the top magician school Ernst Academy can easily become an earl in a kingdom."

"Earl of a kingdom?" Lynnray understood the point.

Ranks of a kingdom were not as difficult to obtain as those of an empire. Every empire among the four could be compared to the entire Holy Alliance, and was much larger than Fenlai Kingdom.

"Oh, good to see you here, Mr. Doyle."

"Heber, I came here for my son. Hess, say hello to uncle Heber."

The nobles in front were chatting with each other. The magic recruitment test cost 10 gold coins. If the student was enrolled by a magic school, tuition would be even higher. Generally, one year's tuition of magic schools was hundreds of gold coins, which was beyond the capacity of ordinary families. But if their children were enrolled, nobles would fund them. But not all magic schools charge high tuition.

For example, the No.1 magic school 'Ernst Academy' only recruited very limited number of students. As far as the student belonged to the Holy Alliance, he would be exempt from tuition. After all, they only enrolled talented students with great potential.

"Hum, the civilians and villagers also came. They are daydreaming." Some nobles at a distance were sneering.

Among the hundreds of people gathering in the square, some were civilians or village nobles such as Lynnray. Village nobles were also held in contempt. Nobles in the capital were generally proud and looked at others with arrogance.

"Lynnray, just neglect them." Hilman said in a low voice.

Lynnray glanced at the nobles and smiled: "Uncle Hilman, I'll not drag myself down to their level." With Hogg's education over these years, Lynnray didn't care about the arrogant nobles in the capital.

People in the square were divided into two crowds -- the capital nobles engaged in grand talks, and the civilians and village nobles. Two warriors with armor were controlling at the church gate and blocking entrance of outsiders.

After a while, a priest in black robe walked slowly to the gate, and said with a clear voice: "Magic test now starts. Recruitment staff of magic schools are ready. Candidates, please follow me into the hall."

Chapter 8 - Magic Test (I)

Under the direction of the priest, people in the square came into the hall in order.

In the hall of church.

The ground was paved with shiny marble, and a large crystal color light was hanging on the ceiling. Hundreds of people were accommodated in the hall without packing.

In the front of the hall were a line of chairs which were seats of recruitment staff. And in the center was the location of test.

The priest in black robe smiled and said with a clear voice: "Test is carried out in the center. Candidates should come one by one, and other people are not allowed to enter the circle in the center. Please stand in line. Parents and relatives, please stand at the side."

"Lynnray, here is your test fee and identity proof. Go now. By the way, leave the shadow mouse to me. It can't follow you into the test." said Hilman.

"Beibei, stay with uncle Hilman. I'll go to the test." Lynnray communicated with the shadow mouse mentally. The shadow mouse moved a bit reluctantly at Lynnray's chest, but under repeated request of Lynnray, it jumped into Hilman's clothes. Lynnray took the 10 gold coins and stood in line. He saw elder children of 17 to 18 years old, and smaller ones at 6 to 7. The children stood in two lines, and the priests of church took the test fee.

The circle in the center was 10 meters in diameter. There were three adults in the circle, two carrying out test and one doing record. The tools for test included one crystal ball and one complex magic hexagram.

"Candidate No.1"

A bald-headed old man pointed at the crystal ball and said: "Put your hand on the crystal ball to test your affinity with elements."

The first was a juvenile of 12 to 13 years old. He placed his hand nervously on the crystal ball, which started glowing in light red with occasional appearance of some cyan rays.

The bald-headed old man looked at his paper in hand and said indifferently: "Age 12, affinity: medium level in fire, low level in wind."

"Now enter the magic circle and test your spiritual force. Stand straight, do not kneel or fall, and hold on for as longer as you can." The old man said with an indifferent voice still, and the juvenile nodded and entered the hexagram magic circle. A divine white beam appeared from the old man's body and merged into the magic circle.

Light magic -- deterrence!

"Test method is still so primitive." Delin flew out to Lynnray's side.

"Grandpa Delin." Lynnray was composed upon seeing Delin.

"Affinity with elements is secondary in the test. The most important part is spiritual force. You should have a spiritual force 16 or 17 times of your peers, cultivated by your meditation practice for half a year." Delin smiled at Lynnray, "These tests should be simple for you."

After a short while, the juvenile in the magic circle collapsed out of fatigue.

"Spiritual force: twice of peers. No possibility for becoming a magician." The bald-headed old man announced indifferently. The magic circle paused, and the juvenile walked out in frustration.

A bustling sound of chit-chat appeared in the crowd.

"Quiet!" The old man ordered, and the nobles stopped talking right away. "Next one."

Delin looked at the process with interest.

Amazingly, among the first ten candidates, none was qualified. Now a young lady entered the magic circle. She held on for longer than the 10 candidates before her.

"Eh?" The old man brightened his eyes and increased the power of magic circle.

After a while, the young lady collapsed on one knee.

The old man nodded satisfactorily and smiled: "Spiritual force: 8 times of peers, bottom level of a magician. Affinity with elements is medium. She can be a magician." The old man's announcement determined the young lady's future.

"Ah, so good!" The first one to shout was not the girl, but her father, a bald-headed gentleman.

"Quiet!" The old man grunted.

A priest came and led the girl and her father to the recruitment staff.

Many people looked at the girl in admiration.

Becoming a magician was a guarantee of power and status.

As time passed, more and more people came into the hall. The magic test lasted for seven days, so most people were not in a hurry. When the turn came to Lynnray, the line of candidates had extended to the outside.

"Next one." said the old man.

Lynnray composed himself and stepped forward. Delin was still beside Lynnray. He believed only a holy fighter could perceive his existence, while these ordinary magicians couldn't.

Lynnray put his hand on the crystal ball.

Suddenly, the crystal ball became brilliant with colors of earth-yellow and cyan, and occasionally, a ray of fire red. The dazzling light made people near it squint. All people in the hall were shocked by the crystal ball as dazzling as the sun.

The bald-headed old man trembled with a piece of paper in his hand. The paper said clearly that Lynnray was eight years old.

"Age 8, affinity with element is super in earth and wind and medium in fire." The old man's heart was beating quickly. Normally, magicians were at medium grade in their affinity with elements. The high grade was rarely seen, and super grade... That was definitely very rare. It could be said that one hour's practice for Lynnray in cultivation of magic force was equal to 10 hours of practice for other people.

"Wow!"

The hall was filled with exclamations of amazement. Super grade in two series -- that was unimaginable.

"Super in wind?" Delin was also surprised.

"Eh, I'm also good at wind magic?" Lynnray was surprised, too, so he asked Delin in the mind.

Delin smiled: "Lynnray, I said I could only test your affinity with earth elements. By the way, did you feel wind elements while practicing magic force?"

"Wind elements?" Lynnray paused a bit, "When you first taught me to cultivate magic force, you said I should not be distracted, so I didn't think much about the cyan light dots around me. Later when I absorbed earth elements, I was surrounded by dots of earth elements, and no cyan dots appeared anymore."

Delin understood it.

When a dual-series magician practiced one series, he would absorb elements of the series he was practicing, while other elements would be rejected.

"Then, when I practiced each time, I was surrounded by earth elements, so I forgot the cyan light dots altogether." Lynnray was very delighted.

He knew that a dual-series magician was slightly more powerful than a single-system.

The next step was to test the spiritual force.

Chapter 9 - Magic Test (II)

"Remember to hold on during test of spiritual force. Hold on as longer as better." Delin said seriously, "I don't know wind magic. You should really study in the magic school. It's a pity you don't learn wind magic with such a strong affinity."

Lynnray understood Delin's point.

"Please enter the magic circle." The old man rarely used the word 'please'.

Even many nobles were looking at Lynnray differently. Super grade in affinity with elements meant he could spend much less time practicing magic force, and save much more time practicing spiritual force. He certainly had a brilliant future.

Lynnray stepped into the magic circle.

A warm white beam appeared in the magic circle to exert force on his soul.

Light magic -- deterrence.

"It's so weak. Much weaker than the black dragon half a year ago." Lynnray was still absorbed in thoughts.

With the passing of time, the magic circle became brighter and was applying stronger pressure. All people in the hall held their breath at the sight. The boy in ordinary wearing would surely become a powerful magician.

"Who know this boy? Which family does he belong to?" The nobles chatted with each other.

If they had association with such a promising boy, they would have a powerful friend in future.

"His name is Lynnray." Some recruitment staff knew his identity from the test personnel.

The recruitment staff of magic schools, who had been engaged in casual talk, now came to the spot and observed. All magic schools wanted to recruit some talented students.

In the magic circle, Lynnray was resisting the deterrence alone.

He was breathing heavily and felt dizzincss in the head. The pressure on him was like a mountain and was gradually increasing. He was insisting.

"The longer I insist, the better school I can enter." He thought.

But when the pressure reached a certain level, he could not resist it any more and collapsed onto his one knee and hands.

All people turned their look to the bald-headed old man.

The old man said clearly with a radiant face: "The boy's spiritual force is 18 times of his peers and is at high grade. His affinity with elements is at super grade."

At this moment, some recruitment staff rushed in: "Hi, Lynnray, I'm from Rand Magic Academy, and we sincerely invite you to enroll in our school. If you can some, we can give you a full waiver of tuition and

1,000 gold coins of scholarship every year. And we will arrange a senior magician to teach you."

"Lynnray, I'm from Willing Magic Academy, we...."

......

Surrounded with a group of warm-hearted recruiters, Lynnray paused for quite a while and was amazed that they knew his name in such a short time.

"Hey, everybody, you'd better go back to your seats. We have to carry on the test." The bald-headed old man said gently.

He could be proud in front of ordinary people, but he was polite towards the personnel of magic schools.

"Lynnray, Ernst Academy sincerely invites you to join." A voice came from afar, and the entire hall quieted down. Even the bald-headed old man stopped talking.

Lynnray turned his head.

A man in white robe came forward and said with a smile: "You are at super grade in affinity with elements and high grade in spiritual force. You are super in both series. Ernst Academy welcomes you, but we don't know if you are willing to join us."

Hilman was stupefied for quite a while and ran to Lynnray. He was trembling in the hand out of excitement.

Ernst Academy? What did it mean to be a member of Ernst Academy, the No.1 magic school on Yulan Continent?

It meant once you graduated, even as an ordinary student, you could easily become an earl in a kingdom. Excellent students were even invited by the four empires.

And on the entire Yulan Continent, Ernst Academy only recruited 100 students every year.

What kind of probability was that?

All students admitted to Ernst Academy were talents.

"Lynnray, say yes to him." Hilman was very excited.

Lynnray was very excited, too, but he remained sober and calm. He knew that the instruction of Ernst Academy and Delin together could help him reach level-7 or level-8 in decades.

His family could rise again.

"Sir, I'm honored to be a member of Ernst Academy." Lynnray said politely.

The middle-aged man in white robe was amazed at Lynnray's calmness, but he continued with a smile: "Lynnray, I will pass on your identity information to the school. By then, you only need to bring your identity proof and pass another test in school to be enrolled."

Cheating was useless, because there was a second test in school.

"One year is divided into two semesters, and the first one starts at February 9th. Arrive at school before the date. Here is a certificate of admission." The man in white robe took out a red letter from his chest.

In fact, he wrote Lynnray's name on the admission letter upon seeing the test results, because he believed no one would decline the invitation of Ernst Academy.

"Thank you." Lynnray took the red letter.

Lynnray did not show excitement apparently, but Hilman was very excited. Every student of Ernst Academy had noble status. Lynnray's achievement in future could be expected.

"Uncle Hilman, let's go." Lynnray put away the red letter in his chest, and followed Hilman to the outside.

In the crowded hall, the capital nobles and civilians gave way to them, and even the nobles who had looked down upon Lynnray as a villager were smiling amicably with the best of their attitudes.

Student of Ernst Academy was itself a symbol of status.

In the vision of nobles, civilians and church clergies, Lynnray and Hilman walked out of the church.

"Chi Chi!" The shadow mouse squeaked upon their exit from the church. It could feel Lynnray's excitement in the heart.

Now Lynnray fully showed his excitement. With a clench of fist, he looked at Hilman with bright eyes and said rapidly: "Uncle Hilman, let's go back now! Go to Wushan Town and tell dad the good news!"

Chapter 10 - Secret Guidebook of Dragonblood (I)

In Baruch mansion, Wushan Town.

Hogg just had his lunch, and was reading a book leisurely on his deck chair.

Two figures entered the mansion fast. They were Lynnray and Hilman who returned quickly from Fenlai City. With still excitement on their face, Lynnray shouted from a distance: "Dad, I'm back."

"Mr. Hogg." Hilman said excitedly.

Hogg had a premonition upon seeing the excited expression of Lynnray and Hilman. He stood up, looked at them, and inquired with a slightly trembling voice: "How's the magic test?"

Baruch family had remained anonymous for quite a long time, and needed a great person to restore its honor.

"Mr. Hogg. It was Ernst. Lynnray was admitted by Ernst Academy." said Hilman excitedly.

Hogg was stupefied at the news, and felt blank in his brain as if in oxygen deficit.

"Mr. Hogg?" Hilman called him twice.

Hogg returned to normal thinking and asked Hilman with a rapid breath for confirmation: "Were you saying Ernst Academy?" Hogg opened his eyes widely.

"Dad, this is the admission letter of Ernst Academy." Lynnray handed the red letter to his father, who paused a bit, opened the letter and read the admission notice.

He saw the titles in red -- 'Ernst Academy', 'Lynnray'.

"Hahahaha, predecessors of Baruch family! We have hope!" Hogg looked up and laughed with a shivering body and tears. "Baruch family has hope!"

His hysteric laughter and tears surprised Lynnray.

"Dad." Lynnray called him gently so as not to disturb him.

He never saw his father laughing in madness, and the tears were a shock to him.

Steward Hilly came and was surprised at Hogg's reaction, without knowing what happened.

Hogg took a deep breath and looked at Lynnray with great excitement: "Good, good."

"Hilman and uncle Hilly!" Hogg looked at both of them, "I'll put on a feast tonight. Prepare it now. I'm very happy today. With such a good son, I'm doing great favor for the predecessors of Baruch family."

"Yes, Mr. Hogg." Hilman and steward Hilly replied.

"Chi Chi..." Suddenly the little shadow mouse BeiBei jumped out of Lynnray's chest and stood on his shoulder. It stared at Hogg with anger in the eyes. Lynnray held back his laughter when he received the shadow mouse's message in the heart.

The shadow mouse had been in sleep, but Hogg's laughter woke it up. As a juvenile, it slept a lot, and hated being awakened, so it was angry.

"Monster shadow mouse?" Hogg turned pale when he saw the shadow mouse.

"Dad." Lynnray was afraid his father might attack the shadow mouse, so he said in a hurry, "The shadow mouse has been in a soul contract with me."

Hogg was stupefied and stared blankly for quite a while: "You subdued this shadow mouse, a monster?"

There were two conditions for subduing a monster: 1. Make it submissive, 2. Lay out a soul contract magic circle.

Hogg believed Lynnray was weak, but even the weakest shadow mouse was at level-3. Besides, how could Lynnray possibly lay out a soul contract magic circle?

"Yes, dad, I subdued it." Lynnray said seriously.

Hogg felt his son was different from before. Totally different!

"Mr. Hogg, Lynnray subdued this shadow mouse. I saw it. The shadow mouse was the lovely animal he fed these days with rabbits and prairie chickens." Hilman explained.

"The animal you were feeding?" Hogg recalled those days and stared at Lynnray with an incredible look, "The shadow mouse is the lovely animal you were feeding at the old houses in the back?"

Lynnray nodded honestly.

Hogg found it unbelievable that a so-called lovely animal was a monster.

He was in doubt how Lynnray entered into a soul contract with the shadow mouse, but he was not in a hurry to ask. He was in a good mood at this moment.

"OK, let's not discuss these things. Uncle Hilly and Hilman, bring some guards to prepare for our feast tonight." Hogg said with a laughter. He was laughing with strength.

Lynnray looked at his father, who had never laughed so happily since he could remember things.

At night.

Baruch family was in a lively atmosphere. Even the dozen guards and their families were invited to the feast. Five dining tables were placed in the front yard. The mansion was filled with laughter.

"It's delicious." Little Warton grabbed food here and there and ate excitedly.

"Young master, congratulations for entering Ernst Academy. You will become a great magician in future." A family guard congratulated Lynnray with a smile.

Lynnray was the main role in the night feast.

Everybody was excited to hear Lynnray would enter Ernst Academy. A glorious path was ahead of him. He had a wider stage to demonstrate himself than the small town.

"Brother, they are making a toast with you. I'm making a toast, too." Little Warton held up his glass of fruit juice.

Lynnray found it interesting to see Warton's oily hand, but he also raised his glass of fruit juice and clinked with Warton's.

"Come on, let's drink as brothers." Lynnray raised his glass with a smile.

......

Lynnray and Hogg together alone in the ancestral temple of Baruch family, late at night.

The door was closed, and it felt warm in the temple with a row of lit candles. Hogg looked at the memorial tablets and said with a deep voice: "Lynnray, since the appearance of the fifth Dragonblood warrior, our family has been declining over generations. It declined to such an extent that even our family heirloom was sold off... I feel ashamed whenever I think about this. We are a glorious family of the Dragonblood."

Lynnray was quietly standing behind Hogg.

The loss of heirloom was also his shame.

Lynnray was proud as a member of an ancient family of 5,000 years, and a family of the Dragonblood. But the family lost its heirloom due to its decline.

"Lynnray." Hogg turned back and looked at Lynnray seriously, "From today, I will not regard you as a child, but the pillar of our family. Our family counts on you for its future."

"Yes, dad." Lynnray replied resolutely.

"Wait a moment. Let me fetch something." Hogg walked to the secret chamber of the ancestral temple, and came out with a book after a while. "Lynnray, read this book and keep in mind its content."

"What's this?"

Lynnray took the book in doubt. There was no script on the cover, but when he opened it, he saw four large words on the first sheet -- Secret Guidebook of Dragonblood.

Chapter 11 – Secret Guidebook of Dragonblood (II)

"Secret Guidebook of Dragon blood?" Lynnray looked up at his father in surprise.

Hogg said with a smile: "The guidebook is only part of it. This book has recorded many events relevant with Baruch family, including Secret Guidebook of Dragonblood, the method of making a Dragonblood needle, and stories of our predecessors."

Lynnray turned over the book carefully.

The first quarter of the book was the guidebook, and the rest was events related to the family.

"Lynnray, this book is of no use to outsiders. Other people cannot practice according to the guidebook, and our family events are of no use to them. Do not worry much. And we have a few copies at home. This one is a copy. The original has turned into ashes over time." Hogg said with a smile.

Lynnray smiled, too.

"Yes, it's no use to others." Lynnray started reading the beginning part of the Secret Guidebook of Dragonblood.

"To practice according to the guidebook, one has to activate his blood of Dragonblood warriors, which requires his density of blood of Dragonblood warriors reaches certain level. If he does not meet this condition, there is another method..."

Lynnray was surprised at these sentences.

Another method for those who did not have required level of blood density? Why didn't anyone ever achieve success?

"The second method is to gulp down a living dragon's blood, or the blood of a dragon which died less than a few minutes ago. If the dragon was dead for a longer time, the effect of its blood would be too weak. By gulping down dragon blood, one can activate his latent blood of Dragonblood warriors. The best effect comes with a dragon in the holy domain. A dragon at level-9 only has low probability of activating the blood of Dragonblood warriors."

Lynnray was a bit surprised.

"How did the predecessors come up with the idea of gulping down a dragon's blood?" Lynnray held back his laughter.

"Gulping down a living dragon's blood, and a dragon in the holy domain. Your predecessors were tough." Delin appeared beside Lynnray, astonished by the first lines of the secret guidebook.

Delin was invisible for Hogg, who smiled bitterly: "As you read, Lynnray, our ancestors provided two methods to activate the blood of Dragonblood warriors deeply latent in our blood. But the second method, gulping down a living dragon's blood is not as easy as it sounds. Besides...turn this page and look by yourself."

Lynnray turned the page and saw the following lines.

"But the second method, gulping down a living dragon's blood is very dangerous. A dragon's blood is an extremely strong liquid. It improves our constitution drastically when poured on our body, but it also causes pain as sharp as skin peeling. That is the result of pouring on the skin. If you drink it, you will feel as if burned by fire. You will even suffer heavy burn injuries, have blood vessels cracked and lose your life."

Lynnray became speechless upon reading these words.

"Dad, who wrote the Secret Guidebook of Dragonblood despite its danger?" Lynnray did not know what to say.

Hogg said seriously: "It was written by Baruch, the founder of our family and the first Dragonblood warrior on Yulan Continent. He had his reasons writing this, although two of our family members in history drank a holy dragon's blood and died of vessel crack."

"So somebody did it?" Lynnray was a bit surprised.

But with a second thought, it was normal.

The family's patriarchs in the first three generations were Dragonblood warriors. So the family was in great power and glory at that time. It was possible that they took a holy dragon and carried out bloodletting.

"The secret events of remote past were not recorded in this book. I only know that the dragon race negotiated with Baruch family in this respect. Since then, nobody tried this method... And with the decline of family, you don't even have a chance to do it." Hogg shook his head and gave a sigh.

Lynnray nodded.

The pride of dragon race was recorded in many books.

Being taken alive and let blood was a great shame for dragon race. Baruch family was luckily not destroyed by the infuriated dragons. But it could also be imagined how prosperous the family had been.

"No, dad. If nobody became a Dragonblood warrior by swallowing dragon blood, why did our ancestors write this guidebook saying we can practice by gulping down a living dragon's blood? And he also said a level-9 dragon was also effective to a limited extent." Lynnray was confused.

Hogg froze at Lynnray's doubt.

"Lynnray, don't question further. I can only get a rough picture of our family history from this book. We can never know what happened 4,000 or 5,000 years ago." Hogg smiled at Lynnray.

Lynnray nodded.

But he was still in doubt. Since the book said nobody ever succeeded by gulping down a dragon's blood, why did it provide this method?

"Lynnray, it's late. Go back and rest." Hogg smiled.

Lynnray nodded.

At night.

Lynnray returned to his bedroom. He was still wondering with this book in hand.

"Grandpa Delin. Nobody ever succeeded by using this method, but why did they know this method as a proven fact?" Lynnray asked in confusion.

Delin was far more intelligent. He said confidently with raised beard: "It's simple. As far as I know, the dragons are a proud race, and they are very powerful. I reckon drinking a living dragon's blood is effective, but under the pressure of the dragon race, your family changed the content of this book."

Lynnray suddenly realized the fact.

That was highly probable.

Under the pressure of dragons, Dragonblood warriors of Baruch family were not allowed any more to seize living dragons for their practice.

"Of course, this is my guesswork." Delin smiled lightly, "And as far as I know, gulping down a living dragon's blood is not a sure way to death. You can contradict the harm of dragon blood by using it with 'Blueheart', a grass. But this secret formula may have been forgotten till now."

Lynnray was a bit surprised.

Then he was wild with joy: "Grandpa Delin, is it safe to drink a living dragon's blood with Blueheart?"

Delin nodded with confidence: "Sure. In the Pron Empire, once a princess was heavily ill. She was cured by using a living dragon's blood and the grass Blueheart. I caught a dragon in the holy domain for them."

"The old palace doctor prescribing the formula said objects in the world inter-restricts each other. All materials have other materials to neutralize. Only he and I knew this secret formula. After 6,000 years, I'm sure few people know it now." Delin said lightly.

Lynnray nodded.

"A living dragon's blood, and grass Blueheart..." Lynnray showed excitement in his eyes, "When I reach level-9 in magic, I will transform Warton into a Dragonblood warrior by using a living dragon's blood and grass Blueheart."

And he even wanted to use it himself, if there was a chance.

He might become a holy magician and Dragonblood warrior at the same time. Of course that was only a dream. Firstly, catching a holy dragon alive was a remote dream.

"There is a long way to go. Let me sleep first. I'll go on practicing next morning."

Chapter 12 - The Request

Several months passed and it was February. With the coming of Spring, many trees sprouted on Wushan Mountain.

Lynnray was sitting cross-legged under an old tree and doing meditation to cultivate magic force.

In the meditative state, Lynnray could clearly feel large amount of light dots in earth-yellow and cyan colors around his body. The light dots were entering him at different parts, penetrating his limbs and torso, refined and gathered at central Dantian in the chest.

Earth-yellow and cyan fog was concentrated at central Dantian.

The fog in earth-yellow and cyan represented magic force in earth series and wind series, respectively.

"Hu." He breathed out and recovered from meditative state.

Delin, in a moon-white robe was sitting cross-legged on the ground and appreciating the scenery around. When he saw Lynnray waking up, he smiled and said: "Lynnray, you'll head for Ernst Academy tomorrow, but you are still practicing with great endeavor today."

Lynnray curled his mouth and smiled: "Grandpa Delin, as you said, a strong person practices with great effort every day without relaxation. Only long-term practice leads to astonishing strength."

"Lad, you are teaching me now." Delin joked with a laugh.

"Heihei." Lynnray grinned.

"Su!" A black shadow swooshed from a distance to Lynnray's shoulder. It was shadow mouse Beibei, which was showing its teeth and pointing at a dead rabbit on the ground.

Lynnray knew what Beibei wanted.

"You want me to roast it for you?" Lynnray smiled.

Beibei nodded.

"Lynnray." Delin passed his voice mentally, "Strangely, the shadow mouse did not grow even a bit in these months. It should grow faster in the juvenile period."

"I don't understand it, either." Lynnray shook his head.

The shadow mouse was not growing in size, but its movement speed increased rapidly.

"It's weird." Delin glanced at Beibei, which did not know a spirit was watching it.

"It's late now. I have to attend the evening training." Lynnray stood up and walked downhill with the dead rabbit in his hand. Delin floated beside him and said with discontent: "Lynnray, you'll be a magician in future. Why are you still doing warrior exercise?"

Lynnray smiled: "Grandpa Delin, I found that warrior training can help me improve fortitude, and consequently spiritual force." "I know it." Delin said with discontent, "The training is most primitive. It's far less effective than meditation."

Lynnray fell silent.

Improving spiritual force was only his excuse to insist on warrior training.

He was still attending warrior training because: "If I have the chance to drink a living dragon's blood, I can practice according to Secret Guidebook of Dragonblood, so I still need to practice my physical body. The body is an important vessel and vital energy is wine. I can lay the foundation for practicing according to the guidebook in future."

Since Lynnray had good affinity with elements, he only needed a short time every day to cultivate magic force.

Most of his time was used to cultivate spiritual force via meditation.

Such practice was energy-consuming and caused fatigue. Warrior training could be used as a form of adjustment and rest.

……

On the morning of the next day, many residents gathered at the streets to see off Lynnray. Wushan Town was in honor to have a magician admitted to Ernst Academy.

Ernst Academy only recruited 100 students on Yulan Continent every year.

Lynnray was in the Baruch mansion at the moment. Hilman and the guards were outside, and in the front yard were Hogg, Lynnray, Warton and steward Hilly.

"Lynnray, you have formally become a member of Ernst Academy. After you graduate from the school, you will be a great magician. I have some words for you before your departure." Hogg had a lot to say before parting with Lynnray.

But after a long pause, he only spoke several simple lines: "Lynnray, remember the wish of our predecessors over hundreds of years, and remember our shame."

Hogg's face turned a bit blue.

"You will be at least a level-6 magician upon graduation. If you practice with effort, you can reach level-7. And as a dual-series magician at level-7, you will surely be a great personality in Fenlai Kingdom and fully capable of seizing back our family heirloom. If you can't even achieve that, I will not forgive you till death." Hogg stared at Lynnray gravely.

"I will not forgive you till death."

The sentence touched Lynnray in the heart.

It was his father's request before his departure.

"Dad, you are assured that I'll seize back our family heirloom in this life. I swear!" Lynnray made his guarantee while looking into his father's eyes. His shiny eyes showed firm determination.

Hogg brightened his eyes and patted on Lynnray's shoulder with his strong hand.

"I trust you, son!"

......

On the path east of Wushan Town, Lynnray looked back at the hundreds of folks seeing him off. His father Hogg and brother Warton were heading the crowd.

"Bye, brother." Warton waved his hand vigorously.

Looking at his father and brother, Lynnray also waved his hand with full strength, and his eyes were turning red.

"Father and Warton." Lynnray's mind was lingering on them.

He had never really left home since childhood. But this time he would be away for a long time. The shadow mouse Beibei remained quiet on Lynnray's shoulder, as if it could feel Lynnray's melancholy. Delin, who was staying at one side in the form of spirit also looked at Lynnray with encouragement.

"Lynnray, let's go." said Hilman. They might come across bandits on the way, so Hilman's duty was to protect Lynnray.

Lynnray looked at his relatives with reluctance, and finally set off for Ernst Academy.

"Bye, my relatives and hometown."

In 9991 of Yulan calendar, the nine-year-old Lynnray left his hometown Wushan Town with guard captain Hilman and shadow mouse Beibei.

Chapter 13 - Gathering Place of Talents

Ernst Academy was the No.1 magic school of Yulan Continent.

Located in the woods 20 li south of holy capital Fenlai City, Ernst Academy was built on the funding of Church of Light. With abundant finances, it occupied a wide area of nearly 10 li in diameter. In the aspect of size, it could be compared to a city. Outside of Ernst Academy was wide areas of mountains and woods with no residents.

Restaurants, clothes shops and bars were set up inside the academy. It could be said that students were living in the academy.

"A grand place." Lynnray made a sigh at the gate of Ernst Academy.

The front gate was 50 meters wide and had a huge half-moon structure with carved mystical magic mantras. Based on level of complexity, the structure was a large magic circle.

It was lively at the gate. Some clerks were working there, and a juvenile was going through procedures with admission letter and identity proof. So Lynnray also started registering himself with his admission letter and identity proof.

"School starts on February 9, but today is February 8. According to notice, students must arrive before February 9. This juvenile is going through procedures today, so he must be living near Ernst Academy." Lynnray said to himself. The juvenile was only a boy, accurately speaking. He was half-a-head lower than Lynnray and accompanied by an old man.

“Hello, I’m Reno from O'Brien Empire.” The boy turned back and greeted Lynnray warmly.

Lynnray was surprised to hear about Reno’s hometown.

O’Brien Empire was one of the four empires located on the east of Monster Mountains, but Ernst Academy was on the west. To arrive at Ernst Academy, he must go around Monster Mountains from the north or south. Except a level-9 fighter or holy fighter, no one dare cross Monster Mountains directly.

Monster Mountains were as long as 10,000 li.

A journey from O’Brien Empire was nearly 20,000 li, and if he lived in the eastern part of O’Brien Empire, it would take even longer.

About one year would be spent on the journey of 20,000 li.

“I’m Lynnray, from Fenlai Kingdom.” Lynnray said to Reno politely.

Reno blinked and sighed: “Fenlai Kingdom? Easy for you. I spent one year arriving at Fenlai Kingdom. You must have spent only a short time.”

“Yes, it took me half a day.” Lynnray replied honestly.

“Er...” Reno made an exaggerated expression.

Half a day for one, but one year for anther.

“Students, quick.” The testing staff urged.

One procedure of enrollment was to test the student’s power once again. The academy was worried about admission letter being taken by some others.

"It's my turn." Reno went in for the test.

Lynnray was surprised at Reno's test results.

Reno had high-grade affinity with elements, and his spiritual force...

"Reno, age 8, spiritual force is 32 times of peers, super grade."

Lynnray opened his eyes widely upon hearing the result, but the testing staff did not show any surprise.

"Why? You are surprised at this?" Reno said carelessly, "This is Ernst Academy. It only recruits 100 students on Yulan Continent every year. Every student is a talent. My power is only medium among all students."

"But Ernst Academy is preferential toward Holy Alliance. They recruit 50 students in Holy Alliance, but 50 students in four empires and Dark Alliance altogether. That's unfair." Reno sighed.

Lynnray only smiled at these words.

Ernst Academy was founded by Church of Light and was certainly inclined toward Holy Alliance.

"It's my turn." Lynnray went in for the test.

Reno twitched his nose and thought confidently: "This boy is from Holy Alliance and benefited from the preferential policy. He must be less talented than me."

But he was then shocked at Lynnray's result.

"High grade in spiritual force and super grade in affinity with elements. dual-series in earth and wind." Reno became speechless.

Super grade of affinity in one series was already rare, but Lynnray was super in dual series. He was more talented than Reno. Anyway, a dual-series magician was very powerful.

"Reno, don't be distracted. Let's go." Lynnray smiled.

"Oh." Reno was only 1 year younger than Lynnray, but he looked 2 or 3 years younger in appearance.

Lynnray and Reno received their student ID and dormitory key. All students had to live in the dormitory regardless of their financial condition. Schooling and boarding were provided free of charge.

But...

"Eh, you are paying the tuition?" Lynnray was surprised to see the old man beside Reno paying tuition.

Hilman, who was together with Lynnray, smiled: "Waiver of tuition and boarding fee was applied to students from Holy Alliance only. Students from other places had to pay their expensive fees."

Reno nodded.

The old man beside Reno smiled to Lynnray: "Yes, and Ernst Academy was not alone in such practice. The No.1 warrior school on the continent -- O'Brien Academy -- is the same. It waives fees for students from the same country, but charges high cost from students from elsewhere."

Lynnray certainly understood his point.

"Lynnray, my young master has the same key with you. You should be living in the same room. I hope you can help each other." The old man said friendly.

Reno said with discontent: "OK, grandpa Loum, you can go back. I'm here at Ernst Academy already."

"Uncle Hilman, you can also return. I can take care of myself." Lynnray smiled at Hilman, who nodded with assurance: "I'll be back then. Study hard." Hilman encouraged Lynnray.

Lynnray nodded with a kidding smile.

"Lynnray, let's go." Reno held Lynnray's hand and ran into the academy.

"Uncle Hilman, bye."

Hilman and the old man watched as the two kids entered the academy, and after a long while, they left.

After bidding farewell with Hilman, Lynnray walked into Ernst Academy with Reno. The academy had shading trees, lakes, stone bridges and old buildings, creating an atmosphere of ancient history. The large trees were telling their age with a thick trunk only surrounded by seven to eight persons.

"The academy does not show off itself like others. This is called cultural deposit." Reno looked around and sighed with emotion.

There were many signboards pointing out the direction, and obviously, they were in the service of freshmen of the academy. "Lynnray, let's go to the dormitory." Lynnray pulled Reno and headed for the dormitory.

Number of dormitory -- 1987.

Lynnray and Reno had gone through the procedures one after another. Generally four students lived in a room. When Lynnray and Reno came to the lodging area, they were amazed to see thousands of single houses.

Apart from the single houses, there were rare two-story apartment buildings.

"1987, 1987..." They glanced at the numbers and kept their direction in the south.

The dormitory rooms were numbered in a regular way. Starting from 0001, every line had 100 single houses, and at the 20th line, they saw 1901. Then they ran east. With Reno gasping quickly, they arrived at the single house of 1987.

Chapter 14 - Brothers in Room 1987 (I)

"Oops, I'm so tired. Why is your stamina so good?" Reno was gasping, but Lynnray was not.

"Tired so soon?" Lynnray laughed. That was a short distance.

He did not feel tired at all on this trip from Wushan Town to Ernst Academy.

"Hey, place it here. Box should be there. Be careful. You can't afford the damage." A juvenile's voice came from the yard of Room 1987. Lynnray and Reno looked at each other and walked in with curiosity. They saw several young men carrying various items.

A juvenile in luxury clothes was standing in the middle and ordering these people.

When the juvenile saw Lynnray and Reno, he showed light in his eyes and ran to them excitedly: "Haha, you must be my roommates. I have been waiting for you alone. Let me introduce myself. I'm Yale, can be counted as one from Holy Alliance"

"Why do you say 'can be counted as one'?" Reno curled his mouth, "I'm Reno from O'Brien Empire."

"I'm Lynnray, from Fenlai Kingdom of Holy Alliance." Lynnray said with a smile.

Since they were roommates, they had to stay together for a long time.

"Ah, Reno, Lynnray, glad to see you. Hey, put the fitness equipment over there." Yale turned around and shouted to his servants.

"Fitness equipment?" Reno stared at Yale with wide-open eyes, "Yale, why do you use those? Do you want to become a warrior?"

Yale twitched his nose and giggled: "We are noble magicians, but we still need to develop shape, otherwise how can we attract beautiful women? There are many beautiful women among magicians, and especially, the beautiful women in Ernst Academy have good temperament besides good looks. You'll be honored to say you have a girlfriend in Ernst Academy."

"Er..." Reno became speechless.

Lynnray also had nothing to say. He thought the equipment was used in physical training, but it was only Yale's tool to cultivate romantic attraction.

"I'm eight. How about you, Yale?" Reno was social.

Yale had a tall stature. Lynnray at nine years old was one and a half meters, but Yale was half-a-head taller than Lynnray.

"I'm ten, but not young. My brother had his first time at 12, and I should be prepared for that." Yale showed light in his eyes.

"What does first time mean?" Reno looked at Yale in confusion.

"Yeah, what does first time mean?" Lynnray also looked at Yale with doubt. Yale became speechless while looking at his roommates. Delin laughed out loud beside Lynnray, who asked him mentally in doubt: "Grandpa Delin, what are you laughing at?"

"Young master, we have had everything in its place." A middle-aged gentleman said respectfully.

"Hmm. You can go back now. Tell my dad that he doesn't need to bother me with trifle affairs. By the way, remember to remit funds to my Magic Crystal Card. As you know, the wand and gem of a magician are costly." Yale said in a casual manner.

The middle-aged man replied with respect: "Yes, young master."

Yale nodded satisfactorily, and waved his hand to dismiss the servants.

"Magic Crystal Card?" Reno looked at Yale in surprise, "It is only provided by the Union Bank of Empires jointly founded by the four empires. It's said the service fee for obtaining the card is 100 gold coins."

"That's true." Yale said clearly, "The initial deposit should not be less than 1,000 gold coins. But 1,000 gold coins may not be enough for my use in one month."

"A rich guy." Lynnray thought to himself upon hearing those words.

Lynnray's father gave him 100 gold coins in a year. In fact, 100 gold coins a year was enough for himself. After all, an ordinary civilian only earned 20 to 30 gold coins from a year's hard work. "You are truly rich. My father only gives me 200 gold coins in a year." Reno said with curled mouth, "And he says I should focus on studying magic."

"Mine is only 100 gold coins." Lynnray smiled, "But it's enough for simple living."

"Hi, brothers, my money is also yours. Ask me if you are short of money. Maybe we'll be together for decades. Brothers of decades should share happiness." Yale was quite generous, but Lynnray and Reno were perplexed by his words.

"Decades?" Lynnray looked at Yale in surprise.

Yale said with assurance: "Students of Ernst Academy graduates at level-6, but on the path of magic, your progress will be harder and harder when you move up the ladder. It generally takes decades to reach level-6."

Lynnray frowned.

Would he live on his father's support for decades?

"Grandpa Delin, why didn't you tell me this?"

Delin's voice appeared in Lynnray's mind: "Don't worry. Ordinary people would spend decades to become a level-6 magician, but with my instruction, you only need 10 years."

Lynnray was relieved to hear 'ten years'. By then, he would be only 19.

"Everybody has arrived?" With a clear voice, a child as tall as Reno walked in, but he looked calm in character. "Hello everyone, I'm George, 10-year-old from Yulan Empire."

Yale, Reno and Lynnray introduced themselves to George.

"Yulan Empire?" Lynnray was a bit surprised.

Yulan Empire was the oldest empire on Yulan Continent. In the first year of Yulan calendar, it unified the entire Yulan Continent, but conflicts over time split it up.

So far, Yulan Empire was only one of the four empires.

But it was the No.1 economic power and the birthplace of many magicians. Magic schools in Yulan Empire were only secondary to Ernst Academy.

"George, magic schools in Yulan Empire are good enough. Why do you need to get here?" Yale asked in surprise.

George smiled: "Magic schools in the empire are very good, but not as good as Ernst Academy. I want the best. Besides, long journey is a trial for me."

"George, you are ten? But you appear in the same age as me." Reno said.

George smiled bitterly.

Eight-year-old Reno and ten-year-old George had similar stature, and were the shortest in the four. Lynnray was half-a-head taller than them, and Yale was the tallest.

"By the way, I checked at enrollment that all the admitted 100 students are at high grade or above in spiritual force and affinity with elements. And I found some are at super grade in both spiritual force and affinity with elements." George seemed to be well informed of events.

Yale said with curled mouth: "It's normal. No one is weak in Ernst. My spiritual force and affinity with elements are both at high grade, basically at the bottom of 100 students. I would not be able to come here if not because of my father's relations in Church of Light."

Lynnray was amazed at Yale's background.

With relations in Church of Light, Yale's father was certainly not ordinary.

"In our room, Lynnray is the most talented, but there is an absolute talent in Ernst Academy. Have you heard of him?" Yale glanced at his roommates.

Lynnray and Reno shook their heads.

But George nodded with a smile: "I know. Ernst Academy has a top talent Dixi over the hundred years. He is a dual-series magician and at super grade in affinity with elements and spiritual force. His spiritual force is 68 times of his peers. Generally, 30 times of peers is considered super grade. His spiritual force can be called top grade, but super grade is the highest, according to the standards."

Lynnray was surprised at these words.

A dual-series magician at super grade in both affinity with elements and spiritual force.

"I'm only a dozen times of my peers but he is 68 times." Lynnray marveled in the heart.

Ernst Academy was indeed a gathering place of talents. With more than half of magic talents on Yulan Continent studying in the academy, Lynnray was only above average. But fortunately, there was a holy magic master of 5,000 years ago in support of him.

Chapter 15 - Brothers in Room 1987 (II)

Students generally stayed for decades in the academy; therefore, juveniles allocated to the same room would form a tight brotherhood at graduation. Although Yale, Reno, George and Lynnray were maturer than their peers, they were still children.

After a short chat, the four established a close rapport with each other.

"Let's get familiar with the school today. I'll treat everyone tonight. Haha." Yale patted on his chest and made a generous proposal.

"He has a Magic Crystal Card. He should treat us." Reno giggled.

George and Lynnray also smiled innocently.

"Chi Chi..." The little shadow mouse Beibei stuck out its head from Lynnray's clothes right after it woke up.

"Ah, what's this?" Reno was startled.

"Beibei, awake now?" Lynnray touched Beibei's head. Beibei squinted to enjoy the touch, and with a glance at Reno, Yale and George with its small eyes, it snorted with contempt.

"This is monster shadow mouse. I read about it in the books." Yale shouted.

"Lynnray, you have a monster?" Reno and George were surprised.

How could they subdue a monster as children?

"Beibei is only a juvenile. I provided some food to it, and it liked me. So it entered into a contract with me." Lynnray said with a smile.

"God, this is a monster. Lynnray, you are great. I dreamed of keeping a monster since small." Yale stared at Beibei with bright eyes, "Although I have a soul contract scroll, I don't have enough power to subdue a monster." Yale said with frustration.

"Why don't you try with a juvenile monster?" Lynnray smiled.

Yale shook his head: "I haven't even reached level-1. With limited power, I can only keep a juvenile of a level-1 or level-2 monster. But what's the use of such a weak monster? The children of level-7 or level-8 monsters are hard to get. Besides, they are much stronger than me even in juvenile stage."

Lynnray agreed with his words.

The shadow mouse Beibei was now nearly at level-5, much stronger than Lynnray. But during half of the year spent with it, it did not grow in size, which was strange for Lynnray and Delin.

"Lynnray, is your shadow mouse called 'Beibei'? Can I hold it?" Reno kept looking at the little shadow mouse.

"Beibei."

Lynnray tried to persuade Beibei in mental communication.

"No." Beibei could also express simple ideas, and it showed teeth angrily in front of Reno: "Chi Chi...".

Reno plumped up his mouth helplessly.

"Reno, I can tell you a way. Beibei likes eating roast meat. You can get some roast ducks or chickens, and it will not be so hostile toward you." Lynnray said with a smile, and Reno brightened his eyes upon hearing his words.

"Good idea."

Reno suddenly frowned and looked at Yale, "Yale, if I don't have enough gold coins sometime, can you lend me some? I'll pay you back when grandpa Loum comes."

"No problem." Yale said generously.

"I guess you haven't visited this academy, right? We can take a tour around and get familiar with it." George smiled.

Among the four brothers, George was the gentlest and calmest, Reno was the most childish, and Yale... was a playboy. Lynnray was the most mysterious in the eyes of the three.

He was at super grade in dual series, and owned a monster.

That was great mystery.

In the aged academy, there were ancient buildings with thousands of years' history as well as relevant introductions, such as well-known persons who studied in the building.

Over thousands of years, Ernst Academy had educated several holy magicians and more level-9 magicians.

The four young students from age 8 to 10 were reading those celebrity biographies with admiration. Especially, when they came across the stories of holy magicians, they were filled with enthusiasm. Every one of them dreamed to be a holy magician.

But a voice came to Lynnray ear: "They were just some newbies. There was no need to boast themselves about killing a purple-black bear. A holy magician who could only kill a level-9 monster but was not able to defeat a holy monster was only a newcomer in the holy domain."

Many so-called celebrities in Ernst Academy were unworthy of their name in the words of Delin.

……

The four brothers of Room 1987 visited the academy to their satisfaction with the little shadow mouse Beibei. After getting a general understanding of the academy, they had an abundant dinner in a luxury hotel near their dormitory. They only ordered fruit juice as their drinks.

The next day was February 9, the day of formal start of semester.

But class started one day after, on February 10. The students only heard the discourse of school leaders on February 9. A hundred children aged from 6 to 12 sat in a large classroom, and without having any idea about the identity of lecturing leaders, they slept through the opening ceremony and left happily in the end.

The four brothers discussed the courses after dinner. They had four chairs in the yard of Room 1987.

"It's so easy with only one class in a day. Oh, Lynnray has two classes as a dual." Yale sighed with emotion, "But Ernst Academy is loose in management. You can freely skip classes."

George had a faint smile, "Yale, don't take it lightly. The school does not force you to attend classes, but they test your power every year. You can only get in a higher grade when you have increased your level of power. If you don't practice diligently, will it be possible for you to stay 100 years in Ernst Academy? And they have rules saying you'll be ejected from school if you cannot reach level-6 in 60 years."

Lynnray nodded while looking at the document of regulations at hand.

Management was loose. You could be a player for 60 years, but if you couldn't reach level-6 in the end, you would be ejected.

"Ejected from school?" Yale stared ahead, "If I'm ejected, my dad's going to kill me." Ejection from Ernst Academy was a bad reputation unbearable for anyone, because admission itself was a proof of their talent.

"Classes will start tomorrow. I don't know how's the capability of teachers here. If they are less competent than my grandpa Loum, I'll regret coming here." Reno murmured.

"Reno, your grandpa Loum is a magician?" Lynnray asked with a bit surprise.

"Certainly, grandpa Loum has taught me magic on the way from O'Brien Empire to Ernst Academy." Reno said proudly.

Lynnray was in a mood of expectation when he chatted with his three brothers.

"The courses in earth magic are not so important. Teachers in the academy are by no means comparable with grandpa Delin. But wind magic is important. I don't know how is their competence in wind series."

Night fell gradually, and the yard of Room 1987 was filled with the children's laughter.

Chapter 16 - Wind Magic

In Ernst Academy, there were classes in the first 28 days of a month, and no class in the last 2 days.

Classes of earth magic were given between 8 and 10 a.m. Fire magic was instructed between 10 and 12 a.m. Water magic was instructed between 2 and 4 p.m. Study of wind series, thunder series and light series should be from 4:30 to 6:30, 7:00 to 9:00 and 9:30 to 11:30, all in the afternoon and night hours, respectively.

But most students were single-series and only needed to study for 2 hours in a day. Lynnray was dual-series and had 4 hours of class. And they were permitted to skip classes.

Earth magic was instructed in 6 grades, and every grade had a building. Beginners and level-1 magicians were at grade 1, level-2 magicians were at grade 2, and level-3 magicians were at grade 3... The final grade was grade 6.

Students in grade 6 could apply for graduation at any time or continue their study if they wished.

In the classroom of grade 1 earth magic, on February 10.

The classroom of grade 1 earth magic was very large with hundreds of seats. More than 20 students had come and taken their seats. Lynnray sat down in a front location. By 8 o'clock, there were 50 students in the classroom. "Maybe only some of them are freshmen, and others may have studied for some time." Lynnray thought to himself.

After all, a beginner would take several years to reach level-2.

"Hello everyone." An amiable middle-aged man with brown hair was standing on the platform, "I'm Wendy, your earth magic teacher. Today we have nearly 20 new students here. As usual, you will give a self-introduction in turn to know each other.."

The students took turns to introduce themselves in the front.

"I'm Golhan from the prairie in far east."

Lynnray was surprised at Golhan's self-introduction: "Students indeed come from different parts of Yulan Continent, and there is even one from the prairie in the far east."

In the geography of Yulan Continent.

The Holy Alliance and Dark Alliance were located on the west of Monster Mountains, and four empires were located on the east of Monster Mountains. On the east of four empires was a large prairie including three kingdoms. The prairie was very far from Ernst Academy, with a one-way trip taking as long as 2 to 3 years..

"I'm Lynnray from Holy Alliance." Lynnray also introduced himself in the front of the classroom.

After the self-introduction process, Wendy first started his boast about earth magic, and only came to his lessons in the second half of the class.

Lynnray and other children were listening carefully when Delin appeared beside Lynnray. "Wendy has a good basis in magic knowledge. He is not powerful, but in giving lessons to level-1 magicians, he is doing better than even level-8 and level-9 magicians." Delin nodded in praise of him.

Lynnray had good knowledge in earth magic and was studying easily.

"Grandpa Delin, he does have a good basis, but he is making things more complex than you put it." said Lynnray.

Delin nodded with a smile and said with raised beard: "That's natural. A holy magician's understanding in magic is deeper than level-9 and level-8. The holy domain opens up a brand new vision. I explain magic in a way easier to understand, and I point at the essence of magic directly."

After the lesson, Lynnray made a decision: "I'll attend one lesson of earth magic in one month." He didn't want to waste time.

Lynnray planned to practice magic outdoors in the daytime. The location of practice was the back mountains of Ernst Academy. The academy was located in a wooded mountainous area.

Four and a half in the afternoon.

Lynnray was hearing the lecture carefully in the classroom of grade 1 wind magic.

"Hello everyone." A golden-hair handsome young man said with a smile: "I'm Trey, grade 6 student of the academy. I'll teach you wind magic from today. I live in dormitory number 0298. You can come to me after class with your questions." In grade 6, the student was a level-6 magician who could apply for graduation at any time. They were qualified to teach students of grade 1 and 2.

"Before we start, let's introduce ourselves." Trey said with a smile.

The students came forward to introduce themselves as a necessary process in the first class.

"Eh, Lynnray, have you found that there are many lovely girls in the wind magic class? Look, the golden-hair girl is smiling at you." Delin said in a dancing manner, "According to her self-introduction, her name seems to be Delia. What a lovely name! Based on my 1,300 years' experience, this girl will become a beauty in future. Smile back at her and build a connection so you can move further."

Lynnray had no free time to listen to Delin's words.

He kept his vision on the wind magic teacher Trey and listened to his explanation.

"Wind magicians are the fastest and agilest, and the only magicians who can fly without attaining the holy level." Trey spoke in high spirits and passed on his love for wind magic, "Do you want to fly in the sky? You will have the most fantastic experience when landscape is passing beneath you."

The children listened with brightened eyes

Fly in the sky?

Everybody wanted it.

"A holy fighter can fly, too, but we hardly have a holy fighter in Ernst Academy in a hundred years. But a wind magician can use 'floating magic' at only level-5." Trey said confidently, "And wind magicians can achieve the fastest speed by using auxiliary magic 'top speed'."

"Of course, those are only ordinary magics. The legendary forbidden magic 'destructive windstorm' is the strongest destructive magic, and we have 'dimension sword', the strongest single-person attack." Tray introduced with a loud voice.

The juveniles listened in a yearning mood and stared with wide-open eyes.

"'Destructive windstorm' is the strongest destructive magic? Then how about 'world crack' and 'meteorite shower' in earth magic?" Delin said with discontent.

"Grandpa Delin, how about the 'dimension sword'?" Lynnray asked.

Grandpa Delin did not mention 'dimension sword', so Lynnray thought maybe it was really the strongest single-person attack.

"The 'dimension sword'? It can rip matter and space, so it's really strong. But it is also a one-time attack. In contrast, our 'guard of land' can be used repeatedly in a fight." Delin argued.

Lynnray could judge the power of these magics.

The 'dimension sword' was really horrible, and it must not be so simple as Delin explained. The opponent might not be able to dodge such a one-time attack.

"If I can become a Dragonblood warrior, and with the assistance of wind magic, I will..." Lynnray had an ambitious thought in mind.

As the teacher explained, Lynnray became more and more interested in wind magic. Every type of magic, including earth, fire, water and wind was as deep and vast as an ocean, and Lynnray was involuntarily immersed in this ocean.

Chapter 17 - Life of Learning (I)

As time passed by, Lynnray had spent half a year in Ernst Academy.

During these days, Lynnray was learning basic magic knowledge like a thirsty tourist drinking water in the desert. He increased his strength and understanding in wind magic, and Delin would also advise him now and then.

On a sunny day.

After lunch, the four brothers in Room 1987 were wearing a sky-blue robe given out by the academy as a uniform. Because of long-term practice, Lynnray had special charms in his robe, no wonder several girls in wind series liked chatting with him after class.

At this moment, the four brothers were walking and engaging in casual talks.

"By the way, Lynnray, we'll attend freshman association this afternoon. Will you come with us?" George smiled.

George liked joining public activity, gathering news information and making friends with students. With only half a year, he became a well-known person in grade 1.

"No." Lynnray replied in a straightforward way.

"Haha, I know Lynnray will not join us." Reno laughed. Yale held Lynnray's shoulder and sighed: "You can't practice too hard. With your talent and some effort, you can certainly reach level-6 in 30 years. Why do you practice so hard? You should enjoy life. There are many lovely girls in the association."

"Yes, very lovely." Reno said with wide-open eyes.

Lynnray only had a smile.

Reno was led astray by playboy Yale.

"Yale, don't pull me now, you playboy. I have to practice now. Tomorrow is the end of month, I can play with you tomorrow." Lynnray said with a smile. He gave himself 2 days' holiday at the end of month.

Yale, Reno and George nodded, since they were familiar with Lynnray's schedule.

Lynnray ran to the mountain in the back of the academy. Personnel of Ernst Academy included thousands of students, magicians carrying out tests and researches and many service staff.

He also saw many students in sky-blue robe.

"Howl..." A low roaring came to his ears.

Lynnray looked in the direction of the roaring and saw a monster in amazement.

"A monster!"

The elegant mane, smooth cyan hair, strong feet, fierce look in the eyes and the claws shiny with luster of metal chilled people's heart.

It was a wind wolf, a monster with the speed of wind.

In the Monster Forest, the most horrible thing was to encounter a group of wind wolves. Wind wolves were speedy and it was difficult for humans to escape from their attack. At this moment, a handsome black-hair young man was sitting on the wind wolf. The young man was looking around and seemed complacent to own such a monster.

"Maybe he is a student in grade 5 or 6." Lynnray guessed.

Many people owned monsters in Ernst Academy, including the teachers specially hired by the school and some students in grade 5 and 6. The students had purchased soul contract scrolls and subdued some monsters as their mounts.

"A monster is nothing to be proud of." Lynnray didn't admire the young man at all.

After exiting from the back gate, Lynnray walked into the back mountains.

The back mountains of Ernst Academy were very wide. There were monsters in the mountains a long time ago, but magicians killed all of them. Now there were only some ordinary beasts.

Lynnray moved rapidly after entering the mountains.

With the auxiliary wind magic 'top speed', Lynnray easily passed through the woods and his body was as light as a leaf. After several li, he reached his destination, an open land near a creek.

"Chi Chi..." Beibei squeaked. Lynnray said with a smile: "You want to play again? Fine, but do not get too far away." Lynnray was not worried about Beibei. After one year since their first meeting, the little shadow mouse was still 20 centimeters long, but it became much faster.

"A warrior at level-8 or 9 may be able to catch the shadow mouse, but no magician can catch it, unless he is in the holy domain." Lynnray was well aware of magicians' physical strength.

Beibei swooshed into the woods.

"Grandpa Delin, come out and guide me." Lynnray called Delin in the mind.

A streak of fog came out and turned into Delin, who looked at Lynnray in an amusing way: "What's up today? Aren't you just doing meditation without talking with me? Why do you need me now? I was sleeping in my sweet dreams."

Lynnray curled his mouth.

Delin was a holy magic master, but over long-term contact, Lynnray could feel his innocence covered under amiable attitudes.

"Grandpa Delin, I feel that I'm at level-2 now, can you test me?" Lynnray explained his purpose.

"Level-2 in magic?"

Delin reckoned with interest: "You only practiced for one year and a half with me. Hmm, use beginner magic 'stone crack' and I want to see your limits."

'Stone crack' was an improving magic skill in both level-1 and forbidden field. But in the forbidden field, 'stone crack' was named 'meteorite shower'. With the increase of magic power, the magician could use 'stone crack' in a more powerful way.

"Yes, grandpa Delin."

Lynnray started chanting magic mantras with a familiarity which skipped the thinking process. Along with the chanting, Lynnray's mind entered a special state.

Earth magic force moved at his chest and attracted elements between sky and earth.

Ground beside him suddenly cracked.

Five stones as large as a man's head rose and hovered above his head. The stones were surrounded with earth-yellow light, and with one sudden low shout of Lynnray, they smashed into the distance with a whiz.

"Pum!"

The stones smashed onto a tree as thick as a bowl. The thunk shook but did not break. And then the stones fell on the ground.

"Good job." Delin brightened up his eyes, "Five stones are controlled at the same time with a wonderful flying speed. You are at level-2." Delin was satisfied with Lynnray's performance.

Lynnray also had a smile.

He had drawn nearer to his goal. He recalled his father's words before his departure: "If you cannot seize it back, I will not forgive you till my death." The sentence was like a sword hanging on his heart, and stimulating him to practice diligently.

Delin said with a smile: "But Lynnray, you should know level-2 is nowhere near the real power. Level 1 and 2 are the beginner grade, level 3 and 4 are intermediate, and level-5 and 6 are high grade. A level-7 magician is called 'great magician', level-8 is called 'magic master', and level-9 is called 'great magic master'. Level-7 to 9 are the real power. You still have a long way to go."

"Yes, I know." Lynnray nodded.

"Continue with your practice." Delin re-entered the Ring of Coiling Dragon.

Lynnray calmed down, sat crossed-legged and continued with his practice. A powerful person must have accumulated his strength little by little since childhood.

Two to three li away from Lynnray's location.

Lynnray's wind magic teacher and level-6 magician Trey thought with knitted brows: "Eh, earth magic 'stone crack', seemingly on level-2 based on its power. Who is that beginner magician practicing in the back mountains?"

When Trey was practicing wind magic 'perception through wind', he perceived magic fluctuation two to three li away. He figured out the magic based on its fluctuation. With curiosity, Trey walked in that direction. As a level-6 magician, he used 'top speed' in a much more powerful way than Lynnray and flew lightly through the woods like a streak of fog.

After a short while, Trey appeared a hundred meters from Lynnray.

He observed Lynnray beside a tree.

"It's him!"

Trey certainly knew his student, "This lad does not speak in class, and when other people are trying magic, he stands at a distance and does not show his power... I didn't expect he is already a level-2 magician. As a freshman, he is really talented."

Lynnray certainly knew how to use magic, but when the teacher asked students to try a toss-out, he was just watching.

As known to all, Lynnray was mysterious because he never participated in group activities.

"Oh, I have a talented student. I guess I can get some bonus after grade 1 competition." Trey smiled brilliantly. And Lynnray, in a meditative state, could not feel Trey's presence a hundred meters away.

Chapter 18 - Life of Learning (II)

One month had passed since Lynnray reached level-2.

In grade 1 classroom of wind magic.

Lynnray attended earth magic class once a month, but he didn't miss any class of wind magic. Today, he sat in his old position.

"Hi, Lynnray." A lovely girl took her seat beside Lynnray.

Lynnray looked at the girl and said with a smile: "Delia, you are early. Still a few minutes before class." Lynnray did not decline the pleasure of sitting with a beautiful girl.

But Delia was not an ordinary girl.

Her brother was Dixi, top talent of Ernst Academy rarely seen in a hundred years. He was a dual-series magician and at super grade in affinity with elements. With a spiritual force 68 times of his peers, he was considered a super talent.

Naturally, Delia was not far behind Dixi as her sister.

"I know you come early." Delia smiled with half-open eyes.

Time slipped through fingers during their chat, and class began quickly. The teacher Trey gave his class with passion, and Lynnray was listening to him carefully. Delia peeped at Lynnray now and then.

"OK, now we end today's class, but before we finish, I have something to tell you." Trey said with a smile.

The students conversed with each other in low voices.

"As known by old students, Ernst Academy holds a 'grade competition' in the last 2 months of a year. The grade competition is the most lively period in our school, and if you win in the competition, you will easily be rated as excellent students at graduation. By then, maybe even the four empires will invite you to join them."

Trey smiled.

The students were filled with excitement right away.

Ernst Academy was a gathering place of talents, and talents liked proving their strength.

Therefore, the grade competition every year became the opportunity for them to gain fame. Almost ninety percent of students would stay in tune with the grade competition, and if they have some power, they would certainly like to join.

"Wind magic students will certainly participate. Tell me if you'd like to join." Trey said with a smile, but he turned his look to Lynnray.

"I'd like to join." Many students started to apply.

"Good." Trey took out paper and feather pen to record their names. But after recording a dozen students, he found Lynnray was still chatting with Delia and showed no intention to apply.

Trey walked down the platform.

Lynnray saw him approaching and called him politely: "Mr. Trey." Delia also offered her respect.

Trey nodded with a smile: "Lynnray, the coming grade competition is a good opportunity to exercise yourself. I believe all elites in grade 1 will join. You don't want to miss this good opportunity, right?"

"I'm not interested." Lynnray said directly.

"Well, winners in the competition are rewarded." Trey tried to persuade him.

"Reward?" Lynnray was in need of money.

His family was not in a good financial condition. If he could get some monetary reward, there was no problem for him to join.

"Yes, as you may now, most students live in ordinary dormitories -- the single houses. But the top 3 students in grade competition can live one year in a two-story apartment building. It is a sign of identity, and provides much more comfort." Trey continued.

Lynnray realized the fact.

There weren't many two-story buildings in the dormitory area, and most of them were occupied by level-7 and level-8 magicians. Now he knew the top 3 in six grades were also qualified to live for one year.

Boarding conditions?

Lynnray did not care about it at all.

"I'm not joining." Lynnray insisted. Trey was a bit anxious. As a grade 6 student, if his students could reach top 3, he would be rewarded himself, and good reputation came with the reward. Young people liked good reputation.

Trey got closer to Lynnray and whispered: "Lynnray, are you afraid of revealing your power? I now you have reached level-2."

Lynnray looked up at Trey in surprise.

How did Mr. Trey know his power? It was very difficult to judge one's power based on his appearance.

Upon seeing Lynnray's expression, Trey knew he had learned the truth, so he said with a smile: "Lynnray, you don't need to hide your power. Even if you don't join the competition, I may reveal your secret to others, too."

"Anyway, I'm not joining."

Lynnray stood up casually and offered his respcct: "Bye, teacher."

Then he left directly in Trey's perplexed look.

"Hey, this lad." Trey suddenly realized something and laughed. At this moment, Delia was giggling while covering her mouth.

It was past 6 o'clock in the evening after wind magic class. The day was reaching its close, so Lynnray ran to his dormitory. The four brothers in Room 1987 were in good relationship with each other, and they usually dined together at night.

"Hi, Lynnray." A juvenile with curly hair in Room 1986 warmly greeted Lynnray.

"Harry, did you have dinner?" Lynnray asked with a smile. Lynnray was in good terms with students in the neighboring yards. Harry nodded: "Sure, your three brothers are waiting for you."

"Lynnray is back. Let's go and have dinner." It was Yale's voice.

Obviously, Yale heard Lynnray's voice in the yard, and Reno and George followed and greeted Lynnray. Then they headed for the restaurant. There were luxury hotels inside Ernst Academy, but Yale was persuaded by Lynnray and George out of the habit of going to large hotels.

Small restaurants were cheap and offered delicious meals.

After ordering some dishes, they started chatting again.

Lynnray could learn of news of activities in the school from his three brothers. Since he often practiced in the back mountains, he had no chance to be informed of school information.

"The first year will end in more than a month. A grade competition will take place in the last 2 months. I heard the top 3 of the grade can live one year in the two-story apartment building." Yale mentioned the competition in the first place.

"Grade competition?" Lynnray smiled, because he just knew the information in classroom.

"Haha, I will surely join." Reno said confidently.

Yale curled his mouth and said: "Bro, you have become a level-1 magician on the way from O'Brien Empire to Ernst Academy. By now, you are not far from level-2, I guess. It's unfair."

Reno took a year to travel from home to the academy.

On the carriage, Reno learned magic from the steward and reached level-1.

George looked at Lynnray with a smile: "Don't forget Lynnray. He was level-1 at enrollment. And he is practicing very diligently in dual series. I think he is the most powerful among us."

Lynnray grinned: "George, I'm not that good."

"Lynnray, have you reached level-2? Tell me the truth." George stared at Lynnray.

"How can it be so fast? With our talent, we only need 1 year to progress from a beginner to level-1, but we need at least 2 years to move up further to level-2." Reno said with a twitched nose.

"Not necessarily. Lynnray was hiding his power." Yale looked at Lynnray and asked, "Lynnray, have you reached level-2?"

Lynnray nodded casually.

Reaching level-2 was not surprising for Lynnray. He was already at level-1 in the magic test, and an attainment to level-2 was worthy of one year's arduous practice.

"You really reached level-2?" Yale, Reno and George stared ahead in surprise.

"Join the grade competition. You must join and defeat others on behalf of Room 1987." Yale said right away.

The waiter served the dishes at this moment.

"Let's have dinner. I'm not interested in the grade competition." Lynnray didn't want to compete with weak people. In his eyes, the grade competition was only a show-off.

The other three looked at each other in surprise.

They knew Lynnray was practicing diligently. There were talents in grade 1 who were at super grade in affinity with elements and spiritual force, but they were less diligent than Lynnray. Besides, Lynnray was talented in two series of magics... So they believed Lynnray was the most powerful in grade 1.

"It's a pity you are not joining. Somebody else will become famous then." Yale curled his mouth, "I'm not as powerful as you, otherwise I will show off myself, and by the way, I may get some girls."

Lynnray smiled: "Let's eat. Don't think too much."

Lynnray did not care about the grade competition at all. But most people were enthusiastic about it. Even some professional magicians of Ernst Academy kept themselves updated on the competition.

Chapter 19 - The Number One (I)

The back mountains of Ernst Academy were in tranquility.

Lynnray sat cross-legged beside the creek, and while listening to the murmuring of water, he entered a meditative state in which the earth elements, wind elements and everything in a dozen meters were clearer than ever.

The elements entered his body from limbs and torso and nurtured his muscles, bones and organs. Lynnray's physical fitness was improving in a slow but steady speed.

Many elements were refined and concentrated at middle Dantian in the center of chest.

The gurgling of water was heard at every moment.

The little shadow mouse Beibei was biting a prairie chicken in a picturesque setting.

Tranquility in the back mountains was in sharp contrast with the lively atmosphere in Ernst Academy. Thousands of students and many magic teachers of the academy were watching the challenge. The audience also included many great personalities outside of the academy.

It was the grade competition.

All students of Ernst Academy were carefully chosen. The games were spectacular. In grade 1, there were exchanges of fire balls, lightning and wind swords. And in grade 3 and 4, the audience could see auxiliary magics and scale-attack magics such as 'stone crack', in which dozens or a hundred large stones fell with lightning striking one after another.

Games in grade 5 and 6 were astonishing.

Dazzling magics came onto stage with continuous sounds of explosion. The audience shouted and applauded loudly in a very active atmosphere. Most people in the academy gathered at the site.

……

The grade competition lasted one month, which was the most lively and crazy time of Ernst Academy. During the period, Lynnray only watched the part in grade 5 and 6. Most of the times he was only practicing all by himself.

"And it requires participants avoid incidents of death. How can it be called a competition with so many restrictions?"

Lynnray was influenced by Delin's opinion and looked at the competition with contempt.

"Lynnray, you task at present is to cultivate power. When you reach level-5, you can gain experience of real fight in the edge of Monster Mountains." Delin persuaded Lynnray.

Watery Hotel was the most luxurious hotel inside Ernst Academy. It was Yale's treat today, and the four brothers of Room 1987 dined together in this hotel.

On the first floor of Watery Hotel.

Several pretty waitresses were standing by on the shiny floor.

Many customers in Watery Hotel were wearing student uniforms and were financially abundant. Even an ordinary meal in the hotel would cost dozens of gold coins, which were beyond Lynnray's capacity to afford.

The grade competition just ended, and many students were talking about it. Most of them were young men, and Lynnray and his brothers were the only children there.

"Bad luck this time. I was nearly in the semi-final. Maybe I could have risen to top 3." Reno said with discontent. He was the smallest in four, but the most self-confident.

Yale smiled: "It's really a pity. The guy named Rand ended up the first."

George smiled without making a comment.

He did not want to offend anybody.

"Rand? I heard he is the one in our group of enrollment who is at super grade in affinity with elements and spiritual force." Lynnray recalled the name.

George smiled: "Yes, that's him. His spiritual force reached the requirement of level-2 even before he practiced anything. He was only accumulating magic force in this year. It's not difficult for a level-2 magician to achieve top position in the competition of grade 1."

"Talent is not something to boast of. Besides, he is not as talented as Dixi." Yale curled his mouth and continued, "I don't like that guy. Lynnray, you didn't see his complacence after getting to the top position. I don't know what will happen if he gets the first in grade 5 or 6."

Practice would be more difficult as the magician moved up the ladder.

Therefore, among thousands of students in Ernst Academy, most were at high grade. Competition would get more fierce at high grade.

Reno also nodded: "I don't like him, either. Just compare him with our first talent Dixi at grade 3, who also won the competition. They had a huge difference. Besides, our number one is not Rand."

"Yes, bro, you didn't participate, otherwise you'll be number one." Yale grunted.

Yale, George, Lynnray and Reno intimately called each other bro, as if they were real brothers.

"Hi, what are you talking about?"

The four brothers saw another group of four walking downstairs from the second floor of Watery Hotel, and the heading golden-hair juvenile looked at Lynnray and his brothers indifferently.

Yale said casually: "Oh, it's Rand. Didn't you hear what we said?"

Lynnray laughed sarcastically in his heart.

Yale was brave and cared much about his reputation.

"Hum, don't think I didn't hear." Rand said coldly.

The brown-hair juvenile beside Rand also sneered and said in an arrogant voice: "Rand, don't argue with the four idiots. They are not worth your attention. Reno, why are you looking at us? You don't admit your failure in the competition?"

Reno stared at the brown-hair juvenile and said with contempt: "What are you, man? You won me by luck. There's nothing to be proud of."

The brown-hair juvenile put on a cold look.

George smiled: "Rand, it's OK. We are wrong by judging you. Let's forgive each other."

"Shut up, George, you are not in a position to speak here." Rand stared at Yale, "Yale, I was not happy with your arrogant attitude in Elm Bar, but you are arrogant toward me again. Why dare not you compete with me on the arena?"

Rand laughed complacently.

Yale was a bit angry, but he was indeed weaker than Rand.

At this moment, other people in the hotel turned their attention to the two groups of juveniles. Many students at high grade stood up and looked at them with interest. The children of both groups were about 10 years old.

"I know the golden-hair lad. His name is Rand, first in grade 1 competition. He'll achieve big in future."

"The brown-hair lad is named Raisen, the third in competition grade 1. It seems they are a stronger group than the other. Their argument is interesting."

The magic students at grade 5 and 6 were chatting and watching both groups.

Rand was proud to hear others commenting on his wonderful performance on the arena, and he looked at Lynnray's group with more contempt.

"Yo." Rand glanced at the table of the four brothers, "Fruit juice? You are drinking fruit juice? Oh, Yale, I'm ashamed for you. We are drinking Kelver, but you are still drinking fruit juice."

Lynnray frowned at Rand's challenge.

"Rand, we are having our meal. Piss off." Lynnray said gravely and stared at the four. If he was practicing and some beast disturbed his practice, he would kill the beast directly.

"Oh, here's another one." Rand stared at Lynnray and said: "I never know there is such a person in Yale's room."

Lynnray turned cold in his look.

He rushed out like a crafty rabbit, and Rand opened his eyes widely in surprise, "You..." Before Rand took any reaction, Lynnray grasped his neck and raised him up on one arm.

"Ah, Ah..." Rand could not make a sound, and his eyes were filled with horror.

Lynnray stared at Rand coldly, and Rand felt he might be killed at every moment.

Once again, Lynnray had a bloodthirsty feeling due to the Dragonblood warrior's blood in his body. But he frowned and persuaded himself: "Here is Ernst Academy. I can't kill anyone for no reason."

The three beside Rand were also petrified.

"Piss off."

Lynnray waved his arm and threw Rand onto ground like a sandbag.

Chapter 20 - The Number One (II)

Lynnray was near level-2 as a warrior, and generally, a level-1 warrior was strong enough to raise an object of 100 jin, and a level-2 warrior could wave such an object easily.

"You, kof, kof..." Rand had several coughs and stared at Lynnray in anger: "You..."

"Good." Yale said loudly with excitement: "Good job, bro. I didn't know you have so much physical strength."

"The lad's strength is too much for his size."

The magicians at level-5 and 6, and some magic teachers in the hotel looked at Lynnray in surprise.

A juvenile about 11 years old raised a person of 80 to 90 jin.

And he was a magician!

"Hi, Rand, didn't you say you were the number one in grade 1?" Yale sneered at him.

Rand blushed with anger and shouted at Lynnray: "Are you a magician? If you are good enough, you should fight with magic. A noble magician does not use the means of a vulgar warrior." Rand was full of shame and anger. He just won the first in the grade competition, but when Lynnray held him at the throat, he was horrified to have his life at Lynnray's disposal. "Yes, you should fight with magic. Are you a student in Ernst Academy?" Raisen and others beside Rand shouted.

But the four were also afraid of Lynnray's strength, which they witnessed with their eyes.

"Magic?"

Reno laughed at this time: "Rand, do you think you are the strongest as the number one? You are daydreaming. Our brother is the real number one in the grade."

"Lynnray, show your power to them." Yale said.

George had been rebuked by Rand just now, so he stopped playing a mediator: "Rand, don't overestimate yourself. Many powerful magicians are not interested in the grade competition. Don't think too high of yourself."

Rand turned even paler in his look.

"Let's try and see. Rand, compete with them." The young men in grade 5 and 6 laughed. The fight among grade 1 students was an interesting event after all.

Rand was only 10 years old, but he considered himself a talent since childhood.

As one of the topmost talents in Ernst Academy, he had never been so humiliated before.

"Number one?" Rand gritted his teeth, "The number one is not in words, but in competition. If you are really good, you should fight with me only by using magic." Rand was confident with his magic power. He won the first in grade competition after all.

"Why don't the hotel management stop them?" The onlookers found it weird, because the management staff of Watery Hotel were standing at a distance and not interfering.

Because they recognized the students.

Not to mention their identity as students of Ernst Academy, they had their individual backgrounds, especially... Yale.

"Young master Yale is here. Just let them do whatever they want. I have nothing to do with their mischief." The management staff shook their head helplessly, because they dare not offend Yale.

Especially, after entering Ernst Academy, Yale had a great raise of status in his family.

"Yes, number one is not in words, but in competition." Lynnray also stood up and looked at Rand coldly.

"Rand, our magic competition should involve a bet. If you win, I will offer my respect to you in future, otherwise you'll offer respect to me."

Rand said coldly: "The bet is too small. I think the loser should offer respect to the winner along with 100 gold coins."

Lynnray knitted his brows.

A hundred gold coins?

His living expense was 100 gold coins a year, and he was not rich.

"Haha, Rand, 100 gold coins are too cheap. Let's say, how about 10,000 gold coins?" Yale said complacently.

"10,000 gold coins?"

Many students in the hotel gasped at the amount. That was a big sum of money. The number of students in the hotel who could take out 10,000 gold coins could be counted on fingers.

"10,000 gold coins?" Rand shivered in the heart.

His family was a big one, but only gave him 3,000 gold coins a year as living expense. And he was not eating in Watery Hotel every day. Today, he was here to celebrate his and Raisen's winning as the first and third in grade competition.

"You dare not make the bet?" Yale took out his Magic Crystal Card and played it in a catch-and-throw motion.

"Rand, say yes to him." Raisen said, "The four of us can afford 10,000 gold coins. I don't think this unknown guy can defeat you."

Rand and his three brothers looked at each other.

"Fine, 10,000 gold coins!"

Rand said aloud, and then sneered at Lynnray: "This place is too small. Let's fight on the arena of grade competition, if you dare." After saying these words, Rand strode out of the hotel with his three brothers.

"Let's go, too." Yale had light in his eyes.

Reno and George were also excited. Lynnray nodded and had a faint smile: "They are giving us 10,000 gold coins. How can we not receive it?"

The four brothers exited the hotel.

People in the hotel started their lively discussion. A competition involving a bet of 10,000 gold coins was rarely seen among even level-6 students. Besides, the competition had two special parties: one was Rand, the winner of grade competition, and the other was an unknown lad.

So the people paid their bills and followed to the outside.

The arena was made of green rock and was tough enough.

Lynnray and Rand were standing on both sides of the arena.

A large group of people gathered below the arena. The competition was spread mouth-to-mouth during dinner and attracted a large audience. The amount of bet was also their point of attention.

Rand was proud to see so many people gathering and watching their fight.

"Today, I'm in a magic competition with this guy named Lynnray. The loser shall provide 10,000 gold coins and offer his respect to the winner. I request everybody to witness." Rand said with a clear voice. He was not afraid to speak in public.

The crowd applauded. After the grade competition, Rand also won many supporters, but few people were supporting Lynnray.

And Lynnray was standing calmly at one side of the arena.

"Have you spoken enough?" Lynnray asked with composure.

Rand smiled confidently: "OK, let's start."

Rand and Lynnray started chanting magic mantras almost at the same time. Both of them were level-2 magicians, and the mantras at level-1 and 2 were relatively simple, including only one and two sentences.

"Hu!"

Seven cyan-color wind swords formed in the air and cut toward Rand.

"Level-2?" Some experienced onlookers figured out Lynnray's level.

Rand also tossed out his magic. Five red fire balls were shot at Lynnray. Wind swords were faster than fire balls, and Rand dodged in an embarrassing gesture -- rolling on the ground. However, Lynnray dodged the fire balls in graceful wide steps. And during his movement, he chanted a mantra and tossed out his second magic.

Earth magic -- 'earth shaking'!

With a buzz, the cyan stones under Rand's feet were fluctuating like waves, which disrupted his mantra chanting. Then Lynnray used another magic when five stones as large as a human's head and surrounded by earth-yellow light were thrown at Rand.

Rand could not stand stably on the shaking ground, and he dodged two stone attacks with difficulty.

"Pum!"

Rand spit blood when a stone hit his belly. He covered his head with his arms. After two hits, Rand rolled off the arena with dust all over his body.

Lynnray won in the fight.

Lynnray glanced at Rand over the arena. He had paid attention to the severity of attack. Rand would recover after one month's rest. If he attacked Rand's head with stones, Rand would be dead already.

"Level-2 and dual-series. I don't know there is such a master in grade 1."

Some grade 1 students off the arena shouted. Even one level-2 magician was rarely seen in grade 1. But Lynnray was level-2 and dual-series. He was definitely a master in grade 1.

"This guy has wonderful control and agile movements."

Some students at grade 5 and 6 were surprised, because when Lynnray was attacked by fire balls, he would dodge and chant a mantra at the same time. He was indeed agile and speedy in movements.

"Haha, Rand, do you really think you are the number one? My bro has defeated you easily with magic." Yale laughed.

"Kof, kof." Rand stood up and put his hand on his chest.

He knew Lynnray showed mercy in the fight.

"Yale, bring Lynnray to Union Bank of Empires tomorrow and I'll transfer him 10,000 gold coins. I'm true to my word." Rand looked at Lynnray deeply. He was awakened from the good feeling about his talent.

A talented person would still be defeated if he did not make effort.

"Thank you, Lynnray." Rand took a bow, which surprised Yale, and then stared at Lynnray: "I'll defeat you one day."

Then he pressed on his chest and headed for the dormitory with the help of his brothers.

"Lynnray, you did great. I'm proud of you." Reno gave Lynnray an embrace when Lynnray stepped down the arena.

Lynnray looked around.

Many people were talking about Lynnray. There were well-known elites in Ernst Academy, but no one expected a person in grade 1 could easily defeat Rand, the number one in grade competition.

"Hello Lynnray, I'm Danny, grade one in water magic. Glad to meet you." A tall golden-hair girl came forward and smiled to Lynnray.

"Hi, I'm Lynnray." Lynnray was not accustomed to talking with strangers, so he took leave: "Sorry, I'll practice meditation."

Then he cast a glance at his three brothers, who understood his point and left with him. Only the girl Danny was frowning with discontent.

Chapter 21 - Brooks Guild Hall (I)

Union Bank of Empires was a bank jointly founded by the four empires on Yulan Continent. The Magic Crystal Card of the bank was only owned by rich people. Besides, ordinary people were unwilling to obtain a card by paying a service fee of 100 gold coins.

10,000 gold coins were placed in 100 small cloth bags, or they would require nearly half of the volume of a home-used rice bag. They had a large total weight.

"I threw away 100 gold coins." Lynnray went out of the Union Bank of Empires and made a sigh. But he got a new Magic Crystal Card.

He knew that placing a pile of gold coins in the dormitory was unsafe. So he deposited them into the Magic Crystal Card.

The Magic Crystal Card was costly in its make. As the result of research of alchemists hundreds of years ago, it identified a person based on his palm print and could be used only by its owner.

That was why obtainment of such a card required 100 gold coins.

"With 10,000 gold coins, I have sufficient funds for my living and a lot of savings. And I can help my father a bit." Lynnray thought gladly.

Yale held Lynnray's shoulder, whistled and looked at Rand and his group proudly. The group of Rand took out their living expense, and maybe they only had less than 1,000 gold coins left. Fortunately the school year was coming to an end.

Reno and George were chatting and joking with Lynnray.

In fact, neither Reno nor George suffered much hardship.

"Brothers, tomorrow is the end of month. My father's people will come tomorrow. I guess I can arrange some carriages and guards and let's look around in the holy capital." Yale made a proposal.

"The holy capital?"

Reno, George and Lynnray showed light in their eyes.

The holy capital Fenlai City was much more prosperous than ordinary cities.

"Good idea. I only stayed 2 days in Fenlai City after the long journey from O'Brien Empire to Ernst Academy. I had no chance to make a visit." Reno said eagerly.

George and Lynnray nodded.

"The holy capital has a lot of good places. We'll have an eye-dazzling trip tomorrow." Yale said in a mysterious tone.

On the morning of the next day, the four had breakfast and went to the front gate of Ernst Academy, where they would wait for the carriage team of Yale's father.

But even after 2 hours, they did not see the arrival of a carriage team.

"Chi Chi..." Beibei squeaked on Lynnray's shoulder.

"Beibei is more anxious than us. Yale, you took us here in the early morning, but there is still no sign of your carriage team." Reno said with discontent, and Yale smiled regretfully: "I don't know. They should arrive now." Lynnray patted on Beibei's head at this time.

"They arrived." Yale shouted.

Reno, George and Lynnray, who almost fell asleep, looked in the distance and saw four carriages and hundreds of guarding riders. Seven or eight griffins were flying over the team. The mounts of the riders included monsters, bloody bulls and wind wolves.

"The team is fancy." Lynnray sighed with emotion, and Reno and George also showed light in their look.

Delin was sitting beside Lynnray and enjoying the sunshine. His eyes were also brightened by the sight of the team. After a short while, four carriages and hundreds of riders arrived at the gate, and three magicians of the academy came out to welcome them.

A middle-aged man got off the carriage in the front. He overlooked the three magicians and came directly to Yale.

"Uncle, why are you so late?" Yale said with discontent.

Yale's 'uncle' smiled: "Take it easy. I have prepared your carriage. The last one in the team has some cargoes, which I'll ask them to unload. You can head for the holy capital directly."

"Cass, protect the young master with another three people." The uncle commanded.

A bald-headed rider got off his horse and offered his respect to Yale, "I'm Cass, pleased to meet you."

Delin showed light in his eyes and said to Lynnray: "Lynnray, your brother Yale is not ordinary. Judging from Cass' walking gesture and look, he is much more powerful than your uncle Hilman. He's a master. And the eagle on his shoulder is a level-7 monster -- 'green-eye thunder eagle'."

Delin regarded Cass as a master. Cass definitely had unusual power.

"Lynnray, get on the carriage. We'll head for the holy capital." Yale called out.

Lynnray and his three brothers entered the carriage. The carriage was spacious, and the four did not feel packed at all. Then the driver led the carriage in the direction of Fenlai City.

Cass and other three guiding riders advanced by the side of the carriage.

In the cabinet of the carriage were various fruits and sealed wine. The four brothers ate and chatted casually all the way. In only half an hour, the carriage completed the trip of only 20 li from Ernst Academy to Fenlai City.

The four brothers got off the carriage and toured the city with the protection of four guards including Cass.

"Hey, where are we going now? There are many interesting places in Fenlai City. In the eastern part are places of luxury purchase, and we can see many beautiful maidens. In the western part are many art galleries such as the well-known Brooks Guild Hall." Yale was very familiar with Fenlai City. "Beautiful maidens? So let's go to the eastern part." Reno said with shiny eyes.

"It's in the morning. Those places are only interesting at night. But sure, we can go there now." Yale said with a smile.

Lynnray didn't like those kind of places, so he said: "No, we are still children. You just mentioned Brooks Guild Hall, which is named after the master Brooks. It should be great. Why not have a look?"

Brooks was the number one stone sculptor on Yulan Continent.

"I heard about Brooks, too. One piece of his work, seemingly named 'Hope', was sold at millions of gold coins. That was a great sum of money." Reno sighed with emotion.

George smiled with confidence: "Countless stone sculptures were circulated around the world since the prehistorical age. Each of the top 10 was priced at millions of gold coins. And among the top 10 pieces, Brooks had three. He is worthy of the title number one."

Lynnray gasped in astonishment.

Millions of gold coins?

It was huge. Suppose his family sold their ancestral house, they could only get 100,000 gold coins.

"Let's go and see." Lynnray said right away.

Chapter 22 - Brooks Guild Hall (II)

Brooks Guild Hall.

As the number one guild hall of stone sculpting, Brooks Guild Hall had branches in several large cities on Yulan Continent. The guild hall occupied a large area, and visitors were people who considered themselves as well nourished in art.

If you wore several magic rings at hand, people might look down upon you, because you were not artistic at all.

This is the place where artistic understanding was valued.

Ticket price was one gold coin per visitor.

Music of landscape genre came out from the guild hall and pacified one's mind. Many visitors were walking into the guild hall, including noble men and women and beautiful girls. All of them were classy in their wearing.

Ordinary civilians would feel inferior at the Brooks Guild Hall.

The four brothers and four guards came directly to the square in front of Brooks Guild Hall. Anyone with a bit knowledge would be respectful upon seeing the school uniform of the four brothers and the green-eye thunder eagle on the shoulder of Cass.

"Uncle Cass, please follow us inside, and you three, please wait outside." Yale requested them. The four brothers and Cass walked into the guild hall. They saw a tall human-figure sculpture in the center, which represented the number one master in stone sculpting -- Master Brooks.

The entire Brooks Guild Hall was in silence.

All the visitors, regardless of their social status, were avoiding disturbance to others.

Yale, Reno, George and Lynnray could feel the beauty and art contained in the stone works.

"The exhibition hall of Brooks Guild Hall is divided into three parts -- the ordinary, senior and master. Amateur sculptors send their works to the ordinary hall to be priced. After one month's exhibition, their works are sold at the highest bidding price. Ordinary works are worth only several gold coins, and some excellent ones are worth dozens of gold coins."

Yale introduced with a smile: "The senior hall is different. It is divided into separate exhibition rooms, and in each exhibition room are the works of one senior sculptor. They are called senior because their skills have been recognized. Senior works are generally worth 1,000 gold coins."

"The master hall is located at the most inside and displays the works of masters, who are only a few in number. A random piece may cost tens of thousands of gold coins, and some famous works may cost hundreds of thousands." Yale introduced to his three brothers in more detail.

Lynnray held his breath upon hearing these words. Any random work of a master was worth tens of thousands of gold coins. Masters in stone sculpting were not short of money.

"But masters hardly produce one piece, because they do not want to leave stains in their career." Yale said with emotion: "A classic work requires wonderful skill, talent and inspiration."

"Works in the ordinary hall only had good looks. Let's go ahead." Yale was guiding the tour.

While walking in the spacious and tranquil guild hall and listening to peaceful music, Lynnray was immersed in the ocean of art. At this moment, Delin came out of the Ring of Coiling Dragon and appreciated the stone sculptures around.

"Poor work. Why do they make a show with these?" Delin said with discontent.

"Grandpa Delin." Lynnray looked at Delin, "This is the ordinary hall of Brooks Guild Hall, and ahead of us are the senior hall and master hall."

"Brooks Guild Hall?" Delin was a bit surprised and fell silent.

"Grandpa Delin? Grandpa Delin?" Lynnray called Delin, but Delin was still absorbed in thoughts. Lynnray followed Yale, Reno and George to the senior hall. Details of every senior sculptor and locations of their independent display room were shown in the senior hall.

The brothers went into the display rooms.

Although Lynnray did not know much about stone sculpting, he could easily feel that the works of senior sculptors carried a special temperament, which was not seen in ordinary works. When Lynnray was appreciating the senior works, Delin's voice came into his mind.

"Good, they are at entry-level." Delin praised, "But they are still far behind Brooks."

Lynnray became speechless.

"Grandpa Delin, how could they be compared with master Brooks?" Lynnray shook his head and smiled bitterly. Anyway, Brooks was the number one in stone sculpting throughout history.

Delin frowned and said with raised beard: "Why? Brooks was not born a master. He grew from an ordinary sculptor and became a master in the end."

Lynnray was a bit surprised.

But Delin's words made sense.

After visiting the independent display rooms, they headed for the master hall most inside.

"Remember not to touch anything in the master hall. It'll be terrible if you broke one." Yale reminded them.

The master hall was in profound tranquility.

There were only a small number of works in the spacious master hall. Number of masters could be counted on fingers, and each of them had four or five pieces. The hall had only 20 to 30 pieces of work in total.

The works were few, but carried a sense of liveliness as if they were alive. "They are good. I didn't expect the art of stone sculpting has developed so far in 5,000 years." Delin sighed with emotion: "If they make some more progress, their works can be compared with Brooks'"

The four brothers were spiritually nourished in the hall of art.

In the evening, Lynnray and his brothers got off the carriage at the gate of Ernst Academy.

"George and Lynnray, I said we should enjoy ourselves in Fenlai City tonight, but you... You are shy. I was playing in such places since six." Yale said with a bit discontent.

"That's true." Reno agreed with him.

George and Lynnray looked at each other and smiled.

"Open the gate, quick!" An anxious voice was heard.

Lynnray looked at one side and saw a young man with curly hair holding another young man who was bleeding. A pretty girl was standing beside them. The bleeding young man looked pale. His left arm had broken with exposed bone, and there were several claw marks on his chest.

"He must be injured in a trial in the Monster Forest. How many groups of students have gone there so far? We saw so many high-grade students injured in their trials within one year." Yale said casually.

Monster Mountains were located on the east of Holy Alliance.

In fact, Monster Mountains were very near Ernst Academy with a distance of only 100 li. A physically strong person may take only half a day to get there.

"I have seen many monsters in the academy, including the flying, running, and all kinds of them. But the owners are mostly magic teachers, and some of them are high-grade students." George sighed with emotion.

When the four reached the gate of academy, Lynnray heard a familiar voice: "Lynnray."

He turned his head and saw the arrival of uncle Hilman. So he addressed Hilman pleasantly: "Uncle Hilman."

Chapter 23 – A Pleasant Surprise

Hilman was waiting at a corner near the gate. He walked toward Lynnray with a smile: "Ernst Academy is strict in management. They don't allow me to get in, so I sent a guard to find you inside, but you came from the outside."

"Yale, you can go back to the dormitory. I'll be back soon." Lynnray turned his head and said to his brothers.

Yale, George and Reno smiled at Hilman and entered the academy.

"Uncle Hilman, why are you coming? I thought you will come in the end of school year." Lynnray asked in surprise.

"Let's talk over there." Hilman pulled Lynnray to one side and said with a pleasant expression: "Lynnray, I want to tell you about a happy event."

Lynnray brightened his eyes.

"What happy event?" Lynnray asked eagerly.

Hilman said with a smile: "Do you know little Warton's birthday?"

"Yes, January 3, what's the matter?" Lynnray was in doubt.

Hilman smiled: "It's December now. Warton is about 6 years old. Last night your father tested his density of Dragonblood warrior's blood in the ancestral temple. Haha..." Hilman started laughing.

Lynnray felt the rapid beating of his heart.

So the result of blood density test was...

Lynnray asked: "Has his blood density reached the required level?"

Hilman nodded: "Yes, and your father was very excited. He drank with me until midnight. He said he is proud of both of you. One is a great magician and the other is a Dragonblood warrior. Haha..."

"That's great."

Lynnray was very glad to hear the news.

As a member of a Dragonblood family of 5,000 years' history, Lynnray had a heavy responsibility on his shoulder before Warton's test came out as having the potential to become a Dragonblood warrior. His responsibility was the result of the past honor of his family.

But today...

He knew his brother could become a powerful Dragonblood warrior with only decades of arduous practice.

"I came to tell you the good news. And your father said the strongest fighters in Wushan Town are only him and me. We are only level-6 warriors. We cannot teach your brother with our experience, and your family records are only armchair strategies." Hilman said gravely, "So your father decided to send your brother to O'Brien Academy in O'Brien Empire. He will receive the best education in the topmost warrior school and the most powerful military empire."

Lynnray agreed with the decision. If one had only force but no skills or experience, he was no more than a gorilla.

"Oh, no." Lynnray frowned and looked at Hilman, "O'Brien Academy provides free education for locals, but charges a high cost on foreign students." Lynnray recalled the high tuition of Ernst Academy charged on Reno.

Hilman nodded: "One year's tuition of O'Brien Academy is 5,000 gold coins. You father decided to send Hilly with Warton to take care of him. 10 years' tuition would be 50,000 gold coins."

The expense of 50,000 gold coins would force Baruch family to sell everything in the house.

"By the way, uncle Hilman."

Hilman looked at Lynnray in doubt, and saw him taking out a Magic Crystal Card from the pocket. Hilman exclaimed with surprise: "Magic Crystal Card?" Hilman had seen Magic Crystal Card when he had served as a captain in the military.

"Lynnray, how did you get a Magic Crystal Card? Even your father doesn't have one." Hilman looked at Lynnray in surprise.

Lynnray pulled Hilman and said: "A wealthy young master lost a lot of money to me in a magic competition. Let's go to the Union Bank of Empires." The guards of Ernst Academy didn't prevent Hilman, because they recognized Lynnray, who went out in the morning.

Lynnray planned to use the gold coins to help his family.

......

In the living room of Baruch mansion, Wushan Town.

Hogg was absorbed in thought.

He had a son whose density of Dragonblood warrior's blood reached the required level, so he must educate his son to the best of his financial ability.

"To whom can I sell the stone screen in bedroom? The miser Philip cannot pay a high price." Hogg kept thinking. The cost would be tremendous if they sent Warton to O'Brien Academy. He was thinking about how to sell some items of family at a high price.

Footsteps came suddenly.

Hogg raised his head and said: "Hilman, you are back. What are you carrying on the shoulder?"

Hilman threw the bag onto ground with a deep sound of clash, which indicated the heavy weight of the bag.

"Mr. Hogg, Lynnray asked me to bring this back." Hilman untied the bag and poured out its content. Many small yellow bags of coins were piled together, producing a clear tinkling sound.

The small yellow bags were specially used by Union Bank of Empires to contain gold coins. One bag had 100 gold coins in it.

"So many gold coins? Maybe 10,000?" Hogg looked at Hilman in surprise, "You said Lynnray asked you to bring them?"

Hilman said solemnly: "9,900 gold coins in total. Lynnray asked me to bring them to you. A wealthy lad had a magic competition with Lynnray and lost to him 10,000 gold coins. Lynnray deposited all of them into his Magic Crystal Card. He withdrew all of them from his account."

Hilman could still remember Lynnray's request to the bank staff: "Take all coins out!"

"9,000 gold coins? Lynnray had them?"

Hogg looked at the bags in front of him and fell silent.

Chapter 24 – The Flat Knife School

In Ernst Academy, several days later.

Lynnray had his breakfast and went to back mountains to practice.

When Lynnray walked on a path in the school, the shadow mouse was standing on Lynnray's shoulder and looking around. Quite a few people in Ernst Academy owned a monster, so Lynnray was not eye-catching with his shadow mouse. At this moment...

"That's Lynnray, our number one magician in grade 1." A clear voice came from ahead.

Lynnray looked in the direction of the voice and saw two lovely girls chatting with each other quietly and looking at himself occasionally. When Lynnray looked at them, they laughed and covered their mouths.

"So I'm famous, huh." Lynnray laughed at himself.

He often heard people talking about him these days. Since he defeated Rand, the number one in grade competition, he was considered the real number one.

"Ah, who's that?" Lynnray saw a thin figure in the distance.

The child had golden short hair and was as thin as Reno. He looked cold overall and walked on the path with a cold expression.

"Dixi?" Lynnray squinted.

Dixi was nine years old, and one month younger than Lynnray. Despite his age, he was already a level-3 magician. For a magician, practice would be more and more difficult as he moved up. A nine-year-old magician at level-3 was very rare.

"He's Dixi. According to the yearly test result yesterday, he is already at level-4." Some girls about 17 years old talked about Dixi.

Most people at grade 3 were above 16 years old, but Dixi was a super talent.

"Level-4 magician!"

Lynnray felt twitching in the heart. Both of them were nine years old, and Dixi was one month younger than him. But Dixi was at level-4, while he was at level-2.

Dixi walked past Lynnray with a cold expression.

As a super talent, Dixi was unique among his peers.

As a light ray came out of Ring of Coiling Dragon, Delin smiled beside Lynnray: "You don't have much difference, actually. When Dixi was enrolled, his spiritual force was 68 times of his peers. It means his spiritual force was at level-3 even before his practice. Therefore, he only needed to strengthen his magic force to reach level-3 in the first year of study. He has been in school for 2 years, so it's natural that he reached level-4."

Lynnray understood the point. Dixi was very talented with a strong spiritual force. Besides, his affinity with elements was at super grade. He could accumulate magic force in a rapid speed.

"His progress was fast, but it would take him 3 to 4 years to reach level-5, and another 4 to 5 years to reach level-6."

"You are at level-2, but I have confidence that you can catch up with him in 10 years." Delin said confidently.

But Lynnray was not so confident.

"With a better talent, he can progress faster than I. Besides, he is already two levels ahead of me. How can I catch up with him in 10 years?" Lynnray certainly knew the difficulty of progress through levels during his study in the academy.

Delin had said he could help Lynnray reach level-6 in 10 years, but Lynnray was in doubt. He was aware of how fast he could progress.

While talking with Delin, Lynnray walked out of the back gate of Ernst Academy and entered the back mountains. While swiftly passing through the woods, Lynnray heard Delin's voice: "Lynnray, find a place against a peak."

"A place against a peak?" Lynnray was in doubt.

"Don't ask too much. I'll tell you then." Delin smiled.

The back mountains were covered with wild grass and tall trees. After a while, Lynnray found a place meeting Delin's requirements. There was a peak hundreds of meters high, and Lynnray stood at its foot.

"Grandpa Delin, why do you ask me to come here?" Lynnray inquired. Delin smiled: "You don't believe I can help you catch up with him in only 10 years. Haha... As a holy magic master, I have a method to increase spiritual force."

"A method to increase spiritual force? Isn't it meditation?" Lynnray looked at Delin in doubt.

Delin said with a smile: "Meditation produces good results, but you will feel drained after meditation."

"Sure, during meditation, we use our spiritual force to a bottom line, and then allow it to recover. It is a tiring practice." Lynnray frowned.

Delin said proudly: "My method is different. It does not consume spiritual force. It is an entertainment activity."

"Entertainment?" Lynnray was confused.

"Yes, and it is sculpting!" Delin said with a proud expression.

"Sculpting?" Lynnray was surprised, "Making stone sculptures like those in Brooks Guild Hall?"

Delin said with a smile: "Yes, others may use a lot of energy and feel tired, but with my method, you may be tired in the beginning, but feel very good in later stages."

"Is it real?" Lynnray found it hard to believe.

Delin stared at Lynnray: "You don't believe it? I was a holy magic master of Pron Empire. Many nobles offered a price about one million gold coins to purchase several works of mine. But I was proud of my works and didn't give them to others." "That's great, but why didn't I hear about you among sculpting masters?" Lynnray asked in doubt.

Delin said with embarrassment: "I hid my works in a secret basement without being known by others. After 5,000 years, I cannot find the location of my basement." The world changed over 5,000 years, and even the capital of Pron Empire perished without trace. How was it possible to find a basement?

"Oh, so no one know about you." Lynnray giggled.

"You don't believe it?" Delin opened his eyes widely, "Brooks, as a young man in those days, asked to have a look at my works. After studying my works, he made a breakthrough and became a master. He could be considered as my student."

Lynnray was struck by surprise.

"Brooks?"

The number one stone sculptor 'Brooks' was only a student of Delin.

"Certainly, if we say Brooks' works embody the pursuit for perfection, then my works were seeking an extreme. I call my sculpting skill the flat knife school. It arrives at a different extreme from other schools of stone sculpting. It is tiring and troublesome in the beginning, but you will enjoy good result in later stages."

Delin said with absolute confidence.

He glanced at Lynnray and smiled: "In the past, I was the only sculptor in the flat knife school, but from today, you are another one."

Lynnray trusted Delin very much, so he decided to learn stone sculpting.

Besides, if things worked out as Delin said, he could increase his magic power and become a stone sculptor at the same time. By stone sculpting, he could earn enough to support his brother's study.

"History recorded in the form of texts had only tens of thousands of years, but stone sculptures existed long before the emergence of texts." Delin sighed with emotion, "Since millions of years ago, our ancestors carved anything the saw or thought of as a way to pass on civilization."

Lynnray nodded.

No artistic work was as old as stone sculptures.

"Since the ancient times, no artistic forms were as old as stone sculpting or could express people's experience and happy and sorrowful feelings in a better way than stone sculpting. That is why stone sculpting has remained popular throughout ages."

"Stones are hard objects difficult to carve. And it is even more difficult to carve out a unique charm. Therefore, successful works created with effort were very precious." Delin sighed with emotion.

Lynnray agreed in the heart.

In painting, you could easily make a natural stroke, but making a natural scrape in sculpting was very difficult, because stones were too hard.

"The form, material, texture, and color of a stone embody an image and beauty itself. By cutting off redundant parts of a stone, a beautiful image will be exposed. That is stone sculpting."

"Sculpting is a process to trim image and space. The sculptor reduces redundant material from outside to inside and makes the outline of a form. In the process of removing redundant material, the form will become clearer and clearer, and you will feel as if the form breaks out from its shell."

......

Delin was eloquent in his introduction to stone sculpting.

Lynnray also felt Delin's love for the art.

"Generally, we need a lot of tools to carry out sculpting, including round knife, flat knife, oblique knife, triangle knife, jade-bowl knife, axe and saw... This is partly because of the rigidity of stone. They use a round knife to make an array, a flat knife to cut, and a triangle knife..."

From Delin's explanation, Lynnray learned the general knowledge of stone sculpting.

Delin laughed suddenly: "But my sculpting technique is different from others. I only use one tool -- flat knife. Therefore my sculpting school is called flat knife school!"

"How's it possible? How do we use only a flat knife?" Lynnray showed disagreement, "For example, how do you carve the scales of fish with a flat knife? That's impossible."

"No, ordinary people can't do that, but earth magicians can."

Delin said confidently, "Earth magicians can feel the texture of stones. As long as you have enough wrist strength, you can carve with a flat knife.

But flat knife carving is not easy. You should buy a sharp flat knife, and from tomorrow, I'll spend three hours a day to teach you sculpting techniques."

Chapter 25 - Six Years

Lynnray was sitting cross-legged beside a creek and holding a flat knife and a stone as large as his palm.

"Let's start from the basics and practice on this small stone..."

In the back mountains of Ernst Academy, Lynnray was studying stone sculpting with Delin. As he learned more knowledge in sculpting, he understood why flat knife carving could help improve spiritual force in middle and later stages.

Other sculptors needed many tools to perform sculpting.

They did a lot of brain work on the selection of tools to use in different places. Every piece of good work was the result of painstaking effort.

But flat knife school was different.

The only tool was a flat knife, and the sculptor need not think about which tools to use. But the use of only one tool came with its own difficulty. For example, the sculptor had to be very familiar with stone texture to carve a part which should be carved with a jade-bowl knife. And it also required good strength.

Some large raw blocks should be cut apart with an axe. If you only used a flat knife, you should have sufficient strength.

Earth magicians had special power to feel the texture of stones, but wrist strength still required training. As a level-2 magician, Lynnray had good wrist strength sufficient for carving small pieces. To carve larger ones, he still needed more training.

But he was just laying the foundation.

After the school year ended, Lynnray went back to Wushan Town.

Little Warton did not spend much time with his brother Lynnray after the new year, because he had to go to O'Brien Empire under the care of steward Hilly. When the 6-year-old left Lynnray, he cried loudly with tears. And at this time, Lynnray was ten.

Time passed quickly.

After returning to Ernst Academy, Lynnray picked up his special way of life, and practiced diligently in the back mountains most of the time.

As he entered puberty, he was eating much more and growing in height, physical strength and stamina. He was also making steady progress in stone sculpting under the guidance of Delin.

……

As seasons rotated, three years passed in one blink.

At a waterfall in the back mountains.

Water poured down into the pond like a curtain, and produced a rumbling sound.

Lynnray was carving on a stone half the height of a man with a 30-centimeter flat knife beside the waterfall. He waved the flat knife in flashing speed, and with each wave, waste material was scraped off the stone. A sculpture was taking its shape.

The outline became clearer and clearer from morning to evening.

Lynnray focused his vision on the stone sculpture and immersed himself in the natural settings. With mind totally absorbed in the work, he could not feel the passing of time. In such a spiritual state, his spiritual force started recovering and growing.

Lynnray was unaware of the growth of spiritual force. He just focused on carving the stone with his flat knife.

With reduction of waste material, a form gradually emerged. At sunset, Lynnray finally stopped waving his knife.

"Hu!"

Lynnray breathed out. When powder was blown off, the sculpture stood out. A mouse half a meter long appeared in front of Lynnray. It looked like real and made the shadow mouse Beibei squeak at one side.

A smooth carving from beginning to end.

"The feeling is wonderful." Now Lynnray felt a substantial increase of his spiritual force.

Delin, in a moon-white robe, was smiling beside him: "Lynnray, from today, you have entered the field of stone sculpting. You got the wonderful feeling? But your work is still on the level of formal similarity and can only be accepted in the ordinary hall. It's a shame on my skills. Destroy it." "Yes, grandpa Delin."

Lynnray waved his flat knife several times and cut the stone sculpture into a dozen pieces. In this year, Lynnray entered the beginning stage of stone sculpting.

And he was 13 years old!

Days and nights passed as he practiced.

Since Lynnray reached entry-level in stone sculpting, he was making rapid progress in spiritual force. To be accurate, he was at level-2 in magic at 9 years old; at age 11, he reached level-3, and then he became a level-4 magician at 13.

Progress would be much more difficult as one rose up through levels. Normally, he should take nearly 3 years to progress from level-4 to level-5.

However, he became a level-5 magician at 14 and a half years old, in the autumn of 9996, Yulan calendar. He took only one year and a half to cross from level-4 to 5, even shorter than the period from level-3 to 4.

That was the amazing result of flat knife sculpting!

……

The spring of 9997. It was the 7th year of Lynnray's study, and he was 15.

Lynnray, in a blue-sky robe, walked on the path of Ernst Academy, and on his shoulder was the lovely shadow mouse Beibei. Even after 7 years, Beibei did not change much in its size. Lynnray was 1.8 meters high and had a stable temperament. His body had been improved by elements of earth and wind, and with continuous practice and the advantages of Dragonblood warriors' blood, Lynnray reached level-4 in warrior power.

He could easily lift a large stone of several hundred jin and smash one with his fist.

Because of the benefits of flat-knife carving, Lynnray had been growing in spiritual force since 13.

In the beginning of 9997, Lynnray entered grade 5 of the school, the same grade as number one talent Dixi. Dixi took 3 years to cross from level-4 to level-5, but he was still unable to reach level-6.

A level-5 magician at 15 years old.

Both Lynnray and Dixi made astonishing progress. Lynnray was even more astonishing when he reached level-5 in only one year, based on record of school tests.

Lynnray's speed of progress was surprising for everybody.

They were viewed as top 2 talents in Ernst Academy.

"Look, Lynnray was at level-4 the year before last, but he reached level-5 last year. He only took one year to cross his level. That's amazing. I guess Lynnray will reach level-6 earlier than Dixi."

"Lynnray practice in the back mountains every day. I heard Dixi is doing the same recently. Maybe he picked that up from Lynnray."

"Probably, Lynnray may replace Dixi and become the number one talent, based on his amazing speed of progress."

......

When people saw Lynnray on the path, they started talking about him. The top 2 talents of Ernst Academy were a great sight and topic for people. But Lynnray still refused to join any grade competition despite his power.

"Talent?" Lynnray laughed.

Lynnray never considered himself a talent. He made achievement by continuous practice and persistence through the six years. And Delin's guidance also played a role.

"Maybe I cannot even defeat Beibei." Lynnray looked at Beibei, "Beibei, what level are you at?"

"Chi Chi..." Beibei grinned and talked to Lynnray mentally, "I don't know. I never fought with a monster. You cannot defeat me anyway." Beibei said those words with pride.

Disregarding people's admiring look and talks, Lynnray walked out of the back gate of Ernst Academy and entered the back mountains. He continued with his diligent practice. His diligence through the six years was the cause of his success.

Lynnray was passing through the woods swiftly when Beibei chatted with him in the heart: "Boss, when will we go on a trial in the Monster Forest? You are at level-5 now. Besides, I can also show myself."

"I'm not in a hurry." Lynnray only gave a short reply. "It's so sad. I'm a monster, but have never been to the Monster Forest. What a sad fact!" Beibei could express itself much better after 6 years.

"Quiet. If you keep talking, I will not roast meat for you today." Upon hearing these words, Beibei shut up right away.

When Lynnray was passing through the woods, Delin was hovering beside him. Delin was also glad to see Lynnray's progress.

"Lynnray." Delin said suddenly.

Lynnray turned around and said with a smile: "What's up, grandpa Delin?"

Delin said with a smile: "Based on your recent works, I can formally tell you, your craftsmanship has reached the beginner level."

Lynnray showed light in his eyes.

Delin had a bad habit that he would destroy all works less than his standard. In his words, "Such works are a shame to flat knife school and myself."

Therefore, Lynnray had to destroy all of his works, which he could have used to sell for money.

"The beginner level? What does it mean?" Lynnray looked at Delin with amazement.

Delin nodded happily: "Yes, from today, you don't need to destroy your works. Let them remain in this world. You can also sell them in Brooks Guild Hall to promote our flat knife school and earn some gold coins."

Episode 3 – Monster Mountains

Chapter 1 – Stone Sculpture (I)

The sunshine was warm and comfortable in spring, and the juveniles of Room 1987 were staying in their yard.

Yale, George and Reno were engaging in idle chat. Yale and George were 16, and Reno was 14. The three grew very fast. Even the shortest one, George was 1.6 meters, and the tallest, Yale was 1.9 meters.

"George, don't pretend to have a pure heart. Reno lost his virginity, but you are Lynnray are still pretending. At the end of month, you and Lynnray can go to the 'Green Water Paradise' in Fenlai City. I can pay for your comfort with a virgin girl, how do you think?" Yale giggled while practicing his chest with two stone dumbbells.

The stone dumbbells weighed 20 to 30 jin each, and were not something Lynnray would take an interest in.

George smiled: "Don't push me, Yale. You'll go to Green Water Paradise, and I'll have a drink with Lynnray, OK?"

Reno curled his mouth: "George, you are not a man."

George smiled bitterly.

Footsteps came from outside. Yale put down his stone dumbbells, looked at the yard gate and said: "I guess Lynnray is coming. Let's go to eat..." He stopped when he saw Lynnray carrying a huge stone one meter high on his shoulder. The stone must weigh several hundred jin.

But Lynnray carried it easily into the yard. In the shocking look of Yale, George and Reno, Lynnray placed the huge stone in a corner of the yard. The sound of heavy clash between the stone and ground made the three brothers shiver in the heart.

"That's weird, bro, I know you have good strength, but you still surprised me." Yale stared at the huge stone, "Is it empty inside?" Yale walked to the stone and tried to lift it.

"Hum!"

Yale tried hard with redness on the face, but the stone was lying still and solid on the ground.

"Bro, don't waste your energy, you can't carry it." Lynnray smiled.

Yale's physical strength was not even at level-1 in warrior standard. How could he carry the stone?

Reno looked at the huge stone, sighed with emotion and asked Lynnray: "Alas, why do you get such a huge stone to the dormitory, Lynnray? Ah, I know." Reno said with brightened eyes, "I saw powerful warriors training their body by doing weightlifting with a huge stone. Are you going to do weightlifting?"

"This stone can crush me into a pancake." George looked at the huge stone, made a sigh and asked Lynnray in confusion, "Bro, what's the use of the stone?"

Lynnray smiled at his brothers and uttered two words: "Stone sculpting!" As Delin said, his works were in the beginner stage now. Carving a stone was a time-consuming task taking more than a couple of days. He used to place his works in the back mountains without caring about damage. But now he had to think about preservation.

"Stone sculpting?"

Yale, Reno and George stared at Lynnray in surprise.

"Surprised?" Lynnray looked at them.

Reno said: "Quite surprised. We have been together for 7 years, but we've never seen you carving a stone. Are you starting from today?"

Lynnray smiled: "I'm not starting from today. I have practiced 5 years in the back mountains. But this one is different, because I'm prepared to send it to Brooks Guild Hall. Let's see if I can sell it."

To support Warton's study in O'Brien Empire under Hilly's care, Baruch family used up all of their wealth.

But Hogg was still happy about that.

Now his elder son Lynnray was a student in Ernst Academy, and was expected to become a noble magician. His younger son could possibly become a Dragonblood warrior.

Hogg could foresee the honor of his family in future!

"Brooks Guild Hall?" The three looked at Lynnray in surprise.

Lynnray was the pride of Room 1987. He entered grade 5 at only 15, and was named with Dixi as top 2 talents of Ernst Academy. His brothers recognized that, but...

Stone sculpting was a very profound art.

Many people learned stone sculpting for decades but did not go beyond the level of ordinary craftsmen. As an art with a long history, it was not easy to learn. But Lynnray wanted to show his work in the topmost exhibition venue -- Brooks Guild Hall.

"Lynnray, don't be impulsive." George joked with him.

"Will someone buy your work?" Reno frowned with disbelief.

Yale laughed at the moment: "What are you guys saying? Bro, you can just show your work, and I'll pay 10,000 gold coins to promote your name."

"I'm serious." Lynnray took out a flat knife from his chest.

"Flat knife?" Reno said with surprise, "It seems you are well prepared. I also tried to learn stone sculpting in the past. There are many tools, such as flat knife, round knife, triangle knife, jade-bowl knife and axe. Are you going to use only one tool?"

All three of them had a general understanding in various art forms.

Lynnray didn't speak much.

With the flat knife in hand, Lynnray entered a state of tranquility and union with nature, and he could feel the flow of elements and the veins in the huge stone. He smiled and started waving his knife.

Lynnray waved his knife in a flashing speed. The sunlight reflected from the knife made the three brothers squint, but they still stared at the huge stone.

"Hu Hu Hu!"

The knife cut at the same place rapidly, and a large block of waste was lifted off the stone.

"How's that possible?" Yale looked at the scene in shock, "Such a huge stone should be chopped with an axe, but it is being scraped with a flat knife. It requires tremendous wrist strength." Reno and George fell silent.

Wrist strength?

It required much more than wrist strength to scrape a stone in an easy way and produce natural and neat surfaces.

Lynnray did his work in a peaceful and natural manner. The flat knife seemed to be an extension of his right hand, and kept cutting on various locations of the stone. Waste material was being thrown off. The carving process was an enjoyable sight for the viewers.

"Lynnray..."

Yale, George and Reno looked at each other and had a feeling that Lynnray was really a stone carving master.

Peaceful, natural, and serene.

Lynnray enjoyed the feeling of sculpting. At his level of proficiency, he could carve different locations with suitable force without even thinking about it. Carving was accomplished with a subconscious feeling.

But sculptors in other schools were not fortunate enough to have such enjoyment. They needed to use different tools to carve different locations, which required a lot of thinking.

In a natural and peaceful state of mind, Lynnray's spiritual force was growing rapidly, which brought him a lot of inner happiness.

Lynnray's right hand suddenly stopped movement.

Waste material was thrown off and fell onto ground. The huge stone now took a rough shape of a reptile.

"Why are you three standing?" Lynnray smiled at his brothers, "Now we only got a simple sketch. It will take a longer time to complete. Let's go and have lunch."

Yale, Reno and George looked at each other.

Judging from the scene just now, the three were assured:

"A master." Yale praised him.

"A talent." Reno sighed with emotion.

"A talent among masters." George added.

A sculpting student like Lynnray, who reached the current proficiency in only 6 years, was rare to find in even a hundred years.

Chapter 2 - Stone Sculpture (II)

In Watery Hotel.

In Yale's words: "Now I know Lynnray is a stone sculptor. Let's go to Watery Hotel and congratulate." So the four entered Watery Hotel when many students in the first floor turned around and looked at them.

Their vision was focused on Lynnray.

Dixi and Lynnray!

They were the top 2 talents of Ernst Academy, and point of focus wherever they went. Many students were conversing in low voices about them.

The four sat down and dishes were served.

"Chi Chi..." Beibei, which was sleeping, held out its head from Lynnray's sleeve and looked at a roast chicken on the table. Reno gave the chicken to the shadow mouse: "Come on, Beibei."

"Boss, I'm eating." Beibei sent a mental message to Lynnray.

Before Lynnray had time to answer, Beibei jumped on the table and started eating the roast chicken. In less than 10 seconds, the roast chicken was finished by the shadow mouse, which was smaller in size.

"Lynnray, my heart twitched every time I saw Beibei eating food." Yale smiled. After eating, Beibei looked at Lynnray, who frowned at Beibei's oily claws.

"Chi Chi..."

Beibei squeaked to Lynnray, squinted contently, and sent out black light all over its body. The air of darkness was spread out. In an instant, the dark light disappeared, and Beibei's oily claws and mouth became clean.

Beibei squeaked toward Lynnray and talked with him mentally: "Boss, now I'm clean."

Lynnray smiled.

"Su!" With one sudden movement, Beibei swooshed into Lynnray's clothes.

Then the four brothers started chatting casually and eating food.

"By the way, Lynnray, if you want to send your stone sculpture to the guild hall, you have something to pay attention to." Yale reminded Lynnray.

"Oh, what should I pay attention to?" Lynnray questioned.

Lynnray knew nothing about the rules of Brooks Guild Hall.

Yale said with a smile: "Generally, stone works should contain the carver's name or title at the bottom left corner for identification purpose. Second, the stone work must be sealed after arrival to prevent damage. A sealed work will be inspected at the warehouse for integrity. They will note down your identity information. Generally, your work will appear in the ordinary hall three days later."

Lynnray nodded. Carving the sculptor's name and title on the work was intended to prevent falsehood.

Sealing was also easy to understand: "Some stone works are carefully made and can be easily damaged during transportation. Sealing them with the protection of papers and cloth waste will offer additional security."

"How does the guild hall price them? And how's commission fee?" Lynnray questioned further.

The purpose of sending his stone sculpture to the guild hall was to make money and improve his family's financial condition.

Yale said contently: "Stone works are priced by buyers. The buyer offering the highest bid will obtain the work, and you will be paid. With a successful transaction, the guild hall will charge a 1% commission not exceeding 10 gold coins. Even if your work can sell at more than 1,000 gold coins, the commission would still be 10 gold coins."

Lynnray got the point.

"Don't worry, bro, I'll arrange everything for you and make you satisfied." Yale held Lynnray's shoulder and said, "If it sells good, I will gain a good reputation, too."

George looked at Lynnray and praised him: "Bro, you are a fifth grade student, and will be a stone carving master in future. You'll achieve much bigger than us."

"A stone carving master? I'm not that good." Lynnray laughed at himself.

The four brothers ate, drank and chatted with each other. "Days in Ernst Academy are really good." Yale put down his glass and sighed with emotion, "I remember when I was at home, training was much harder than this."

Reno curled his mouth and said: "We are students of Ernst Academy. I heard from my grandpa Loum that the world is filled with fight and slaughter. No one dare meddle with Ernst Academy because the Church of Light is supporting it. That's why we are living a quiet life here. After we get out and go on a trial in the world, we will know how cruel it is."

"That's right."

Lynnray nodded, "I'm in grade 5 now. Many students have trained outside. As they said, some students lost their lives, got disabled or were seriously injured. We can't grow if we don't experience the real battle."

"We are like pets kept by nobles and live a comfortable life, but how can we face the ferocity of beasts outside?" George sighed with emotion, "I admire the battles of life and death high-grade students are experiencing. The days of burning blood must be very exciting."

Yale, George, Reno and Lynnray were at about 16 years old now. They all desired for the passionate life outside. But except Lynnray, they were still too weak to experience life and death.

"Lynnray, you are at grade 5 now, right?" Reno said suddenly.

Yale and George looked at Lynnray with brightened eyes.

Lynnray took a deep breath and nodded: "Yes, I'm at level-5 and can be called a senior. In June, I will go on a trial in Monster Mountains for two months. I'll be back by August." Lynnray had plans for himself.

"Monster Mountains?"

Yale, George and Reno gasped.

Monster Mountains were the first mountain range of Yulan Continent, less than a hundred li on the east of Ernst Academy. It was the place of second and third trials of many high-grade students. In the first trial, generally they would do something ordinary, such as escorting cargo delivery, which was less dangerous.

"Lynnray, you'll go to Monster Mountains on the first trial?" Reno asked. And Yale and George were worried.

"Don't worry, I can protect myself."

Lynnray was confident about himself. He was both a level-5 magician and level-4 warrior. A level-4 warrior moved fast, and with the help of wind magic 'top speed', he could reach the speed of level-6 warriors.

Most importantly, he was able to use senior wind magic 'floating'.

Chapter 3 - Night in Green Water Paradise

Time passed quickly, and it was the end of May.

During the two months, Lynnray spent most of his times in meditation, and sometimes he did sculpting and reading. There were an enormous number of books in the library of the school, and Lynnray was expanding his knowledge in reading.

On the morning of May 29.

Lynnray, Yale, Reno and George stood in the square in front of Brooks Guild Hall. Three wooden boxes were placed in the carriage beside them. During the two months, Lynnray completed 9 stone works. But today he was sending three works to the guild hall to see the result.

"Carry the three wooden boxes." Yale ordered.

Servants of Yale's family carried up the three wooden boxes.

"Lynnray, follow me." Yale knew the way and directly headed to the side of Brooks Guild Hall. The guild hall occupied a very large area, and hundreds of meters beside the front gate was a small gate. Beside the small gate was standing a middle-aged gentleman.

The middle-aged man saw Yale and his companions, so he smiled and offered his respect: "Young master, you are welcome."

Yale nodded with a smile: "I think you already know my purpose. This is my brother Lynnray, who is the creator of the three stone works. Where are your warehouse staff? Carry the sculptures inside."

"Wait a minute." The middle-aged man nodded with a smile.

Several porters came to the spot. The middle-aged man said to Lynnray: "Lynnray, according to our rules, you should leave your identity information. So please show me your student ID."

The student ID of Ernst Academy was sufficient to prove their identity.

Lynnray took out his student ID.

The middle-aged man opened the student ID and said with surprise: "Grade 5?" Lynnray's age was obvious, but it was astonishing that he reached level-5 at such a young age.

Yale said proudly: "Lynnray is one of the top 2 talents of Ernst Academy. Last year he was 14, but he was proved to have reached level-5 in yearly test."

The top 2 talents of Ernst Academy?

The middle-aged man knew Lynnray had a brilliant future, so he put on a much humbler attitude. He recorded Lynnray's identity and made a mark on the three wooden boxes.

"Everything is OK, Lynnray, you can come back in one month to receive your payment." The middle-aged man smiled.

"After one month? I don't have time after one month. How about two or three months later?" Lynnray asked. He was about to go to Monster Mountains in 2 weeks, and he decided to stay there for 2 months.

"We are not in a hurry. As long as your item can sell, you can receive your payment at any time." The middle-aged man nodded.

Yale frowned: "Eh? I remember you would check the inside when you receive stone works, but why don't you check them now?"

The middle-aged man replied: "We check the inside of the wooden boxes because we are worried that some people may send some damaged items and cheat money from us. But the stone works are sent by you and Lynnray. I believe a personality like you will not do such a thing."

The middle-aged man was clear what kind of person Yale was.

Even if he cheated Brooks Guild Hall, the money he obtained would not be enough for his short-term squandering. And the creator of stone works -- Lynnray -- was one of the top 2 talents of Ernst Academy. Such a person would not degrade himself to be a cheater.

......

Late night on the same day. Floor 3 of Green Water Paradise deep in Champs Avenue, eastern part of Fenlai City. Lynnray and his pals were in an independent room.

The night of Fenlai City was bustling.

The night of Green Water Paradise reached the most bustling point. The chatting and laughter of women and men were heard at every moment. The four brothers were drinking and having a casual talk in the company of four good-looking girls.

"George and Lynnray, Reno and I will go to sleep now, you two..." Yale held a girl with green long hair and said with an alcoholic smell. "Fine, boss, I'm not interested." Lynnray interrupted.

Yale looked at Reno, and then glanced at Lynnray and George in contempt, and then held a girl each to leave the room. Since two years ago, the brothers often visited this place.

Generally, Yale and Reno would enjoy with women, and Lynnray and Reno would drink and chat with the girls.

"Young master, we've known each other for two years, but you..." The green-hair girl beside Lynnray said with discontent.

Lynnray was troubled at her words.

"Ella, take some rest if you are tired. I'll pay you in full." Lynnray said coldly. The girl dare not speak anymore. It was rare to play in Green Water Paradise but only drank alcohol.

A ray of light came out of the Ring of Coiling Dragon and turned into Delin.

Delin looked at Lynnray with a smile and teased him: "Hey, you are behaving strangely in front of women. Sadly I'm existing in spirit form, otherwise I can enjoy women, too. Why are you so indifferent?"

"Grandpa Delin." Lynnray frowned and talked to Delin mentally.

Delin curled his mouth and said: "You haven't enjoyed a woman, otherwise you'll think differently."

Lynnray looked through the window and neglected Delin's words. When cool air touched his face, he made up his mind.

"What will it be like to be in Monster Mountains?" Lynnray was about to depart in 2 weeks. He heard many legends on Monster Mountains in

Ernst Academy and from Delin. But he had never been there. He could only explore the mountains in his imagination.

"I'll set off in one week."

Lynnray looked at the night sky through the window and made his decision.

Chapter 4 - Price (I)

In Brooks Guild Hall, music touched everyone's heart, and visitors were quietly appreciating every stone sculpture.

The guild hall was divided into three halls, the ordinary hall, senior hall and master hall.

The ordinary hall had the largest area and displayed most works. On the northeast corner of the hall were three stone works. The three stone works contained a special temperament, and anyone with a bit knowledge in stone sculpting could feel such temperament. Tens of thousands of stone works were displayed in the ordinary hall, and the three pieces were like a needle in the sea, hard to be noticed.

"These works have more form than essence."

Earl Juno, aged 160 was slowly walking in the hall and glancing at the stone sculptures. Juno had no other hobbies except stone sculptures. He would spend an entire morning every day in the guild hall.

But in the ordinary hall, hardly one piece could attract his attention.

"Mr. Earl, which stone sculpture do you like?" A beautiful female attendant came. Because Juno came every day, the service staff were very familiar with him.

Juno shook his head: "I haven't found one yet." "Mr. Earl, works in the ordinary hall could never be compared with those in senior hall or master hall. Why do you spend so much time every day in the ordinary hall?" The female attendant asked curiously.

Juno said with a mysterious smile: "You don't understand. There are a large number of works here, and spotting a good one is like finding gold in sandy mud. It's a pleasant experience."

"Oh?" The female attendant looked at Juno with confusion.

Juno stopped speaking and continued to appreciate the stone sculptures. When he walked to the three pieces created by Lynnray, he showed light in his eyes. Based on his one hundred years' experience, he knew at first sight the special characteristics of the three pieces.

"Cool, natural and proud..."

Juno said involuntarily.

That was the kind of temperament which a stone sculpture should have to be called an excellent piece. Earl Juno was touched by the temperament of the three stone works.

"Come here and price them. I offer 100 gold coins for the three pieces." Juno said to the female attendant beside him.

The female attendant took out his notebook and recorded the numbers and prices of the works. Then she took out three tags and pasted them onto the works. Each of the tag said '100 gold coins'.

When the female attendant was taking note, Juno appreciated the three pieces in detail. "Eh? Something is not right." Juno opened his eyes widely and stared at the stone sculpture of a 'raptor'. "Why are the lines of scales and legs so continuous? Generally, the scales should be carved with a round knife, and leg outline should be carved with a flat knife. No matter how careful the carver is, he cannot make it so natural and smooth."

Juno studied stone sculpting for over a hundred years.

He had not been a wealthy noble, but by buying low and selling high with his special insight, he made a fortune and became a rich man in Fenlai City.

"Was it carved with only one tool? No, based on the curves and depression on the scales, only a round knife can make it perfect." Juno frowned, because he had never seen such a work before.

"Mr. Earl?" The female attendant called him in a low voice.

Juno thought to himself: "I didn't expect there is such a special piece in the ordinary hall. If I offer my price of 100 gold coins, other people may notice it and observe it. It will rise substantially in price."

Earl Juno made his decision.

He should offer his price in the final one or two days.

"Cancel my offering." Juno said to the female attendant.

"Cancel it?" According to the rules, offered price could not be canceled, but Juno was their old customer, so the female attendant took off the three tags quickly.

"May I ask why you canceled your offering?" She inquired.

Juno smiled mysteriously: "I can't tell you. By the way, what's the deadline for exhibition of the three pieces?"

The female attendant looked into her notebook and smiled: "The final day was June 30. And the three pieces were sent here for exhibition yesterday afternoon."

Juno nodded.

"OK, I'll look around, don't worry about me." Juno said with a smile.

Juno felt delighted in the heart. He could say every piece of the three was worth 3,000 gold coins, in real price. A senior's work was worth 1,000 gold coins generally, but the three pieces were carved with special techniques, which could increase their price twofold.

……

Earl Juno visited Brooks Guild Hall every day. As he expected, there were so many stone works in the ordinary hall that the three wonderful works were not noticed. Even if someone noticed them, they would feel the sculptures were good, but could not see their real value.

On June 10.

Juno arrived at Brooks Guild Hall and casually looked around in the ordinary hall, but when he walked to the three pieces of Lynnray, his face changed, because all three pieces had a price tag.

The price for each one of them was '300 gold coins'. Juno cursed the bidder in the heart: "Idiot! The stone sculptures are good, but you should not price so high. You are attracting others' attention." Juno was angry, but he had no right to cancel other people's bidding.

As expected, when Juno came back on June 12, the price on the tag changed.

"500 gold coins?" Juno squinted: "It seems we have many people learned in the art."

Chapter 5 – Price (II)

Earl Juno decided not to offer until June 30. With the passing of time, the price of the three pieces was slowly rising. Because a senior's work was about 1,000 gold coins, the price was rising much slower afterwards.

500 gold coins, 510 gold coins, 515 gold coins...

Price slowly rose to only 625 gold coins by June 29.

On June 30.

Juno did not come in the morning, which was rare. He decided to come at night, because Brooks Guild Hall closed at 12 p.m. And Lynnray's works would be taken off the shelf after 12 p.m.

"Yesterday's offer was 625 gold coins, I'll wait till the last moment." Juno walked to the three stone pieces with a smile.

"900 gold coins? Which idiot offered this price?" Juno cursed.

In the last day it was only 625 gold coins, but it reached 900 today. Juno could do nothing but wait, despite his anger. After quite a while, he looked at the wall clock.

"It's eleven now, still one hour before close." Juno smiled.

Earl Juno was an intermediate noble in Fenlai City. In his younger days, he was very poor, but he increased his wealth by collecting stone sculptures. Now he had hundreds of thousands of gold coins and could be considered a rich man.

"Earl Juno, nice to see you here." A middle-aged man with a handlebar and tail coat walked to him with a smile.

Juno changed his face upon seeing this man, but he still smiled: "Oh, Earl Demu. Why are you coming here at eleven?" Juno felt something was not right.

Earl Juno and Earl Demu were two famous collectors in the circle of stone sculpting.

"I'm coming for the three pieces of stone work." Demu raised his handlebar and said with content: "Earl Juno, you see, the unique temperament of the three pieces is so attractive. I believe their creator must be a special person."

Juno's heart shivered.

Earl Demu wanted to get the three pieces, too. And he is arriving at eleven with the same purpose as him.

"Miss, come over here." Demu said politely to the female attendant, who walked to him with a smile. Demu pointed at the three pieces of Lynnray: "I offer 1,000 gold coins for each of the three."

The female attendant nodded politely: "Wait a moment."

She took out her notebook, recorded the numbers and offered price and pasted tags on the works.

"1,000 gold coins?" Juno twitched in the corner of the eye.

Demu looked at Juno and said: "Juno, the three pieces are really wonderful. By the way, why do you come here instead of sleeping at night? Are you coming for the three pieces, too?"

Juno nodded.

"I didn't expect you like the three pieces. I didn't quite notice them. Let's me have a look." Juno smiled and started observing the three pieces, and gave no heed to Demu beside him.

Demu sneered in the heart: "Your intention is so obvious."

Music as sweet as spring was sounding in Brooks Guild Hall. Demu and Juno were observing other works, and the hall was in tranquility.

"Dang, Dang..." The wall clock ticked.

It was twelve o'clock.

"Miss, come over here." Juno called to the female attendant, who ran to him right away.

"I offer 1,010 gold coins for each of the three." Juno made his offer.

The female attendant saw the tagged price 1,000 gold coins of the stone works, and thought of Juno sarcastically: "Good, he added 10 gold coins instead of one."

"Wait a minute." She took out her notebook.

"Juno, you only added 10 gold coins? I offer 1,100 gold coins!" Demu said. Juno looked at him, and saw him walking from a distance with a content look.

Obviously, Demu had been paying attention to Juno, and he came to the spot when Juno offered.

"I offer 1,200 gold coins." Juno said with a low voice, and his anger was obvious. The female attendant could also feel the competition between the two nobles. He closed his notebook and watched at one side. In Brooks Guild Hall, the attendants liked to see people making offers in competition.

Demu looked at Juno in surprise: "Mr. Juno, works in the senior hall are only worth 1,000 gold coins. You are a money-saving guy, why do you offer 1,200 gold coins?"

Money-saving?

It should be called miserliness, for which Juno was famous.

"You are at 1,200 gold coins. I will be more generous, 1,300 gold coins!" Demu smiled.

Juno turned cold in his look: "I offer at a high price because I like the three pieces. Their real value is only a bit more than 1,000. I offer 1,500 gold coins. If you make a higher offer, they are yours." Juno made his last offer at 1,500 gold coins.

In fact, Demu was less than Juno in his insight. He did not notice the bizarre details of carving on the stone works.

In the eyes of Demu, he only saw the good temperament of the three works, and considered their price as a little more than 1,000 gold coins. It made no sense to bid higher. "Haha." Demu laughed, "Since you are so generous, I can't take them from you. They are yours."

The female attendant made notes of the numbers and final offering.

"Two respected earls, it's twelve o'clock now. We are closing. Earl Juno, we will send the three pieces to your place tomorrow." The female attendant said with a smile. And only at this moment Juno had a smile.

Juno glanced at Demu and held him in contempt in the heart: "Dude, I studied stone sculpting for many years. You don't have enough insight to compete with me."

Chapter 6 - Invitation

"Eh? The three pieces in ordinary hall were sold at 1,500 gold coins?" Ostony, a management staff member of Brooks Guild Hall looked at the record in amazement. He searched for Lynnray's information and was surprised, "All three pieces were created by Lynnray? He is only 15?"

The circle of stone sculpting was like a pyramid.

In the Holy Alliance, only five or six sculpting masters are at the top of the pyramid, and seniors may be 100 in number. Therefore, senior sculptors were rare. They were the people who had their feelings about life, and could merge their feelings in their works. In this way, the provided a temperament in their works.

A senior sculptor at the age of 15?

It was indeed rare.

"Lynnray is a student in Ernst Academy?" Ostony was even more surprised. Ernst Academy was the number one magic school on Yulan Continent. "And he is a grade-5 student? Only at the age of 15?"

Ostony gasped.

Lynnray was really a talent.

"Although the three pieces were only worth about 1,000 gold coins, the identity of their creator can increase their value multiple times." Ostony was assured. Generally, stone works created by a 15-year-old at this level had high values.

And this sculptor was at grade 5 of Ernst Academy. He was indeed a top talent. And the value of his works would rise much higher.

"In the afternoon, I'll go to Ernst Academy. We haven't got a new senior for a time." Ostony made his decision to have a visit. The price of Lynnray's works has indicated his capabilities.

That was enough for Brooks Guild Hall to open an independent display room in the senior hall.

In the afternoon of the same day.

A carriage arrived at Ernst Academy. Ostony came with two of his guards. He took out his ID showing he was a member of Brooks Guild Hall, and Ernst Academy sent a guard to lead him.

The teaching affair office, grade 5 of Ernst Academy.

"Mr. Ostony, this is the place of magic teachers of grade 5." The guards opened the door, and a dozen magic teachers were chatting with each other inside. Teachers of grade 5 were themselves on the level or 7 or 8, generally.

The door opened, and the noble magicians turned around.

"Respected magicians, Mr. Ostony is from Brooks Guild Hall, he is asking for a favor." The guard said respectfully.

The magicians nodded.

Brooks Guild Hall had its branches in several large cities of Yulan Continent. And he had astonishing force of arms. Therefore, the noble magicians were treating them with respect.

"Respected magicians." Ostony smiled, "I came here for a grade 5 student -- Lynnray."

"Lynnray?"

The magicians smiled. A purple-gown middle-aged man said: "Lynnray is one of our top 2 talents. He is practicing in earth and wind series. You can ask his two teachers."

"Don't ask me. I only saw him twice in my earth magic courses over the three months." A red-beard old man said with discontent, "But he attends every class in wind series."

A gray-hair old man in white robe said with a smile: "I'm Lynnray's magic teacher in wind series. I'm familiar with him. You can ask me."

Ostony nodded: "Lynnray sent three stone works to our guild hall one month ago. His works carry a recognized temperament. Based on the price offering, we determine that he is qualified to open an independent room in the senior hall. So I arrived here to give him a silver-color Magic Crystal Card."

"An independent show room?"

The magicians were shocked.

As noble magicians, they knew about stone carving art, and they knew that carving a vivid stone sculpture was very difficult, not to mention providing a temperament in the stone sculpture. Opening an independent room in Brooks Guild Hall was the dream of every stone sculptor. "Are you sure he's Lynnray? He practices diligently and he's only 15." The wind magic teacher said with astonishment.

Ostony smiled: "There is no doubt. We have our record with his student ID. And according to record, Yale accompanied him to our guild hall."

The magicians nodded.

Then they were in a heated discussion. One of the top 2 talents became a stone sculptor qualified to open an independent room in Brooks Guild Hall. That's a pieces of news unheard in a thousand years.

The magicians were naturally very surprised.

"Can you tell me where he is?" Ostony asked.

The old man in white robe said with a smile: "He lives in Room 1987."

"Room 1987?" Ostony wanted to pay a visit.

But the old man in white robe continued: "Wait a moment, although Lynnray was living in Room 1987, he set off for a trial outside of our school. So you'll not see him."

"Trial?" Ostony was a bit surprised.

He knew that senior magicians at grade 5 and 6 were qualified to go on a trial, and the school encourage them.

Ostony made a sigh in the heart.

The result was not expected.

"Then I have to leave, respected magicians." Ostony offered his respect. The magicians nodded and gave no heed to Ostony. Then they started chatting in excitement. "Lynnray is great..." The magicians were amazed to hear that Lynnray was qualified to open an independent show room in Brooks Guild Hall.

Chapter 7 - The Journey (I)

Back to June 5.

In the morning, after bidding farewell to his brothers, Lynnray carried a leather bag and went on the journey to Monster Mountains.

"Chi Chi..." Little shadow mouse jumped happily on Lynnray's shoulder.

"Boss, we are finally heading for the Monster Mountains. I'm so excited." The shadow mouse's voice sounded in Lynnray's mind. Lynnray had a faint smile when Delin in a moon-white robe was also walking beside him.

Delin enjoined him: "Be careful when you are alone. We may come across bandits."

"I know, grandpa Delin." Lynnray smiled.

As to the precautions of staying outside, grandpa Delin had said many times. Lynnray was wearing a pair of linen trousers and a sleeveless vest. Judging from his muscles, he seemed to be a warrior.

According to Delin, wearing a magician's robe in Monster Mountains was a burden. It was better to wear lightly.

Lynnray was moving fast. Although the journey was difficult, Lynnray moved forward 40 li with the power of a level-4 warrior. At this time, he saw three people in front.

"Eh?" Lynnray looked at one of them.

That person was wearing a robe uniform of Ernst Academy. As to other two persons, one had a strong body and carried a huge saber, and the other was thin with a short knife on his waist. The thin young man looked at Lynnray in alert.

Lynnray disregarded the three and decided to overtake them.

"Lynnray, it's you!" A voice was heard.

Lynnray turned around and saw the young man in robe shouting to him: "Lynnray, I'm Desat, do you remember me?"

"Oh, nice to see you, Desat." Lynnray stopped.

Lynnrey knew him.

Desat was also a grade 5 student in wind magic. They were not close, but were in the same class.

Desat brought two warriors and smiled warmly: "Lynnray, I didn't expect you are dressed like this. I almost didn't recognize you. When I saw the shadow mouse on your shoulder and looked at you carefully, I knew it's you."

"Kava, Matt, let me do an introduction. He is Lynnray, one of the top 2 talents of Ernst Academy. He is at level-5 in only 15 years old." Desat introduced Lynnray to his pals.

Kava was the man as strong as a bear, and Matt was the thin warrior.

"Desat talked about the top 2 talents before. I'm fortunate to meet you today." Matt said politely, and Kava said in a surprise: "Are you are magician? But I think you are more like a warrior."

Lynnray didn't answer, but asked them: "Are you going to Monster Mountains, too?"

Desat nodded: "Yes, Kava and Matt practiced with me last year and we cooperated very well. In this year, we'll carry out an exploration in the edge areas of Monster Mountains. You can go together with us. It will be safer."

Lynnray nodded.

"I can go with them temporarily. Desat can be trusted because we are in the same school. We can part after arriving at Monster Mountains." After making the decision, Lynnray continued his journey to Monster Mountains with the three.

All four of them advanced fast on the way.

Even Desat, the weakest in physical strength, used the auxiliary magic 'top speed' to advance fast on the deserted road.

Kava said with a loud voice: "Lynnray, if you join us, we'll have two level-5 magicians. Then four of us can kill a level-6 monster. The magic crystal core of a level-6 monster is worth 1,000 gold coins. If we kill a few more, we won't worry about our livelihood in a hundred years."

The living cost of an ordinary person was only dozens of gold coins a year.

1,000 gold coins were a great amount of money. Lynnray suddenly thought of the books he read in the library of Ernst Academy. The books introduced the monsters' energetic core -- magic crystal core.

"Magic crystal core is formed in the brain of a monster at or above level-3. But those of monsters below level-6 did not have a high price, and maybe were cheaper than my stone sculptures." Lynnray thought to himself.

A level-6 magic crystal core was worth 1,000 gold coins.

According to Delin's judgment, Lynnray's stone sculptures had reached the senior level of Brooks Guild Hall and were worth more than a thousand gold coins. Fighting with a level-6 monster was far more dangerous and difficult than creating a stone sculpture.

"Practicing through trial was the most important thing. The magic crystal core was only an occasional obtainment." Lynnray thought to himself, and looked at the other three.

The three men talked excitedly, and they desired to obtain a magic crystal core.

"The magic crystal cores of level-3, level-4 and level-5 monsters are not priced high, and that of a level-6 monster is only worth 1,000 gold coins." Desat shook his head, "If we can kill a level-7 monster, we will earn a lot of money." Desat showed light in his eyes.

Similar to humans, there was a leap of power between level-6 and level-7 in monsters.

The magic crystal core of a level-7 monster was worth tens of thousands of gold coins.

If they could kill one of level-7 monsters, they could live an abundant life in the countryside.

"A level-7 monster? I guess we can't survive if we fight with one." Lynnray said casully.

He saw a level-7 monster before. That was the raptor. Even today, he still could not penetrate such a monster's powerful defense, not to mention killing one.

Matt, who appeared to be the smartest among the three, said: "We don't even know if we can defeat a level-6 monster, not to mention level-7. It'll lead to a dead end."

"I was just saying." Kava patted his head and curled his mouth.

When the four were talking and laughing, a man in green clothes and with green juice on his face was holding a strong bow a hundred of meters on the rear side of them, and stared at them coldly.

The man was moving his lips, seemingly murmuring a mantra.

The bow was pulled in full, and arrow was shot swiftly with cyan light on the tip. The arrow reached a horrible speed. It split the air and flew across a hundred meters quickly.

Lynnray, who was talking with his buddies, chilled all over and felt the thumping of heart.

"Danger!"

Lynnray dodged immediately. "Pu!" The arrow penetrated the neck of Desat at the nape. After making a hole in his neck, the arrow flew dozens of meters ahead before falling to the ground. Desat covered his throat and opened his eyes widely. He kept uttering unclear sounds, and blood was flowing from his throat.

"Ah, Ah..." Desat desired to live, and in great horror, as blood came out, his eyes darkened, and he fell down feebly.

Lynnray, Kava and Matt lied face down in the grass and looked to the rear side.

Chapter 8 - The Journey (II)

"A wind magic archer. Based on his magic of 'top speed' and 'accuracy', he is at level-5." Delin's voice appeared in Lynnray's mind. "Based on the power of his bow and arrow, you will be serious injured within 50 meters, even if you have dodged his arrow. Flee!"

Lynnray's heart shivered.

"Hand over all your money and I'll spare your lives." A cold voice was heard. Then a dozen people in green clothes rushed out from the woods. All of them carried a bow and arrows, with a short knife at the waist. The dozen people looked at Lynnray and his other two buddies, and moved toward them.

But the one who spoke did not came out.

Lynnray and his pals looked at each other. They did not hand over their money, instead, they looked at the dozen people in alert.

"Shoot!" The cold voice came again. The wind magic archer was very decisive. When Lynnray and his pals didn't surrender, he ordered the kill.

"Su""Su""Su""Su"...

A dozen arrows were shot from the archers. Lynnray, Kava and Matt dodged. Kava used his huge saber to block the arrows. Lynnray used the wind magic 'top speed' and dodged quickly. He had time to see his pals at this moment. Matt was carefully dodging and blocking with his short knife.

But Kava was not flexible enough with his huge saber. He only carried out defense with his huge saber and thin Qi shield. The arrows did not carry much power, so Kava could block them as a level-5 warrior.

"Ah, I'll kill you." Kava shouted and rushed to the archers with his huge saber.

The wind magic archer hiding in the woods saw the scene. He showed coldness in his eyes and pulled his bow in full. After chanting mantras of 'top speed' and 'accuracy', cyan light appeared at the tip of arrow. Kava shouted and rushed to the archers, but half on his way, he saw some cyan light in front of him, and before he took any reaction, an arrow came to his face. He chilled in the back and immediately used his huge saber to defend.

But with a "Puchi!" sound, the arrow penetrated his head.

"Ah..." Kava showed disbelief in his eyes. He blocked the arrow with his saber, but why was he shot? With doubt and disbelief, his eye color darkened, and he fell down like a mountain.

Lynnray shivered in the heart.

"It was wind magic 'accuracy'. As Lynnray was a wind magician, he knew that 'accuracy' could change the direction of arrow slightly in its range.

The arrow should be blocked by the saber, but it changed its direction and penetrated Kava's head.

"Wind magic combined with a bow was really horrible." Lynnray sighed with emotion. But in an instant, he started chanting mantras, too.

"You'd better hand over your properties." The cold voice came again. The archers were also shouting. Wind magic archers should have enough strength to use the strong bow.

A wind magic archer was a powerful distance attacker.

Lynnray had a thought to kill, and looked at the dozen archers like looking at corpses.

"Puchi!""Puchi!""Puchi!""Puchi!"

With earth shaking, ground spears stuck out under the archers' feet. The spears shiny in earth-yellow light penetrated the archers' legs and bellies. Blood tainted the ground and screams of pain were all over the place.

Level-5 earth magic -- ground spear!

"Ah..." Painful screams came one after another.

Dozens of spears rose from ground. With a length of 1 meters, they could penetrate a person easily. A dense array of spears plunged the archers into a painful situation.

"Captain, help! Help!" An archer penetrated at the crotch screamed in pain.

Four of the archers died, and about 10 of them were seriously injured. All of them lost the capability of fighting.

"An earth magician!"

The archer hidden in the woods was shocked. He robbed and killed many people who came out of or tried to enter Monster Mountains, and gathered a lot of wealth.

And when he killed, he killed the magicians first.

Magicians could attack at a distance and were a great threat to him. He didn't expect there were two magicians in the team.

"Go!"

Lynnray used auxiliary magic 'top speed' in the chaotic situation, and moved forward fast. Soon he vanished in the distance. He was sure that he could not attack the archer hidden in the woods.

Magic had limitations of range, while they had a distance between each other. Once he drew near, he could not defend against the attack of the wind magician.

Lynnray passed 20 to 30 li on the way in an amazing speed.

"Boss, why are you running? If the archer is a threat, I can kill him easily. Why don't you let me fight?" Beibei's voice showed its discontent with the escape.

Lynnray was aware of Beibei's strength.

When he was only eight, Beibei's speed had exceeded a level-6 warrior. Now he was 15, Beibei did not grow in size, but its speed could be compared with a level-9 warrior.

With such speed, maybe the magic archer did not have time to set up an aim.

"It's my trial. I have to depend on myself." Lynnray replied.

The little shadow mouse jumped onto Lynnray's shoulder, scratched him, and squeaked in anger. And it talked to Lynnray mentally: "That's too much for me. I want to go on a trial and fight!"

Lynnray laughed: "OK, when we are in Monster Mountains and see some powerful monsters, it's your turn. All right?"

"That's a good idea." The shadow mouse stood straight, placed its front legs at the chest, twitched its nose and squinted with content.

A lightning crossed the sky with thunder. Lynnray looked up and saw flashlights with echoed roars.

"It's going to rain." Lynnray frowned.

He sped up in the direction of Monster Mountains. When he was about 10 li to the mountain range, rain drops began to fall. Then a storm came and swept across the land.

"Boom..."

Thunder kept striking, and storm devoured the entire area. A heavy rain and water mist filled the space.

But Lynnray, who was swiftly moving forward did not have raindrops on his clothes, because 10 centimeters above his head was a 'wind shield' several meters in diameter. Wind shield was strong in protection against raindrops, and could be maintained with only a little magic force.

Wind had no shape, and the wind shield was light cyan in color.

No one could see the wind shield at a distance. Lynnray continued to move forward rapidly with the wind shield over his head. Soon he saw an infinitely long range crossing the south and north. The huge range dividing Yulan Continent into two was the first range in the continent -- Monster Mountains.

Lynnray held his breath at the huge and infinite range several li away.

"A very, very long range."

The range was so long that at one sight, on the east were unending mountains, and on the south and north was still the range. The Monster Mountains were boundless, like an ocean.

Boundless!

"This is the Monster Mountains, the first range of the continent, and the residence of numerous monsters and many holy monsters." Delin appeared beside Lynnray and said with a wandering look: "I haven't been to Monster Mountains for a long time."

Lynnray showed excitement in his eyes.

"Set off!"

Lynnray headed for Monster Mountains in heavy rain with great vigor. And the shadow mouse Beibei also squeaked happily on Lynnray's shoulder. In the boundless rain curtain, Lynnray's sight soon vanished in the range far away.

Chapter 9 – Monster Mountains (I)

Monster Mountains were boundless.

The old trees with unknown age reached up to the sky, and the ground was covered with wild grass and thorns. Rotten leaves fell down, and there were sounds when stepping on them. In the surroundings were densely grown vines and wild grass.

"Such old forest is full of wild grass and vines. I can't even see a monster hiding 10 meters away." Lynnray shivered in the heart.

Delin was beside him.

"Not to mention 10 meters away. Maybe a large python is hiding in the grass right in front of you." Delin smiled.

Lynnray looked at the wild grass in front of him. The grass was very dense and was half the height of a human. A python could really hide in it. Lynnray took a deep breath, stood still and chanted magic mantras.

A light wind spread from Lynnray to all sides and vanished in the distance.

Wind magic -- perception through wind!

Generally a magician could use 'perception through wind' at level-3. The higher level he was at, the broader the range he could perceive. At level-3, the perception was within a dozen meters, but the perception of a level-5 magician was over 100 meters.

"In a range of 200 meters, there was a level-1 monster the bubble rabbit, and several level-2 monsters 'soil scorpion'". Lynnray said confidently.

By using the sensing wind, he could perceive living creatures' shape and smell.

"Don't be overly self-confident. A strong monster can lurk underground. Some holy monsters can disguise themselves." Delin reminded Lynnray, "Certainly, you are only a small character. The powerful monsters do not need to disguise or hide themselves."

Lynnray now became more careful.

"Lurking? Disguising? It was said in the books that monsters have intelligence similar to humans. It must be true." Lynnray thought to himself. He looked at Beibei on his shoulder, "Let's say, Beibei has high intelligence. So I must be careful."

Air was flowing around his feet, and it was the result of wind magic 'top speed'.

Lynnray quietly passed through the Monster Mountains and looked around. The shadow mouse was also looking around on Lynnray's shoulder. In this way, a person and a monster were getting deep into the Monster Mountains.

"Monster Mountains are more than 10,000 li long, with a width of 700 to 800 li. In the a hundred li at the edge, low-level monsters dwell. In another 100 li deeper, there are many level-5 and level-6 monsters. And to get deeper, one would face monsters at level-7, 8 and 9, and even holy monsters." Delin was providing Lynnray with information of Monster Mountains.

"The division was not absolute, because some level-9 monster may be bored and get to the edge." Delin said humorously, "You may also encounter a group of monster wolves as many as 10,000. If that happens, you can only blame your misfortune."

Lynnray curled his mouth upon hearing the words.

Crap!

Why should such misfortune happen to him in the vast area of Monster Mountains? And if that happened, Delin, who existed in spirit form, could not help him. A holy magic master without magic force could not launch an attack.

"Grandpa Delin, I know. Stay quiet and do not distract me." Lynnray complained.

Delin touched his white beard and stopped talking.

In the old forest of Monster Mountains, the dense leaves of old tree blocked all the rain drops, and only some drops occasionally fell. Lynnray walked a while in the mountains. He knew the edge area was not dangerous.

Lynnray made a leap with his feet to a tree branch seven meters high, and looked into the distance.

"Boss, there is a wind boar on the rear right side." Beibei's voice appeared in his mind. Lynnray looked back and saw a single-horned wild boar carefully observing its surrounding at 100 meters away. If not because of the height, Lynnray would not be able to see the wild boar.

"Single-horned boar, level-3 monster, earth series. It can only use ground spear." Lynnray recalled information of the monster.

"Although it is a level-3 monster, I can eat it as lunch. Boar meat tastes good." Lynnray passed through the wood swiftly and drew near to the single-horned boar. Because of dense grass and thorns, the boar did not notice Lynnray.

When Lynnray was at a 10-meter distance, he would only dimly saw the boar through wild grass.

"Hu!"

Lynnray suddenly leaped out from grass. When the boar noticed his movement, Lynnray was already in front of it, as if he came from the sky. The boar roared and attacked Lynnray with its horn.

"Hu!" Lynnray grabbed the horn with his right hand and made a throwing movement.

The boar, several hundred jin in weight, was thrown to seven meters high. Lynnray leaped again, and kicked out his right leg on the boar's head.

"Pum!" With a crack of bone, the boar was heavily thrown onto a large tree and fell to the ground heavily. Even the ground shook a bit. The head bone of the boar cracked, with its brain flowing from the bone crack. It was still bleeding in the mouth. After trembling a few moments in the limbs, it stopped moving.

Killing a level-3 monster with a warrior's strength was not difficult for Lynnray.

"The magic crystal core of a level-3 monster was only worth 10 gold coins, but it should not be wasted." Lynnray took out his flat knife, opened the boar's head bone, and removed an earth-yellow crystal core from the brain. Lynnray wiped the crystal core on the grass and put it in his bag.

Then he used the flat knife to cut the boar's leg skin and obtained its four legs.

After cutting off some branches, he lit a fire with one wave of hand. Then he set up a simple grill and started roasting boar legs.

The shadow mouse Beibei drooled and stared at the boar legs: "The boar legs must be delicious. Can't you roast them quick with fire magic?"

"Fire magic? I only know a little of it. Besides, we can't roast meat fast by lighting a larger fire and increasing the temperature." Lynnray curled his mouth, and sprinkled some salt on the meat.

Based on Lynnray's magic test, he was at super grade in affinity with earth and wind elements, and medium grade in fire series. In fact, a medium grade was good enough for an ordinary person. But Lynnray did not want to waste his energy in fire magic.

To make similar achievement in fire magic as in earth and wind, he needed to make 10 times of the effort.

Therefore, he only casually practiced some magic force in fire series. It was easy for him to set out a fire ball.

After roasting two boar legs, one for himself and one for Beibei, he continued with other two boar legs.

"Wow, so delicious." Beibei ate excitedly and talked with Lynnray, "Boar leg is much more delicious than home-kept pigs. And you did a good job in roasting." Beibei praised Lynnray a bit.

Lynnray laughed.

"Boss, I want to eat more." After finishing one leg, Beibei looked at Lynnray with a pitiful expression.

But Lynnray didn't soften his heart. He said directly: "One boar leg is much larger than a roast chicken. One is enough. The other two legs are for dinner." Then, disregarding Beibei's pitiful expression, he waited until the other two legs were roasted, wrapped them up with large leaves and put them into his bag. Then he set off with Beibei again.

Chapter 10 - Monster Mountains (II)

Monster Mountains were a continuous range with various plants of unknown age. Traveling through the mountains was troublesome because the traveler had to cross mountains and sometimes took detours.

"Do not remove the thorns on the way. We prefer to take a detour." Delin explained to Lynnray.

Lynnray heard Delin's explanation carefully and kept going.

"Remember, do not always make noise in case being discovered by monsters. If you have made some noise, leave the spot quickly." Delin continued, "And if you get wounded, cover your blood stain, because a bloody smell can attract monsters. They have a much sensitive nose than us."

Lynnray looked up at the sky.

The tree crowns almost covered the entire sky. Lynnray thought of the knowledge he learned in the library of Ernst Academy on how to live in an old forest. In such a place where even the sun was covered, you had to distinguish the directions.

Lynnray crossed over branches and vines as flexibly as a monkey, but he gasped at the scene he saw suddenly.

The corpses of three men and two women were a dozen meters ahead. They had not rotten, but there were obvious signs of consumption. None of their corpses were intact. One man was eaten in half, with a hole in the stomach, and intestines flowing to the ground. A woman's head was eaten in half, with one eyeball still remaining. The pale skeleton had some worms on it.

Lynnray held his breath at the scene.

"They should be dead two or three days ago." Delin appeared beside Lynnray and observed the corpses. He still looked peaceful, "Just carefully observe. Every one of them had an insignificant bloodstain at the location of heart. They were killed by a human, and the same human."

Lynnray was surprised.

"Grandpa Delin, they were killed by a human?" Lynnray looked at Delin in surprise.

Delin smiled lightly: "It's your first time to enter Monster Mountains. If you are experienced, you will know you need to defend the attack both from monsters and from humans."

"Human attack? Why should they attack each other?" Lynnray was a bit angry.

In Monster Mountains, the numerous monsters were already a problem, but humans killed each other instead of uniting with each other.

"It is normal. Why do people enter the Monster Mountains? They come for magic crystal cores. You only get one if you kill a monster, but if you kill a human, maybe he has several, or more in his bag." Delin touched his white beard.

Lynnray suddenly understood.

It was greed!

Because of greed, some people wanted to obtain more magic crystal cores easily. And killing other people was indeed the quickest way.

"Lynnray, you must be careful. In my observation, the murderer of the five was powerful. All of the five people, maybe four warriors and one magician, were killed by stabbing in the heart. The quick attack was shocking. But we don't know the power of the five people, so we cannot figure out the real power of their murderer." Delin frowned and continued, "But the five people dare enter Monster Mountains. It means they are not weak. So the murderer should be more powerful than you."

Lynnray stepped forward, examined the corpses and agreed with Delin's point.

It was quick attack and kill.

"Now we are still in the edge area of Monster Mountains. Go ahead." Delin smiled.

Lynnray nodded and continued with his journey into the deeper area of Monster Mountains. He often saw the remnants of monsters and humans as well as many rusty weapons. And he also came across some weaker monsters.

At night, Lynnray and the shadow mouse ate one boar leg each and took rest. Lynnray sat on the ground, and the shadow mouse shrank beside Lynnray. "We can't light a fire in Monster Mountains." Delin enjoined. "I see, grandpa Delin." Lynnray was aware of the know-hows of surviving in Monster Mountains. Monsters were not ordinary beasts. They were not afraid of fire.

Sitting on the ground, Lynnray closed his eyes in a peaceful mental state. He could feel the flow of earth and wind elements, and it was like returning to the arms of the parents.

Lynnray was at super grade in affinity with wind and earth elements, so he could feel those elements in clarity.

"The pulsation of land and wind." Lynnray smiled and fell asleep.

In this state, Lynnray could be easily warned of any shaking or movement in the air.

That was the capability of a magician in wind and earth series.

Late in the night, the shadow mouse Beibei also started snoring. Wind cooled down, but it was summer, and coolness could only be felt in late night. The temperature in the day was humid and hot.

Everything was in darkness.

"Su Su..." The sound of friction between flesh and grass was heard.

Two wind wolves with cyan hair were walking through the woods. They were watching the surroundings with green eyes; meanwhile, they walked quietly on their feet.

The pale teeth of wind wolves were shiny in cold light.

Chapter 11 - Group of Wolves (I)

Lynnray suddenly opened his eyes and looked in the south. But there were only messy thorns. It was a place of rest chosen by Lynnray. Ordinary monsters could not discover him even in close range since he hid himself in the grass and thorns.

"Two monsters are drawing near, maybe 40 meters from me." Lynnray discovered two monsters based on the fluctuation of wind elements.

Lynnray quietly came to the edge of the thorns, and through the thorns, he saw two strong wind wolves with green eyes 30 meters away. The wind wolves were advancing in his direction. Lynnray felt some weight coming onto his shoulder, and it was the little shadow mouse Beibei.

"Boss, aren't they wind wolves? We saw them several times in the school." Beibei was not worried, and talked with Lynnray mentally.

Lynnray stared at the wind wolves and said: "Yes, they are wind wolves. Monster wolves are classified into tooth wolves, wind wolves and snow wolves. The snow wolves were the strongest, and tooth wolves were the weakest. Wind wolves are in the middle. Even the most ordinary wind wolves are level-4 monsters. Elites may be at level-5 or 6. I heard the topmost wind wolves are at level-8."

Even the most ordinary are level-4 monsters. This is not something to be compared with wild boar. "I'm only at level-4 in warrior strength. I can't defeat them with only warrior strength." Lynnray said with a bit excitement, "I like taking challenges."

When the wind wolves quietly approached, Lynnray moved his lips and chanted magic mantras, with a cold look in his eyes.

"Boom!""Boom!""Boom!""Boom!"...

With a low rumbling, a dozen large stones with earth-yellow light flew toward the wind wolves, which raised their head in alert and tried to keep away.

A low sound of strike.

When the large stones were thrown toward the wind wolves, they escaped in a fast speed. One wind wolf was hit in the back leg, and the other barely dodged.

"Wind wolves are so fast."

Lynnray chanted magic mantras and used the auxiliary wind magic 'top speed', and meanwhile, he held his flat knife and rushed out of the thorns to the injured wolf.

A level-4 warrior with 'top speed' was as fast as the non-injured wind wolf. Of course, the injured one was much slower than Lynnray. It tried to escape, and grinned toward Lynnray.

"Su!""Su!""Su!"...

A series of wind swords cut toward Lynnray.

"Wolves are strong in the head and tail, but weak in the waist." Lynnray moved flexibly, and with three light steps, he dodged from the attack of the injured wolf. His right leg kicked at the waist of the wind wolf like an iron whip.

"Pum!" The wind wolf was kicked into the air, and howled in pain.

Lynnray made another leap and cut the wind wolf's belly with his flat knife. He felt the knife had cut on a firm piece of leather. With difficulty, it made a wound. Blood was spilled into the air.

"The wind wolf has a weak waist, but its skin is firm. No, the knife is not sharp enough. It can be used to cut ordinary stones, but it will be difficult to cut the skin of a level-4 monster." Lynnray thought, and looked at the other wind wolf in alert.

The other wind wolf did not move. It stared at Lynnray with the intention to kill in its eyes. And it was making howls in a deep sound.

"If the wind wolf is not injured, I cannot kill it with warrior strength, based on its flexibility." Lynnray knew that wind wolves are fast monsters. If he did not use wind magic, he could not fight with the wind wolf.

But when Lynnray was half way in his chanting, he suddenly looked pale.

"Terrible!"

The low roaring of wind wolves was heard in all directions. Lynnray had a glance and saw green eyes all around him. In darkness, such green eyes were indeed frightening.

"Not one, but a group of them."

Lynnray got nervous, and Beibei, who was yawning, now straightened its hair and looked around in alert.

"Boss, it's dangerous."

"Grandpa Delin, your words came true." Lynnray said bitterly.

In the Monster Mountains, there was no chance of survival if one met with a super powerful monster or a group of wind wolves.

"Not at all. I mean a group of tens of thousands. In that case, you will die for sure, unless you can fly. But we are in a better situation, there are 20 to 30 wind wolves at most." Delin said easily, but with a grave expression, "But you should know I'm a spirit with no magic force. I cannot hep you. You have to depend on yourself."

Lynnray felt bitter in the heart.

"20 to 30 wind wolves, and they are at least in level-4. They are fast and can use magic. But I'm only a level-5 magician." Lynnray felt a heavy pressure. At this moment, the wind wolves stopped roaring.

Two strong wind wolves walked out of the group. Their sizes were larger than the two he saw just now. The surviving wind wolf stood beside the two wolves respectfully and made a low crying sound. Lynnray had no idea what they were communicating.

The larger size and green eyes shook Lynnray in the heart.

"They are elites in the group. At least, they are at level-5 or, in a worse case, level-6." Lynnray got nervous and started thinking of solutions.

Suppose they were level-5 monsters. Two level-5 monsters and a group of level-4 monsters attacked one person together. Lynnray had no confidence to win. The speed of level-4 wind wolf was already the limit for Lynnray. And Lynnray could not be faster than a level-5 wind wolf, even if he used 'top speed'.

The two heading wind wolves were staring at Lynnray with a killing intent in their eyes.

"It seems I have to fight desperately." Surrounded by a group of wind wolves, Lynnray sweated in the forehead and the back. He had rapid beating of heart and chanted magic mantras in a faster speed.

"Awl..."

One of the two heading wolves made a low howling, and instantly, the 20 to 30 strong wind wolves started their attack on all directions. Their pale teeth were trying to bite Lynnray, and more than a hundred wind swords in green color appeared in the air.

Chapter 12 - Group of Wolves (II)

At this moment, more than 20 wind wolves surrounded Lynnray. More than 100 wind swords in deep green filled the narrow space.

There was no place to hide!

Lynnray made a leap on the feet, and his body was like an arrow shooting onto a large tree. But there were too many wind swords, a dozen of which cut on Lynnray's body.

"Pum!""Pum!""Pum!""Pum!"...

The wind swords seemed to be cutting on firm leather. Lynnray was forced to change direction by the wind swords. He grasped a horizontal branch and climbed onto the tree. He reached a height 20 to 30 meters, and looked downward.

"It was really dangerous."

Lynnray took a deep breath in relief. At this moment, on his body was an armor in the same color as rocks. The armor was shining in earth-yellow light, sending out an air of earth elements.

Earth magic -- holy armor of land guard!

Holy armor of land guard required at least level-5 to deploy one. Magicians at level-5 and 6 could deploy a holy armor of land guard which was in the form of rock consisting of gathered earth elements. A holy armor in the form of rock had great defense and could defend against attacks on the same level several times.

The wind swords only had power at level-3 or 4.

"Howl..." An angry low roaring.

Lynnray looked downward and saw more than 20 wind wolves jumping up. The heading two wind wolves made a leap of a dozen meters onto the branch of the tree. Their powerful claws grasped the branch and stood stably.

Wind wolves had good balance, so climbing trees was not difficult for them.

"I'm only afraid that you don't climb." Lynnray felt the surge of blood in his body. He was excited at the dangerous situation on the verge of life and death.

As to capability of climbing trees, wind wolves were weaker than humans. Lynnray swiftly jumped between trees, and the wind wolves followed.

In the peripheral area of Monster Mountains, wind wolves were the strongest. Even if a level-6 warrior came across them, he had to escape. The physical strength of a level-6 warrior was not enough to defend the claws of wind wolves.

So Lynnray and the wind wolves were playing catch and chase 20 meters above ground. The heading two wind wolves were even faster than Lynnray, who could only dodge quickly. The heading wolf shoot out several wind swords, and Lynnray had to change his direction.

"Hua!" Several branches were cut off by wind sword and fell down to ground.

"Puchi!"

The claw of one heading wolf scratched Lynnray's back. The holy armor of land guard shivered several times, and blinked in earth-yellow light.

"Su!""Su!""Su!"...

The head wolf moved very fast and flexibly. Its claws scratched Lynnray's torso, head and neck. Luckily the holy armor of land guard was a cluster of elements and could change its form or create a helmet for protection. But under the attack of wolf head, the armor was twinkling.

"The wind wolf moved too fast, and the holy armor of land guard is about to break."

Lynnray clenched his teeth and climbed higher. Humans were lighter than wind wolves, and were more flexible in climbing. When Lynnray reached 80 meters high, the wind wolves could not move higher. They could only spit wind swords to Lynnray. Lynnray dodged the wind swords at first, and for those he couldn't dodge, he defended with holy armor of land guard.

"You will die by falling from such height." Lynnray chanted magic mantras quickly. He could keep calm in such a dangerous situation, as a result of practice in stone sculpting.

"Pum!"

A wind sword cut on the holy armor, which could not resist any more, and broke apart. It turned into earth-yellow light and vanished. A next wind sword came and was spotted by Lynnray.

"The wind swords of ordinary wind wolves were like those sent out by a level-3 magician. They could not kill me, a level-4 warrior." Lynnray continued to chant magic mangras and allowed the wind swords to cut on his body. "Shi..." With bleeding, a horrible wound appeared on Lynnray's chest.

Lynnray only frowned and continued to chant mantras.

"Boom!""Boom!""Boom!""Boom!"...

More than 100 stones as large as a head, with earth-yellow light on the surface, smashed toward the wind wolves. About 30 stones hit heavily on the heading wolves' body. They were smashed down to ground. The stones came in a large quantity and great density, with several "Awl..." sounds, the wind wolves fell down, and even tree branches were broken.

Most wind wolves were hit and fell. But they were flexible monsters, and with good defense in the skin, their claws held tightly to the tree branches. Some wind wolves were lightly injured, and no wolf died.

"The wound looks scary, but is not deep. However, I can't let it bleed in this way." Lynnray conjured up flame with his right hand, and pressed his right hand at the wound. With a "Shi" sound, a smell of roast meat spread into the air, and Lynnray frowned and gasped. His wound at the chest sealed, but left an ugly scar.

When Lynnray was making the movement, he quickly jumped between branches and covered a long distance. Then he jumped to the ground directly. He fell from a height of 80 meters. With air flow covering his body, he was not falling in a fast speed, and at the time he chanted magic mantras.

The wind wolves chased him and caught up with him in a short while.

The head wolves landed on the ground most quickly, looked at Lynnray and made a roar. They had confusion in their eyes. Why wasn't Lynnray running? A monster with high intelligence worried Lynnray might have some tricks.

"Howl..." One head wolf roared in a deep sound, and a level-4 wolf obeyed the command and jumped toward Lynnray.

Lynnray took a leap and pointed at the gathering wind wolves in the distance. He shouted with a deep voice: "Gravity control!"

Earth magic -- gravity control!

This was a very terrifying earth magic. It used the earth element flow that controlled the earth to adjust the gravitational force within a certain area of the land, causing the pressure on the attacked person to increase sharply. Gravity control could be performed by a magician of level-5 at least.

And the stronger the earth-based magician was, the greater the power of the'gravity control' could be shown.

"Om..."

The air trembled, centered on Lynnray, and the ground within a hundred meters of the area was earth-yellow in color. All the wind wolves within this range felt astonishing pressure, and the leaping wind wolf was also affected by the sharp increase in pressure. Unable to fall, there was a hint of panic in the eyes of the other group of wind wolves, but the two wind wolves headed by it roared desperately towards

Lynnray, but it was obvious that the speed of these two wind wolves was not even half of the past.

“Your speed has been drastically reduced, but I’m not experiencing any influence.” The earth-yellow light circulated on Lynnray’s body, which seemed to complement the earthy yellow light on the ground.

The earth element of gravity had special fluctuations, and different earth magicians had some differences in their display. As long as you fully grasped the fluctuation of the earth element, you could rely on the earth element to offset the influence of gravity.

The wolves’ speed dropped sharply, and Lynnray’s speed was much faster than them. Lynnray dodged flexibly, and at the same time, he chanted a magic mantra quickly in his mouth.

“Puchi!” “Puchi!” “Puchi!” “Puchi!”...

Dozens of ground spears suddenly emerged from under the feet of the wind wolves. The sharp ground spears directly pierced the abdomen of the seven wind wolves, bleeding all over the place. Several wind wolves were also severely injured by the sharp stabbing.

"Howl..."

The two wind wolves became anxious.

Within the range of gravity, their speed was not as fast as half of the past, and they couldn’tblock the flexible Lynnray. If face to face, level-5 wind wolves could definitely kill Lynnray, but they couldn’t get close to him! With the power as a level-5 magician, it was not difficult to deal with the wind wolves.

"Howl..." A low growl.

The two wind wolves in the lead did not hesitate to turn their heads and ran away, and the other dozen wind wolves that were alive also slid away immediately. In the dark night, these wind wolves disappeared from Lynnray's vision in a blink of an eye. At this time, Lynnray's rushed over, like a strong wind, passing three severely wounded wind wolves who had no time to escape.

"Pum!""Pum!""Pum!"

Three consecutive legs kicked hard on the heads of the three severely wounded wind wolves. There was a cracking sound of skulls, and the wind wolves immediately fell to the ground. Including the seven wind wolves that had been pierced by ground spears, a total of ten wind wolves died, and because of violent movement, Lynnray's chest wounds that had been sealed by the fire opened again, and blood leaked out.

Chapter 13 - Crisis (I)

"Huh, finally gone." Lynnray let out a sigh of relief.

Lynnray knew very well that he himself had the strength of a level-4 warrior, and fighting in close combat with a level-5 wind wolf would only lead to death. Magic was the only resort. But if you didn't have enough speed, how could you have time to chant the magic spell? Fortunately, your speed was fast enoughto lead to such a result.

"Even a level-6 cannot do better than me. If a level-6 magician came, at the speed of an average level-6 magician, he couldn't escape the chasing of the wind wolf. If besieged by a group of wind wolves, he didn't even have the time to use magic."Lynnray felt it was a wise decision to cultivate his physical strength.

Lynnray glanced at the Ring of Coiling Dragon on his left middle finger. This ringhad been worn on the finger since he grew up.

"It's also fortunate to have the Ring of Coiling Dragon, otherwise how could I use so many level-5 magics in one go!"

A general level-5 magician may have no magic power after using level-5 magic twice, but Lynnraywas different. He had just cast a level-5 earth magic'stone crack' three times, 'gravity control' one time, 'holy armor of land guard' once, and 'ground spear' once. He used level-5 magic six times.

He benefited from the Ring of Coiling Dragon.

The Ring of Coiling Dragon was obtained by Delinaccidentally. Delin was shocked to discover when he cast a magic once. If the same magic was cast through the Ring of Coiling Dragon, only a sixth of the original magic force and spiritual force was needed.

With the Ring of Coiling Dragon, the magician could obviously communicate with and manipulate earth elements in a better way. The burden on mental power and magic power was very low.

One sixth, what did it mean?

For example, a holy magician can only cast the 'destructive storm' once, and after owning the Ring of Coiling Dragon, he can cast the magic six times. Such a horrible treasure was initially considered to be a gift from Mother Earth, so it was named the "Ring of the Land".

The divine tool 'Ring of the Land'.

This name was givenby Delin. According to Delin's words, although there were other wonderful treasures on Yulan Continent which could make it easier for magicians to cast magic, they had none to have the effect of 'Ring of the Land'.

And after Lynnray got the Ring of Coiling Dragon, he found during his training:

"I only need to use one sixth of required spiritual force by using the ring to communicate with elements in the magics of earth, wind and even fire series."Lynnray looked at the Ring of Coiling Dragon happily.

Delin appeared beside Lynnray at this time.

"Don't observe it anymore. After I got this precious item, I dare not tell others. If the news gets out, many holy fighters will come to grab it. I didn't know this ring can help the magician in wind and fire series besides earth series." Delin praised the ring.

Lynnray nodded: "I will not tell others about the secret." Lynnray knew the preciousness of the ring. Only news got out, he might be torn into pieces by holy fighter of Yulan Continent.

"Boss, it's the end?" Beibei's voice came. Beibei was staying in grass at a distance. It did not join the fight, but observed it quietly.

Lynnray smiled.

"Huh, it's a little painful." Lynnray looked at his wound at the chest. His upper clothes were torn apart, and the wound at chest was still bleeding. He carefully cleaned his wound, and by healing it with earth elements, the wound was gradually closing. Beibei looked at Lynnray at this moment, and felt nervous for him.

"Boss, next time I will join the fight." Beibei talked mentally.

"No, you can fight when you find that I would be dead fighting alone. Otherwise...why am I here?" Lynnray insisted, and Beibei stopped talking. It had the intention to kill, but Lynnray didn't allow it to do so.

At this time, a black figure was lurking in the grass 30 meters from Lynnray.

"This young man used level-5 earth magic six times. Although the force was level-5, he used it six times, which means he is a level-6 magician. His warrior strength is level-4. And based on his auxiliary wind magic, he is also a wind magician. Overall, he is a dual-series magician at level-6 and a warrior at level-4."

The black figure calculated in the mind.

"I have 90% of probability of killing him. I can attack." The black figure made his judgment.

Lynnray just experienced a battle, so he relaxed himself. The black figure remained motionless and quiet in darkness. Not to mention Lynnray, even the shadow mouse Beibei did not notice his presence.

The time of gravity effect had passed.

"At this time!" The lurking black figure rush out to Lynnray like a elusive shadow.

Lynnray was taken by surprise. He dodged, turned his head and saw a man in black stabbing him with a knife. The knife's cold light surprised him, and the indifferent eyes with the intention to kill caused a shivering of his heart.

"Fast speed." Lynnray stepped back, but the black figure was faster, with the shiny knife reaching him.

"Kang!"

Lynnray withstood with his flat knife, which hit the man's knife. With a clear striking sound, the flat knife was broken, and a piece of broken blade crossed Lynnray's face and left a blood trace.

"Pu!""Pu!""Pu!""Pu!"...

Eight wind swords appeared in front of Lynnray and cut toward the black figure. Lynnray was able to cast wind swords without chanting a mantra. The wind swords cut at the black figure, who had a flow of black light, dissolving the wind swords.

"Vital energy in dark property." Lynnray made his judgment.

The eight wind swords did not prevent the black figure, but distracted him. Lynnray took a leap on one side, and the black figure reacted quickly and leaped toward Lynnray.

The knife with black light was reaching Lynnray in a rapid speed, pointing at his heart. At this moment, Lynnray thought of the scene of the five corpses, who were stabbed in the heart.

"Go to hell!"

The black figure said with confidence, and pushed his knife onto Lynnray's chest. Above ground, Lynnray had no means to dodge. He could only use the simplest defense magic -- earth shield. A small earth shield only 1/3 of the size of a normal one appeared at his chest location.

"Hum!"

The black shadow grunted, and pushed his knife into the earth shield. Such a low-level magic was not a hindrance for the man in black.

The earth shield still had strong defense despite its small size. However, it could only reduce the speed of knife attack, but could not block it. Lynnray felt a sharp pain at the chest. In moments, the knife penetrated the earth shield.

"Yo..."

With a horrible squeak, shadow mouse Beibei appeared beside the black figure's wrist. The shadow mouse opened its mouse in a size enough to swallow a fist. Its sharp teeth bit on the black figure's wrist. With a painful scream, the black figure's wrist was bit off.

Only a broken hand was holding the knife inserted on Lynnray's chest.

Chapter 14 - Crisis (II)

"Ah, Ah..." The pain of losing a hand made the black figure scream.

The shadow mouse swooshed to the black figure again. The black figure looked at the pet-like shadow mouse: "What a monster is this?" He didn't believe it was a shadow mouse. He saw shadow mice before, and none was as horrible as this. Tolerating the pain of losing a hand, the black figure summoned a vital energy shield, and tried to escape.

The black figure felt the little creature was turning elusive. Then he felt a sharp pain. The shadow mouse bit at his throat and penetrated his dark vital energy shield.

"Crunch!"

With a trembling sound of crunch, the black figure's neck was bit off in half. The head and torso was connected only by skin. The black figure's eye darkened and he fell onto ground.

Lynnray jumped onto ground at this time and took out the short knife. Blood tainted his clothes. He shivered upon seeing his wound at chest. If the knife went a few inches deeper, maybe his heart was pierced.

"I was only a bit from death."

After the battle, Lynnray looked at the shadow mouse which saved his life. Beibei said nervously: "How are you, boss?"

"I'm good. I'm still living." Lynnray smiled at Beibei. If not because of Beibei, he would be dead already.

Beibei relaxed when he heard these words. It stood straight, shook its hips and said contently: "Boss, you are too weak for the trial. You were almost killed by a man hidden in the dark." Beibei said with sarcasm.

Lynnray only smiled.

"Beibei, thank you for saving my life." Lynnray looked at his horrible wound at the chest and sighed with emotion: "This is the first day."

Delin appeared and exclaimed: "This killer is good at lurking. And the shadow mouse really helped. I'm only a spirit and cannot save your life." Lynnray understood that his holy magic master only existed in a spirit form.

"Grandpa Delin, why was this killer so fast? I used auxiliary wind magic but was not as good as him." Lynnray found it unbelievable.

Delin explained: "This killer should be a level-6 warrior, but he practiced vital energy maneuvering in the property of darkness, which was strange. And he underwent special training of lurking and holding breath. A level-6 warrior like him was more powerful than an ordinary level-6 warrior. Vital energy maneuvering in the property of darkness was a strange art, and he might have used a secret method of accelerate himself."

Lynnray slightly nodded.

Magic or vital energy maneuvering in the property of darkness was forbidden in the Holy Alliance, but allowed in four empires and Dark Alliance. Similarly, light magic and vital energy techniques in the property of light were forbidden in the Dark Alliance.

“Boss, come.” The shadow mouse Beibei jumped beside the killer’s body.

Lynnray looked at the scene in surprise: “Beibei, what’s the matter?”

“The killer is carrying a bag.” Beibei said excitedly. Lynnray looked at the killer’s body. The killer’s black clothes in the back was scratched open. It was done by the shadow mouse.

Under the black clothes, there was a bag tied to the body.

“Lynnray, the five people should also have been killed by this killer. Judging from his strength, I don’t know how many people he had killed. The magic crystal cores hidden in his bag are definitely in a great number.” Delin said with a smile.

Lynnray couldn't help but feel excited in the heart. Based on his strength, maybe an ordinary level-6 warrior would be killed by him. Maybe he collected a lot of treasures.

"Chi Chi..." Little shadow mouse picked up the bag with its mouth and leaped onto Lynnray's shoulder.

Upon seeing this scene, Lynnray also secretly exclaimed: "Beibei’s speed is too fast. Although the speed of the killer is fast, he is only a little faster than me. Beibei’s speed is so fast that I can't react at all. No wonder that the killer was bitten to death by Beibei, with no time to escape.."

"Chi Chi..." Beibei carried the bag in its mouth, stood on Lynnray's shoulder and shook it, "Boss, open it up and take a look." Beibei talked anxiously to Lynnray in the mind.

Beibei was also curious about what was in it.

Lynnray smiled and took this bag. This bag was dark and made of leather, but it was obvious that the quality of this bag was much better than that of Lynnray. It seemed to be made of the skin of a powerful monster. Lynnray unbuttoned the bag.

Looking at the contents of the package, Lynnray's eyes lit up. In the middle of the package, there was a set of clothes and some barbecue ingredients, the other was a bag of gold coins, and the largest inter-layer of the package was a big bag of items. Lynnray untied this big bag and took a look. He could not help but took a breath.

"How many people and monsters did this killer kill?"Lynnray was a little shocked, this big bag turned out to be full of colorful crystal cores of monsters, and occasionally a few transparent cores mixed with them.

"Maybe there are dozens."Lynnray was excited.

Lynnray immediately began to count, and at the same time distinguished the level of the monster core. It is not difficult for a magician to distinguish the energy of the monster core. In a short while, Lynnray figured out the quantities and types of crystal cores inside.

"There are a total of 102 monster crystal cores, a total of 7 magic crystal stones, among which, there are 5 cores of level-6 monsters, 26 cores of level-5 monsters, 71 cores of level-4 monsters, and none of level-3 monsters. Of the seven magic crystal stones, 6 are medium grade and one is high grade."

Lynnray felt his heart beating quickly. He didn't know that this killer had also obtained level-3 cores, but didn't bother to take it.

Magic crystal coreswere generally inlaid on the magic wand, which was used to quickly restore magic force. When the killer killed the magician, he pried off the magic crystal core on the magic wand.

"102 monster crystal cores are worth about 13,000 gold coins, while seven magic crystal cores are worth 1,600 gold coins. Add up to about 15,000 gold coins."Lynnray calculated this number with surprise. There are so many in one killer's package.

What about your own family?

To send Warton to study in O'Brien Empire, Lynnray's family was almost drained in wealthBaruch family would feel difficult to gather even 10,000 gold coins today.

"I didn't expect to have so much gains on the first day in the Monster Mountains. How much will I gain in the next two months?"Lynnrayreflected with hope.

However, Lynnray also knew that it would be impossible to encounter such a big "fat sheep" every time in the future, and the big "fat sheep" was also strong, and Lynnray almost lost his life this time. Thinking of the scene just now, Lynnray couldn't help feeling the wound on his chest and the wound on his face that was cracked by a flat knife.

Lynnray suddenly glanced at the ten wind wolves that had died.

"Ten level-4 monster crystal cores, which add up to several hundred gold coins. I have to take them."Lynnrayused the short knife of the killer to pry out the magic crystal cores in the skulls of the ten dead wind wolves. He found that the short knife was much sharper than his flat knife.

Chapter 15 - Cruelty (I)

Lynnraycleaned his wound at a water sourceand absorbed earth elements to heal himself. He was grateful for the compassion and selfless love of Mother Earth. Stepping on the ground, he felt the slow improvement of his body and peace in the heart.

Lynnray's package has now changed. The quality of his own package was far inferior to that of the killer's package in terms of leather quality and internal design. The killer's package had internal layering and locks. As long as the lock was tightened, the contents inside would be clamped tightly, and it would not affect his movement when carried on the back. And that killer's black short knife was also much sharper, and was easy to use.

"Hu!"

Lynnraypassed through the woods in agile movement. He only fought with level-3 and 4 monsters and neglected the lower levels. He also dare fight with a level-5 if the monster was alone.

As he went into the depth ofMonster Mountains, he experienced bloody and cruel battles, and encountered hidden killers. He had more wounds after the battles, and his character was getting tough.

The battle between life and death made Lynnray's heart more tenacious and his methods more fierce.

In a blink of an eye, Lynnray had already stayed in the Monster Mountains for a month.

On top of a big tree beside a creek.

With a shallow scar on his left face, Lynnray bowed his body like a cheetah lurking in a tree.

At this moment, Lynnray was hiding among dense leaves and looking down carefully. There was a stream tens of meters away from the big tree where Lynnray was, and beside the stream was a strong bloody boar with a scarlet horn on its nose. It had prominent muscles and blue veins similar to the old roots of a tree.

Bloody boar, level-5 monster, fire magic!

"This bloody boar has thick skin and very strong defense. I am afraid that the ground spearcannot penetrate its thick skin."

Lynnraymade a quick decision, and moved his lips silently to chant the magic spell. Gradually, the wind elements beside Lynnray began to gather, and then a cyan translucent javelin appeared in front of Lynnray. At the tip of the javelin, there was a wind surging.

Level-5 wind magic -- roaring of the wind!

"Su!"

With a sharp whiz, the air javelin suddenly shot downward at a terrifying speed, and Lynnray suddenly jumped towards the canopy of the big tree, almost following the translucent javelin and rushed downward.

The bloody boar who was drinking water heard the harsh sound and couldn't help but look up, but the speed of the javelin was too fast, and for a while, it was only a few meters away from the bloody boar. Because of the speed of the javelin, a circular airflow is formed at the end of the gun.

"Howl" The bloody boar roared angrily, and its scarlet horn rose against the javelin.

"Pum!"

The air javelin formed by magic hit the bloody boar's forehead and broke apart immediately. When attacked by the level-5 magic of the wind element, the bloody boar couldn't help but knelt down in half. There was even a trace of blood on its forehead.

"Puchi!"

The bloody boar hadn't reacted yet, and Lynnray, who followed 'roaring of the wind', held the sharp short knife, and pierced the center of the bloody boar's forehead. The black short knifedirectly penetrated the boar's head, and at the moment of piercing, Lynnray quickly backed away.

"Howl..."

The bloody boarwhich was piercedroared frantically, flames all over his body, and at the same time rushed frantically toward the front, the terrifying aura was extremely shocking. But after rushing for more than ten meters, it fell to the ground feebly, with limbs twitched and trembling for two or three times and then he stopped moving, and the flames all over its body disappeared.

"Among level-5 monsters, bloody boars and bloody bulls might have the lowest wisdom."Lynnray walked to the bloody boar's corpse, pulled out the short knife, and also took out the magic crystal core of level-5, fire property.

Recalling his life in the Monster Mountains this month, Lynnray had to admit that although he was still a level-5 dual-series magician and a level-4 warrior, his combat power was much stronger than when he first entered the Monster Mountains.

After experiencing life and death several times, the scars on his body represented the cruelty of this month.

Especially, there was a terrifying wound on his abdomen. That time he really got to the gate of the death, and in the end it was the shadow mousewhich rescued him.

This wound was not left by a monster, but by a very lovely girl.

"I really believed her at the beginning. I believe her friends were killed, and there was only one wounded woman left."Lynnray felt scared after thinking about what happened two weeks ago. The girl looked really kind and innocent.

When Lynnray discovered her, the other three men and another girl were dead, leaving her in horror.

Lynnray involuntarily went to comfort her, help her, and take care of her. The girl seemed to have been hit hard at the beginning, and was terrified. Every night, Lynnray had to hug her so that she could sleep peacefully. Every day, seeing this girl sleeping peacefully, Lynnray felt a burst of joy in his heart. This kind of day passed for three days, and on the third day, she also slept quietly in Lynnray's arms.

But suddenly this girl pierced the abdomen of Lynnray with a dagger.

And then, the furious shadow mouse Beibei grew in its size strangely, and the girl's entire head was suddenly crushed by its mouth, killed on the spot. Then Beibei returned to its original state.

However, Lynnray's abdominal wound bled more and more, and the little shadow mouse Beibei finally used dark magic to seal the wound.

"I should have listened to grandpa Delin back then, because I had too little experience."Lynnray thought of it and sighed in the heart. At first Delin warned him several times, but he finally saw Lynnray stubbornly taking care of the seemingly poor girl. Delin had no way to interfere, but he still requested Lynnray to avoid being leaned against, if he really wanted to help the girl.

However, the girl was extremely frightened at the time and couldn't sleep soundly without holding Lynnray. In the end, Lynnrayhugged her to provide comfort and they slept peacefully together.

"I really didn't expect she was such a good actress. I treated her so nice, but she was relentless"Lynnray sighed in his heart. He chilled in the heart every time he thought of the girl's fierce look when she pierced his abdomen.

What caused this girl to be so cruel?

Wasn't she touched by the care she had taken for three days?

"Fortunately, Grandpa Delin warned me again and again not to tell her about Beibei's real strength."Lynnray had to admit that grandpa Delin and Beibei saved his life.

"Lynnray, are you thinking about the girl again?" Delin appeared beside Lynnray.

Delin could guess that when he saw Lynnray's expression. The girl's attack with the dagger caused pain in Lynnray's heart and body. From that day on, Lynnraycould not put trust in people easily.

Delin saw through the girl much earlier. Would anyone who dare enter the Monster Mountains be terrified to that point because of dead people?

It's a pity that Lynnray was still cheated by that girl'sperformance, thinking how pitiful she was.

"Lynnray, the girl's capability of acting was not unique. When I was in Pron Empire, I saw many spies from other countries who could disguise themselves for decades without being noticed. Their skills of acting were far beyond your imagination."Delin said with a light smile, "Remember, don't let your guard down on a stranger."

Lynnray nodded slightly.

"Chi, Chi..." the little shadow mouse Beibei called out next to Lynnray.

Lynnray looked up.

Beibei also jumped from the side at this time, onto the bloody boar's dead body.

"Boss, when are you going to the core area of the Monster Mountains?" Beibei said with some discontent. "In these places now, the strongest one to encounter is a level-6monster. It is not that challenging. I want a challenge. Level-7 monster, boss, I want to fight with a level-7 monster!"

Lynnray glanced at the little shadow mouse: "Well, don't be too proud. You are saying a level-6 monster is not challenging. The last time you saw the heading cyan-wind vulture, you weren't able to do anything."

"Don't blame me." Beibei's little paw touched her nose and snorted, "Boss, as you saw, heading cyan-wind vulture didn't come down. It threw out wind swords in a crazy manner. How could I tolerate that?"

Lynnray smiled.

After several battles, Lynnray has already gained a certain understanding of the strength of the little shadow mouse Beibei. In terms of speed alone, Beibei has reached a terrifying point, but because of its size limitation, its attack could only rely on paws and mouth. It could fight with a level-6, but not so easily with a level-7.

At this moment, Lynnray frowned, turned his head vigilantly and looked in the distance. He saw a thin young man running toward him.

Chapter 16 - Cruelty (II)

"Lynnray, glad to see you again."With a pleasant voice, a thin young man ran to him. This young man met Lynnray on the way to Monster Mountains.The other two, his classmate Desat and reckless Kava were all dead.

At that time, facing the wind magic archer, when Lynnray used the earth magic 'ground spear', the agile level-5 fighter 'Matt' took the opportunity to escape, but Lynnray didn't care about the flee. After all, Matt didn't have much friendship with him.

To be honest, among the three, Lynnray also had a little trust in his fellow student Desat, and the big manKava gave him a good impression, but Matt only left an ordinary impression.

"Matt, I didn't expect that we could meet in the Monster Mountains after one month of separation."Lynnray was still very calm.

Matt was very excited: "It's really great. I almost became a monster's snack in the Monster Mountains several times this month. I have been lucky, huh, the bloody boar? Lynnray, you killed the bloody boar? Amazing."

Lynnray smiled.

"I'm hungry. I heard people say that the meat of bloody bulls and bloody boars was very delicious, and offered a good chewing feeling. I haven't eaten lunch yet. Would you mind giving me a bit of bloody boar?"Matt said jokingly.

The bloody boarwas so big, the weight of its meat was definitely several hundred jin, maybe enough for 10 people to have a feast.

"Of course I don't mind."Lynnraytook out his short knifeand tried to dismember the bloody boar.

"Lynnray, you don't need to do it yourself. It's your game. How can I trouble you in preparation? I'll do it. My barbecue skills are very good." Matt walked towards the bloody boar, and pulled out a short knife from his waist.

Matt waved the knife in his hand and dismemberedbloody boar. He also separated the bloody boar's limbs, tongue, and tail, and washed them in the nearby stream.

"Boss, his technique is quite proficient, he seems to be not worse than you." The little shadow mouse Beibei jumped onto Lynnray's shoulder.

Lynnray turned his head and glanced at Beibei, but he sighed in his heart. When outsiders saw such a little black shadow mouse, they might think it was ordinary without much threat.

But in fact, Lynnray still remembered the scene of horror in which the shadow mouse killed the man in black and the hypocritical girl.

"We can't judge people or monsters by their appearance"Lynnray sighed in his heart.

AndMatt set up the grill very quickly at this time, and took out some coarse salt from the package on his body: "Lynnray, the thigh meat of this bloody boarhas a firm taste, and the tongue is tender and delicious. The tail is also a good part to eat."

As he spoke, Matt expertly cut the tongue and tail of the boar into several pieces. Watching Matt ignite the wood with flint, even if Lynnray knows fire magic, he hasn't interfered with him all the time, watching Matt as he roasted quickly.

After a long time.

"It's almost done, taste it." Matt handed a boar thigh to Lynnray very enthusiastically.

Lynnraygave the boar thigh to Beibei next to him, and Beibei immediately took it happily and ate it in big mouthfuls. This boar thigh was about three or four times the size of Beibei, but Beibei just ate it up in just a short while.

This scene also stunned Matt.

"The black shadow mouse eats so fast. It deserved the title of a monster." Matt sighed, and at the same time he handed a piece of roasted boar tongue to Lynnray, "Lynnray, come and taste my piece of cooking art."

Lynnray smiled and refused: "No, I'm not used to eating it, the thigh meat is fine."Lynnray grabbed a boar thigh and ate it quickly. Matt next to him also smiled and said: "That I won't push you anymore. If you don't eat it, I will eat it, haha."

Matt enjoyed eating pig tongue and pig tail.

After Lynnrayfinished the entire thigh of the boar, Matt didn't eat even a bit of the thigh beside him. "Have you finished eating? Haha, that's okay, now I'm half full, I'll eat this boar thigh when I'm hungry." Matt took out a piece of tarp from his package, wrapped the boar thigh and put it in the package.

Lynnray glanced at Matt.

It seemed that Matt wanted to walk together with him.

"Matt, I want to stay alone inMonster Mountains, let's go our separate ways here."Lynnray said directly.

Matt frowned and said: "Lynnray, the Monster Mountains are very dangerous, and we should be much safer together. To be honest, for a month, I have been frightened, and I didn't even sleep at night."

"Then it's up to you."

Lynnray stopped talking, and headed deeper into the mountains and forest. Matt immediately rushed up from behind with a smile on his face, but heglanced at the leather package on Lynnray's back with a sinister intention in his eyes.

"This package is different from the one that Lynnray carried on his back a month ago, and it is also a lot bigger." Matt sneered in his heart, but his smile became more cordial. Matt was not like Lynnray. Hehad went on many trials in other places before entering the Monster Mountains.

Matt quickly followed. He giggled and said:"Lynnray, you are so kind, and I feel more at ease following you, after all, two people are better than one, and you can sleep in a different direction at night. No need to be careful all night." Lynnray was silent, glancing around from time to time, paying attention to any monster which might appear.

...

Lynnray headed northward slowly in Monster Mountains. He dare not go east anymore, because on the east was the danger zone. In his current location, monsters were generally at level-5 or 6.

And Matt followed along the way, and seemed very happy.

Two days later.

In the evening, it was dim, and Lynnray and Matt continued to move forward, one in front and one in the back.

"Lynnray, do you think we can go back? To be honest, we have been in the Monster Mountains for such a long time." Matt was on the road, whispering to Lynnray.

Lynnray just shook his head lightly, but made no sound.

Matt also had a bit of resentment in his heart: "Lynnray is very alert at night, not giving me any chance." Matt was not sure whether he could kill Lynnray; after all, staying in the Monster Mountains for such a long time was a proof of strength.

"En?"Lynnray turned his head abruptly and looked into the thorn bushes in the distance as if he had noticed it. There was a vague dark shadow hiding in the bushes.

And Matt, who was walking next to Lynnray, saw Lynnray turn his head and turn his back to him, with a hint of greed and excitement in his eyes. The short knife in Matt's hand was very skillful, and without hesitation, it stabbed Lynnray's back as quickly as possible——

Lynnray turned around abruptly and grabbed Matt's right wrist where he stabbed him, holding the short knife with one hand. At the same time, he looked at Matt indifferently, his eyes were even colder, and he said in a cold voice, "What are you going to do?"

"You--" Matt was startled, and Matt couldn't believe that he was attacking from behind, and the other party stopped him as if he could detect it.

Matt immediately smiled and looked at Lynnray: "What am I going to do? Great magician genius, I tell you, I want to kill you." Matt was confident that when the two were close together, as a level-5 warrior, he could easily kill a level-5 magician.

Matt's right arm suddenly used force, with vital energy surrounding it, and suddenly shocked Lynnray's hand.

"Go to hell!" Matt stared at Lynnray ferociously, slashing at Lynnray with a short knife in his hand.

"Howl~~~"

A terrifying sound, "What?" Matt couldn't help but tremble when he heard that voice, and then Matt saw a small black shadow appearing in front of his eyes instantly.

"This, what is this?" After Matt saw the black shadow clearly, it was the little shadow mouse Beibei who had played with Lynnray all day, but the little shadow mouse opened its mouth full of densely interlaced sharp teeth. He bit Matt in the face.

"No!"

Matt quickly backed away, and dodged his head sideways.

"Puchi!"

The speed of the little shadow mouse was far beyond Matt's imagination, and how could Matt be able to dodge it? With a sudden wave of the right front paw, the little shadow mouse cut off most of Matt's neck like a sharp sickle, and blood keeps pouring out.

"Uh, ah..." Covering his throat, Matt's eyes stared like a bull's eyes. He looked at the little shadow mouse in disbelief and horror."Black shadow mouse? Is it a black shadow mouse?"

At the moment of death, when his consciousness dissipated, Matt had a lot of doubts and panic in his heart. He had been preparing for this shot for a long time, but he did not pay attention to the black shadow mouse.

Black shadow mouse was at the weakest level of shadow mice.

But at the moment of death, Matt knew that this cute little shadow mouse was the scariest monster.

"Boom!"

In the end, Matt's hands covering his throat drooped, and his bodyfell down to ground. Blood stained his clothes and the ground.

Chapter 17 -- Beibei's Strength (I)

Lynnray stood in front of Matt's body, looked at it for a moment, only sighed, and couldn't help touching the position of his abdomen.

There was also a wound here, a wound that almost killed him.

"You are far worse than Nina."Lynnray shook his head and sighed. Matt didn't actually have much friendship with him, and only had a brief acquaintance on the way. That was far less than enough to gain trust.

Besides, after his experience with Nina, Lynnray would never be rest assured with his back side.

"Chi, Chi..."Beibei took the package on Matt's back at this time, and eagerly talked to Lynnray mentally, "Boss, open it and see how many magic crystal cores are there. Ah, no killer in this month has as many magic crystal cores as the first one."

Delin appeared beside Lynnray.

"Lynnray, this little shadow mouseseems to like to count magic crystal cores."Delin said with a smile.

"It seems to be true."Lynnray stretched out his hand to untie the package, and at the same time joked with Beibei, "Beibei, this time you killed this guy named Matt, as if you didn't use your sharp teeth, but your claws. Why don't you use teeth?"

Babe stood upright, screamed proudly, and said: "Boss, I'm stronger than you think. My claws are not worse than my teeth. And this Matt is too sinister. I don't want to pollute my teeth." At the same time, Beibei made a spitting gesture.

Lynnray laughed upon seeing Beibei's lovely, human-like gesture.

"Okay, eh, Beibei, you see, there are still a lot of magic crystal coresin Matt's package, there are more than 30, it seems that he has not been idle this month. But among them, the best are those of level-5."

Lynnray carefully calculated.

In the past 30 days, he killed monsters, or counterattacked and killed some people who wanted to kill him. The total amount of magic crystal cores he obtained was more than 300. The total price of those magic crystal cores, according to Lynnray, was around 40,000 gold coins!

"40,000 gold coins, if my father knew, then..."Lynnray felt a burst of joy in his heart when he thought of sending 40,000 gold coins to his father.

"It's normal for you to harvest so much."Delin said next to him. "Among the 300 magic crystal cores, only 50 were obtained from monsters. All the others were retrieved from killers' packages."

Lynnray nodded and admitted.

The first killer who wanted to kill himself at the beginning brought him a full 15,000 gold coins, and the other killers added up slightly more than the first killer.

"The Monster Mountains are very dangerous, so entering the Monster Mountains usually involves many people joining together. The killer generally does not attack a group of people, because the killer is best at killing the enemy in an instant. So the killer will usually attack a single person. ."

Delin suddenly laughed, curling up his beard, "Lynnray, you are innocent despite your big stature, and the hair on your lips proved one thing:"

"You are still a teenager!"

Delin laughed loudly, "Lynnray, in the vast Monster Mountains, the killers will not spare a teenager who shows innocent on the face. So, In just one month, you have encountered several of them."

"And those who come with friends may not encounter a killer in a month. Of course, the five people we saw soon after our entrance were an exception. One reason was that they were not strong enough, and the other was that the killer was too strong. But the killer was killed by Beibei in the end."

Lynnray also smiled and nodded.

He was only 15 years old despite his 1.8-meter stature. One with a bit insight would know he was a teenager.

"Generally, a level-5 or level-6 magician can only get a few thousand gold coins a month in the Monster Mountains. Moreover, these gold coins are obtained at the risk of their lives. After all, the Monster Mountains are too dangerous."Delin sighed.

Lynnray nodded in agreement: "It's very dangerous. I have been accepting my trial in the peripheral area until now. I have encountered up to level-6monsters, but I have been injured a few times. I would have been dead if not because of the Ring of Coiling Dragon, my capability in dual series, my grade-4 warrior strength and Beibei."

He looked at the little shadow mouse Beibei, which was playing with the monster core at this time.

After calming down, Lynnray packed up the monster crystal cores, and then set off again with the shadow mouse to continue with the trial journey in the Monster Mountains. After all, according to Lynnray's original plan, he would spend two months in the Monster Mountains.

......

Every day, Lynnrayfought with the beasts, the magic and the warrior's attacks were more sophisticated, the actual use experience of the earth and wind magic were also enriched, and the probability of Lynnray's injury is getting less and less, of course. As Lynnray couldn't help but approached the core area ofthe Monster Mountains slightly, the number of level-6 monsters also increased, and Lynnray became more vigilant every day.

In the forty-sixth day of Lynnray's entering the Monster Mountains.

"Wow~~~"

The calm lake surface suddenly produced ripples, and saw a figure emerge from the bottom of the lake, it was Lynnray, and Lynnray used a cloth to wipe his whole body.

The little shadow mouse Beibei watched Lynnraytaking a bath on the shore and was very envious. He squeaked and jumped directly into the air before rushing directly into the lake. Lynnray just smiled when he saw this scene, and then went on taking a bath.

"Haha, don't scratch, Beibei, don't scratch."Lynnray suddenly couldn't help laughing.

"So boss, you are also afraid of scratching." Little Shadow Mouse jumped up from the lake excitedly, a trace of content in his lovely eyes.

Lynnray smiled and went ashore, took a set of clean clothes from the package and changed it. After taking a bath, it was really refreshing and comfortable to put on clean clothes. Then Lynnray washed the original set of dirty clothes by the lake, and it cooled on the branch next to him. Lynnray jumped to the branch of another big tree and lay half down and watched the little shadow mouse playing in the lake.

He saw Beibei happily jumping out of the water for a while, rushing to the bottom of the water again, and wandering on the lake for a while...

"Pum!""Pum!""Pum!""Pum!"...

Suddenly, there was a slight vibration from the ground, and the rhythm of the vibration was very similar to the rhythm of stepping, Lynnrayfelt shivering in the heart. When he looked directly at the sound source, a hundred meters away from the south, he saw a tall and fuzzy shadow appearing. In the dense forest south of the lake, Lynnraysaw the target in a short while.

It has a huge body two stories high, a piece of fiery red scale armor as big as a shield, and thick limbs covered with scale armor, especially the tail that is more than half the body, like a whip. Just as agile and fast, those strange eyes that were the size of a lantern and red as rubies stared at the lake, and the white air currents containing sulfur scent spurted from the nostrils.

Lynnray got nervous and excited like a cat with its tail stepped on.

"Raptor, a level-7 monster!"

Chapter 18 - Beibei's Strength (II)

Since childhood, the only time when he was made interested in 'monster' was the moment he saw the raptor. The raptor demonstrated its amazing power. In Wushan Town, a raptor was an insurmountable existence. Houses were destroyed. The terrible force...

The raptor really shocked Lynnray.

When he saw the raptor, he was only an eight-year-old child, but now he was 15, and a dual-series magician at level-5.

"Boss, boss, it's mine!" Beibei's voice appeared in his mind.

Lynnray looked at the lake and saw Beibei's hair straight up like steel pins, and its muscles were plumping up. Its claws and head were getting bigger. A shadow mouse only 20 centimeters long became nearly half a meter. The size of half a meter was the limit of its change, as Lynnray observed.

But despite the size, the shadow mouse was tiny in front of the raptor.

The raptor's red eyes and cold look were focused on Beibei. The raptor made an angry roar, which echoed in the mountains. The shadow mouse also raised its head and produced a sharp squeak.

The roars and squeaks were heard at the same time.

Lynnray, who was observing the scene on a tree suddenly felt the raptor and shadow mouse were on the same level.

"Howl..." An angry roar was heard.

The raptor spit fire, which covered a space of dozens of meters. A "Shi Shi" sound was heard at the surface of the lake. Water was evaporated, but Beibei stayed still in the fire.

Beibei was unharmed by the fire.

"Beibei does not have a large size, but it has good defense. The flame with power at level-5 or 6 could not harm it." Lynnray looked at the scene quietly. After entering the Monster Mountains, Beibei had not encountered an opponent which he could fight with the best of its ability.

Beibei suddenly moved in the fire.

"Yo..."

A horrible squeak sounded, and Beibei turned into a black shadow rushing to the raptor. The raptor's eyes turned red, and its tail swept across the sky like a whip. The tail of raptor was near the speed of the shadow mouse.

"Hu!" Beibei moved in a strange way. It got around the fastest tail and bit on the neck of the raptor. The raptor turned its head and tried to bite Beibei.

Beibei was much faster. It bit heavily at the neck. With a crunch sound, the raptor's scales at the neck was bit off, or eaten by Beibei. Beibei ate stones and bones as food, so it could also eat the scales. At this moment the tail whipped to the spot. "Pa!" The tail's whipping sound made Lynnray feel numb in the scalp. Then Beibei swooshed off.

"The raptor had a thick skin at the neck. Beibei only injured it lightly." Lynnray held his breath and looked at the battle between the monsters. "The raptor's tail was moving in a bizarre way, and it can make quick turns while walking."

The raptor's tail was fast and elusive in direction.

"Yo..."

Beibei changed into a black shadow, broke up from the water and avoided the raptor's tail. But after its dodge, the tail changed its direction quickly and whipped in the opposite direction, heavily on Beibei's body. The black shadow was whipped deep into the woods.

"Beibei!" Lynnray was a bit nervous.

But the raptor was looking into the woods in alert. Beibei rushed downward from a tall high. The raptor attacked it with its tail immediately. Now Beibei took his lesson and also changed its direction by swinging its tail.

Two shadows, one the shadow mouse, and the other the raptor's tail were chasing each other! Sometimes the shadow mouse was whipped away, but it bit heavily on the raptor. They fought from the lakeside to the woods. The trees were broken by the tail and fell, but their fought saw no signs of an end.

"It seems Beibei is at an advantageous position."

Lynnray looked at the fight nervously. The raptor's scales had seven or eight bleeding holes. Blood tainted half of the raptor's body, and the raptor kept roaring in anger.

The raptor whipped its tail and the trees were broken in its range. Woods in hundreds of meters were destroyed.

"But can Beibei resist the whips?"

Lynnray became worried, because the raptor's tail was too strong. It could smash stones and break trees. It was heart shivering. Lynnray was confident that he would lose his life if attacked by the tail.

"Hu!" Beibei was whipped off again, but it turned into a black shadow and swooshed back.

The raptor was tainted with blood, with wounds all over its body. It looked miserable.

"Howl!"

The raptor escaped quickly to the woods, and vanished from the sight of Lynnray. Beibei chased it for a distance and ran back.

Lynnray jumped down from the branch, and Beibei ran to him, with its size returning to normal.

"Beibei, are you alright?" Lynnray communicated with it.

Beibei jumped onto Lynnray's shoulder, stood on its back legs, and looked at Lynnray proudly: "What kind of monster I am? I'm not afraid of a raptor." Beibei's lovely face showed complacence.

But it also moved a bit and said: "The raptor's tail was powerful. I had some pain when I was whipped." Lynnray smiled. The raptor's tail was very fierce. Lynnray was glad that Beibei was not injured despite the numerous attacks.

"The raptor's scales and skin were thick. I expanded myself to the limit, but could not bite through its skin."

Beibei sighed, "But if I insisted, I could let it bleed to death. But the raptor was cunning. It moved in the muscles and avoided being bitten at the same wound."

Lynnray smiled.

There was a huge gap from level-6 to level-7. A level-7 monster had a much higher attack force. The raptor had an intelligence similar to humans. It certainly understood the point.

Although the raptor had thick skin, it could not be bitten several times at the same spot. It knew it could not last long in the fight, so it fled.

"Beibei, do you want to fight with a level-8 monster?" Lynnray joked with it.

Beibei opened its eyes widely: "Boss, you are kidding. I was tired fighting with the level-7, but I heard a level-8 is 10 times more powerful than a level-7. They may not be faster than me in movement, but they can attack quicker than me."

Speed of movement is different from speed of attack.

The raptor moved slowly, but it whipped its tail in a flashing speed. Some large-sized monsters moved slowly, but attacked as quick as lightning!

Level-8 monsters were much more powerful than level-7.

"You are humble now." Lynnray patted on Beibei's head, "Um, my clothes are about to get dry. Let's take a rest on the tree, eat something and set off again." Lynnray made a leap to a height of eight meters, then made a few more steps to reach a branch 20 to 30 meters high. He leaned on the branch to rest.

Chapter 19 - Black Short Knife

It was the 51st day since they entered the Monster Mountains.

"Those killers thought I was easy to be bullied?"Lynnray looked at the dead woman in black. The woman in black was at about level-5, warrior strength. Lynnray killed her alone, only with magic.

Delin laughed: "With only a second look, one will know you are a daring young man thinking too high of himself and walking alone in the Monster Mountains. Who doesn't want to come and kill you?"

Lynnrayhad a resigned feeling.

He was only 15 years old. Although taller than an adult, he had innocence shown on his face.

"This woman, attacked me even after her falling. I'm fine with scars, but my clothes were damaged. Now I only have the last piece of wearing."Lynnray looked at the torn clothes on her body with upset.

Along the way, Lynnray had already obtained some clothes from killers, but clothes were the most easily damaged items inMonster Mountains.

"Boss, the magic crystal cores in this killer's package are also worth several thousand gold coins. Can a piece of clothing be worth several thousand gold coins?" Beibei retorted.

Lynnrayhad a smile. During one month in Monster Mountains, he got more and more scars, but the number of magic crystal cores he obtained was increasing.

"Forget it, I don't have any clothes on my upper body. I save the only piece of clothes to wear when I go back. No one will see me in the Monster Mountains anyway."Lynnray simply threw the damaged clothes away and left his upper body naked. He continued forward while holding his black short knife.

This black short knife has also given Lynnray a lot of help in these days.

After walking for a certain distance, Lynnray naturally recited the magic spell silently. After a while, a breeze spread from him to all sides. It was 'perception through wind'. Monsters and people within two or three hundred meters could all be discovered by Lynnray.

Lynnray generally used the 'perception through wind' cautiously every time he advanced a long distance. When Lynnray had walked for a long time, he used the 'perception through wind' again:

"Huh, a group of people? Why are those people hiding in the tree?"Lynnray was puzzled.

At this time, there was a very sturdy tree more than 100 meters south of Lynnray, and in estimation, it would require seven or eight people to embrace. No one knew how many years it had existed. A dozen people were hiding in the tree, and Lynnray drew near them out of curiosity.

Approaching very slowly and carefully, Lynnray only saw the people in the old tree more than 30 meters away when he entered a thorny bush.

There were more than a dozen people in black clothes, and every one of them had a black knife at the waist.

"Black short knife?"Lynnray focused on one of the black short knifes.

Both the style and the color were exactly the same as the black short knife that Lynnrayhad in his own hands. At the same time, the dozen people hiding in the old tree give Lynnray a grim feeling, which was the same as the first killer he encountered.

"It's all black clothes, all black short knives, and..."Lynnray also discovered that all of them had a protruding part on their back.

Lynnray recalled that his first killer had put the package tightly on his body at the beginning, inside the clothes. At that time, Beibei tore the killer's back clothes before they discovered the package.

"They are in the same organization."Even a fool could tell at this moment.

Lynnray had a fast beating of heart, and at this time more than a dozen people in black in this ancient tree were still talking quietly.

"Why haven't No.18 and No.7 arrived yet?"One of the men in black said with discontent.

"He might be dead." A man in black said indifferently.

"According to the time, when it gets dark, if they have not arrived, whether they are dead or alive, they are considered to have not passed." One of the people in black said coldly, and the other people in black fell silent upon his words.

Lynnray, who was hiding in the messy grass, could also guess that the man in black who was talking was probably the leader of this small team. He was shocked in his heart: "The killers who wanted to kill me were all level-6warriors who practiced vital energy techniques in the property of darkness. The leader of this team was probably more powerful."

Lynnray was about to retreat immediately, but after only a few steps, the man in black who was talking suddenly frowned, and cast his glance at Lynnray's place.

"Su!"

At the same time, a black light flux shot at Lynnray's location at extreme speed. Lynnray was startled to realize he was exposed.He used auxiliary wind magic 'top speed' instantly and headed to the depth of Monster Forest with the fastest speed.

In Lynnray's view, Monster Forest would get more dangerous as he pushed inside. The enemy might think twice before chasing him. Lynnray was prepared to take another direction after running several li.

When the man in black saw the bag on Lynnray's back and the black short knife, he put on a different look.

"No. 2, go and kill him." The leader in black ordered.

The higher the number, the stronger the strength. From Lynnray's reaction of escape, the leader in black made a judgment of comparative strength.

"Yes, sir." One of the men in black immediately swooped down from the tree and chased Lynnray at an extremely alarming speed. However, Lynnray was already at a distance from them, and he ran away first. The distance between the two was 70 or 80 meters at the beginning.

But this man in black was really fast, it seemed that he was even faster than the first killer who wanted to kill Lynnray.

"It's amazing speed."Lynnray flexibly shuttled between the mountains and forests, sometimes climbing and sometimes jumping.

But the man in black at the back chased indifferently, the distance between the two of them was shortened quickly, 60 meters, 50 meters, 40 meters, 30 meters... the more Lynnrayfled, the killer got closer to him.

10 meters, 9 meters, 8 meters, 7 meters!

Lynnray seemed to panic, but just rushed towards the depths of the Monster Mountains.

"Auxiliary wind magic?" The man in black could see that Lynnray was using an auxiliary wind magic, "He is so slow in spite of his magic. He is at level-4, at most" With full confidence in killing Lynnray, the man in black was getting close to him.

Lynnraypanickedapparently, but he was calm in the heart.

"It's almost been a few li away, and the dozen killers in the distance could not know the situation here."Lynnray, who had been fleeing in a panic, flashed a cold look in his eyes, and at the same time, the shadow mouse who seemed to be scared on Lynnray's shoulderssuddenly moved.

“Hu!”

In the man’s pupils, the shadow mouse enlarged, and came instantly to his location. He could even saw its sharp teeth.

Chapter 20 - Black Short Knife (II)

The man in black, who was only four or five meters away from Lynnray, gave no heed to the shadow mouse, but at this time, his usual indifferent heart started to panic: "What kind of speed?" He swiftly pulled out his black short knife.

Obviously, this man in black was better than the first killer who wanted to kill Lynnray, at least he had time to wield a short knife in front of the black shadow rat.

"Hu!" Beibei's waved its sharp claws.

"Bang!"

Beibei's claws hit the black short knife violently, and the black short knife burst open. Then, Beibei's claws slammed the black man's head and grabbed the black man directly. With head shattered, he died tragically on the spot.

"The gap between level-6 and level 7 is so big."Lynnray also sighed when he saw this scene.

Beibei was a horrible shadow mouse which made a level-7 raptor flee. With Beibei's sharp teeth and claws, killing a level-6 warriorwas as easy as eating food.

"Hiss..."Lynnray tore the clothes on the back of the man, grabbed his black package directly, turned his head and fled north again. The wind was blowing under Lynnray's feet, and the whole person was elegant and flexible. There was almost no trace of Lynnray's escape.

After a while, a group of people in black finally arrived at the spot. Looking at the scar on the head of No.2's corpse, the leader of the black man frowned.

"A monster?" A lot of monsters appeared in the black man's mind. "Is it a level-6 cyan shadow mouse? Or a level-7 purple? Or a level-7 stone biting mouse in golden color?"The small claw mark indicated a mouse species.

In the Monster Mountains, some people said that the most frightening thing was to encounter a monster at level-8 or 9. Some people said it was an encounter of a group of monster wolves, but in the hearts of the people in black, the most horrible thing was to encounter a group of stone-biting mice or shadow mice.

Stone-biting mice had strong defense and sharp teeth and claws.

Shadow mice was fast and also had sharp teeth and claws.

If thousands of shadow mice or stone-biting mice rushed out, not to mention their dozen or so killers, even an army could be swallowed up and clean.

"Let's go back!" Without hesitation, the head of the man in black gave the order.

With the lofty mountains and rugged rocks, Lynnray had already ran into a mountain peak at this time and ran a hundred li in one breath.

Lynnray believed that even if they chased him, they would not be able to catch him.

"Boss, see what's in the package?" Beibei urged him at this time.

Lynnray also had some expectations in his heart. The more powerful the killer was, the more magic crystal cores were in the package. The first killer left him magic crystal cores and magic crystal stones worth nearly 15,000 gold coins, and he didn't know how much the man named No.2 left him.

He opened the bag.

"Two more pieces of clean clothes."Lynnray glanced at the clothes in the package, and then took out the bulging bag from the inter-layer. This man named No.2 stayed in the Monster Mountains one month longer than the first one and had more strength.

Lynnraygasped at the number of magic crystal cores in the bag.

"So many, and most of them are level-5 magic crystal cores, and there are many level-6 magic crystal cores." He often got magic crystal cores, so he could judge the level of magic crystal cores based on their color. Then he began to calculate.

"9 of level-6, 56 of level-5, 12 of level-4 and 7 magic crystal stones. Total value was 20,000 gold coins.With the 50,000 he already had, the total harvest was 70,000 gold coins."Lynnraygasped at his earnings.

70,000 gold coins!

His father would be shocked at so much wealth.

During his 51 days in Monster Mountains, two killers who belonged to the same organization gave him 35,000 gold coins. There were other killers in more than a month, and they provided 30,000 gold coins. He only earned 5,000 by killing monsters.

Delin came out of the Ring of Coiling Dragon at this time, with a smile on his face.

"I finally know why many people in the Monster Mountains like to kill other people. They can earn only a few thousand gold coins for a month. But by killing other people, they can take away their earnings of 1 or 2 months."Lynnray put the two bags of magic crystal cores in his package, and threw the original into the messy grass.

"Of these 70,000 gold coins, only 5,000 were obtained by killing the monster myself, and the others were obtained from killers."Lynnray shook his head and sighed.

Delin touched his white beard and smiled: "It seems that your age has helped you a lot. If you weren't mature enough, it is estimated that there would not be so many killers against you."

"Haha."Lynnray couldn't help but smile.

"Grandpa Delin, what the killer team said just now, it seems that entering the Monster Mountains was their test?"Lynnray was a little confused.

Delin smiled lightly: "Lynnray, all powers standing long-term on Yulan Continent had their own forces, and forces were cultivated through training. Some large organizations often sent their people to train in Monster Mountains."

Lynnray nodded.

"Lynnray, there are many forces on this continent that you don't know. Actually...I don't know, either. For more than 5,000 years, the forces during Pron Empire might have fallen long ago."Delin laughed.

Lynnray didn't ask further, but at this time he felt a pressure. Yulan Continent was more complicated than he thought.

After sorting out the package, Lynnray put on a set of carapace and carried the package on his back and moved on. He flexibly moved forward in the mountains and forests, sometimes jumping over rocks, sometimes climbing big trees, all the way forward, but when Lynnray climbed over a mountain, he found itwas hundreds of li in length and there were a lot of trees on the mountain. Lynnraywas standing on the edge of the cliff at this time. If he wanted to reach the opposite cliff, he needed to fly hundreds of meters.

"What a weird canyon!"

Lynnray found that the cliffs became closer to each other in positions reaching out to both sides, and Lynnray ran along the cliff towards the edge. The more he ran to the side, the closer the distance to the opposite cliff was. After entering, the cliffs on the two sides are only one meter away, and he could cross it in one step.

"This is the case here, is it the same on the other side?"

Lynnray stepped on both cliffs with his feet. Looking at the other end of the canyon, it seemed that the two cliffs were close and connected again in the distance.

"It’s weird."

Lynnrayhad been in the Monster Mountains for a while, but he had never seen such strange cliffs. Lynnray looked down and saw the canyon was filled with white mist, it was vague and impossible to see what was inside.

"Unfathomable."Lynnray was very curious, but he was also wary of the misty valley.

Walking along the edge of the canyon cliff while looking down, Lynnraywanted to discover with his bare eyes what were there. In addition to the two cliff walls connected at both ends, there was another weird thing in this misty canyon.

The further downward, the farther the distance between the two cliffs.

For example, the two cliffs above were only a few hundred meters away, but the distance between the two cliffs below may be thousands of meters, or even dozens of li.

"Huh? That's..."

Lynnray was as surprised as being struck by lightning. He carefully looked at a blade of grass looming in the mist above and below the opposite cliff. The grass growing on the cliff was all green, but this blade had a blue glow of light.

"Blueheart grass, it is Blueheart grass!" Recalling the images and descriptions of plants in the library of Ernst Academy, Lynnray brightened up his eyes. It was exactly the precious medicine which could contradict damages to the body caused by a living dragon’s blood.

Chapter 21 - Misty Valley (I)

In order to practice Secret Guidebook of Dragonblood, one must mobilize the blood of the dragon blood soldiers in the body. There are only two ways to mobilize the blood of the dragon blood soldiers in the body. One is that the blood of the dragon blood soldiers in the body reaches the most basic limit, and the second is pain. Drink invigorating dragon blood to arouse.

Drinking the Dragon's Blood is very dangerous.

The dragon blood poured into the body is so painful, let alone drink it in the belly. Then everything in the world falls into one thing, and Blueheart grass is the best plant for living dragon blood. However, Blueheart grass is extremely precious, and Lynnray also asked about the price.

A Blueheart grass, worth tens of thousands of gold coins, was still priceless. And Delin also said at the beginning: "Living dragon blood is extremely overbearing. Generally, a Blueheart grass is not enough. If you drink more dragon blood, you need more Blueheart grass."

A Blueheart grass is so expensive, can Lynnray buy it? I am afraid that for the 70,000 gold coins I have earned in more than a month, I can only buy one Blueheart grass.

"Blueheart grass, Blueheart grass, God really takes care of me."Lynnray felt joy in his heart. Lynnray used force at his feet, suddenly jumped over a dozen meters and landed on the opposite cliff, and then immediately muttered the magic spell. In just a short while, Lynnray's body was wrapped in wind elements, and his body was still surrounded by air currents.

The level-5 of wind magic-floating technique.

Lynnray can only float physically but can't fly. floating just can go straight up and down. Lynnray took a step forward and stood above the canyon in the air, then Lynnray slowly began to descend, gradually deepening into the misty canyon. Beibei stood enviously on the shoulders of Lynnray and followed Lynnray's depth. Although Beibei was relatively strong, he could not fly. He is not a flying beast, so if he wants to fly himself, he can only break through and become a holy beast.

In the misty canyon, the mist is full of white mist that rolls around. As it goes deeper, Lynnray also finds that the distance between the two cliffs is getting farther and farther, and at this moment Lynnray has flown to the side of the Blueheart grass.

"Blueheart grass, green leaves are green, with a faint blue halo flowing, Blueheart grass starts to be cold, the grass leaves tearing up and there is aquamarine liquid, the entrance is refreshing."Lynnray still remembers the explanation of Blueheart grass in the Ernst Academy Library The most basic sentences in

Looking at the Blueheart grass growing on the cliff and the Blueheart grass undulating in the breeze, Lynnray took a deep breath, and then carefully pulled out the Blueheart grass.

"It is really cold."Lynnray grasped the Blueheart grass and felt that the Blueheart grass was like ice cubes. He immediately put the Blueheart grass into the package behind him, and then looked carefully in all directions, "I don't know if there is any Blueheart. Heart grass!"

If you can grow a Blueheart grass, you can grow a second Blueheart grass.

Under the floating technique, Lynnray carefully and slowly descended downward, and at the same time, Lynnray tried his best to watch downwards, the white mist rolled around, everything looked vague, Lynnray also vaguely saw the vines entangled on the cliff. .

"So big!"

The more he flew down, Lynnray discovered how wide the range below this canyon is. The maximum distance between the two sides of the canyon above is only a few hundred meters, and now Lynnray is sure that the distance between the two cliffs is at least a few thousand meters away, because he It has been flying close to one side of the cliff. It can be inferred only by the angle of the cliff and the distance of the flight.

"Howl..."

"Hu..."

Various low-pitched roars occasionally sounded below, and they sounded in different directions. Just listening to the sound at least had over a hundred beasts, Lynnray couldn't help but trembled: "Monster, there are a lot of beasts below!"Lynnray could easily tell from the sound alone. Judge it out.

Lynnray couldn't help but get close to the stone wall, and at the same time grabbed the vines with his hands, and slowly descended carefully.

"Boss, I feel that there is danger below." Beibei suddenly communicated to Lynnray's soul.

Lynnray also felt his throat mentioned in his heart, and the lower the sound of the monsters became clearer, those roars were low and powerful, they must be those of large monsters, and none of the large monsters were weak. A powerful monster is not necessarily large, but a large one must be powerful.

"Blueheart grass!"

Suddenly Lynnray saw a Blueheart grass growing on the stone wall in the distance below. The Blueheart grass was surrounded by green vines and other plants, and Lynnray was not a timid person. Lynnray was climbing the vine with both hands, controlling himself to levitate over.

However, Lynnray didn't notice at this time--

Among the green vines around the Blueheart grass, there is a huge green python with a length of more than 20 meters and two people embracing it. The giant green python is also surrounded by vines, and it is itself Green, in the faint mist, Lynnray hadn't found such a giant python at all.

As it descended, Lynnray got closer and closer to the Blueheart grass.

"Boss, be careful, it's a monster snake!" Beibei suddenly said in an eager soul.

"Python?"Lynnray trembled in his heart. Most snake-like monsters are extremely strong, even the weakest triangular viper is a level-6 monster. Lynnray immediately carefully observes the front. At this moment,

Lynnray is only less than a hundred meters away from the green giant python. Observing this closely, he suddenly discovered Such a giant python.

"Huh!"Lynnray took a deep breath.

It was twenty to thirty meters long, and its huge body as thick as a water tank made Lynnray's heart tremble: "Green-patterned python, a seventh-level beast,'green-patterned python'."Lynnray's heart suddenly appeared about green patterns. The message of the python.

Lynnray also knows why this canyon has so much white fog at this time.

"Water mist is only a first-level water magic. The seventh-level water monster'Green Veined Giant Python' can form endless white water mist around it. And this canyon is so dense and dense that there is definitely more than one green pattern. Python."

Lynnray inferred at once.

The bottom of the canyon is tens of li wide and tens of li deep. Such a large canyon is completely filled with white mist. From this one can imagine how many green pythons there are. The green python lurking among the green plants on the cliff suddenly moved, its huge head facing towards Lynnray, and the chilling eyes of the python head stared at Lynnray.

"Hey..."

A terrifying cry sounded from the green-patterned python's mouth, and at the same time, the green-patterned python flew at extremely fast.

"Hoo...""Oh...""Oh..."The sounds of various beasts sounded one after another in the bottom of the valley, as well as the sound of heavy and speedy running. Lynnray glanced at the bottom and saw ten A few huge reptiles came over, and these dozen or so were only a few of them, and there were more beasts covered in white mist.

"Go!"

Facing the attack of the green-stranded python, Lynnray only flew upwards at high speed, controlling the force of the wind element. When the levitation force far exceeded the body weight, the whole person flew upwards at an amazing speed. During the flight, Lynnray had already seen In the other direction, there was also a green python swiftly stalking along the cliff wall, and the cold eyes stared at Lynnray, yellingconstantly.

"Ga Ga..."

There was a sharp chirping sound, and dozens of huge flying birds at the bottom of the gorge were chasing.

"Pterosaur, it's Pterosaur!"Lynnray's face turned pale.

Chapter 22 - Misty Valley (II)

More than a dozen pterodactyls, which are several times larger than a griffon, quickly caught up. Lynnray immediately passed the ring of the dragon and tried to make his ascent as fast as possible. At the same time, he began to meditate on the word "Guardian of the Earth" Kai' magic spell.

"call!"

With only the sound of strong wind, Lynnray had already thrown away the green-patterned python, but the pterosaur was very fast, and the distance to itself was getting closer and closer. When Lynnray flew over the canyon cliff, The dozen or so pterosaurs rushed to chase directly and continued to chase and kill Lynnray.

Lynnray jumped and fled in the mountains and forests at great speed, but no matter how fast his legs were, how could he compare with the flying speed of a pterodactyl.

"Ga..." The pterodactyl's ear-piercing chirp sounded.

The wings of the pterosaur spread over 20 meters, and the dozen or so pterosaurs spread their wings and almost covered the sky above the Lynnray. Lynnray only felt that the surrounding area was darkened, and the dozen pterosaurs immediately swooped down. At the same time, a dozen pterodactyls spewed fiery flames from their mouths, and all the surrounding trees burned all at once. The 'sacred armor of the earth's guardian' on Lynnray's body circulates, protecting all parts of Lynnray's body.

"Chichi~~" The flame burned on the surface of the body, and the earthy yellow light circulated on the surface of the earth guard saint armor in the form of rock.

Among the dragons, Pterodactyls and ground-walking dragons belong to the lowest level of dragons, but even the weakest dragons are level-6 monsters. In particular, ground-walking dragons and pterosaurs lived in groups. More than a dozen six-level monsters attacked from the air, and even seven-level fighters had to flee for their lives.

A dozen pterosaurs swooped down--

"Shit!" The claw of the pterodactyl was fiercely a claw on Lynnray's holy armor of protection of the earth, the holy armor of the earth's protection trembled a little, and the golden light on the surface flickered slightly.

"Can't resist!"

Lynnray was frightened by the attack power of this paw, and the whole person immediately sprinted through the mountains and forests quickly and desperately, rushing towards the hard-to-walk places. Flapping, jumping, climbing...Lynnray was desperate at this time, and the dozen pterodactyls were scrambling to catch Lynnray with their claws on top of Lynnray's head.

"Yo!"

Beibei screamed angrily and expanded, from twenty centimeters long to half a meter long. But Beibei, half a meter long, is still small compared to the pterodactyl whose wings spread out to be more than 20 meters wide. "Shoo!" Beibei put a point on Lynnray's shoulder, turning into a black afterimage and rushing to a swooping pterodactyl.

Hearing only the cracking of bones and the terrifying chirping of the pterosaur, the pterosaur fell from the air, and Beibei jumped on the pterosaur to the other pterosaur. Facing the neck of the pterodactyl, there were two mouthfuls, and they directly killed each other.

Pterodactyl is only a sixth-level beast, and Beibei can even escape from the attack of the seventh-level beast "raptor".

and--

From level-6 to level 7, that is an extremely large watershed, with a huge gap in strength. Beibei just can't fly, but once on the pterosaur, the pterosaur is bound to die. In just a while, three out of a dozen pterosaurs died.

The other pterodactyls immediately flew high in horror, and Beibei looked at the high pterodactyl and had nothing to do. It couldn't fly.

The pterosaurs hovered in the high air for a while, and finally wailed a few times before flying back towards the misty canyon.

"What a terrifying canyon."Lynnray breathed a sigh of relief at this moment.

Lynnray took out the magic crystal cores of the three pterodactyls while thinking about the Misty Canyon.

"Grandpa Delin."Lynnray immediately called, and Delin also flew out of the Ring of the Dragon. Delin still wore the forever clean moon-white robe and looked at Lynnray with a smile: "Lynnray, what's the matter?"

Lynnray's mood was not calm at this time.

"Grandpa Delin, I entered a misty canyon just now. I didn't expect that there are a lot of monsters, green pythons, and huge reptiles in the canyon. I didn't see it clearly at the time, but the size is not smaller than the Velociraptor. Pterodactyl... and what I saw was only a small part of the Misty Canyon. I didn't see the entire Misty Canyon."

Thinking about Lynnray was shocked, there is such a canyon where monsters gather.

"Oh?"

Delin was a little surprised, "There are so many monsters in the Misty Canyon? Interesting. Generally, the monsters are of the same clan and gather together. The monsters you just mentioned are not the same kind, they actually gather in the Misty Canyon. Interesting, really interesting. If I'm still alive, I'm afraid I will go inside and explore."

Lynnray shook his head and smiled helplessly: "In that gorge, there is still Blueheart grass. Just now there was a plant I didn't have time to pick, only one plant was picked."

"Blueheart grass?"Delin's eyes lit up. "The place where Blueheart grass grows is definitely not an ordinary place. There must be some treasures in the misty valley, or super monsters, such as ninth level. Monster, and even Sanctuary Monster. But..."

Delin frowned: "Generally powerful monsters have territorial awareness. If there are powerful monsters in them, they should not allow pterodactyls, green snakes and other monsters in them."

"But, why can pterosaurs, green-stranded pythons, and many of the reptile beasts you talk about can get along together? Strange things, strange things."Delin also couldn't figure it out. The situation in the Misty Canyon seems to be very contradiction.

Lynnray smiled: "Grandpa Delin, don't think too much about it. Let's explore again when I reach the seventh-level magician and can perform 'flying'."

Reached the seventh-level magician, the earth guardian holy armor also reached the 'jade' level, and even the power of auxiliary magic such as speed increased greatly. At that time, Lynnray has absolute confidence to face those pterosaurs, and with the 'flying skills', Lynnray is naturally confident to go to the misty canyon.

"Level-7 magician? You are only a level-5 magician now. It's early."Delin said, cooling down Lynnray's pride.

Lynnray also understood in his heart.

It might not be difficult to reach level-6 in magic, but there was a big gap from level-6 to level-7.

"We build our own pathway."Lynnray smiled slightly, "I have been in the Monster Mountains for almost two months, and now I start to go back. It will take several days to cover a distance of nearly 1,000 li, but it's a good opportunity to practice myself."

With Beibei on his shoulders, Lynnray began to return.

Chapter 23 - The Girl Named Alice (I)

On the way home, the monsters encountered were getting weaker and weaker. When Lynnray stepped into the outer area, almost all the monsters encountered were level 3or 4, and there was no threat at all. But even so, Lynnray did not dare to relax his vigilance completely.

Delin and Lynnray walked side by side, but Delin always had worries in his heart. Today, Lynnray has a calm aura in his whole person, but he will not tolerate it when he does it. In those eyes there was also a cold indifference that was far away.

Delin still remembered that before stepping into the Monster Mountains, Lynnray's eyes contained sincerity, and it was easy to trust people.

After thinking about it for a long time, Delin finally said through his soul: "Lynnray."

Lynnray, who was swiftly moving through the mountains and forests, couldn't help turning his head, and looked at Delin in confusion: "Grandpa Delin, what's the matter?"

Delinkovo nodded his head and solemnly said: "Lynnray, before entering the Monster Mountains, I once reminded you that the human heart is separated by the belly, and you cannot easily trust others, so that you can remain vigilant towards others."

Lynnray nodded and said, "Grandpa Delin, you are right. People really can't believe it easily. If I believed Grandpa Delin earlier, I'm afraid I won't be hit in the abdomen."

Delin shook his head and said, "Although you can't trust others easily, you can't be too vigilant. How can you get along with others in the future if you think about it now? Remember, you can't be too indifferent to others, and maybe you can't be too indifferent. Trust. Trust is gradually established in long-term communication. Don't be easily influenced by the other party's language."

Lynnray is very smart. He has read a lot of books at home and at Ernst Academy. When Grandpa Delin said so, he understood a little bit in his heart. But after two months of cruel life, Lynnray had already seen the cruelty of human nature very clearly, and it was really difficult to make him believe in people.

"Grandpa Delin, I understand."Lynnray nodded and said.

Delin sighed inwardly, but Delin was also grateful in his heart: "Fortunately, Lynnray is accompanied by the little shadow mouse and some good friends from Ernst Academy. He will not become too indifferent."

Delin still remembers that when the Pron Empire existed thousands of years ago, there was a white-clothed man who was a powerful sword master and was extremely solitary.

"Grandpa Delin, how will my father think after seeing so many monster crystal cores?"Lynnray suddenly looked at Delin and asked with a smile. At this time, Lynnray looked forward to his father's praise.

He was like a child who expected the father's praise for his good scores in the exam. "Lynnray, are you going to give all of these monster cores to your father?"Delin asked with a smile.

Lynnray nodded and said, "Of course, these monster cores are worth more than 70,000 gold coins, and I don’t need anything more than food. Dozens of gold coins a year are enough. My dad is in charge of the family and needs to cover Warton’s tuition. I should give these to my dad."

Lynnray didn't want to sell the monster cores by himself. After all, he had no experience in trading, and he might not even know that he was deceived.

"Haha, I believe your father will be startled with pleasure."Delin said with a laugh.

Lynnray couldn't help but grinned, and immediately sped up and walked on the way back.

Lynnray didn’t bother to kill level-3 and level-4 monsters. He passed in the Monster Mountains swiftly and flexibly. When he crossed a creek, he heard a loud roaring of a monster and humans’ intense shouting.

"Huh? Those who dare to come to the Monster Mountains are at least level-5 fighters, and the outer areas are generally occupied by monsters at level-3 and 4. How can the battle be so fierce?"Lynnray was a little confused.

In the inner area of the Monster Mountains, where the fifth and sixth level monsters were scattered, and even the places where the seventh-level monsters occasionally appeared, such violent fights might occur. However, such things rarely happen in the peripheral area, where battles ended quickly.

With a kick on his legs, he jumped up to seven or eight meters, jumping between the trees very easily, and came to the battlefield in just a while.

Standing on a tree branch, Lynnray looked quietly.

He saw two teenagers and two girls fighting fiercely with a bloody boar. One of the teenagers in white armor was shouting to command the battle: "Bro, don't run around, protect Alice. I'll guide this stupid pig. Niya, don't panic, aim at its critical part."

These four obviously had very little experience, and even panicked in the face of danger. Only the heading juvenile in white armor was stabler.

"These four people are really bold enough. The white armor boy should have the strength of a level-5warrior, but the other three, up to a level-4 strength."Lynnray shook his head in his heart. The other three came to Monster Mountains before reaching level-5.

Another red-haired boy also shouted in panic, "Boss Karan, didn't you say that the periphery is occupied by monsters at level-3 and 4? This is a level-5."

The young man named Karan, heading the four, was in a helpless situation. As a level-5warrior, he was going on a trial in the outer area of Monster Mountains with three good friends. There should be no danger. But they didn't expect to encounter a level-5 monster.

"Pu!" A dozen ground spears suddenly appeared from around the bloody boar, and three of them stabbed on it, but were broken by the thick skin of the bloody boar.

"Howl..."

The bloody boar immediately roared at the only magician among the four, and then rushed over. The bloody boar dashed with a shocking momentum, and there were flames from the nostrils. Suddenly, another teenager panicked.

"Hide, Alice, run away." Karan shouted.

The girl named Alice has long blond hair and dim eyes like a dream. At this time, Alice also wants to flee in a panic, but after all, the bloody boarwas a level 5 monster, with an intelligence not good enough, but much higher than beasts.

The bloody boar rushed toward Alice.

Seeing the bloody boar rushing towards her, Alice was terrified and tried to run, but she was tripped by vines under her feet, and fell to ground. When she looked back, she saw the bloody boar rushing in a crazy manner. Her weak body might be trampled.

Alice was stunned for a while.

The other two teenagers and a young girl were also frightened and overwhelmed. They had no time to save others.

"Alice!" the boy named Karan could only shout in pain and anxiety. Although he was a level-5warrior, his experience was obviously far worse.

"Puchi!"Seven or eight sharp ground spears with a rich earth-yellow light suddenly appeared. Although the level-5 monster bloody boar had thick skin, it was still pierced into the hard muscles by two of the ground spears, blood flowed from the belly of the bloody boar.

Unfortunately……

The ground spear just pierced into the muscles and did not damage the internal organs.

"Howl..." The bloody boar snarled up in pain.

"Puchi!" From above, a black short knife pierced directly into the bloody boar's eye like lightning. The eyeball burst, the black short knife pierced through the entire head, and the bloody boar couldn't help but trembled like chaff. It stopped moving after a while.

Karan, Niya, and Alice were so scared that their hearts beat fast.

They watched as the strong junvnile in the blue warrior outfit took out the bloody boar's monster crystal core very skillfully, and then the juvenile turned around and was about to leave. But Karan was the first of the four to return to senses, and immediately addressed the juvenile: "Buddy, wait a minute."

Chapter 24 - The Girl Named Alice (II)

"En?"Lynnray turned his head, frowning.

Karan came over immediately and said gratefully: "My name is Karan, thank you very much for your help, if it weren't for you, I'm afraid Alice would be dead."

The girl named Alice also ran over at this time. She apparently still had lingering fears, her panting chest kept rising and falling, but those dim eyes stared at Lynnray curiously: "Thank you for saving my life, my name is Alice, full name Alice Duff, I am also an earth magician."

Lynnray's eyes lingered on Alice for a while.

I have to say that Alice is a very temperamental girl, that kind of pitiful temperament is innate and does not need any voice or makeup to create.

"Lynnray, you don't usually save people from danger in Monster Mountains, right? Why do you rescue them?"Delin's teasing voice sounded in Lynnray's mind, "Ah, I know, you must like the girl named Alice."

Lynnray frowned.

"Grandpa Delin, it wasn't that I didn't want to save people in the past, but in the Monster Mountains, the monsters were at leve-6 or 7, and came in groups. I was unable to come to rescue. But killing a level-5 monster is not that difficult, so I did the favor."Lynnray explained to Delin.

Delin smiled and said no more.

"My name is Tony. May I know your name?" Another juvenile also said aloud.

Lynnray looked at this group of people indifferently: "How long have you been in the Monster Mountains?"

"It's our first day." Karan said helplessly, "We didn't expect to encounter a level five monster on the first day of entering the Monster Mountains. It was really unlucky. According to the book, the outer area should be occupied by monsters at level 3 or 4. It shouldn't be too dangerous for the four of us to come here."

"Stupid."Lynnray shook his head and said.

The female archer named Niya immediately turned angry: "Hey, why are you arrogant? You just saved Alice, why do you scold us?"

"Niya." Karan scolded.

Lynnray said directly: "I really admire your courage to venture into the Monster Mountains. At the same time, I have to say that you are lucky, because you haven't come across any bandits."

"Bandits?"The group of people glanced at each other. It was real they had not come across bandits.

The Monster Mountains stretched for more than 10,000 li, and could be entered at all sides and locations. It was normal that they had not encountered any bandit. "Let me tell you, if you don't want to die, leave the Monster Mountains immediately now."Lynnray said directly.

"Why? Are there a lot of level-5 monsters in the peripheral area?" the juvenile called Tony asked in confusion.

Lynnray said lightly: "In the Monster Mountains, especially the outer parts, the most dangerous thing is not monsters, but humans. The four of you are not only weak, but you have no experience. I believe that any greedy person will not leave you alone. It is estimated that you just entered the Monster Mountains on the first day and were not discovered by others, otherwise the four of you would have been killed."

"The most dangerous are the humans?"Karan frowned, but his face soon changed drastically.

Karan said respectfully to Lynnray: "Mr. Magician, we have just entered the Monster Mountains today, and we only know some general information. This time I also decided to come here privately. I hope you can help us leaveMonster Mountains together."

Lynnray frowned.

He doesn't like trouble, but if these five people encounter robbers on the way back, it was really very dangerous.

"Mr. Magician, please help." Alice also begged.

Lynnray glanced at Alice, looked at Alice's pleading eyes, thinking of the scene where Alice was killed by the bandits, Lynnray softened, nodded and agreed: "Well, I will also go out by the way, I'll lead you on the way. But if I encounter robbers on the way back, I can only promise to help as much as possible. If any of you are killed, I can't help it." Karan was overjoyed and immediately nodded and said: "We are very grateful for your help."

Lynnray nodded and went straight ahead, then turned his back to the four people and said directly: "Follow me." The four immediately followed Lynnray and walked out of the Monster Mountains under Lynnray's protection and walked towards the city.

On the way back, Karan and the other four also learned of Lynnray's name, and the "Alice" who was also an earth magician admired Lynnray very much. Alice was also fifteen years old this year, a top talent in Willing Magic School.

But even so, Alice just reached level-4 this year. This kind of performance can only be regarded as medium at Ernst Academy.

When the journey stopped, Lynnray, Karan, Alice and others began to eat, while Lynnray and Alice were sitting together.

"Brother Lynnray, you are so amazing. You reached the level-5 when you were fourteen. I guess you will have to wait until you are twenty." Alice looked at Lynnray in admiration.

"I'm nothing. Dixi, the top talent in our academy, was a level-4 magician at the age of 9, and a level-5 magician at the age of 12."Lynnray said casually, but he did not say... he was at level-4 at 13, but came to level-5 at 14.

Just over a year, he made a three-year progress and caught up with Dixi.

"Level-4 at the age of 9? I just became a level-4 magician at 15. I'm the top talent in our academy. Our Willing Magic School is far behind your Ernst Academy." Alice sighed.

"Brother Lynnray, I feel that your ground spear seems to be very powerful, even more powerful than some fifth-grade students in our academy. Why is that?" Alice was also an earth magician, and naturally found Lynnrayout of the ordinary.

Lynnray smiled lightly, not only for power, but actually the speed at which the burst of spears emerged was extremely fast.

"Earth magic is originally derived from the Earth Element..."Lynnray explained to Alice. In fact, Lynnraywas more sophisticated than the teacher of Ernst Academy in the knowledge of earth magicians, because He had a holy-level teacher.

Alice looked up at Lynnray and listened attentively.

One spoke and the other listened, and the two were getting closer physically. Lynnray was absorbed in his explanation, and when he rested, he found their faces were only one fist apart.

Lynnray was startled. This was the first time he was so close to a girl, especially looking at Alice's dim eyes and small nose so closely. Lynnray could even feel herbreath and smell her fragrance.

"Lynnray, why are you not talking now?" Alice asked in doubt, but after only a while, Alice knew the reason and pulled away from Lynnray, blushing.

Lynnray pacified himself, and then stood up and said to everyone as if nothing happened: "OK, we are full now. Let's march forward to the city."

Chapter 25 - Purple in Night Wind (I)

Many luxury mansions were located on Green Leaf Road of Fenlai City, the capital of Fenlai Kingdom, Holy Alliance. In front of one mansion, a dozen people were gathering.

"We, the family of Debus, thank you for your help. If it weren't for you this time, Kalan would really suffer." An old man with gray hair said to Lynnray with a smile. Beside the gray-hair old man was Karan, Alice, Tony, and Niya. Behind them were a group of servants of the Debus family.

The gray-hair old man turned around and nodded to a servant behind, and that servant took out a yellow pouch from his arms.

The gray-hair old man took the yellow pouch and handed it to Lynnray with a smile, and said, "Here are100 gold coins, although it is not too much, it also represents the heart of our Debus family. I hope you can accept it."

"No, I only did a little favor."Lynnray said politely, "I have to leave now."

The gray-hair old man did not insist, watching Lynnray leave with a smile.

"Tony, you three can go home too. Your parents must be very worried." The gray-hair old man said with a smile, and after bidding farewell to Karan, Alice, Niya and Tony went home. When Karan and the gray-hair old man walked into the living room, the gray-hair old man's face suddenly turned cold, and he said with a cold voice, "Kneel down!"

Karan immediately slammed his knee on the groundand said, "Grandpa, I was wrong. This time I did not learn of the danger of the Monster Mountains, so I took three good friends and entered. I'm really sorry for that."

"Huh, it was a terrible adventure."

The gray-hair old man glanced at Karan coldly: "Kalan, you are already an adult, and you are also the future heir of Debus family. How can you make such a stupid mistake? How can the danger of the Monster Mountains be within your imagination? You took the risk without consulting with the family. I'll leave it to your father to decide how to punish you. I just want to remind you that if always make stupid mistakes, you will ruin the family when you are in charge."

Karan lowered his head to listen, not daring to speak.

The Debus familyranked among the top 3 in the entire Fenlai Kingdom. The Debus familywas strong not because of its high position, but because it was the partner of Dawson Chamber of Commerce in Fenlai Kingdom. And Dawson was one of the three major chambers of commerce on Yulan Continent.

Dawson Chamber of Commerce had tremendous wealth, and businesses distributed across Yulan Continent.

The financial and military power of any of the three major chambers of commerce on the Yulan continent was terrifying. Even in Fenlai Kingdom, there were many families which want to cooperate with Dawson Chamber of Commerce. Being able to cooperate with the

Dawson Chamber of Commerce was equivalent to getting on a giant chariot.

The Debus familyhad a relationship with Dawson, which was remarkable.

Even the two alliances and four empires tried to get along with Dawson.

Lynnray left Fenlai City for Ernst Academy. Beibei was looking around on Lynnray's shoulder, and Delin was walking side-by-side with Lynnray.

"Grandpa Delin, do you think this world is a bit scary?"Lynnray said mentally.

Delin nodded and listened, without saying a word.

"I didn't feel anything when I went to Fenlai in the past, but this time when I came back from the Monster Mountains, I found a lot. The cruelty in the Monster Mountains, the natural selection of the species was so obvious and bloody, without any covering."

"However, the nobles, magicians, and powerful warriors in FenlaiCity are well-dressed and courteous. But in this prosperous city, the division of social strata is strict and ruthless."

"Even in the law, the rights of the nobility greatly exceed the common people. Although Fenlai City is prosperous with endless laughter, there are hidden rules much more complex than in Monster Mountains. In Monster Mountains, there are no nobles or civilians; power determines your life and death."

Lynnray gradually came to know the world at this time.

In this world, the great nobles are at the top, and the civilians are exploited. No matter how gentle and hypocritical the nobles acted, they could not hide the strict hierarchical system. If you want to gain status, you can only become a great warrior or a great magician.

If you don't work hard, you will be eliminated.

"Human society is more complicated than the world in the Monster Mountains. They put a gorgeous coat on the cruel competition in the Monster Mountains. But sometimes, this gorgeous coat is very useful."Lynnraywas now looking at the hypocritical nobles with contempt.

The sharp contrast between Fenlai City's bustling life and the cruelty in Monster Mountains changed Lynnray's mood.

"Are you afraid of competition?"Delinasked suddenly.

Lynnray grinned: "Fear? No, I like it. If there is no competition in the world and all days are mediocre, what's the use of living? I like exciting competitions. I like the passion of dancing on the tip of a knife."

"Chi Chi..." Beibei beside her also screamed cheerfully.

......

Back in Ernst Academy.

Once entered the Monster Mountains and realized the sinister nature of human nature, Lynnray cherished the brotherly feelings in the academy even more, and walked to the door of the dormitory but heard a voice from inside:

"Boss Yale, Lynnray hasn't come back yet. There is no danger for him to enter the Monster Mountains, right?"

"Bro, shut your stinky mouth, Lynnray will definitely come back safely. Let's go and eat..." Yale looked up and and was stunned to see the figure in front of the yard gate.George and Reno were next to him. Then Yale, George, and Reno all rushed over excitedly.

"Haha, bro, you are finally back." Yale was the first to rush over and gave Lynnray a hug.

Reno also yelled loudly: "Wow, Lynnray, Yale and George talked about you every day, and worried about you, but I believed you will come back safely."

"Reno," George stared, "you were worried that Lynnray would be in danger just now."

"Me?"Reno looked puzzled. "Did I say?"

Lynnray looked at his three good brothers, and felt warm in the heart. Yale immediately waved his hand and said with pride: "Well, you two, don't talk nonsense. Lynnray's safe return is a big happy event. Let's go and celebrate."

"George and Reno,"Lynnray also said with a smile, "let's have a drink. My treat."

"Ah?"Renostared at him. "You'll treat us?"

Yale laughed loudly: "Yes, it's Lynnray's treat, don't forget, the Brooks Guild Hall sent the invitation letter a few days ago. The three works of Lynnray sold more than 4,000 gold coins. Let's eat with his money."

"Invitation letter from Brooks Guild Hall?"Lynnray was a bit surprised.

Yale said in a hurry: "Bro, your stone carving works have sold for a high price, and the Brooks Guild Hall has fully agreed with your carving standards, so you are invited to set up an independent exhibition room in the hall's senior room. I'll bring you the letter of invitation." Yale ran toward the dormitory room.

Reno said mysteriously to Lynnray: "Lynnray, don't you know that since the people from the Brooks Guild Hall came to the academy, the fact that you were invited to set up an independent exhibition room in the hall has spread to all. You became famous."

"It spread all over the school?"Lynnray was a little confused at the news.

"Yes, I'm afraid you are the last one to know" George said with a smile.

"Lynnray, this is the invitation letter from the Brooks Guild Hall." Yale ran out of the dormitory holding a white envelope inlaid with gold.

Chapter 26 - Purple in Night Wind (II)

In the evening, the four brothers of Room 1987 walked on the quiet road of Ernst Academy, chatting casually about the past two months.

"So fierce?"Reno lifted Lynnray's short shirt in shock and couldn't help holding his breath when he saw the earthworm-like wounds on Lynnray's abdominal muscles. George next to him was silent for a while, only Yale grinned and said, "Haha, you have too little knowledge, I have seen something worse than this when I was a child."

"Yale, really?"Reno asked in surprise.

Yale smiled and said: "Of course it is true, and I have seen a lot of them, like torturing and killing prisoners, and watching real people fighting with a monsterbare-handed. When real people were fighting with a monster, there were a group of rich people watching them. The scene was very bloody. ."

Lynnray could fully imagine that kind of scene after hearing what Yale said.

"It's good in here." George exclaimed.

Lynnray also nodded in agreement. Now in the evening, on the quiet road of the academy, you could often see a couple of men and women walking together, or holding hands, or sitting on the monsters together. It is very leisurely in the academy. "By the way, Yale, don't you want to accompany your girlfriend tonight, why are you not going today?"Reno said suddenly.

Yale said casually: "Girlfriend? Today, Lynnray is back from the great danger ofMonster Mountains, so I have to accompanyhim. Reno, remember, brothers are like hands and feet, but women are clothes for wearing."

Reno immediately made a look of contempt.

"Lynnray!" Suddenly a surprised voice came from a distance.

Lynnray and the other four couldn't help but turn their heads and look, only to see a tall beauty with a long flowing blonde hair happily running over, ran to Lynnray and said in surprise: "Lynnray, you are back from Monster Mountains, it is true that's great. It's been two months since you went this time. I was very worried. Were you hurt or something?"

"Delia, I'm fine."Lynnray replied with a smile.

Delia also met Lynnray when she entered the Ernst Academy, and the relationship between the two was very good. When he was with Delia, Lynnray felt that he could relax completely without any mental burden, just like when he was with his brothers.

"Delia, uncle's carriage is still outside, don't waste time." A cold voice sounded.

Lynnray looked up and saw a juvenile wearing school robe standing in the distance He was Delia's brother Dixi, one of the top 2 talents of Ernst Academy. Dixi's robe was clean without any stain. Dixi had eyes as clear as water. "Oh." Delia replied with a little disappointment, and then looked at Lynnray, "Lynnray, my father asked me and my brother to go back. The carriage is still waiting outside, so I will leave first."

"OK, Delia, let's talk again when you come back."Lynnray said with a smile.

"Well, goodbye." Delia was obviously disappointed that she didn't have time to talk with Lynnray, and Dixi in the distance also came over and glanced at Dedia. Delia walked towards Dixi, who looked at Lynnray and said:"Lynnray, I heard that you have went on a trial in the Monster Mountains. Congratulations for your successful return."

Lynnraywas surprised.

Dixi was talking to him!

Dixi's indifference is very famous at Ernst Academy. Most people felt pressure together with Dixi, especially when those clear eyes were staring at someone, that kind of psychological pressure could make the other person feel broken.

"Oh, thank you."Lynnray replied.

Dixi nodded slightly, and then took his sister Delia to the entrance of the Academy.

......

In Brooks Guild Hall, Fenlai City, the morning of the next day.

"Ah, Lynnray, please sit down."Ostony said enthusiastically, "Yale, you guys also sit down and rest."

Ostony looked at Lynnray carefully and exclaimed: "Lynnray, I have to say, you are really a genius, a super genius! A fifteen-year-old boy can become a genius student at the No. 1 School of Magic on Yulan

Continent. Not only that, but your skill level in stone carving has reached an extremely high level."

"What you have done is a miracle."

"Not to mention you are a talent in magic, in the circle of stone sculpting, those allowed to open an independent show room in our guild hall are generally above 40 years old, and your age is certainly the smallest. Even in history, only two top talents can compare with you. But what makes you different from them is... you are not only a genius in stone carving, but also a genius in magic. Oh... genius."

Lynnray was a bit embarrassed at Ostony's praises.

"Ostony, don't waste your time, finish the matter as soon as possible, and we four have to go out and play." Yale urged.

Ostony looked astonished. He quickly took out a silver-color Magic Crystal Card from the folder next to him and handed it to Lynnray with a smile: "Lynnray, this silver Magic Crystal Card was customized for us by the Union Bank of Empires. It represents your identity as a senior sculptor. All the gold coins you earn in the future will be directly transferred to your Magic Crystal Card."

"Now this silver card has not been activated. Please record your fingerprint, and you'll be able to use it."Ostony handed the magic crystal card to Lynnray, and then whispered, "Lynnray, have you brought stone sculptures here this time?"

Lynnray nodded slightly: "I brought three pieces."

Ostony smiled even more brilliantly.

……

At night, in the private room of Green Water Paradise, only Lynnray and George were drinking and talking with two women, while Reno and Yale had already went to bed with beautiful women in their arms.

"Yale and Reno are always like this."Lynnray drank a glass of wine and said to George who was talking to the girl next to him. "Bro, I'm a little dizzy. I want to go out and refresh myself in cool air."

"OK." George replied, and then continued to chat with the girl next to him.

Lynnray went downstairs and left the Green Water Paradise. As soon as he walked out of the noisy venue, and felt the cool breeze in the middle of the night, he became clearer in the mind. Compared with the Green Water Paradise, the outside was obviously much quieter, and Lynnray wandered casually on the roads of Fenlai City.

The night wind carried coolness and comfort.

There were mansions of nobles beside the streets of Ganmo Road, but compared with Green Leaf Road, some mansions on Ganmo Road were obviously less luxurious. On the balcony of a two-story building, Alice was enjoying the cool night wind.

Looking at the bright moon in the sky, Alice couldn't help but think of Lynnray who had saved her life.

In the moment of life and death, when she was desperate, Lynnray jumped over and directly killed the bloody boar and saved her life. At the moment of despair, Lynnray's swift movement was undoubtedly a great shock to her, and even left a deep impression in her heart.

"Lynnray was silent, but when he talked about magic, he was also very handsome." Alice thought for a while, with a smile on his face.

Suddenly, Alice noticed that there was a familiar figure on the street downstairs. After carefully recognizing it, Alice showed surprise on her face and hurriedly waved her hand: "Lynnray, Lynnray!"

Lynnray was strolling on the street and enjoying the peace of night when he heard someone calling him. So he looked up in the direction.

On the balcony of a small building in the distance, he saw a figure in purple with a moon on her back. In his eyes, the figure was like a spirit in moonlight, with purple clothes and elegant hair fluttering in night wind. And in a daze, he seemed to have smelt again the fragrance of Alice's hair.

The fragrance was so charming.

"Alice." Lynnray walked toward the small building.

Episode 4 – Dragonblood Warrior

Chapter 1 – Homecoming (I)

The yard wall of Alice's mansion was only two meters high. Lynnray leaped from ground, stepped on the wall and reached the balcony like a flying eagle.

"Squat." Alice pulled Lynnray.

Lynnray squatted with doubt.

"Hush." Alice looked down carefully, and said to Lynnray with relief: "Luckily the gatekeeper is sleeping. I'll be in trouble if we are discovered."

Lynnrayseemed to realize something.

"We'll sit behind the wall of balcony so that no one will see us." Alice smiled contently like a cunning little fox. After wiping with linen cloth, they sat on the ground.

Lynnray was very happy to see Alice.

"Lynnray, it's late at night. Why are you still on the streets? I remember you are a student of Ernst Academy. What are you doing in Fenlai City?" Alice asked several questions curiously.

What was he doing in Fenlai City?

Lynnray was a bit embarrassment. Anyway, he couldn't tell her he went to Green Water Paradise with his roommates.

"My friends and I were touring the city. I was bored at night, so I came out to the streets." Lynnray could only give a rough answer.

Alice nodded.

"Alice, why don't you sleep in such late night hours?"Lynnray raised the question.

Alice curled her mouth helplessly: "I slept early, but my drunk father disrupted my sweet dreams. He is a bad father who gambles, gets drunk, and creates disturbance at home every day. It's annoying."

"It's my misfortune to have such a father. How's your father, by the way?" Alice looked at Lynnray, who was sitting by her side.

"My dad?" Lynnray evoked memories since his childhood, "My dad does not gamble. He drinks but does not get drunk. However, he has been harsh on me in education."

Alice sighed with envy: "You have a happy childhood, not like me."

In the moonlight of late night, a boy and a girl chatted in this way on education, the school, the friends, and interesting things shared with friends...

Lynnray talked very happily, and was gradually familiar with Alice's life.

Long night passed, and a streak white appeared in the eastern horizon. Fresh air of the morning was spread across the land. Lynnray and Alice, absorbed in their talks, were only aware of the passing of time when the day came.

"Ah, it's dawn." Lynnray noticed the time.

Alice was reminded and said: "Sorry for keeping you through the night."

"Well, I should go now." Lynnray felt an unusual air, got nervous and stood up.

"Lynnray, will you come to Fenlai City in future?" Alice asked.

"Yes, I will come when I have time." Lynnray pressed on the balcony, made a flip and landed on the yard wall. Then he stepped on the wall and leaped out to the streets a dozen meters away.

Lynnraywaved goodbye to the girl behind him, without looking back.

Alice watched as Lynnray vanished at the end of streets, and entered her own room.

...

The sun in late August was like a big fireball emitting scorching heat to the world. After having lunch with his brothers, Lynnray headed back to his home in Wushan Town. He was carrying a bag of magic crystal cores worth 70,000 gold coins.

"Chi Chi..." Beibei was joyfully squeaking on Lynnray's shoulder.

Lynnray looked at Beibei, smiled and asked it: "You are happy back, right? By the way, I have never asked you why you were in the old house of our family?"

"I don't know." Beibei shook its head, "I have been in the old house since I could remember things. I don't know who were my mom and dad, but there was a voice in my memory saying, 'Stay here and do not run away.'"

"Stay here and do not run away?" Lynnray felt a bit strange.

Could this voice be made by Beibei's parents?

"I ate stones in the beginning, and obeyed the voice not to leave. Later you gave me chickens and rabbits. I liked you and didn't want to leave you." Beibei twitched its nose.

Lynnray also recalled that scene.

Beibei was hesitating at the entrance of Wushan Town, but it entered into the soul contract when he was about to leave.

"OK, Beibei, we will be together forever." Lynnray patted Beibei's head with care, and Beibei squinted comfortably.

Lynnray was walking in a medium speed of 20 li per hour. He arrived at the border of Wushan Town at dusk. As he kept going, he heard a familiar voice:

"Straighten your waist. Don't bend. If your butt touches the dyed branch, you fail, and should double your training."

Lynnray looked at a nearby location.

On the familiar open land east of Wushan Town and beside the white poplars, children from 6 years old to 16 years old were divided into three groups and were training under the direction of three instructors. All of their clothes were soaked in sweat.

“I trained in this way in those years.” Lynnray sighed with emotion.

"Lynnray?"Hilman saw Lynnray at a distance. He gave some requests to Rory and Roger, ran to Lynnray, and embraced him.

“Uncle Hilman, I haven’t seen you for long.” Lynnray said happily.

“Haha, let’s go home. Mr. Hogg will be glad to see you.” Hilman smiled, and then they went into Wushan Town.

“Young master.” Rory and Roger greeted Lynnray.

“Uncle Rory and Roger.” Lynnray waved his hand and went with Hilman to the Baruch mansion.

“Lynnray, you are bringing a bag full of things. What’s in it?”

Lynnray gave a mysterious smile: “It’s my gift for dad!”

Chapter 2 - Homecoming (II)

In the courtyard of Baruch mansion, Hogg was lying on a chair flipping through an extremely thick book and reading it carefully.

"Master Hogg, dinner is ready." A maid walked over and said respectfully.

Since steward Hilly took little Warton to the O'Brien Empire, there had not been a single servant in the entire family. Hogg was, even in the worst case, still the patriarch of a Dragonblood warrior's family. He couldn't do the job of servants himself, so he hired a housemaid.

"Oh." Hogg closed the book in his hand, glanced at the maid next to him, and sighed in his heart, "Fortunately, those nobles know that my son is now a genius magician at Ernst Academy, and are willing to lend me gold coins, otherwise my life will be more difficult."

"The tax rate of Wushan Town could barely cover the kingdom's tax and salaries of guards." Hogg felt aggrieved even after thinking about it. When the family passed to his generation, most of the things that could be sold were sold out.

But fortunately, he had two great sons.

"Lynnray is now a level-5 magician, and graduation is coming soon. Then the family can hand it over to him, and I can do what I always wanted to do."

Hogg got up and walked towards the living room.

"Mr. Hogg."Hilman's voice suddenly came from afar.

Hogg looked at the gate of the mansion in doubt, but Hilman stepped in after a while, and beside Hilman was a strong juvenile.

Seeing the smile on the young Hogg's face immediately bloomed, he greeted him with a big smile: "Lynnray, you are back, haha, it is great, this is really a big surprise."

"Agatha, please prepare a rich dinner." Hogg patted Lynnray's shoulder affectionately, "Good boy, you are as tall as me now. By the way, I think you will be back by the end of year. Why do you return so early?"

Lynnray smiled mysteriously: "Dad, I'll tell you that after dinner."

"So mysterious?" Hogg frowned deliberately.

Hilman smiled and said: "Mr. Hogg, Lynnray told me that he prepared a mysterious gift for you. I asked him, he didn't say it yet."

"Uncle Hilman."Lynnray frowned and looked at Hilman.

"Well, I won't say, I won't say."Hilman laughed.

As night fell, darkness covered the land, and several candles were burning, illuminating the entire living room. After dinner, maid Agatha cleaned up the table, and when Lynnray and Hogg were alone together, Lynnray placed his parcel in front of Hogg.

"What's this?" Hogg looked at Lynnrayin doubt. "Wait a minute."Lynnray got up and closed the door of the living room. Hogg couldn't help but laughed: "So mysterious that you need to close the door?"

Lynnray sat down confidently: "Dad, you can open the package now."

"I want to see what you have in it." Hogg curiously opened the package. In surprise, he saw a big bag inside the package.The mouth of the bag was tightened, and the bag was expanded by large numbers of magic crystal cores inside.

Hogg touched the big bag and wondered: "The content should not be gold coins. Is it gravel?" Hogg was a little confused, and while talking, he opened the bag. .

At this moment, colorful magic crystal cores exuded brilliant light, and Hogg's eyes couldn't help but look at it. This is a big bag of various magic crystal cores, which Hogg had never seen in his life.

"Magic crystal cores?" Hogg opened his eyes widely and looked at Lynnray in shock, and then swallowed his saliva with difficulty. Hogg had also seen magic crystal cores, but he had never seen so many of them. The quantity produced a strong visual impact.

Lynnray nodded and said, "Yes, most of them are magic crystal cores, and only a dozen are magic crystal stones. According to books, these magic crystal cores should be worth more than 70,000 gold coins."

"70,000 gold coins?"Hogg felt a twitch in the heart.

Hogg had been troubled by money all these years, and now he might need to borrow if asked to pay even 500 gold coins.

More than 70,000 gold coins! What did it mean? 70,000 gold coins could definitely feed the entire Baruch family for a hundred years.

"Of course, the figure was calculated according to prices recorded in the book, which were prices in the past.They should sell at a higher price today. It is estimated that they could sell for 80,000 gold coins."Lynnray answered honestly.

Hogg looked at the colorful pile of magic crystal cores in front of him, and felt like he was dreaming.

"Huh, huh!"

Hogg took a few deep breaths before pacifying himself.

"Lynnray, where did you get these magic crystal cores?" Hogg suddenly realized something and stared at Lynnray, "You went to the Monster Mountains?"

Lynnray nodded: "Yes, dad, these magic crystal coreswere obtained from the Monster Mountains."

"You, you..." Hogg was a little annoyed. "The Monster Mountains are the most dangerous district on the entire continent. It was such a big decision. Why didn't you discuss with me before entering it? Do you know how dangerous it is?"

Hogg laughed at himself as soon as he spoke.

Lynnray has been in, of course he knows how dangerous it is.

Hogg looked down at Lynnray, who remained silent while listening to his rebukes, shook his head and said with a sigh: "Lynnray, I'm not rebuking you, but you have to know that you are a talented magician in Ernst Academy. Your have a bright future and are responsible for our family. After all, your brother is still young, and I don't know how long it will take him to become a real Dragonblood warrior. You are shouldering the hope of me and Baruch family, so you can't take your life lightly."

Lynnraydare not speak at this moment.

"Take off your shirt and let me see if you were injured." Hogg said suddenly.

Take off the shirt?

Lynnray hesitated. He appeared normal with clothes on, but only he himself knew how horrible the scars looked.

"Take it off." Hogg frowned.

Lynnray hesitated for a moment, but finally took off his short shirt to reveal a strong upper body. It was densely covered with scars, with even a few fatal ones.

Seeing the scars on Lynnray's body, Hogg felt trembling of heart.

Hogg, with hand trembling, slowly touched Lynnray's chest and the fatal scars in his abdomen. Seeing these scars, Hogg felt bitter in the heart. He dare not think about how his son survived the hardships.

"Lynnray, you..." Hogg choked.

"Dad, I'm fine."Lynnray comforted his father. Hogg looked at the pile of magic crystal cores that represented huge amount of wealth next to him, and then looked at the scars on Lynnray's body, which were like tree roots intertwined. Hogg trembled slightly.

He hated it!

He hated his own incompetence!

After taking a deep breath, Hogg looked up at the sky and said in a low voice, "Lynnray, you have been tired all day on the road, so go and rest early."

"Yes, dad."

Lynnray quietly left, leaving Hogg sitting quietly in the candle-lit living room...

Chapter 3 - Hogg

On the next morning, at the dining table in the living room of the Baruch family, Lynnray was surprised to find that his father was radiant and his mental appearance was completely different.

Putting down the knife and fork in his hand, Hogg smiled and looked at Lynnray: "Lynnray, stay at home for a while this time, and my father hasn't seen you for a long time. Let's get together, father and son."

Father let himself stay at home for a while longer?

Lynnray was a little surprised, after all, his father had never said such things for so many years. Originally, Lynnray also planned to go to Fenlai City to stroll around, so I had a look at Alice by the way. But by this time Alice had already been forgotten by him.

"OK, father."Lynnray nodded happily.

Hogg nodded happily, but he had some special thought shown in his eyes.

...

Lynnray stayed in Wushan Town for more than ten days, and even when the next semester of Ernst Academy arrived, he didn't worry about going back. Hogg did not urge Lynnray to go to the academy.

On the Wushan Mountain east of Wushan Town, beside the gurgling stream, Lynnray sat cross-legged and quietly meditated to refine magic force.

Earth and wind elements penetrate into the body from all over Lynnray's body. Bones, muscles, and meridians throughout the body naturally absorbed elements to improve physical fitness. After a small amount of these earth and wind elements were absorbed, most of them were refined. The transformation eventually flowed into the pubic position in the chest.

The sea was filled with rivers, and the elements flowing through the meridians all over the body eventually gatheredthere.

Lynnray sat like this for half a day, when he opened his eyes, it was already sunset.

"It's time to go back to academy."Lynnray stood up and exhaled, "Since I gave those magic crystal cores to my father, my father's attitude towards me has become much better and kinder."

These ten days should be the period of time when Lynnray and Hogg got along the most harmoniously.

"What caused the father to make such a big change? The magic crystal core? My father shouldn't be because of money. Or...the scars on my body?"Lynnray thought about it, but couldn't be completely sure why his father would be so good to him.

The word "courteous caring" could fully explain Hogg's attitude towards Lynnray.

Walking into Baruch mansion, Lynnray saw his father who was reading the book at a glance: "Dad, it is getting darker, so let's wait until tomorrow to read the books."

"Oh, Lynnray is back." Hogg smiled and closed the book, "what you said makes sense, I will see it tomorrow."

"Lynnray, you've been thirsty after cultivating for so long." Hogg picked up the kettle placed on the coffee table next to him and poured a glass of boiled water. "Come on, moisten your throat. The temperature of this water is just right, it's not hot or cold."

"Thank you,dad."Lynnray felt warm.

This is how Hogg has treated Lynnray over the past ten days. It's very good. In the past, Hogg was always serious. He rarely showed such a warm side.

While drinking tea, Lynnray said, "Dad, I have been at home for a while, and I am going to academy tomorrow."

"Tomorrow?" Hogg was stunned, then nodded, "Well then. At the end of this year, you have to come back earlier."

"Em."Lynnray answered.

Hogg said softly: "Lynnray, your father doesn't have much skills. The family will rely on you in the future. You gave me this magic crystal core, which is enough for your brother to spend in the O'Brien Empire. At this point, I I'm very satisfied, but I still remember the shame of our family in my heart. I hope you don't forget that the treasure of our family is still out there."

Lynnray felt his father's expectations for him, took a deep breath and nodded slightly. "I don't have any other desires now, I just hope to see the saber slaughter before I die." Hogg's voice was very low.

Lynnray felt that the atmosphere was not right, and immediately said, "Father, don't be so negative. You are only forty years old now, and you will grow up in the future. I am confident that in less than ten years, I will bring the saber back and put it in our ancestral temple."

"Ten years, good, good." Hogg nodded slightly.

...

Lynnray left Wushan Town at noon the next day, and in the living room of the Baruch family that night, there were two people, Hogg and Hilman. The door of the living room was closed tightly, and that generation of magic crystal cores was placed on the dining table in the living room.

Hilman was stunned by such a bag of magic crystal cores, and Hogg said: "Hilman, I will sell these magic crystal cores in the near future, and I hope you will keep these gold coins."

Hilman suddenly came to his senses and quickly said, "Master Hogg, no, how can you give me such a large fortune. Can't you be in charge of it yourself?"

"Hilman, don't call me Lord Hogg, just call me Brother Hogg." Hogg smiled very kindly.

Suddenly Hogg stood up and faced the east: "You said I am in charge? Haha... Hilman, you probably know the Baruch family and my Hogg the best."

Hilman was startled, he didn't know why Hogg mentioned this.

"It's been almost eleven years since that incident was hidden in your heart. Over the past eleven years, I have felt that my heart is being bitten by ants. I have been enduring it, day after day, year after year... It's been eleven years in a blink of an eye."

Hogg's whole body trembled slightly.

Hilman's face changed, he stood up abruptly, and said in horror: "Master Hogg, you want?"

"Yes, I have to investigate what happened back then, and I have to avenge Linna." Hogg's face was grim and furious.

"Master Hogg."Hilman said hurriedly, "Didn't we check it out? The enemy's power is very large, and only that part is found to be terrifying. You may lose your life if you go to check it."

Hogg snarled, "Death? I'm still afraid of death? Hilman, you don't know my pain and the kind of spiritual torture in the past eleven years. I have had enough. Now Lynnray gave me this magic The value of the crystal core should be around 80,000 gold coins. It is completely enough for Warton's expenses. With this gold coin, I have no burden."

"For so many years, I have been forbearing, for what? Not two sons, now Lynnray is growing up, Warton is also in the O'Brien Empire. I have nothing to worry about."

Hogg held Hilman's shoulders with both hands and stared into Hilman's eyes: "Hilman, although you call me Lord Hogg, we have been brothers for so many years. For this reason, I I hope you can fulfill me."

"Hogg, you..."Hilman was very anxious.

Hilman knew very well that once Hogg really went to investigate what happened back then, he would probably lose his life.

"I've made up my mind, Hilman, you know, I'm better off living in these days." Hogg's eyes were a little red, and Hilman felt helpless when he saw Hogg like this. He can understand Hogg's thoughts.

Why has Hogg been so harsh and indifferent over the years?

Others didn't know, Hilman knew very well that Hogg was a very cheerful person before Lynnray and Warton's mother "Linna" died. Then since Linna died, Hogg's temperament changed.

Although Hogg said that Linna had died in childbirth, Hilman, steward Hilly and others still knew the facts.

"Hilman, you don't have to persuade me anymore, I just ask you, will you help me?" Hogg stared at Hilman.

Hilman stared at Hogg for a moment, and finally sighed weakly: "Well, I'll help you." Hogg's face couldn't help showing a smile, it was a smile of relief.

Chapter 4 - Price of Stone Sculpture

On the road in Fenlai City, Alice was on the balcony of her two-story small building, with her hands on her chin watching the pedestrians passing by in the street ahead.

Since Lynnray left last time, Alice has been watching pedestrians on the balcony almost every day, hoping that Lynnray will come again. however......

"Class will start tomorrow, and I will go today." Alice sighed inwardly, and finally took a look at the street.

She just expected Lynnray to come to see her again, but unfortunately, Lynnray hadn't been here once in the past ten days, and at this time the voice of her good friend Niya sounded at the door below: "Alice, hurry up." Niya, Tony, The Karan trio were waiting at the door below.

Karan, Niya, and Tony belonged to the Warrior Academy, and the academy for the three of them was closer to the Welling School of Magic where Alice was. In addition, the four of them are in Fenlai City, so the relationship is better.

"Okay, I will come down."

Alice glanced at the street in front of the mansion, and the package prepared on her back went downstairs.... On the evening of the third day after Alice left Fenlai City, Lynnray came to Alice's courtyard and looked up at the balcony of the two-story building, but there was no one on the balcony.

"Hey, what are you doing?" The middle-aged man at the door of Alice's house called to Lynnray.

Lynnray turned his head and looked around and asked with a smile, "Hello, I am from the Welling School of Magic and I am good friends with Alice. I wonder if Alice is still at home now?"

"Oh." The middle-aged man said with a smile upon hearing these words, "Miss Alice has been away from home for almost three days and has already been to the Magic Academy."

"I see, thank you."Lynnray said politely.

Lynnray turned around and left along Ganmo Road, but when he reached the end of Ganmo Road, he still looked back at the balcony of the two-story building, feeling a little helpless in his heart.

Go to the streets of Ernst Academy.

A white streamer flew out from the ring of the dragon, and turned into a white-haired and white-bearded Delin wearing a moon-white robe. Delin looked at Lynnray with a smile: "Lynnray, do you like Alice?"

"Somewhat."Lynnray did not deny either.

Delin touched the white beard and laughed: "I didn't expect that you kid will finally be tempted by women, but Lynnray, you and Alice are in different magic schools, and they are separated in two places. It's very difficult to make any emotional progress."

"I know, let the fate, if there is a result, there will be a result, then forget it."Lynnray couldn't help but think about being with Alice in his mind.

For the first time, he looked panicked under the bloody boar.

On the way back from the Monster Mountains, Alice looked shy when the two talked.

There are also those who look like moonlight elves under the moonlight.

...

"Is this my first love?"Lynnray laughed at himself. When he was his age, the four brothers often talked about some girls when they were in the dormitory, and even Yale and Reno had girlfriends for a long time.

For feelings, Lynnray also has some expectations in his heart.

At the Ernst Academy of Magic, Lynnray practiced as seriously as he used to, and spent part of the time every day on the carving of the "Flat Knife School", both mental power and magic power were steadily and rapidly improved.

One month passed in a blink of an eye.

According to the old rules, Lynnray and the four brothers set off with three stone sculptures to the city of Fenlai, in Ostony's room in the Brooks Guild Hall of Fenlai.

"Nearly 15,000 gold coins? So many?"Lynnray was a little surprised at the price of the three stone sculptures last time.

Ostony laughed and said: "Lynnray, this is normal. The price of the works of ordinary stone carving masters can reach about one thousand gold coins. Our Brooks Guild Hall emphasized your identity, a fifteen-year-old man. The stone sculptures created by magical geniuses are enough to double the price of the stone sculptures just because of your identity."

"The most important thing is...your stone carving works are very peculiar, while other people's stone carving works are beautiful, but there are certain flaws in the degree of fluency. Your works have very smooth lines, such as the use of flat knives and jade bowl knives. Everywhere, people can't detect the break, and the connection is perfect."

Lynnray couldn't help laughing when he heard this.

Broken?

The stone carving works of my own flat knife genre only use a flat knife from beginning to end. There is no need to switch to various carving knives. The natural lines will be very perfect.

"Because of this special point, coupled with the arrogant temperament contained in your work itself, coupled with your identity, the price of the work has reached nearly five thousand gold coins. It is just that there is a slight lack in the treatment of some fine lines. Otherwise the price may be higher."Ostony praised.

Lynnray also understood in his heart.

"Detailed pattern treatment?"Lynnray shook his head secretly. He uses a flat knife. Although he can barely get some other special patterns, the effect is definitely weaker than that of other professional carving knives such as oblique knives and round knives. some.

Lynnray also sighed in his heart.

Three stone carvings can be sold for 15,000 gold coins. The money came too easily. If Lynnray devoted himself to carving, he would definitely be able to carve ten works in a month.

Ten works are worth nearly fifty thousand gold coins!

"I spent two months in the Monster Mountains and experienced life and death crises several times. I only got seven or eighty thousand gold coins by killing some killers. The master stone carving expert is simply stealing money."Lynnray sighed.

The price of Lynnray's works is also top-notch among master stone carving masters.

"Stone carving masters can be regarded as stealing money, the stone carving master..."Lynnray sighed.

The more he understands, the more sighs Lynnray. In the stone carving circle, the income gap is too obvious. There are only a hundred masters of stone carving in the entire Holy Alliance. The scarcity of the quantity can be imagined.

"Lynnray, work hard, I believe you will become a great stone carving master in the future."Ostony encouraged him.

The stone carving master not only possesses amazing wealth, but also has a very high status. They stood at the pinnacle of this oldest art, and even the ordinary noblemen did not dare to be arrogant when they met them.

Master!

This is an amazing title.

That is not what money or rights can get. It is a person who can reach the top in a certain industry and be recognized by everyone before he can be honored as a master.

Chapter 5 - Rose in Winter (I)

In the evening of the same day, Lynnray, Yale and others walked out of a hotel. According to the old rules, the next stop should be Green Water Paradise.

"Boss Yale, the three of you go first, I'll just stroll around first."Lynnray said as soon as he walked out of the hotel.

Yale, Reno, and George all looked at Lynnray in surprise.

"I don't like the atmosphere of clear water and heaven. I don't like it. You go first, and I will meet you again in two or three hours."Lynnray explained, while Beibei standing on Lynnray's shoulder squeaked. 'Called twice, and at the same time the soul transmitted: "Boss, you are going to Alice's house."

Beibei has been following Lynnray, and naturally knows about Lynnray.

Even though Beibei has not grown up, but this mind can catch up with the average human teenager.

"Little creature."Lynnray glanced at Beibei in a joking expression.

"Okay, Lynnray, you should go out for shopping first, but don't go for too long, we will wait for you in the old place." Yale smiled and said, then Lynnray separated from the three good brothers and walked towards Ganmo Road. There is not much traffic in Ganmo Road, and it seems much quieter. There will also be some pubs and restaurants on both sides of the street. Most of these pubs and restaurants are surrounding residents.

Walked not far from Alice's house and looked at the balcony of the two-story building.

The balcony was still empty.

Lynnray laughed at himself. In fact, he only had very little hope in his heart. Lynnray immediately turned and walked into a tavern next to him and chose a position by the window. Through the window, Lynnray could see the balcony of Alice's house.

"Bring me a bottle of emerald green and two wine glasses."Lynnray ordered a bottle of very mild wine at random.

"Yes, sir."

Although the waiter wondered why Lynnray wanted two wine glasses, he didn't ask much.

"Babe, drink slowly."Lynnray put a glass aside for Beibei, and Beibei immediately jumped to the table, learning from Lynnray and started drinking slowly.

Lynnray was holding the wine glass and looking at the balcony, drinking slowly.

One person and one Monster slowly drank like this, and after nearly two hours of drinking three bottles, Lynnray paid the bill and took Beibei to get up and leave the tavern. "Boss, are you very disappointed?" Beibei stood on Lynnray's shoulder and said through the voice of the soul.

Lynnray reached out and touched Beibei's little head, and said with a smile: "You little fellow." Then Lynnray strolled on the streets of Fenlai City, walking towards the Green Water Paradise, while enjoying the night view of Fenlai City.

The next day, that is, September 30th, the four brothers of Lynnray left Fenlai City and returned to Ernst School of Witchcraft and Wizardry. Then in the evening of the next day, Alice and Karan returned to Fenlai City.

The reason for this coincidence is that the holidays at Ernst Witchcraft and Wizardry Academy and Welling Witchcraft and Wizardry are different.

Ernst School of Magic, the 29th and 30th of each month are holidays. However, the Welling School of Witchcraft and Wizardry and the Welling of Warriors Academy are holidays on the 1st and 2nd of each month. Alice came back in the evening on the 30th.

unfortunately......

Alice was on the balcony, holding her chin with her hands on her chin and watching the crowds on the street. Occasionally, some silhouettes resembling Lynnray in the distance would excite Alice, but whenever a figure came near, she would be disappointed.

On the afternoon of October 2, Alice had no choice but to return to the Magic Academy.

On October 29th, on this day, Lynnray sent three more stone sculptures to the Prussian Hall, and in the evening, Lynnray came to the tavern on Ganmo Road again, and he still chose the position by the window, and the order was still emerald. Green wine, Lynnray and Bei Bei drank slowly together.

"Boss, it seems that you are going to be disappointed again this time."Beibei looked at Lynnray and said.

"Disappointment is disappointment, it can only be regarded as no fate."Lynnray raised his head and drank the small half cup in his hand. By this time, Lynnray and Beibei had finished drinking two bottles of emerald green, and Lynnray still did not appear on the balcony. Looking forward to the silhouette.

And the waiter on the side also came over.

"One more bottle of jade..."Lynnray stopped halfway through his words, his eyes lit up, staring at the balcony of the second-story building of Alice's house. At this time, a girl dressed in white appeared on the balcony.

"Check out."Lynnray stood up suddenly.

The waiter who was going to get the wine was startled for a while, and he reacted in a moment. After paying the bill, Lynnray walked directly outside, and Beibei also jumped from the table onto Lynnray's shoulder.

At this time, it was almost eight o'clock in the evening, and Ganmo Road was also a bit dim. Because Ganmo Road was not a major road, people were still very few at night.

"It's Alice."Lynnray was sure in his heart. "Wow, boss, you finally saw this beauty, haha, are you happy, excited, excited?" Beibei also kept talking proudly from the side.

Lynnray didn't care about Beibei, but ran towards the courtyard wall of Alice's house very flexibly. With both hands supporting, the whole person drew a black afterimage and fell onto the balcony.

Alice just saw Lynnray coming from the direction of the courtyard wall at this time.

"Brother Lynnray." Alice recognized it all at once, the speed of her heartbeat suddenly increased, and her face flushed. Alice was also somewhat lucky.

The last time she didn't wait for Lynnray, she also checked after returning to the Welling School of Witchcraft and Wizardry, only to know that Ernst Academy's holidays were on the 29th and 30th. So Alice came back two days before skipping class this time.

"Brother Lynnray, what a coincidence." Alice said with a smile.

Lynnray was startled: "Alice, it's a coincidence."

Alice couldn't help but laughed, and then she reacted and immediately pulled Lynnray: "Sit down, don't be found by the janitor."Lynnray also sat down. The two of them hid under the balcony parapet and talked in a low voice.

Delin also appeared nearby.

"Lynnray."

"Grandpa Delin, is there something?"Lynnray was a little unhappy.Delin laughed and said: "Boy, don't talk to this girl about the insignificant things, be more intimate, be proactive. What a fool. Looking at the appearance of Alice, he also has a heart for you. "

"Not in a hurry, not in a hurry." Although Lynnray was not very afraid of life and death, but at this time he was a little lacking in confidence.

"What an idiot."Delin was anxious.

Lynnray then ignored Delin and chatted with Alice specifically.

Delin looked at the two, but finally turned into a stream of light and returned to the Ring of the Dragon. Lynnray didn't feel that time had passed in the chat with Alice.

"Brother Lynnray, you are so powerful. There must be a lot of girls chasing you at Ernst School of Magic and Magic." Alice asked casually, but when asked, Alice's heartbeat intensified.

"It's okay, it's okay."Lynnray talked to Alice, speaking a little bit through his brain.

"Idiot."Delin's voice sounded in Lynnray's mind.

Chapter 6 - Rose in Winter (II)

With Alice, Lynnray felt a burst of joy from deep in his heart, and the night passed without being aware of it. Neither Lynnray nor Alice felt tired from not sleeping all night.

There was a hint of white fish in the sky, and there was already a hint of green light between the sky and the earth.

"It's dawn, Alice, I'm leaving first."Lynnray stood up.

"En." Alice answered.

Alice also stood up, looking at Lynnray reluctantly, Lynnray smiled or held his hands together, and the air flow around her body floated onto the street like fallen leaves.

When Lynnray returned to the Green Water Paradise, after the good brothers got up, they were 'interrogated' by Yale and the other three.

After returning to Ernst Academy, Lynnray still practiced as seriously as before, but when he was resting, Lynnray often thought of Alice, Lynnray had a feeling that he seemed to be hit by the god of love.

Yulan calendar year 9997, the evening of November 29.

Alice had been waiting directly in front of her house a long time ago. When she waited for a while, she saw Lynnray at the end of Ganmo Street and ran over immediately. "Brother Lynnray." Alice yelled with excitement. She hadn't seen each other for a month, and when they met, Alice couldn't help feeling a little excited.

Lynnray was also very excited. After all, he hadn't seen each other for a month, but at this moment Lynnray was a little excited: "Although I didn't tell Alice the time to meet again, she is waiting for me today.

Last time I chatted with Alice, Lynnray knew about the 1st and 2nd of each month during the holidays of the Welling School of Magic. Alice is skipping class to meet with herself now, Lynnray also understands the meaning.

"Lynnray, come on, be brave this time."Delin's voice also appeared in Lynnray's mind.

Lynnray also secretly made up his mind, he didn't want to bear with him for another month.

"Alice, why are you outside today, not on the balcony?"Lynnray and Alice walked side by side on the street, Alice smiled: "We can't hide in the balcony, right?"

Lynnray couldn't help but smile when he thought of the two hiding in the balcony.

"By the way, if you don't go back to sleep at night, your father doesn't care?"Lynnray asked.

"He?" Alice pouted. "My father is a drunkard or a gambler. I'm afraid he doesn't even know when he will be back the next day, so he will care about me?"

"Brother Lynnray, I grew up in Fenlai City, and Fenlai City is very big. You must have never been to many places. Let me take you there." Alice said with a smile.

Lynnray and Alice walked side by side on the street. It is winter now. December and January are the coldest days in Yulan. The evening wind is also very cold and there are not many pedestrians on the street. .

However, Lynnray and Alice talked while walking, ignoring the others at all.

"Huh, it's snowing?" Alice looked up at the night sky, and saw flakes of snow slowly falling down, "I like snow the most. This snow is the first snow this winter."

"I like snow too."Lynnray looked up at the night sky, and the snow fell on his face and melted.

It is still very romantic to stroll along the snowy night with the beloved girl, and the two of them wandered the streets of Fenlai like this.

"Brother Lynnray, do you have a girlfriend?" Alice asked suddenly, and then pretended to say lightly, "Brother Lynnray, you must be so good."

"No, absolutely not."Lynnray said immediately.

After listening to it, Alice groaned without speaking.

"Alice, do you have a boyfriend?"Lynnray pondered for a long time, and finally asked.

Alice's face turned red all of a sudden, even the skin on her neck was red, but she couldn't see clearly at night when it was dim: "Why don't I have any boyfriend? Who wants me to be a girlfriend?"

"Oh." Lynnray took a deep breath and suddenly said, "Or, are you my girlfriend?"

"Uh—" Alice looked up at Lynnray in amazement, seeming to be silly. Lynnray was chatting with him just now, and even said this suddenly so suddenly, Alice was a little surprised.

It is very normal for young men and women to be together in the Holy League. Alice's non-girl classmates also have boyfriends, and she also thought about her own boyfriend.

But she didn't expect that Lynnray would ask so directly.

"You want me to be your girlfriend?" Alice asked.

At this time Lynnray felt his heart beating faster than ever before. Even if he faced life and death in the Monster Mountains, he was not so nervous: "Yes, are you willing?"

Alice blushed, her big eyes staring at Lynnray: "Brother Lynnray, in fact, I may not be as good as you think."

"I believe in my vision, Alice, I ask you, do you agree?"Lynnray was almost mad, he wanted to hear Alice's answer now, Lynnray couldn't help but tremble a little.

Alice pondered for a moment, then lowered her head and nodded slightly.

"call."

Lynnray's heart was excited, and he couldn't help but hugged Alice, and Alice also shyly buried her face in Lynnray's chest. At this time Lynnray saw the flower shop next to him.

Just a moment...

"Alice, here." Alice raised her head, but found a bright rose in front of her.

Alice took the rose with a blushing face, Lynnray looked at Alice, the bright color of the rose matched Alice's red face, and it was indescribable. This scene was also carved into Lynnray's memory.

Lynnray took Alice's hand, and the two walked on the street like this.

Snow flies, and the pair of boys and girls are walking on the streets of Fenlai at night. The rose in Alice's hand is so bright.

There are a total of seven people in the elegant room of Green Water Paradise, namely Yale, Reno, George, and four beautiful women.

"Lynnray doesn't know what's going on. The last time he didn't come all night, this time he hasn't come here yet." Yale said helplessly, shaking his head.

"Hey, that person seems to be Lynnray."Reno leaning against the window suddenly shouted in shock. "He is still holding hands with a woman. Damn, Lynnray actually hooked up with the beauty behind us."

"Swipe." Yale and George also ran to the window, staring down carefully.

At this time, Lynnray, who was immersed in the wonderful feeling of first love, did not even notice that there was a Green Water Paradise next to him! Lynnray and Alice walked through the Green Water Paradise like this, and continued to walk towards the far side of the Champs Avenue.

"Hey, when did the youngest be so good?" Yale's eyes lit up.

George and Reno were also excited, and Reno even suggested: "Haha, when the youngest comes in the morning, we have to interrogate him."

...

In the early morning of the next day, Lynnray happily came to the private room of the Green Water Paradise. According to the rules, Reno and Yale should sleep in the private room with the beautiful woman, but—

Pushing open the door of the private room, Lynnray looked inside in surprise: "Boss Yale, why are the three of you here?"

"You ask us, why are we all here?"Reno chuckled. George and Yale also smiled maliciously and approached.

"Say!"Reno glared. "Who was the beauty that was with you last night?"

"Say it quickly." Yale and George also stared at each other.

"Uh, you--"Lynnray was completely taken aback.

Chapter 7 - Gathering of Masters (I)

Being so forced by his own brother, Lynnray also confessed his affairs with Alice very honestly, which amazed the two dudes Reno and Yale.

Since confirming the relationship between boyfriend and girlfriend with Alice, although the two are separated in two schools, they have also decided to meet at the middle and end of each month.

In a blink of an eye, almost a month passed, on December 28th, because tomorrow I will go to Fenlai City again to meet Alice, so Lynnray is in a good mood.

"Hi, Lynnray."

"Oh, David."

Lynnray walked on the road of Ernst School of Magic and Witchcraft and enthusiastically greeted some friends and classmates he knew.

"Boss, are you so excited when you got involved with that Alice?" Beibei wrinkled her nose on Lynnray's shoulder and said with disdain, "Look at how stupid you are, you've been smiling all day long this month. "

Although Lynnray's treatment of people in the past was not cold and ruthless, it was not so enthusiastic. But this month Lynnray's mood was obviously very good, and he often laughed at people.

"You little guy, what do you know?"Lynnray glanced at Beibei badly, and then Lynnray still entered the library vigorously, slightly selected two books on wind magic, Lynnray entered the reading room and started reading .

In the reading room, it was very quiet, and there were only twenty or thirty people in the spacious reading room.

Lynnray chose a position aside and began to read quietly. In the library of Ernst Academy, about history, Monster, mainland geography, various departments of magic... Lynnray almost dabbled in a little bit, and then Lynnray spent the most energy Or wind magic.

After all, Lynnray majored in earth and wind magic, and earth magic was taught by the holy master Delin, but the wind system was different.

While reading, Lynnray also realized something, and couldn't help nodding his head in admiration.

During the reading, two hours passed quickly, and Lynnray closed the book in his hand: "Grandpa Delin, it's already very difficult to fully understand the meaning of wind magic, let alone create some wind magic. Up."

Casting magic, mostly chanting magic spells, is performed step by step. It is to know the reason and not know why, but to comprehend some magic principles, and even to simplify the 'magic spell', or to control the mind, to make the use of magic power as efficient as possible.

"Of course, do you think magic is so easy to create?"Delin's voice sounded in Lynnray's mind.

"It doesn't matter if you create, it would be nice to let me know some magic above level seven, but unfortunately the academy is too stingy.

Seventh, eighth, ninth and even taboo magic are not disclosed at all."Lynnray was very dissatisfied with this, but Lynnray is also very clear that behind Ernst Magic Academy is the Church of Light, and the Church of Light will not pass on powerful magic to people from other countries.

Lynnray was also a little grateful, but fortunately he had Grandpa Delin's guidance, at least he didn't have to worry about magic.

Reading another wind magic book, Lynnray continued to read...

"Together, it's not just the wind element, in fact, some high-level magic of other schools is the same, most of which are extensions of basic magic. For example, the wind blade of our wind element, the higher chain of the wind blade. , The higher "Wind Blade Xiang Flurry" up to the ninth-level wind magic "Vacuum Binding Technique", all belong to one branch. Of course, the wind blade develops according to another branch and can eventually become the strongest taboo magic. Dimensional Blade'..."

Lynnray was very excited when he read this book's detailed description of the wind blade.

The description in this book belongs to the highest point of the magic world, and then unified description. This book is very good for some people with a strong foundation, and it can make them form a complete system of magic in their minds.

"Floating is actually a relatively simple type of magic, but it is not easy to use, because this kind of magic attaches the most importance to the affinity of the elements of the wind element. The higher the affinity, the more delicately you can control the magic force and elements of wind, and reach very fast speed. And the "flying technique" is a higher level than the "levitating technique", the floating technique is only straight up and down, and the flying technique can fly in all directions. It seems to be in all directions, but in fact it is just There are four more directions of "front, back, left, and right" than floating. For example, if you fly to the bottom left, you only need to control yourself to fly down and to the left at the same time. In fact, from this principle, plus the magic spell of floating, It's easier to introduce the magic spell of flying..."

Reading this, Lynnray couldn't help but flash in his mind.

Yes, compared to the floating technique, the flying technique actually has four more flying directions of 'front, back, left, and right'. In essence, it is the use of wind magic to control the wind elements and control the body to fly in the four directions of 'front, back, left, and right'.

"Yes, it's just four winds, front, back, left, and right. If that's the case, it won't be difficult to launch the magic 'fly'."Lynnray imagined several magic spells all at once.

Of course, whether these kinds of magic spells are correct still needs to be confirmed through experimentation.

In the past, Lynnray only thought that flying skills needed to fly in all directions, and it was difficult to set magic spells.

But now it seems that the flying technique has four more directions than the'floating technique', and only four more winds are needed, which is not that difficult for Lynnray.

Lynnray continued reading excitedly.

"Of course, high-level magic that can be simply inferred is extremely rare. For example, higher than 'fly' is 'wings in the wind', which forms two wings in the wind. This is very difficult. Magic spells are also very different from flying spells. It is impossible to reason out."

Lynnray also nodded slightly.

The more I read, the more Lynnray believes that the author of this book is definitely a master of creating magic, because most of the explanations in this book are based on the principles of magic, telling how to study magic spells and how to control elements Arrangement and so on. He didn't say how to increase the power of magic.

If it is an average person, who sees the arrangement of some magic elements so complicated, they will not read this book.

But Lynnray understood that if he understood the principle, he would naturally know how to control magic so as to use the same magic with greater power.

"Lynnray." Just as Lynnray was immersed in the book, a clear voice sounded next to him.

Lynnray looked up and looked to the side, only to see a tall, beautiful girl standing next to him, it was Lynnray's good friend Delia, but Delia's face was not pretty.

"Delia, what's the matter?"Lynnray asked with a smile.

Delia pursed her lips and said after a long silence: "Lynnray, I heard that you have a girlfriend?" Delia's big moving eyes stared at Lynnray.

Chapter 8 - Gathering of Masters (II)

Lynnray was startled slightly, at this moment Lynnray hesitated, thinking a lot in his heart, but still nodded: "Yes, her name is Alice."

Delia's eyes turned red: "Congratulations."

Delia quickly turned around, tears that could not be suppressed flowed down, and then Delia ran out of the reading room directly and quickly.

Lynnray herself did not notice Delia's tears.

"Huh." Saying this directly to Delia, Lynnray felt a little relaxed even though he felt bored.

After this incident, Lynnray was not in the mood to continue reading, and he noted the name of the magic book in his heart, and then stored the book back.

Lynnray felt a little bored on the way back to the dormitory.

"Boss, I know, you also like Delia, don't you?" Beibei said gleefully, "I think Delia is good, better than Alice."

"Shut up."Lynnray's soul transmission shouted.

"Hum, I was right." Beibei said proudly.

Lynnray took a deep breath, and then slowly exhaled, with a smile on his face: "It doesn't matter, since I have made it clear to Delia, I don't have too much burden in my heart. Well, I will meet Alice tomorrow. , Prepare a gift."

Thinking of Alice, Lynnray felt a lot easier.

...

On the evening of December 29th, Lynnray and Yale separated and went to Ganmo Road alone to join Alice. This time Lynnray and Alice spent a lot of time together.

Because every January 1st is called the "Yulan Festival", the Yulan Festival is the largest festival in the entire Yulan mainland. The brightest Holy See will also hold the most grand mass on this day.

Fenlai City is the holy capital of Church of Light. The headquarter of Church of Lightwas located in the western part of the city. Naturally, the Mass of Fenlai Citywas the largest Mass on the entire Yulan Continent. When the time comes, the Pope of the Church of Lightwould host it himself. It was an unbelievable ceremony, and many and many people would attend the ceremony.

January 1.

Western part of Fenlai City, the headquarter of the Church of Light, the Temple of Light, was a huge building nearly 100 meters high. This huge building could be clearly seen in other places of Fenlai City.

In front of the Temple of Light is a large square with a length of several kilometers. The ground of the square is paved with flat white rocks. At this moment, the square is full of people, and Lynnray and Alice are in it.

The knights of the Holy See knights orderly controlled the square, and the people gathered here were also very disciplined.

"Brother Lynnray, when it's eight o'clock, a group of upper-class figures from the Church of Light will come out, as well as the Pope of Light himself." Alice said softly to Lynnray.

Lynnray nodded and glanced at the knights of the Holy See: "Alice, looking at the number of knights maintaining order, there are at least thousands of knights. It seems that the strength of these knights should not be weak."

"Of course, today is the Yulan Day. It is also the Ace Knights of the Temple of Light to maintain order. Every knight is at least a level-5 knight." Alice had lived in Fenlai since she was a child, and she knew much more than Lynnray.

Lynnray was shocked.

Level 5 knight? The lowest level are all five-level knights. The knight group composed of such powerful knights was so strong that you could imagine how powerful it wa. A level-5 magician himself was nothing compared with them.

Alice pointed to some gorgeously dressed people in the distance: "Look, there are a lot of great nobles coming today, and the royal families of the six kingdoms of our Holy League will come soon."

Time passed quickly, and it was eight o'clock in a blink of an eye.

Suddenly, the 100-meter-high spire of the Temple of Light was lit up, and the white light radiated downward. The giant angel statue in the center of the square also faintly circulated, and at the same time, the whole square reverberated with a wonderful divine song that seemed to come from the gods. ...

At this time, a group of people walked out of the side hall next to the Church of Light. At the front of this group were rows of temple knights wearing white armor and red feathers on their helmets. Each of these temple knights has the unique aura of a master, especially the row of knights with a hundred people marching in orderly steps together, the sense of oppression made the entire square suddenly silent.

"Unexpectedly, the strength of the Holy See is so strong. I am afraid that the lowest level of over a hundred knights is a seventh-level warrior."Delin appeared next to Lynnray, carefully consolidating the group of people, "There is a saint today. The domain powerhouse appears, forget it, enter the Ring of Coiling Dragon."

After talking about Delin, he disappeared.

"Sanctuary powerhouse?"Lynnray couldn't help but looked at the group of people carefully.

After more than a hundred temple knights in white armor, there were more than a dozen priests in white robes, and after the white ceremonies were bald-headed and silver-robed elders surrounded by several red archbishops.

"pope!"

The bald-headed and silver-robed old man was obviously the central figure of this group of people. Lynnray couldn't help but focus entirely on this person. The Pope of Light was tall and he was estimated to be nearly two meters tall. Pope Illuminati also holds a scepter about the height of the Pope in his left hand.

Behind the Pope of Light and the Archbishop in red, there are four old men in black robes and over a hundred soldiers in purple robes. This large group of people walks in the middle of the road in an orderly manner. No one dares to gather hundreds of thousands of people in the square. Noisy.

"Grandpa Delin, you said that the sanctuary is strong, who is the sanctuary strong?"Lynnray asked in his heart.

"I could tell at a glance that the Pope of Light and one of the four black-robed elders behind him are all powerful in the sanctuary. They are also confident that they are not restraining their aura. After more than five thousand years, The little Holy See, which was shrouded in the Pron Empire, has grown to such a point."Delin sighed.

"Doesn't converge?"

Lynnray stared at the group of people in a daze. To tell the truth, the archbishop in red, the pope of light, and the four old men in black robes behind him, Lynnray only felt their majesty, but could not feel the breath of the strongest.

But Delin said... the two sanctuary powerhouses did not converge?

"Lynnray, you are still early, a level-5 magician is nothing on the Yulan continent. Only when he reaches the seventh level can he be qualified to be called a strong. And the seventh-level strong, dominates the continent like the Bright Holy See In front of one of the giants, they are just small people."

"On the mainland, the Bright Holy See, the Dark Holy See, the Four Great Empires, and many mysterious organizations. The number of masters in the entire Yulan Continent is far beyond your imagination. You are weak now and have not yet come into contact with that level. At that time, you will understand."Delin said with a smile, "Your greatest advantage is being young. The strength of those who are strong is only gained through years of hard work. You will become a strong in the future."

Lynnray nodded slightly.

Known as a genius at Ernst Academy, Lynnray really thought he was a little bit remarkable, and then at this moment Lynnray woke up, and on the entire continent, Lynnray was nothing at all.

When the pope passed by, the people in the square began to speak in a low voice.

"Brother Lynnray, you see, the six great royal clans are here, and the first one is the royal clans of our Fenlai Kingdom. That blond man is our King, and the strongest fighter in our Fenlai Kingdom, the ninth-level powerhouse. "Alice whispered in Lynnray's ear.

Chapter 9 - The Split (I)

"Your Majesty?"Lynnray looked over.

The sturdy middle-aged man wearing dazzling golden armor, a sturdy body, and a blond hair like a lion turned out to be the king of the Kingdom of Fenlai. Moreover, he is also a powerful ninth-level powerhouse, which is simply incredible.

As a citizen of the Kingdom of Fenlai, Lynnray had heard about the pride of the Kingdom of Fenlai a long time ago -- the legend of the golden lion'Clyde'. The king of a kingdom was a super fighter, which was the pride of all citizens of the kingdom.

In the square in front of the Temple of Light, hundreds of thousands of people stood in an orderly manner. In front of the angel statue, a group of people such as the Pope of Light, the Red Archbishop, the priest in white, and the Knights of the Temple stood quietly. The Pope of Light is undoubtedly the most dazzling.

The six kings of the Holy League and the princes of many principalities also stood silently.

Suddenly, with the Pope of Light at the center, a clearly visible milky white ripple spread out, and the square where hundreds of thousands of people gathered suddenly became silent. Almost everyone had a quiet smile on their faces, and their souls were unprecedentedly peaceful."It is really terrifying to emit the holy light covering hundreds of thousands of people so easily."Lynnray, as a magician, can see how powerful the Pope is.

The whole square was quietly heard only by the breeze.

"In the name of the Lord!" Pope of Light said calmly, but his voice resounded throughout the world, shaking the soul.

Everyone on the court felt a pressure emanating from the Pope of Light, and Lynnray also bowed respectfully without any resistance. This pressure was stronger than the two sanctuary powerhouses Lynnray had encountered in Wushan Town. , And the coercion of the Monster"Black Dragon" is even terrifying.

This kind of coercion does not need to oppress people, but makes people worship from the soul.

The coercion of God!

Except for the Pope of Brightness, hundreds of thousands of people in the square, from the cardinal bishop, the kings of the six kingdoms, to the common people, all bowed respectfully and listened to the instructions.

"May the Lord's mercy, favor, and gifts be with you."

The voice of the Pope of Light seemed not loud, but it resounded through the world and shocked the soul.

Waves of holy light spread from the spire of the Temple of Light, covering everyone. Almost everyone on the court felt a peaceful mind and body, and reached an unprecedented state. Everyone is very respectful.

"May the Lord grant you grace and peace."

At the same time, the Glory Pope exudes a peaceful glory, "The Lord's people, let us confess our sins and repent religiously for our mistakes in our thoughts, actions, and words. May the Lord have mercy on us, forgive our sins, and let us have eternal life. ."

Suddenly--

The whole world also reverberated with holy singing, and all the believers in the Temple of Light also sang religiously. The singing of the believers and the singing echoed between the heaven and the earth are in harmony with each other, and everyone is pious and respectful.

...

The process of Mass was very complicated, from repentance, to pity, to praise, then prayer, then thanksgiving, and finally singing.

Most of the people on the square are followers of the Church of Light, and most of them are immersed in the light of the Temple of Light. Even the people who didn't believe in the Temple of Light very much were driven by the atmosphere of the scene. When the chanting was over, everyone was completely awake, and it was already noon.

The mass was over and the people on the court left in an orderly manner. Lynnray and Alice walked hand in hand side by side: "Brother Lynnray, how do you feel? Is it very comfortable?"

Lynnray shook his head: "I feel affected by the atmosphere, and the whole person can't stay absolutely awake and absolutely autonomous. Maybe people who have no spiritual support will like this feeling very much, but I don't like it, I don't like being affected by other influences. ."

I have to admit that during the mass, Lynnray was indeed affected, and that sense of ease even made Lynnray addicted.

But after all, Lynnray came from a life and death battle in the Monster Mountains, and when the mass was over, he would wake up. Thinking about it, I was afraid for a while. The ability of the Bright Holy See to attract believers is really terrifying.

"Impact, no, the Lord is like our parents. We are the Lord's people. We are favored and favored by the Lord. Brother Lynnray, why do you think that?" Alice was a little unhappy.

Alice has lived in the city of Fenlai since she was a child. As a holy city, the city of Fenlai holds such a large mass every year on the'Yulan Festival'. Most of the residents in the holy capital are believers in the Temple of Light. Just believe in the Holy See, this kind of spiritual belief is not so easy to change.

"Alice, you can't think like this. Isn't your current strength a result of your own hard work? How can it be the Lord's grace? Since the Lord favors you, why would you have such a father, that kind of Mother!"Lynnray knows Alice's family very well.

Alice couldn't help being silent, just staring at Lynnray.

"Brother Lynnray, I'm going back, don't send me away." Alice turned and walked towards her home. Lynnray watched Alice go away, but her heart was a little upset, and she looked back at the towering cloud. Temple of Light: "The Church of Light is indeed harmful."

Quarrels between young men and women are also relatively common. When Lynnray met Alice for the second time, the relationship was in a mess. Both of them are interested in avoiding questions about faith. From meeting twice a month, when they were in love, they even met four times in January. The two even slept well together, but they still did not break through. The last line of defense.

According to Alice's words: "Save the first time until we get married." The second year, that is, the first half of 9998, was the six months that Lynnray and Alice had the best relationship.

But after a long time together, some small problems will naturally arise.

The day of September 29, 9998 in the Yulan calendar.

"Oh, Alice doesn't tell me if there is anything in her belly."Lynnray and his three brothers were walking on the way to the city of Fenlai, thinking of the last time they broke up, Lynnray felt helpless.

Alice and Lynnray live in a different environment, and many of them have different ideas. The most important thing is... Alice is a very strong and independent girl. It's definitely not the kind of girl who compromises easily, what makes Lynnray feel helpless the most is-Alice is a dull gourd.

"Lynnray, are you in conflict with your Alice?" Yale said jokingly beside him. Reno and George also laughed, and Reno patted Lynnray's shoulder and said: "Lynnray, I feel that you value that Alice too much. Be careful of the loss of love. It's very miserable. Look at me. I have a few girlfriends, so I have a happy life."

Lynnray glanced at Reno and couldn't help being speechless.

"The fourth child, don't talk nonsense, Lynnray is going to be married to Alice." Yale said with a smile, and after Yale patted Lynnray's shoulder, "but Lynnray, I also want to talk about you, man, If you want more women, don't wrong yourself too much."

Lynnray smiled and said nothing.

In the city of Fenlai, when Lynnray separated from the four brothers, he walked directly to the house of Alice, Ganmo Road.

"Uncle Hadd."Lynnray warmly greeted the gatekeeper of Alice's house and said. During these days, Lynnray has been very close to Alice, and he has also known the gatekeeper Harder.

Harder smiled and looked at Lynnray: "Oh, Lynnray is here, do you see Miss Alice? Ah, Miss Alice has not come back yet, she should come back according to the rules. I don't know what's going on this time."

"Not back?"Lynnray was startled.

Immediately, Lynnray smiled at Harder: "Then I will wait a while, maybe she will be back later."Lynnray then walked to the tavern close to Alice's house and ordered the familiar jade. Green wine, waiting quietly while drinking.

Chapter 10 - The Split (II)

It was getting dark, and Lynnray was still drinking slowly. Alice's figure never appeared, and there were fewer and fewer people in the tavern. The Beibei next to him was so excited to drink, usually Lynnray wouldn't allow him to drink much, this time It's a great drink.

"Sir, we are going to close here." The waiter in the tavern walked to Lynnray's side and said respectfully.

"Closed?"Lynnray was startled.

"Oh, how much."Lynnray stood up, but felt a little dizzy in his head.

He has drunk six full bottles of emerald green wine. Fortunately, Lynnray's physique is so strong that he would have fallen down long ago. Beibei next to him drank the most exaggerated, drank a full twelve bottles.

After paying the fee, Lynnray walked out of the tavern. It was late at night by this time, and there were not a few people on Ganmo Road.

"This is Alice's first missed appointment."Lynnray took a long breath.

Looking back at the two-story small building in the dark night, Lynnray turned around and walked directly towards the 'clear water heaven' on the Champs Avenue.

Clear water heaven. "Lynnray is probably going to be with his girlfriend again." Yale, Reno, and George were talking and drinking.

"Hey, Yale, do you think Lynnray is still a virgin?"Reno said with a smile.

Yale wrinkled his nose and said confidently: "It needs to be said, just look at Lynnray, a 100% virgin. Hey, fourth, let's rest." Yale walked outside with a pretty beauty in his arms. Reno also walked outside with his arms around him.

"Squeak."

The door suddenly opened.

Yale and Reno looked up in amazement, Yale couldn't help but said in surprise: "Lynnray, why are you back?"

"It's nothing, come, Yale, fourth child, second child, come and drink with me."Lynnray's voice was a little low.

Yale, Reno, and George looked at each other. Yale laughed first: "Okay, it's rare that Lynnray is so refreshing. Today, the brothers will accompany you for a good night." Yale, Reno, and George all sat down. They all started drinking with Lynnray.

The next day, Lynnray went to Alice's house again, but Alice still did not come back.

Among the Ernst School of Magic.

"Alice is she really angry?"Lynnray was walking down the street of the Academy, not feeling very good.

Lynnray casually glanced at a shop inside the academy and saw the papers about various magic props pasted in front of the store. Suddenly, Lynnray focused his eyes on a crystal ball, but remembered in his mind that Alice had been with What I said: "Brother Lynnray, we are separated in two places. Every time I see other men and women in the Academy together, I think of you, but it is very difficult for us to see one side. Alas, if we are all the time It would be great to be able to be together."

Lynnray's heart moved.

I walked directly into this store and said to the salesperson: "How much is your memory crystal ball?"

"800 gold coins." The salesperson's eyes lit up, and the memory crystal ball is a luxury consumer product. "Our memory crystal ball has a very good effect. This memory crystal ball is specially made by the eighth-level magic master of the water department of the Academy. "

Lynnray is very aware of the principle of memory crystal ball.

Attach the water magic 'floating shadow technique' to this crystal ball by alchemy. At that time, just input a little magic power, you can start the memory crystal ball, and automatically record a length of scene. When the enrollment is completed, the memory crystal ball will be activated again in the future, and the memory crystal ball will play the video repeatedly.

After counter-offering, Lynnray spent 1,200 gold coins to purchase two memory crystal balls.

"One crystal ball records some of my sights in the academy, and I let Alice record the other crystal ball. If you don't see Alice in the future, you can also look at the memory crystal ball."Lynnray looked at the two memory crystal balls in his hand. , A smile appeared on his face.

...

Stone carving in the dormitory, cultivating in the back mountain, listening to class in the classroom... Lynnray recorded them in sections until they were completely saturated and could no longer record. However, when Lynnray rushed to the Fenlai City in mid-October with two crystal balls, he found that...Alice still hadn't returned.

October 29.

The four brothers set off for Fenlai City once again. In Fenlai City, Lynnray parted with his brothers.

Yale, Reno and George watched as Lynnray left, and had a serious expression on their face.

"I have known Lynnray for 7 years. He is a talent in both magic and stone sculpting, but obviously, he is giving too much in his relationship with Alice. If he loses the loved one, he will feel very frustrated." Yale frowned and said.

Reno nodded: "I have a feeling that they are having a problem, because Alice did not show up a couple of times."

"Actually, a setback in love is not a bad thing." Yale smiled, "How does a man grow without getting frustrated in love? I think Lynnray cares too much about Alice. I will dump a woman if she goes overboard."

Goerge smiled: "Yale, I appreciate Lynnray's attitude in love. You are holding the view of a player." George shook his head. "I appreciate Yale's attitude in relationships." Reno said, raising his eyebrows.

"Stop our bullshit and go to Green Water Paradise."

Yale, Reno and George headed for Green Water Paradise, but half on the way, Reno pulled Yale and George: "Hey, look over there. Who's that?"

Chapter 11 - The Meeting (first chapter on shelf)

The Champs Avenue was packed with people, but Yale, George and Reno saw clearly the girl not far away. Lynnray had been with Alice for such a long time, so the three brothers recognized Alice as well.

"She's Alice." George whispered.

Alice was walking hand-in-hand with a juvenile and had a smile on her face. If Lynnray was there, he could easily spot the guy as Karan.

"Bitch." Yale showed hatred in his eyes.

Reno said angrily: "Lynnray waited for her several times during these two months, and recorded some events with the memory crystal ball like an idiot. And he said he would marry this girl named Alice. What a joke!"

George felt unfair: "Lynnray has no fault and shouldn't be treated this way."

Yale grunted: "We cannot interfere with this. Let's go to Green Water Paradise and wait for Lynnray's return. We should prepare him for this, otherwise he'll feel difficult to accept it."

George and Reno nodded.

......

In the private room of Green Water Paradise, Yale, George and Reno knitted their brows. They were drinking fruit juice this time, and did not ask for women's company. They didn't want to talk with Lynnray in a drunk state.

"I know Lynnray very well." George said with worries, "He doesn't speak much, and practices diligently. Many girls chased him, but he accepted none. Such a person will be entangled deeper in love than a person like Yale and Reno."

Yale and Renoboth nodded.

Changing a woman was not a big deal for Yale and Reno. But when they joked with Lynnray in dormitory at night during the year, they could feel how much Lynnray loved Alice, judging from his reactions.

"It's annoying." Yale drank up the fruit juice in his glass.

Reno grunted and said: "Yale, we don't need to bother much. A woman is not that important. Lynnray will be painful, but he will turn much better afterwards."

Yale nodded.

Yale, Reno and George were raised in a large family, and women were part of their lives. Reno and George had a strict home education, but Yale was accompanied by women since small.

The three brothers were waiting quietly as time passed.

At about 1 a.m. in midnight, the door opened, and Lynnray went in with his alcoholic smell: "Eh, why are you here?"

Yale laughed: "We are all waiting for you."

"Lynnray, Alice didn't show up, right?" George said casually.

Lynnray nodded quietly and sat down: "Why aren't you drinking?" Lynnray took out several bottles of liquor, pulled off the wooden plug and started filling the glass.

"Lynnray, I'll tell you about one thing." Yale said with a smile.

"Say it." Lynnray was in a bad mood.

Yale said softly: "Today, we saw a girl very similar to Alice on our way. She was far from us so we couldn't make sure. But she was together with a boy."

"You are lying." Lynnray said directly.

Yale was a bit surprised.

Reno patted Lynnray's shoulder and smiled: "Lynnray, we are men. We cannot be crossed over by women. The girl named Alice failed to show up several times. If I were you, I would dump her straight and neglect her even if she kneels before me afterwards."

"Reno, you don't understand." Lynnray smiled, with an alcoholic smell in his mouth, "Don't talk bullshit. I'm in a bad mood. Let's drink."

Yale, Reno and George looked at each other, and started drinking with Lynnray.

On the next morning, Lynnray woke up the first while his brothers were still sleeping on the table. Lynnray had a bitter feeling when he looked at his brothers: "Bros, I know what you were talking about when you drank with me and persuaded me. Alice failed to show up several times, and I do have a bad premonition, but I'm still reluctant to admit it."

Lynnray walked to the window and looked down.

At 5 to 6 a.m., Fenlai City seemed to have just woken up from a slumber. Only a few people were commuting on the streets, while most were staying home.

"Lynnray."Delin flew out from the Ring of Coiling Dragon.

Delin was always wearing a moon-white robe, and his length of white beard never changed.

"Grandpa Delin." Lynnray suddenly felt as if he drifted to the harbor on a boat.

Delin looked at the sleeping brothers and said: "Lynnray, you have three good brothers. As to romantic relationship, I can tell you in my 1,300 years' experience that maybe only one in ten had a successful first love."

"I understand." Lynnray nodded, "But I trust her."

Delin nodded, without speaking much.

......

In mid-November, Lynnray carried a bag containing two memory crystal balls on his back. He went to Fenlai City again and came to the two-story building.

"Uncle Hadd, is Alice back?" Lynnray addressed the gatekeeper politely.

Hadd shook his head and said: "No, Miss Alice has never been back in a month."

"Never?"" Lynnray frowned, "OK, I'll go now." Lynnray took leave.

Lynnray walked alone on Ganmo Road. When he arrived at the tavern, he did not enter. Beibei talked with him mentally: "Boss, you don't need to worry much. Maybe Alice has something important to do, such as going on a trial. There are all kinds of possibilities. Don't think too much."

"True, maybe she has been entangled." Lynnray suddenly had light in his eyes.

Upon seeing Lynnray's reaction, Beibei twitched its nose: "Boss, you are simple-minded in love. A simple lie can make you so excited."

"Little dude, I'll punish you by not giving you a drink." Lynnray said jokingly.

However, he had to admit that Beibei lit up his mood.

......

November 29, a heavy snow. Everything was covered in white, and the four brothers, Lynnray, Reno, Yale and George were sitting in a carriage. The carriage was driven by a rider of Yale's family, and several other riders were escorting some stone works behind.

"Lynnray, yearly test will come soon. We don't know if our top talent has reached level-6." Yale said with a smile.

George and Reno were very proud of Lynnray.

In fact, Lynnray had reached level-6 one week ago.

Lynnray was at level-4 at 13 years old, at level-5 at 14 and a half, and he was going to be 17 years old at the end of year. He crossed from level-5 to level-6 in only two and a half years.

Two and a half years!

How about Dixi, who was once called the No.1 talent of Ernst Academy?

Dixi was at level-5 at 12 years old, and after 5 years, he was about 17. Dixi was progressing fast, too, but he was slower than Lynnray, who benefited from flat knife sculpting.

If Lynnray was found to be at level-6 at the end of year, while Dixi was not, then Lynnray would be the No.1 talent of the academy.

"Lynnray, smile a bit. You don't smile, although you have reached level-6." Reno curled his mouth.

Lynnray grinned.

"Is that a smile?" Reno joked with Lynnray.

Lynnray finally squeezed out a smile: "Fine, bro, let me have some quiet moments." Lynnray decided to meet Alice anyway. If he couldn't find her in Fenlai City, he would look for her in Willing Magic School.

He had to make things clear with Alice in all cases.

After lifting the curtain of the carriage, cold air came in and Lynnray squinted. The world outside was in pure white. Snowflakes like goose feather were all over the sky. When he appreciated the snow scenery outside, he reached Fenlai City.

After sending three stone works to Brooks Guild Hall, the four brothers dined and parted.

Lynnray had a high income of nearly 20,000 gold coins each month. He didn't regard money as a matter of importance. With a bag of two memory crystal balls on his back, he walked to Alice's home.

"Boss, if I'm right, it's your fourth time to come to Fenlai City with the two memory crystal balls." Beibei joked with him: "Maybe you can give the memory crystal balls to Delia. I like Delia."

Since mid-October, it was indeed his fourth time to arrive in Fenlai City with two crystal balls.

"Beibei, don't talk nonsense." Lynnray frowned.

Snow fell from sky and covered the streets. With crunching sounds of stepping on the snow, Lynnray soon came to the familiar two-story building.

After exchanging a few words with gatekeeper Hadd, Lynnray had to turn back.

"She has not returned." Lynnray frowned deeply, "Willing Magic School!" He decided to go to Willing Magic School.

......

On Champs Avenue, Fenlai City.

Alice and Karan were walking on the street, hand-in-hand. Karan said lightly: "Alice, don't you want to make things clear with Lynnray?"

"I still need some time." Alice shook her head.

Karan nodded slightly and didn't press her.

Karan smiled when he looked at Alice, who was holding his hand. He grew up with Alice as childhood friends and liked Alice, but he didn't expect Alice entered a relationship with Lynnray so quickly.

Karan had been angry at the news of their relationship.

Karan had believed Alice was his lover. Although Lynnray helped him before, he would not make concession in the aspect of love. Therefore, he only used some tricks unnoticed.

"Love at first sight? Rescue of a beauty?" Karan thought with contempt: "All such love was fragile in front of reality."

Karan held Alice's hand with content.

"Alice, when are you going to tell Lynnray?" Karan asked again, because he didn't like her ambiguous relation with Lynnray.

Alice shook her head: "I don't know, but I think if I haven't met him for a long time, our love will fade away. Then I can break up with him with less intense reactions on his side."

"You are right. After all, Lynnray saved us before." Karan nodded and said. When they walked to the intersection of Champs Avenue and Ganmo Road, Alice stopped suddenly. Karan looked at her in confusion, and found her staring in the direction of Ganmo Road with a pale face. So Karan turned his head.

A young man in moon-white robe was standing still and looking at them in surprise. The man had no trace of brilliant redness on his pale face.

"Lynnray!" Karan frowned suddenly.

Made in the USA
Las Vegas, NV
30 April 2024

89343983R00286